Green Fields #10

Adrienne Lecter

Uprising

Green Fields #10

ISBN: 9781795710022

Editing by Marti Lynch
Interior design & cover by Adrienne Lecter

www.adriennelecter.com

Give feedback on the book at:
adrienne@adriennelecter.com

Twitter: @AdrienneLecter

First Print Edition February 2019
Produced and published by Barbara Klein, Vienna, Austria

To M

Because, salad.

Chapter 1

"Initializing pre-flight check in three, two, one, go!"

I flipped the switch, then pushed the button. Music started blaring from the speakers, making me laugh as I sagged into my seat, my pulse racing from the sudden systemic shock. A thread of civilization back in my life—how I have missed thee! Over the com, I could hear Nate mutter under his breath, mostly because I knew he was doing it; the electric guitar solo was too loud to even hear myself think. And because there was no time like after the apocalypse to enjoy life to the fullest, I did a perfect rendition of air drums if there'd ever been one, my imaginary sticks flying inches away from the wheel and console. Anything less than a full minute would have been sacrilegious.

"Do you have to do this every single time?" Nate complained when I finally took a bow and turned down the volume.

For good measure, I added another fifteen seconds of the chorus. "Yes. Absolutely."

He was still shaking his head as he powered his own buggy up, the small vehicle giving barely more than a high-pitched tweep as the electric engine engaged. He hadn't bothered with rigging up a sound system to his, let alone spent months searching for a car stereo that could hold up to five CDs at once… and find and select the perfect albums. And he wasn't done blaspheming yet. "Can we, just maybe, not do this next time? Just once I want to get the vehicles out and running without every shambler in the state getting alerted to our presence."

"Just be glad I didn't choose Bohemian Rhapsody this time or you would have had to wait the entire five minutes and fifty-five seconds," I told him, but was only half paying attention. The by-far-more-focused part of my mind was checking on the battery status—fully charged, no surprise after five days connected to the solar panels—and whatever else the very minimal cockpit showed me.

I had my music back—right now I didn't care about much else.

Well, except for zooming across the flats at sixty miles per hour with my music blaring from the speakers. That trumped pretty much everything.

Except for sex, but I really didn't see how I could have added that to the mix in this beloved but admittedly rickety deathtrap on four wheels.

Still grinning about my observation, I pulled my aviator goggles over my eyes—spectacular find that they had been—and made sure that my com battery was fully charged as well. I'd forgotten about that once and figured Nate's silence was a sign that he was okay with my idea of going on a long round trip. Alas, that hadn't been the case, and he'd berated me all of the—admittedly long—way back after he'd caught up with me and managed to make me stop with wild gesticulations. Ah, good times!

"Buggy One, ready for takeoff," I reported, beaming a dazzling smile over to the hulk of welded-together scrap metal sitting next to mine.

Nate flipped me off blindly; his focus was still on his console. "LSV-2, all systems nominal."

I'd rather walk than call this deathtrap by what he claimed was the official designation—Light Strike Vehicle. A dune buggy was a dune buggy, whether it could be airdropped out of some fancy helicopter or not. Considering the hundreds of hours that we'd spent remodeling them to make them run on electric motors—not to mention getting all the parts, and the textbooks teaching us to build said motors—I felt vindicated in giving it the designation it deserved. So "buggy" it was, and Nate could suck his dick for all I cared.

"We do the usual perimeter round?" I asked, snapping myself into the harness. Knowing that I'd survive a crash was one thing; facing months of physical therapy because of broken bones, quite another.

Nate's sigh preceded his response. "Take it easy, bronco. Just the small one today. We need to go check on the southeastern quadrant tomorrow so we can keep to this side of the river."

I made a face, but rather than tell him that he was a spoilsport, I gunned the engine—which didn't even give me a satisfying whine because, electric—and took off, turning the dial on the sound system up to maximum volume once more. I may or may not have whooped loud enough to still be heard over the drums. Gravel spewed as the tires found grip and propelled me forward, and down the plain we went. Wind and dust whipped my face and tore at my clothes, making me whoop again as the first heat of day was replaced by a rush of coolness. It had only been five days but, God, I'd missed this!

The track ended just as I shot over the nearby access road, the terrain turning bumpy as the buggy surged into the high grass. I grimaced, and with overwhelming reluctance turned down the volume to where my mind could once more concentrate, aiming for the rock formations a few miles beyond the grassland. Nate fell into formation with me about a hundred yards behind and to my right, closer to where the elevation picked up on this side of the basin. I lost myself in the rocking, irregular motions of the buggy, letting it lull me into an alert state of relaxation until we reached the dirt path that led up onto the rock outcropping that was our westernmost outlook. I may have accelerated a little harder on the first few serpentines up to make Nate eat the dust my buggy churned up. Once I reached the small plateau on top, I put the buggy into idle, grabbing my binoculars as I climbed out. Nate joined me, both of us standing near the ledge, scanning the plains below.

"See anything?" he asked, still studying the way we had come.

I wasn't entirely sure, squinting because of the glare of the sunlight. "Might be something over by the plantation." Not an actual plantation, but the building had reminded me of colonial-style architecture enough for the name to stick.

"Movement?"

I shook my head. "Birds circling. Could be a larger cougar kill, or…" I trailed off, grinning at the hopeful tone in my voice.

Nate glanced my way for a second and snorted before he found the spot I'd mentioned. "Worth checking it out. That's only a mile from where the mother raised her cub last year. If she's back, I'd rather stay out of her territory for now."

"Or you're secretly hoping to get a good workout in," I teased.

"Nope, that would be you," he responded succinctly.

Putting the binoculars away in my light pack, I grinned. "Maybe if you'd do a better job meeting my needs—"

"Get in your damn buggy, you bloodlusty minx," he growled, the look he gave me speaking of very different ideas that might best be executed outside of the buggies. They really weren't built for anything but transportation—I'd tried in the past, and while ending in laughing fits, those attempts hadn't been very fruitful.

"You say the sweetest things," I drawled, already swinging myself back behind the wheel.

It took us a good fifteen minutes to get to our new destination. When it became obvious that those were vultures circling and not other birds, I cut the volume of my music, grumbling under my breath about inconveniences. I slowed the buggy down further so for the last mile near where we'd seen the disturbance, we made almost no sound besides the rustling of grass and crunch of gravel. It soon became obvious that it wasn't simply a cadaver left by one of the few apex predators in the region, prompting me to bring the buggy to a stop so I could go investigate. Before swinging myself out of the vehicle, I deliberated over my choice of weapons but then went with my favorite and its twin backup, a baseball bat made of oak—heavy enough to be a good stand-in for a much heavier weapon that might have torn itself right out of my grasp in the heat of the moment. I didn't intend to get up close and personal so I'd have to use one of my knives, or my beloved Beretta. I left the buggy idling, trusting that the ninety percent battery charge wouldn't be all gone by the time I returned. If whatever was agitating the vultures like this turned out to be more than Nate and I could handle in a pinch, running for a bit so we could regroup and go about things in a more strategic way was always a good idea. Not what I preferred, but I could be smart and calculating if I had to.

I just really didn't want to—not today.

Humming under my breath, I slowly and deliberately made my way forward, the building a few hundred feet to my right. The front lawn looked undisturbed so it hadn't just been a group of deer trampling through the vegetable patch I'd painstakingly set up there a few weeks ago—it happened, but they were usually deterred by the fence. The light wind came from behind us, carrying my scent forward to any predator hunting by that—a surefire way of making cougars and the likes decide to go linger elsewhere. It was only the stupid bipeds that didn't heed warnings like that.

A whiff of decay hit my nose, strong enough to reach me across what used to be a well-manicured lawn from the other side of the house, making me smile. Yup, no cougar cubs to avoid today. Tightening my grip around the black wraps the bat's handle was covered in, I strode forward with purpose, but made sure to keep my peripheral vision on high. It had been a while since one of the sneaky fuckers had gotten a jump on me, but you never knew.

As soon as I rounded the building and got a glimpse at the gently sloping meadow behind it, I knew we had some work to do. How they'd gotten the jump on no less than five—no, make that six—deer, I couldn't say; the resident deer were usually hard enough to track that it still took me two to three attempts with bow and arrow each time we were out for some venison. Even Nate had an even fifty percent chance of startling them. Maybe the small herd had tried to save their fawns? Whatever the cause, the deer had been too stupid to take off, and had become quite the banquet for the undead. I counted eighteen at a preliminary perusal, with maybe a few more hidden further toward the trees by what had been the natural border of the property, back when such things had been of interest to anyone. I waited for Nate to catch up to me, then raised my brows at him. Almost twenty to two—not the best odds. Then again, they were distracted and likely sluggish from decimating their prey to a few tufts of fur and the odd cracked bone; probably a hoof or two, as well.

Nate considered, then shrugged, leaving the choice up to me.

There was no telling from where they had come—except not from the east, toward the river, where our base was; we would have noticed that. Even less certain was what they would do once they recovered from their food coma. The last thing we needed was for them to take up residence in the building, or squat somewhere else in our territory. Those deer would have easily fed us for a month, and their reeking presence would ensure that other prey animals would steer clear of the site of the slaughter at least until the next heavy rainfall. That alone pissed me off enough that I could feel the muscles in my upper back tense with anticipation of all the work they were about to do.

Yup, screwing with my primary source of protein? A surefire way to make me gear up for a fight.

We wasted another thirty seconds trying to distribute the load between us—which was mostly Nate pointing out which shamblers I should be going for in what order, and me flipping him off—but the undead didn't mind. Not a single one had noticed us yet, let alone focused on us long enough to see us as a threat. Nate finally gave up, giving my shoulder a light shove in a silent, "You're on your own, bitch," if there ever was one, which only served to make me grin in anticipation. Rolling my shoulders and rotating my head from side to side, I exhaled slowly, then let excitement and, well, unbridled lust for violence take over. My pulse sped up, and my amygdala flipped the switch from potential flight to all-out fight mode, adrenaline flooding my system. Euphoria licked at the back of my mind like flames on dry kindling, and a moment later, I exploded forward, coming for the closest zombie. The only thing that would have made it even better might have been screaming at the top of my lungs, but since I didn't need them all to come for me at the same time, I was okay with a semi stealthy approach.

Heavy bat met mottled skin stretched over misshapen cranium—haphazardly covered with hair and lesions—resulting in a very satisfying "thunk" as the shambler sagged forward onto the half-eaten deer corpse. Suddenly finding its food source covered by a decidedly less appetizing piece of meat, the next shambler looked up, just in time to let me hit it right in the face, the bat destroying what was left of it. A third zombie was so surprised by what was going on that it didn't resist as I kicked it in the shoulder, making it sprawl on its back, the prone target even easier to hit. I glanced up for a second, checking that none of the other huddles had become alarmed yet, then turned back to my three targets and did some more bashing in of brains to make sure they'd stay down for good. None of them showed the intelligence or resilience to give even a hint of them being anything but the lowest level of undead—easy to dispatch, and barely smart enough to become a menace to us.

Obviously, those hadn't been the masterminds that had managed to slaughter half a herd of deer, but I was happy to start the cleanup with them.

Nate meanwhile finished off four more, and I moved on to the next cadaver, a little more cautiously now, checking the high grass away from the trampled field of slaughter. I didn't come up with anything so I went for the next easy target, and the next, and the next—until the last shambler lay dead for good on the ground, none of them putting up much resistance. My muscles sang with exertion but rather than feel satisfied at a task completed, my mind was on fire with alertness as I kept checking our surroundings. Nate, panting a little from the work he'd done, was watching me as much as the grass around us, only outwardly relaxing as he straightened. Any tracks had been destroyed by the feeding frenzy, leaving us nothing except for a clear pointer where the horde had come from—south by southwest, but we'd already known that, seeing as we patrolled the northern and eastern parts of the basin.

Propping my bat against my leg for a second, I flashed a quick slew of hand signals at him—just coincidentally bad luck for the deer? He shook his head, still scanning the territory. We waited a good five minutes, but except for a few vultures drawing closer to the heap of corpses farthest away from us, nothing moved. I kicked at one of the shamblers, mostly to vent energy and frustration than to get it off the deer cadaver, but as it rolled away from there, I checked on the dead animal. Nothing useful to be gleaned from it anymore, half-eaten as it already was. Nate spent a few moments checking a few of the corpses while I kept scanning the meadow, returning to me with another negating jerk of his head. No signs that any of them had been special—or had been simulating. We'd had a few incidents of that in the past, although not with a bunch like this one. Like many predators hunting in groups, they seemed happy to establish hierarchies, and if any one of them would have been smart enough to be the boss, that one would likely have come for us before we'd had a chance to come for it.

So where was that boss hiding?

Since I was already worked up and sweaty—not to mention keyed up and still ready for a fight—I whipped through the ground floor of the building next, using the established room-by-room route we'd prepped in the past, but found nothing. None of our traps were disturbed, not a single stumbling obstacle out of place. Sure, someone as smart as us could have avoided them—which technically included the juiced-up fuckers, but without a reason to, why would it have gone to such lengths? Nate was waiting at the second entry for me, acknowledging my silent "nothing" with a light frown. He didn't like this any more than I did. The vultures were descending on the corpses in earnest now, and I could see a few coyotes in the field next to the meadow, called by the same signals as us. The birds made enough sound that calling out was useless to try to scare any other undead out of hiding—they would have come had they still been around.

Well, at least my lettuce was coming along nicely. Next time we'd come by on our usual tour, I'd be able to take the first seven or ten heads with me.

While I was busy checking on my produce, Nate took out a small, dilapidated notebook and wrote down the date and location of the encounter. Together, we returned to the buggies, and after a routine cleanup, we hopped back in to resume our trek. Whistling under my breath, my fingers kept drumming on the wheel, tension taking its sweet time to leak from my body. The music remained off—if we had some smart ones in our territory now, I'd need my full attention. Too bad, really—I could have done with a few more tunes for the week.

It went without saying that we extended our usual route in the direction the shamblers had come from, but we soon lost the trail they'd left behind where it veered off on one of the old highways. Just to be sure that they hadn't left behind a few squatters in the wrecks peppering the cracked lanes, we wasted a good thirty minutes on that but came up blank. I was still jumpy but the tension was slowly draining from my muscles, leaving me with a thread of exhaustion and a latent need to burn off energy—that other kind of energy that didn't necessarily require weapons and gear. Unable to do anything about that right now—or unwilling, considering how Nate kept ignoring my imploring glances his way—I felt anger flicker alive in the depth of my stomach but did my best to put a lid on it.

The noon heat beating down on us only made me cranky, so I hopped back into the buggy so we could finish our round. Roughly three hours after we'd hauled the second set of batteries from the charging station to the buggies, we unplugged them once more, switched out the batteries for the next set, and left everything so it would be ready the next time we'd need it.

Sweaty and covered in grime from the dust the buggy had stirred up, I would have loved to aim for the river, but Nate's reproachful look reminded me that we had something else to do before that. Plastering a placid smile on my face, I pretended that I wasn't still wound up as hell as I grabbed my compound bow and arrows. I was sure I was fooling no one, but I wasn't quite in the mood to escalate things into a fight that might well end with me getting ignored for the next couple of days straight rather than, well, the much more energetic alternate outcome.

An hour later, we reached the patch of forest where we'd seen plenty of deer and rabbit trails this morning and waded into the underbrush, separating. I considered finding myself a nice perch high up in a tree and twiddling my thumbs until some game wandered into my line of sight. Hell, I even had a paperback with me that I could read in the meantime. The idea of how much me doing that would vex Nate made me smile, but only for a minute. We weren't necessarily here to hunt, or not only to hunt; and wasting the exercise like that when I actually needed to clear my head wasn't exactly efficient. But I really could have done with getting up to virtually anything else than this.

I couldn't be entirely sure whether Nate hadn't turned around and was stalking me rather than any other prey, but since I hadn't heard a single sound not belonging to the forest, I presumed he was leaving me to my own devices. I was still tempted to forgo trying to center my mind first, but with a loud sigh I dropped my weapon and pack at a nearby tree before parking my ass, cross-legged with my hands partly open on my knees, in the high grass, choosing a patch of sunlight-speckled birch trees to gaze at.

Follow your breath, my ass. If there was one thing I hated more than meditating, it was meditating when my body and mind were keyed up, but I didn't need Nate's silent reminders to know that it was vital that I kept my parasympathetic nervous system in check. It had been a while since I'd almost lost it, but there was no reason whatsoever to provoke a repeat performance today.

A brief inhale, followed by a long, slow exhale. I forced my eyes to lose focus, instead concentrating on the rustling of the wind in the tall grass, the scent of sunshine in the air, the pounding of my own heart like a steady drum beat, growing slower by the minute. I let my mind idle, doing my best not to chase the millions of bunnies stampeding through my thoughts.

How had the shamblers managed to kill those deer? Reset.

Maybe I should redo the wraps on the bat handle. My right hand felt a little bruised… Reset.

Just how—

Reset.

Anger snaked its way into the stampede, a bright, red light so much easier to latch onto than it was to let everything else go. My pulse increased immediately, the world in front of my eyes snapping into laser-sharp focus. Muscles tensed, my body going from somewhat relaxed to alert in a second.

I forced out the air in my lungs rather than let it escape, the annoyance at my failure to calm down only exacerbating the moment. Two more breaths, equally pressed, and I gave up, coming to my feet in one fluid motion that ended with picking up my gear. I paused for a moment, checking on what was going on around me, before I set out east, letting my mind lose itself in motion and attention rather than nothingness.

Sometimes, that even worked. Today, not so much, but I stopped caring when I caught sight of something disappearing into the underbrush maybe two hundred feet to my left, toward the river. I welcomed the spike of adrenaline that zoomed through my veins, my feet carrying me faster as I sped up into an easy lope without much thought required. A deer, if I wasn't mistaken. Venison, not the worst kind of dinner, particularly after today's find.

Tracking it was easy enough as I hadn't startled it and the animal was gravitating toward the river, stopping to graze or listen every so often. I let my feet pick their own way, moving much slower now that I was closing in on it, my attention divided between my prey and the forest ground. Nocking an arrow, I tracked the animal for a while, but eased up eventually, letting it traipse away when I decided to let it fatten up a few more weeks. My thoughts kept snapping back to the shamblers we'd stumbled upon, something about that encounter still not sitting right with me. Try as I might, I couldn't shake that latent unease that I was missing something.

A cracking sound came from behind me, alerting me to the fact that I was no longer alone. It could have been a boar but I doubted it; it sounded much more like a hunter giving up on his own stalking. It took me a few minutes until I found his tracks, and a little longer to come upon the man himself. I couldn't hide a smirk when I caught Nate, crouching in the shade, munching on some early blueberries. He hadn't seen me yet, and the murmur of the river in the distance muted the inevitable sounds I made well enough. I considered what to do, but only a single option sounded vaguely enticing.

So I did what was only logical—to do away with my abundance of energy and to calm my mind—and pounced.

Food-related distraction aside, Nate must have heard me coming—or all that mulling things over in silence that he, too often, had going on was giving him supernatural senses after all—as he reacted a split second before I crashed into him. He couldn't avoid me, but rather than him going down underneath me, I somehow ended up on my back with him perched above me. Before inertia could pin me to the ground, I did my best to grab him and throw us both into a tumble, but he shamelessly used what strength and reach he had on me, forcing me into a similar position, only now further away from the bushes.

He allowed himself a slight, if slightly winded, smirk. "Hunting, remember?"

"Yeah, I'm not really hungry for food right now," I offered—lied, really, but we still had some leftovers from yesterday, so filling my stomach wasn't my top priority at the moment. His smirk deepened as he got my meaning, as hard to misinterpret as my words had been. When I reached up, he didn't try to break my hold on him, same as he didn't protest when a quick hook of my leg and thrust of my pelvis got him falling onto his back, with me now above him. I grinned down at him, allowing my breathing to slow down for a second before it would, inevitably, pick up once more. "If that's you protesting, you're doing it wrong," I snidely remarked.

"Not protesting," he shot back, his hands warm on my sweaty skin as they found their way inside my clothes at my lower back.

"Thought so."

Then we were busy with something other than talking, or stalking deer, or thinking about the damn shambler incursion—and all was right with the world.

An undefined time later we picked up our discarded clothes and gear and trudged over to the river, following the silver band to where the water had dug out some deeper pools at the shore next to boulders jutting out into the rapids. The shock as I jumped into the icy depth was jarring, making me feel quite awake as it chased away the last tendrils of the mellowness that had previously spread through my body and mind. I stayed in the water just long enough to sluice away sweat and grime before I swam over to the boulders, using a few familiar hand- and footholds to pull myself out of the water and onto the sun-warmed rock. Nate was already waiting for me, lazing, stretched out in the sun, his head pillowed on one arm. I might have spent a moment longer than necessary following the familiar curves and hollows the muscles and tendons of his body formed as I stood there, letting the cold water drip down my own. It had taken some getting used to not feeling vulnerable and utterly exposed whenever we went skinny-dipping, but the spring had started strong enough that, already, I barely had any tan lines except for my face relative to the rest of my body. Just because I could stand there, unafraid and strong, before plunking down next to him to let the sun dry my shivering skin didn't mean I was stupid enough to go toe-to-toe with the undead or other predators in our territory. But that easy-to-defend, hard-to-reach boulder jutting out into the river had a lot going for it, that much was true.

I was just about to doze off when I noticed that Nate was studying me, if stealthily so. Forcing my attention to snap back from drowsiness, I wriggled my eyebrows suggestively at him. "Up for round two?"

He snorted his amusement under his breath, but that wasn't exactly a "no." Yet instead of pushing himself up and crawling over to where I still lay, relaxed and stretched out next to him, he simply shrugged. "If we get all sweaty, we have to clean up again. If I'm honest, I'm too fucking lazy to move right now."

"Spoilsport," I teased, briefly considering if I should initiate something—but found that I was really comfortable right now, and the stark temperature of the water wasn't exactly inviting. I couldn't help but laugh at myself. "Do you ever think we're getting too complacent?"

It never ceased to amaze me how much contempt he could put into a second of side-eye. "Just because we're not fucking like rabbits doesn't mean you have any reason to complain. Besides, nothing is keeping you from laying a hand on me." And because we were quickly regressing into stupid-teenager territory, he had the audacity to pointedly look down at his crotch.

That made me laugh—and consider. Mostly to keep teasing him, I quipped, "I really miss electricity sometimes."

Nate's snort was shy of derisive. "I know I've said it before, but you always feel so special to me when I know you mean because of sex toys rather than washing clothes or dishes, or industrial production."

"You know me too well, husband."

He let out another snort but turned pensive. "It's been seven weeks since we moved here. Might be time to break camp and check on the caves."

I couldn't quite keep a frown off my face. "Isn't that a little drastic? I know it's getting hot out here in the plains, but…" I trailed off, letting that sentence hang in the air between us.

"We can switch up the routine and stay at the lake house for a few days," he mused, ignoring my implied question.

"But my salad's just about ready—"

His low laugh cut me off, but he was smiling slightly as his gaze dropped from the sky overhead to my face. "We both know you only planted that because you finally managed to grow the saplings, or whatever you'd call them, after failing for over a year straight."

I grimaced and chose to ignore that barb. "We can harvest them early, I guess. Some fiber in your diet won't kill you."

"With shamblers rotting nearby, it just might," he griped, but the fact that he didn't continue to rub my nose in my less-than-stellar agricultural attempts made me slightly uneasy.

"It's getting late," I observed, although the shadows of the trees hadn't quite reached our boulder yet. "We should check the snares. With a bit of luck we've caught a couple of rabbits, enough for a stew. No offense to your penchant to salt and air-dry everything you catch, but if I eat another dinner made up of jerky I might as well bathe in brine to preserve myself on the outside to match my insides."

"Let's," Nate suggested rather than answer to his heinous culinary crimes, so back to the shore and our gear we went.

We got lucky. Two of the fifteen snares we'd set had caught some unlucky rabbits—not enough for a feast, but definitely warranting getting a fire started to turn them into a lovely stew. Lovely, presumably, and as usual I let Nate do the seasoning to his likings while I cleaned up the knives and got rid of the remains that we weren't using for anything else. With the next move looming closer than I liked, there was no sense keeping the bones to cook them out for some hearty broth. Once the stew was done, we extinguished the fire and took the pot up into our tree house, me not protesting when Nate offered to haul me up rather than forcing me to climb the rope ladder. As much as it smarted my ego that I'd never have a perfect grip again, it was easily ignored for comfort's sake. We ate in silence, watching the sun set over the treetops, before we went inside, Nate choosing to do some extended weapons check and maintenance while I gravitated to the one thing that made this location my favorite: the bookshelf.

"Not sure I'm feeling like electrical engineering tonight," I mused as I let my attention drift over the three rows of books crammed onto the shelf that mostly served to separate our living space from where we kept a thick mattress on the floor for a bed—also a plus.

"Don't kid yourself. You haven't touched any of those books since we finished rebuilding the charging station for the buggies," Nate muttered under his breath, his motions precise and sure in the gloom the single candle he had lit produced.

I allowed myself a small smile at him using my preferred term for our DIY mode of transportation but wisely hid it from him as I kept perusing the tomes.

"It's not like I need to since you're doing all the maintenance on that as well."

The curse that followed did its own to brighten my smile. "You could try crocheting again," came Nate's acerbic remark from behind me. "That went so well last time."

Now it was my turn to grimace, but I did my best to swallow my ire—as I gave him the finger, or what was left of it on my left hand. "I still did a better job than you," I remarked. "And what's your excuse?"

Silence fell, but I'd long since gotten used to not reading too much into it. Sometimes days passed where I'd need to strike up a conversation with myself if I wanted to hear someone talk.

I was still judging my options when Nate putting down one of the shotguns with a little too much emphasis made me pause and glance over at him. He was staring at the weapon on the table in front of him, hands relaxed and empty, but it was impossible to miss the set of his shoulders. As if he could feel my gaze, he looked up, locking eyes with me for a second. "You don't want to leave yet." A statement, not a question.

I did my best to mirror his calm expression, knowing I was likely failing. "What can I say. I like it here. And there's the salad."

"You like the lake house, too," he pointed out.

"In summer, yes. But it's not warm enough yet that the water is balmy. If I have to swim as hard as I can not to freeze my tits off, it's a workout, not a relaxing soak."

"We can fill the tub on the patio. A good scrubbing to get rid of whatever died in there over the winter, plus a few hours with buckets, and we're set. Give the sun a few days and it should be just right to keep all parts of your anatomy in prime working condition."

I cut down on the impulse to stick my tongue out at him and let my silence be my response.

Nate glanced back at the shotgun before he leaned back in his chair, crossing his arms over his chest. "You think I'm just being a paranoid freak again?"

Stranger things had happened. But still… "The shamblers have me on edge, too," I admitted. "But that doesn't have to mean anything sinister. And if they followed a crafty, smart one here that managed to hide from us, that's reason to stay and hunt it down."

Nate considered my point. "Fair enough. I still think we should move."

It wasn't that hard to hide my disappointment, particularly as his decision wasn't exactly a surprise. "Should I start packing already? The batteries of the buggies should be good to go tomorrow morning if we don't mind stopping early to recharge."

His amused grin had a decidedly wry twist to it. "So you do think I'm being paranoid."

My temper was ready to rear its ugly head but I did my best to keep my voice measured and calm. "Yes, but that has kept us alive for the past two years. Not that we ever found any signs that it was warranted, but no harm done. Except to the salad, of course."

"Of course." He continued to consider but eventually came to his feet with a soft laugh, abandoning his weapon cleaning supplies in favor of sauntering over to me. "Let's give it another week. That's enough time to stock up on jerky for the road and check whether we've dealt with the threat of incursion or just culled the herd a little." He stared at the books just as I had before, then shook his head slightly. "How about we don't head to the lake, or the caves? Let's do something fun. Check on a town, or scout a new location."

"Because looting another creepy time capsule of an abandoned attic isn't weird at all," I snarked, looking away when the frown on his face got a little too imploring. I ended up staring at my hands as I forced my fingers to unclench, the scars—faded and looking older than they were—standing out in familiar light and raised lines. With all the liquids involved in killing the rabbits and prepping dinner, I hadn't bothered with donning my gloves again. Usually, I didn't wear them inside the house, but right then I could have done without the reminder.

To distract myself, I looked back at Nate, finding him doing pretty much the same. "Creepy attic it is," he offered, speaking softer than before. Because, "I miss them, too," was what he wasn't saying out loud.

"But we both know we're doing this for a reason," was what I didn't reply. And we both knew that we weren't not-talking about my wayward appendages. Unbidden, my gaze crept over to the arsenal on the table, and on to the stacks of ammo boxes stashed by the door, and the bed, and on the kitchen counter. Yeah, we had a damn good reason for sitting here in the middle of nowhere, armed to the teeth, jumping at shadows.

"How about you finish up there while I do a last perimeter check?" I suggested, already heading toward the makeshift porch and rope ladder. "That way I don't have to feel like I'm hanging off a cliff just because I need to hit the head one more time."

"Suit yourself," Nate muttered, already falling back into ignoring me and my barbs. It hadn't been my bright idea not to include some kind of bathroom in the construction of the building, if one wanted to call it that. Walking backward for the last three steps, I blew him a kiss, and down off the platform I went.

Chapter 2

I was well aware of the fact that Nate was simply being paranoid, but still walked the entirety of the close perimeter we kept around the house. It had been months since we'd last seen—fully sentient—human beings, and only from a distance. There was absolutely no reason to believe that now would be different. And it wasn't, not really. The forest around me was alive with the sounds of nocturnal animals going about their night, my near-silent passing barely muting their productive scurrying. Stopping for a second, I inhaled deeply and found only the normal scents lingering around me—no hint of decay except for the normal cycles of nature.

It was pretty much the most unremarkable night-time sortie I'd ever been on. Time to take a shit and be done with this.

We kept an extra spade by the roots of the tree that served as the main support for our base high up in the canopy, so quickly digging a pit wasn't much work, although I did end up tripping over a root that I hadn't seen in the pitch-darkness of the forest at night. Done, I paused for a moment to listen once more, coming up with the same findings as before. Yeah, paranoid, all right. Satisfied with my findings, I got down to business, hard-pressed to keep from humming to myself to keep the latent unease at bay that finding absolutely nothing that could have tripped up my senses caused. Shouldn't there have been some crafty predators doing away with the rabbit carcasses? The still-lingering scent coming from our fire pit usually didn't keep them away for long—and was, likely, ringing the dinner bell for them as sure as my own musk and sweat must be keeping them away. Animals in the wild weren't stupid, and after years of civilization being a thing of the past, it was as if humanity had never taken over the globe—at least around here where even then we hadn't had that large of a foothold yet. The more active part of my imagination still expected that I was about to get jumped, so it took me a while to conclude what had me staying down here still. But nothing happened, so I cleaned up, chuckling to myself, and went about filling in the pit I'd dug once more. Better not tell Nate exactly how jumpy I was or else I wouldn't live that down for a week.

The stock of a rifle crashed down on my temple with me still completely unaware.

Pain exploded through my head and vertigo hit when my body tried to compensate as I both stumbled and started to go down while my instincts kicked in and my senses snapped to full focus. My vision was useless, the pain making red and white splotches dance all over the darkness of what my eyes were actually seeing, and for a second, I was so disoriented that I tripped and ended up on the ground, likely because of the same blasted root as before.

But vision wasn't the only sense I was relying on, and while that was still giving haywire disconnect signals, the others picked up the slack. Beyond the sounds my own body was making, I could pick up the scrape of fabric against harder materials as whoever had clobbered me lowered the rifle once more, clearly audible in the sudden silence my stumble and groan had brought on. I could sense his physical presence somewhere behind and to my left side—and call me jaded, but my money was on it being a "him," going on experience. Also, that blow must have come from slightly above, speaking of inches in height my opponent must have on me. Now that I knew what I was looking for, I caught a hint of sweat and weapon oil in the air that was both familiar yet not at the same time—not Nate, and not what our living space was reeking of at the moment.

My empty palms hit the mossy ground, and I allowed myself a second to try to decide what to do. Call out a warning? Chances were, Nate was already on alert after how much noise I'd just made, and there was little sense in letting my assailant know that there were more people around. Then again, if he didn't know our numbers, making him believe that the cavalry would arrive in force momentarily could be a bonus—or make him act more ruthlessly to take me out quicker.

I felt him move toward me and decided he'd already chosen to go for option two, so rather than waste my breath, I inhaled silently to get as much air into my lungs as possible, and went about dissuading him of the notion that I was an easy target.

Giving the adrenaline in my system free reign to whip me into a frenzy, I shot up and pounced at my attacker, never mind wasting seconds to cast around in the dark for a suitable weapon. He was nice enough to have one at hand, literally, so there was no need for me to find another. As I shot toward him, I had a moment of "oh shit" as my senses were triggered by something else—and, a few feet shy of my target, a second body slammed into my side, taking me down in a perfect tackle. We rolled, which gave me the chance to bounce up and tear myself free before he could bury me under his much heavier weight. Thank fuck for all the times Nate had pulled that very move on me as I'd gotten pretty good at evading it.

My triumph was short-lived as the first assailant was right there as soon as I staggered to my feet—only that, really, he was the third, I realized, when my spatial awareness caught up with the motions my body had gone through. My vision finally snapped into focus but I could feel blood trickle down my temple, a reminder that I wasn't quite as unscathed as my body momentarily felt. With that, I finally got a look at my opponents, even as two of them came rushing me again. They all wore heavy gear, and the two currently on their feet were in rather impressively intricate ghillie suits, their faces mostly hidden by night vision goggles. That made me wonder exactly how long they had already been hiding in the bushes that the surrounding wildlife hadn't gotten triggered by their presence. I vaguely remembered doing a nude streak through the forest last night when a late evening need to relieve myself ended with Nate and me—

It was easy to push those thoughts away and ignore them for now as I did my best to block a kick coming toward my face while at the same time keeping my back toward the forest. That gave the third one enough time to get to his feet, and they immediately did a great job surrounding me. They also didn't do me the courtesy of only attacking me one at a time so I could show off my impressive kung-fu moves, like they always do in bad movies. While I was busy trying not to get kicked or tackled, a rifle stock came crashing down at the back of my head, making me see stars all over again as my knees threatened to give out.

Their strategy gave away a few things that I rapidly tried to analyze to find my way out of this. Obviously, their gear and tactics spoke of a well-trained unit, not just a bunch of weirdos who just happened to be preying on hapless women digging latrine pits in the forest at night. From what I could see of the non-ghillied-up one's gear it was as patched up and mismatched as our own, which was the first—and, really, only—good news. Unless they were trying to be confusing and difficult to pin down, that was. My guess was still on scavengers over a certain special-ops hit squat, which was more of a relief than my current situation let on.

The pain from the hit radiated through my skull, making thinking impossible for a second, but my body was more than happy to pick up the slack. I blocked, weaved, and dropped to the ground when I couldn't evade another kick. While down there, I grabbed grass, moss, leaves, and dirt to throw at the next face appearing above me, hoping that if I could make it stick to the goggles, I'd temporarily blind one of them. Yet my fling went wide and I got a boot heel to my right shoulder for my trouble, which hurt like hell but also gave me some extra momentum as I writhed away from it. With no time to try to get my feet underneath me, I made a grab for the next leg I found. No idea who it belonged to, but since his other leg was raised for another kick at the moment, I managed to unbalance him enough that he came crashing down. Seizing the opportunity, I pounced on him, immediately punching for his throat with as much force as my body could muster. In near-perfect timing, my fist hit just as his head rolled to the side on impact, leaving his throat exposed. Bone crunched and cartilage gave, the sounds audible even over the general ruckus of the fight. Triumph flared alive in me when I realized that it was a killing blow unless they had a really good medic along with them—too bad.

I paid dearly for that moment of bloodthirsty elation as it left my entire back exposed, and the seconds I spent staring down at my victim and gloating about just how precise my blow had been cost me time I didn't have. The downed man underneath me tried, in vain, to take a rattling breath as another kick landed squarely between my shoulder blades, sending me forward and pushing me off him. I tried to roll but they anticipated it, and I had to take two more kicks to my lower back and stomach before I could get one in on my own. Yet, it was badly aimed and only warded off another boot instead of sending anyone crashing to the ground. Again, the stock of a rifle smashed into my head, hitting my other temple, and this time the pain was strong enough to make me vomit. I tried to fight the urge but my body was already leaning to the side to leave my airways clear as I hurled up stomach acid and chunks of rabbit, my body going into panic mode with my lungs screaming for air. Before I could get a grip on myself, I was grabbed underneath my arms and pulled upright, and the last bits of upchucked dinner landed squarely in the face of the guy getting ready to punch me. That was a small win in turn for him socking me two good ones, the first hitting me in the jaw, the second breaking my nose.

This wasn't looking good.

It looked even worse when three more figures materialized out of thin air behind the one giving my face a good work-over. It was about time that I turned the tables on them—

And that's when another asshole that I hadn't seen coming jabbed a needle into the side of my neck, leaving behind a burning sensation that rapidly started to spread into the center of my body and then further out into my limbs.

Uh-oh. Not good. So not good!

It wasn't a paralytic—or at least not the same potent stuff that, back in the day, Emily Raynor had shot me up with that had completely and utterly immobilized me—but it was definitely some kind of tranquilizer. The asshole who had been holding me let go, yet as much as I willed my body to lash out—or, failing that, to run—all I managed was a staggering step, and it took all my strength to remain upright. That quickly changed when another punch hit my jaw. I went down like the proverbial sack of rice, incapable of breaking my fall as my arms wouldn't cooperate fast enough. I waited for panic to set in, to maybe undercut the need to fight and give me that extra bit of strength to fight through the haze of the drugs, but there was nothing but that ever-seething pool of rage deep inside of me—that I suddenly couldn't access anymore. Oh, my pulse was still racing and I could feel the jitters left by the adrenaline all right, but try as I might to grasp that extra strength and stamina that should have been there, it was like I was attempting to hold on to water in a gurgling stream.

Sounds of fighting coming from farther into the forest pulled my attention away from my frustration. They must have found Nate; or he had found them. I waited for shots to be fired, dying screams to be uttered, but wasn't rewarded. One of the idiots kicked me again, hitting my left thigh, right where titanium met bone. It hurt like hell, and for a moment, that pain cut through the effects of the drug. Gathering what strength I could, I launched myself forward in something between a crawl and a four-legged pounce, toward where I saw something straight and solid on the ground. Nothing in nature was ever that perfectly geometrical—and I was right, I realized, as my fingers closed around the spade.

Gone was my perception of who or what moved around me, but I still hit solid flesh when I rolled over onto my back and flailed at whatever might be coming for me, doing my best to orient myself once more. The scent of freshly turned earth—among other things—made me guess that I was very close to my pit once more, which meant that my shotgun should have been somewhere around here as well. The sounds of fighting I could still hear didn't come from where I guessed the tree house was, so that must be going on down on the ground as well. Bright as the sky seemed compared to the trees all around me, it was still so dark here that I could barely make out the shapes converging on me as they drew closer. With their gear, it would be the same to them where this went down, but I'd definitely have an advantage if I made it to the small forest clearing that I knew must be around a hundred feet to the south of where I was. Out there, I would be able to see them, and if I saw what was coming, maybe I could better react. But my shotgun wasn't out there in the brighter light coming from the stars and what little illumination the moon cast tonight.

Decisions, decisions.

It was then that I started to wonder why none of them had shot me yet. It wasn't like I hadn't earned it. The conclusion was obvious—they wanted me alive, if not necessarily un-concussed, because that latent woozy feeling that just wouldn't go away anymore let me know that my brain had gotten pretty stirred and shaken. As much as I appreciated being alive—and not in even more pain from a bullet wound or ten—I didn't like the odds of well-trained men coming in overwhelming force who knew they needed to incapacitate us so they could drag us off. Just, no. It could all be coincidence, but so could be my aversion to small, white-tiled cells—and that certainly wasn't.

Shotgun it was, if I could just find it!

The spade helped a lot to get me back on my feet, both because I could use it as a crutch, and because it was a great weapon that gave me something I could normally not rely on: reach. On the first swing, I managed to hit one of my assailants in the head using the blade to best capacity. Yet on the second, I got enough force going on that my grip on the handle slipped for good and only the fact that my other hand found purchase when it slipped back along the shaft let me keep it. I did my best to back away to keep all five of them where I could see them, but they were in no hurry to put me down, I realized. They must be waiting for the drugs to do all the work for them. I staggered and wavered enough that I could see what gave them that idea but at the same time I hoped that my body was very busy churning through that shit and rendering it ineffective.

The sounds of fighting weren't coming any closer but hadn't died down yet, so I saw that as a good sign as well. With Nate, they wouldn't be stupid enough to miscalculate doses, and sooner or later they'd realize that had happened with me. So I kept stabbing the shovel blade in the direction of anything trying to advance on me, turning the fight into what must have looked like a hilarious standoff. That was working for now, but it was definitely not a solution.

After a full minute of that—and my arms slowly getting heavier, not a good sign—I decided that unless I tripped over it, the shotgun was a no-show, and started casting around for other options. I could try getting close to one of them to divest them of their weapons, but I wasn't sure if I'd get a chance to use it once I went down the next time—or whether I'd even be able to get up if they miraculously let me. That left option two: one of the many caches we had hidden around the forest. Some of those had come from paranoia but most from practicality—who wanted to run back the entire way to the base if a gun and some ammo was easily hidden in this old tree stump or behind that boulder? And as good as I'd become hunting deer or boar with a bow, I didn't mind using a gun over a knife for a last killing blow.

Now all I needed to do was find one of those caches.

Easier said than done since I couldn't quite pinpoint my location with the world dipping and swaying like a small boat on a big, big ocean at the moment.

The clearing—right. I could find that easily enough as through the gloom of the tree canopies I could see lighter patches to my very far left, almost behind me. So that's where I started backing toward, step by step, my five heavily armed shadows following me. They were definitely biding their time.

Suddenly, silence fell, the other fight having come to an end. I considered shouting—my inner optimist still expected Nate to have come up on top—but moving and keeping the shovel blade up was hard enough without additional distraction. If he was still conscious—or alive, for that matter—Nate would find me. If not, no need to draw even more attention that I couldn't handle.

The mossy ground turned increasingly more grassy, letting me know that I was heading in the right direction. And then I saw it from the corner of my eye—that crooked birch tree, so out of place right there next to the other trees, easy enough to notice when, say, you were running through the forest, chased by rabid boars. I was a good twenty yards off direction-wise, but a brief halt and some useless stabbing the air with my spade gave me a good excuse to change it up. The idiots were humoring me, keeping just out of reach as they followed, step by step.

As soon as I was next to the birch, I didn't hesitate or look around, but made a jump for the hole in the ground underneath the roots for the neighboring tree, ignoring the dead leaves and other rotting debris my fingers dug through. My fingers brushed cold, wet steel, and all it took was a light yank and the handgun was free. It was fully loaded but with no round chambered, so I quickly rectified that—and as soon as my eyes would focus on a dark shape looming over me, I fired.

One, two, then switch to the next one. Three, four, five, and a second body hit the ground. Two shots went wide as my vision swam too much to properly focus, but then a third was too close to miss and I squeezed the trigger two more times. Just my luck that he fell on me and buried me under his weight, and the next thing I felt was pain radiating from my right hand as someone stepped on it to keep the gun pinned to the ground. I tried squeezing the trigger one last time but my fingers broke before I could get there, agony exploding and racing up my arm.

An impassive face, mostly obscured by the night vision goggles, loomed over mine, followed by a boot—and then, nothing.

Chapter 3

I came to—something resembling consciousness pushing through the blackness—not much later, I guessed, as the musty scent of the forest was still surrounding me. Also the sharp twang of blood, likely my own. Gravity was heavily pulling on my head, and I couldn't move. Some blinking revealed that the reason I could only see out my right eye was because the other side of my face was mashed into whatever I was lying on. The slight motion of blinking my eyelid was almost too much effort, but I managed to keep it open for a bit. There was pain radiating from several points in my body—and more of that chemical burning from the side of my neck—and it took me a little to sort out the differences and realize why my arms and legs were feeling weird. They'd pretty much hog-tied me, wrists and ankles bound together behind my back, leaving me completely helpless and with a lot of strain on my chest—enough so that breathing was hard, and the likely cause for why my vision was swimming so much: the joys of latent hypoxia.

Whatever I was lying on suddenly started to vibrate, with a lot of noise—a vehicle, its engine starting up. Particularly the agony in my head skyrocketed, making it hard to hold on to consciousness—although I asked myself, why was I even trying? Even if I could somehow roll myself off whatever I was stashed on, I'd die of thirst, incapable of freeing myself, or get eaten by all sorts of critters.

Blinding light hit my eye, making me squint, but once it passed, I managed to get a slightly better look at my surroundings. What had passed must have been an ATV like the one I saw idling a few feet away, making me guess I was stashed away on a similar vehicle. And in the back of that ATV I could just make out another tied-up form—Nate. It was too dark to see colors with no direct light, but his hair was heavily matted—with blood, I figured.

I must have made some sound of distress because a figure stepped into my line of vision, obscuring my sight of anything but him. I tried in vain to raise my head—to do what I had no idea—but a fist smashing into my jaw put a stark end to that action.

I welcomed the blackness enveloping me, hoping that things would look less bleak when I came to once again.

If I came to again.

I did, and not in a good way. My mouth was completely dried out, my tongue feeling like a swollen, foreign object. My body hurt with every rocking motion of the ATV underneath me, and there was a lot of jostling going on. I didn't recognize the landscape, cast in the early light of dawn, but gone were the trees, and the plains looked different than over by the plantation where I grew my salad. Salad that would now go to waste, I realized.

Random thoughts—your best friend when you have a concussion and can't think straight.

I tried to get my bearings, but other than a few glimpses of another ATV following the one I was tied to, there was nothing to focus on that didn't make me want to vomit. Mercifully, I blacked out before it got to that.

By noon, the drugs were starting to wear off, allowing me longer stretches of being lucid—which was no consolation whatsoever. It mostly meant that I felt the sun beating down on me, the severe dehydration that added to my splitting headache, and immense cramps in my thighs and upper arms in particular. I wasn't hungry— duh!—but could feel myself getting weaker and weaker as my body burned through reserves it shouldn't have had a need to touch yet, but fighting the drugs in my system and healing my injuries took its toll. My right hand was a mess, sticky with blood from what I could tell and a constant, pounding source of pain, often surpassing what was going on in my temple—and I didn't care at all for how my addled mind loved mixing the actual pain with agony from my memories.

A few times I got a glimpse of Nate, but he never stirred. Nobody came to check on either of us, obviously trusting that between the ropes and the drugs, we were down for the count. There were ten vehicles from what I could tell, all of them running with conventional engines which made me guess that it wasn't simply a raiding party gone bad—as if everything else I knew about them hadn't told me as much yet. They stopped every small eternity—likely intervals of two to three hours—until, later in the still-scorching-hot afternoon, they were joined by two trucks and another group of ATVs.

I must have blacked out for a longer stretch of time then because it was sudden vertigo that startled me awake as someone pulled me off the back of the ATV and onto the grass, wet with dew. It was much cooler, the sky above almost black once more, and in the near distance I could hear the sounds of many more people moving around. My wrists and ankles were still tied together but my limbs had long since lost sensation—a very small respite at the moment since motion made the pain in my head flare up once more. All around where I was dumped, people were busy unloading cargo from the vehicles, only part of which was human—but Nate and I weren't the only living pretzels that I could see. One by one, their bonds were cut but none made any efforts to flee. I realized all too well why when it was my turn—my entire body had turned into a wad of dough, most of my muscles unresponsive except for the pain that slowly but surely rose as blood returned to the parts of me furthest from my heart. All I managed to do was turn my head and finally locate the lump that I identified as my husband—

And then they took him away—two men grabbing his lifeless body underneath the arms, his legs dragging behind—while I was left behind.

That couldn't be good.

As I watched, I realized it was up to two men who made the rounds and pointed out which heaps from the ground were dragged off the way Nate had disappeared, and what others in a different direction. It took me a few minutes to figure out, but I didn't like the conclusion my mind jumped to when I realized that all the remaining prisoners appeared to be women.

Finally, they reached me. I'd tried to work some circulation back into my limbs but the drugs hadn't worn off completely yet, or dehydration was messing with me to the point where it rendered me useless. Either way, I stopped, pretending to be out cold still. That turned out to be impossible to keep up when someone behind my back kicked me hard in my remaining kidney, making me groan and seize up before I could cut down on the impulse to react.

"That's a special case," the kicker ground out, addressing the two men. "Darius wants her in the pits. Says he doesn't care what happens to the bitch as long as it's painful, humiliating, and ends with her dead."

Gee, sounded like I had a new fan. I distinctly felt like telling him to get in line, but then my thoughts caught up to the implications. This didn't sound like what I had expected. My first—and, so far, only—guess had been that Nate's past had finally caught up with him, and while I saw a lot of torture and possible brainwashing in my future, I'd been pretty much convinced they'd want me alive, if only to put more pressure on him. Guess I was wrong.

The two men shared glances, looking less than impressed by the other's statement.

"She'll be more use to us in the kennels," one of them said, sounding rather bored. Somehow I got the feeling he wasn't talking about turning me into dog food.

Kicker would have none of that. "That bitch and the bastard who we picked up at the same place killed five of our people and wounded three more! She deserves so much worse!"

"Then put her on twenty-four-hour duty," the second, so far silent, guy suggested. "They usually don't make it much more than a week of that." He and his buddy shared a laugh.

Kicker wasn't impressed, doing once more what he knew to do best, which made me end up on my stomach, my hands uselessly splayed out on either side of my body. The laughter stopped. Kicker sounded vaguely disgusted, but more satisfied than before. "As if anyone wants to stick his dick into that kind of a deformed cunt." Gee, my ego definitely needed that—much impact as it had, coming from a lowlife like him.

"Then how about you don't make her give you a hand job?" the one with the funny suggestions offered. "From behind, on their knees, they all look the same." And thus they moved on, leaving the less-than-happy kicker alone with me, grumbling under his breath.

"You find that funny, bitch?" he snarled, obviously mistaking my attempt to keep breathing as a wheezing laugh. Or maybe I was the mistaken one because if I could have, I would have laughed him in the face. But before I got a chance to set the record straight, he wandered off, not even gracing me with another round of physical or verbal abuse. That would have left me feeling better if I hadn't had the distinct feeling that I had lots more of both coming, all too soon.

Once the two assholes were done checking on the remaining human cargo, they instructed a bunch of guys that came sauntering over to haul off the last of us. I couldn't tell if those were the same men who'd taken Nate and the other male prisoners away but I got the sense that there were people aplenty around here with nothing better to do than spread misery to newcomers. Before long, I was picked up and thrown over someone's shoulder, not even requiring two men to haul me off as an added insult. I did my best to hold on to my wits but my mind went woozy once more, although I didn't quite lose consciousness this time—a small victory, but not one I was certain I would consider as such very soon. It kept me from getting a feel for the terrain for sure, which wasn't something I appreciated.

They dropped me and the five other women off in what looked like a part of a barn, the floor, if you wanted to call it that, hard-packed earth, with bits of straw gathering in the corners. It stunk of urine and feces, and enough of that to overpower the less than rosy scents that must have been coming from all of us after hours of not being able to move at all. I tried to sit up—or at least roll over so I could get a good look at my broken fingers—but my body was still too unresponsive.

A handful of men remained, presumably to stand guard although it was obviously not necessary. I was surprised when they herded in several women who were quite capable of moving, all of them in simple, dirty clothes; nothing like what anyone out on the road would be wearing, but even sub-standard from what I'd seen in the settlements back before our trip to France. The women quickly set to the task of undressing and cleaning us, using coarse washrags and water that was in itself a health hazard, had I still been concerned with catching anything. I would have still drunk it all down if they'd offered me some. They didn't. The two who were working on me never looked at my face except when they had to wipe away the crusted blood, and wouldn't catch my eyes. That boded well. They also didn't make an attempt to fix up my nose or hand, and the only reaction either of them gave was when they turned me over to get to my back and found my tattoos, which brought them up short.

"Any issues, girls?" one of the men asked, stepping closer. They both cringed away from him even though he was still out of spitting distance, which made me feel even better about laying there, naked and completely defenseless.

"N-n-no," one of them stuttered

The other, quite the traitor, pointed at my back. "She has the marks."

The man scoffed, but still told them, "Show me." It didn't take much effort for them to roll me fully onto my front, leaving my entire back exposed. The man leaned closer but didn't sound impressed. "I bet they aren't real. I overheard one guy from the raiding party claim that they lost a bunch of good people when they picked her and one other guy up." He paused, making me wonder whether he was studying my naked ass, or what else was on display now. "Jesus, just look at those scars! Doesn't look like that one could have inflicted much damage on anything. He probably marked her up so stupid cunts like you'd fall for it and think she's dangerous. Actually, I bet a week's booze rations that there was a whole colony there and those two were the only ones that made it. That's why the heavy losses on our side. Just get her ready. I bet whoever's going first can tell you very soon that she's not the bogeyman. Hell, might even be me." He left, laughing to himself.

The women resumed, but the one who'd kept her trap shut hissed to the other, "Are you fucking crazy? We agreed not to tell them if we found anything!"

The traitor snorted but sounded dejected rather than annoyed. "You know that Madam always checks herself to make sure we don't keep anything from her. You remember what happened to Beth last month? She tried to be sneaky. See what good that did her."

The other looked ready to protest but shut up when two women entered, both wearing dresses that were, if not brand spanking new, in much better condition than what the cleaning crew was dressed in. One appeared to be in her early fifties and she was clearly in charge, the girls cringing away from her as much, if not more, as from the guards, her tall, curvy figure pressed into red velvet and black leather that made her look comically like the proverbial hooker with a heart of gold from a western flick. The cold, calculating way she studied the merchandise on the floor made me revert my guess about the level of empathy she was rocking. The other woman was dressed a little more simply, her blonde hair still untouched by gray, and I guessed she must have been around my age. Her gaze wasn't less calculating but there was some warmth left in her eyes. Both went from prisoner to prisoner, the older giving judgment with few words wasted while the younger remained kneeling at the women's sides, doing some checks and whatnot before they moved on. They kept me for last, probably because I'd needed the most cleanup. As soon as the two in charge arrived, my cleaners moved away, heads deferentially bowed.

"She has the marks," the traitor repeated, her voice trembling. "Zeke thinks they're fake."

The woman in charge—I presumed the Madam, definitely with a capital M, they'd spoken about before—barely glanced at me, but I was sure that she picked up on the damage immediately. Rather than lean closer, she turned to the other woman. "What do you think, Cindy?"

Cindy dropped into a crouch next to me, her hand firm on my arm as she took a better look at my exposed back—and if I wasn't wrong, did a quick check on just how firm my bicep was. I did my best to appear as slack as possible, which wasn't that hard, except that my muscles were starting to get some great cramping and pins-and-needles sensation going on. The fingers of her free hand briefly ghosted across the back of my neck, then down my spine to my tramp stamp where they lingered a little longer. It was a small mercy that she didn't make a grab for my ass, but the way I was lying on my side, maybe she'd missed Nate's name spelled out there.

"The tats are all around the same age," she gave her verdict. "None of them new, with moderate sun exposure." So much for my lack of tan marks. She paused, then added, "I can't tell if they are genuine, but none of them are a complete hack job, which is in and of itself remarkable if she really is a scavenger. I'd say there's a good chance she found someone who did them all for her to distract from her obvious shortcomings. If we let the drugs wear off, it will be easier to tell."

She got a grunt for her assessment. "Doesn't really matter. Darius wants to take out his anger on her so I say, prep her and get her ready. Unless you want to wait and take her place in the meantime?" She got no response but none was needed, and with business obviously concluded for her, the madam left.

Cindy remained behind, rummaging around in the satchel she had brought with her. I really didn't care for the syringe she produced, filled with a translucent brown liquid. She must have noticed the look of derision on my face—and had no issues with holding my gaze once she caught it—as she leaned closer and whispered into my ear. "She's right, you know? It doesn't matter whether you're the real deal or not. Whether you're a decorated war vet or the scourge of the roads out there. But this will help take the edge off a little." Rather than ram the syringe into my neck, she got a tourniquet ready and then fed it into one of the veins in my right arm, all the while keeping up her jibber-jabber. "The first time's always the worst. It gets better after ten or twenty, if you survive that long. Don't worry, that will easily last through the entire night. And if I'm wrong and you really are the real deal? The less you fight, the longer your body will need to break this shit down. So do yourself a favor and just don't."

I had no idea what she'd injected me with, but it was already taking effect even as her words still echoed through my mind—and echo they did as everything seemed increasingly more distant, and decidedly less important. I felt my body relax, even the parts that were still in pain from having been forced into unnatural contortions for far too long. I could still think—somewhat—but what had been pressing concerns moments ago seemed like almost-forgotten memories now. And it was so much easier to give in to that siren song of ignorance. Didn't they say that was bliss?

"Pick her up and get her ready. Last room on the left should do. I don't think we need to waste a good pair of sheets on what's to come," I heard the woman instruct the guards. The words didn't feel like they concerned me, and didn't trigger any alarms. Also not the rough hands that picked me up and carried me out of the room into the main part of the barn. I noticed a central corridor running the entire length with compartments walled off, with doors or curtains, on the sides. Not a barn—a former stable, I realized. Oddly fitting, the nasty voice at the back of my head supplied, but went easily ignored. What did I care? Not. One. Bit.

It got increasingly hard to focus on anything in particular by the time I was put down on something scratchy that gave a little under my weight—a mattress, maybe? It was incredibly hard to force my eyes to focus on anything, and I barely caught more than the glint of flickering fire from a torch on blonde hair as someone—hands soft and gentle—snapped handcuffs on my left wrist, then brought both my arms up and made cool steel close around my right wrist as well. That hurt, but the sensation was so distant that it barely bothered me, like the humming of a bee outside the window. All I wanted to do was drift off and sleep, with not a care in the world…

"You done yet?" a gruff, deep male voice asked from somewhere in the direction of my feet. "I can't wait to put that bitch in her place." Raucous laughter followed.

"Well, get in line," a different voice responded. "Darius already called dibs on that, and not sure there'll be much left for sloppy seconds. He seemed mighty livid when they came back."

Some grumbling along the lines of "not fair" followed that, quickly cut off when another man stormed into the room—Darius presumably. My eyes refused to properly focus on him, but he didn't look familiar. None of them did. The nasty voice was back, whispering, asking if I was really disappointed not to see a familiar face. Because the one I had expected wouldn't have let anyone give me anything to take the edge off, and would have spent plenty of time goading me on. Nothing compared to him, I figured—and about the rest I couldn't give less of a shit about.

I knew I should, but I simply couldn't.

The others left, the door banging shut behind them a million miles away. They took the torch with them, leaving just a single candle flickering by the door, casting the room into dusk and shadows. It was cozy, comforting.

Why wasn't I afraid? At least some residual panic and disgust would have been nice, but even the rage in my gut was gone, for the first time in forever. Huh. Maybe I should track that Cindy woman down and make her tell me what she'd shot me up with once I got out of here? Way better than meditation. Or hunting. Or fighting. Maybe even sex, although the jury was still out on that one. Probably not. It certainly did a good job letting me ignore the string of insults that imbecile kept spewing as he tore off his clothes. Amateur. I could swear up a better storm—when cutting onions made me cry. I couldn't remember the last time I'd had onions. Hmmm, onions...

The mattress dipped and rusty bedsprings groaned as he climbed onto me, his grime-smeared face scrunched up into a grimace of hate. His knees were straddling my thighs, and my first impulse was to tell him that, sorry to point it out, but that wasn't going to work this way. It was surprisingly easy to keep my trap shut—probably for the first time in my life—as the flickering flame of the lone candle drew my attention away from the hulk crouching over me. That really was some potent shit—

My unuttered remark turned out to be unnecessary as instead of wrenching my useless legs apart—or turning me onto my side or whatnot to gain access—he brought his fist down on my already broken nose. Blood sprayed. Pain... flowed and ebbed away, not gone but hard to grasp or focus on. I felt something in my abdomen churn, but hours of dehydration must have left me with not enough acid in my stomach to puke anything up. Too bad.

Two more punches followed, both hitting my jaw. More pain... and again, impossible to focus on. The impacts made my head rock back into the sorry excuse for a pillow, which left the candle outside of my field of vision. That made me feel vaguely sad, but it was hard to hold on to that sentiment as well. The rafters above weren't that interesting to focus on, either. Maybe the sounds around—

That was a resounding "nope," and for a fraction of a second, my mind snapped into sharp focus. I needed to get out of here, and stat, and for that to happen I had to fight off that fucking drug—

And then it was gone once more, leaving me mellow and relaxed with blood running down the back of my throat...

Apparently he'd done enough damage to my face for now—or my lack of a reaction was sorely disappointing—because the next few jabs landed in my abdomen. Yup, that hurt, and although I still couldn't find it in me to care and try to evade, my body reacted, hunching in on itself as much as possible with him still straddling my legs, his disgusting dick, partly erect, dragging across the sea of scars on my left thigh, which made me want to hurl—

The nasty voice was back, laughing at my antics. Really, after everything that went on with that leg—including zombie bites and necrotizing bacteria—one dirty, unwashed dick was too much? Oh, please, just wait and see what happens when—

His fist connected with my temple, exactly where I'd been brained with the rifle stocks—twice—last night, followed by another punch, this one missing my nose but perfectly connecting with my brow, cheek bone, and my eye. Maybe it was the repeat offense; maybe he finally reached the threshold—whatever it was, that punch that would, without a doubt, give me a black eye was one punch too much.

My head lit up with pain, immediately making me rue that the drug must have lost its effectiveness when that didn't stop after a moment or two. I couldn't think because it hurt so fucking much that even trying to make sense of anything was out of the question. I tried to curl up on myself and bring my hands down to protect my exploding cranium, but couldn't; there was a deranged bear sitting on my legs, and whisper-thin steel kept my wrists connected to the rusty bed rail.

Well, that so wouldn't do.

Another punch connected to my jaw, rocking my head back and making alarm bells go off in my mind. The agony it created was staggering, but also made me feel like my entire body had just been dunked into ice-cold water, if cold water felt like molten lava, really. Muscles tensed, synapses fired, and—finally!—my mind started to work again, action steps forming, a neat sequence stacked on top of each other.

First, get rid of the fucking handcuffs. That was surprisingly easy as my right hand, already severely maimed by missing the last two fingers, and now the others broken yet with the swelling already going down reduced to their normal size, only needed one hard yank and my arms were free. Did it hurt like a bitch? You bet, but since that only added to the fire burning within me, I welcomed it.

Step two, punch that wannabe rapist asshole in the face to show him just how much fun it was to be on the receiving end of it. I used my left hand, which still wasn't my dominant hand, but Nate had spent a lot of time on drills and practice to turn me pretty much ambidextrous where fighting was concerned. Darius was so taken aback to find me suddenly rearing up underneath him that he didn't even try to defend himself, so I added a second punch just for good measure.

Step three, get that revolting asshole off me. My thighs were alight with agony from the abuse they'd suffered all day, but now that the serum was doing its thing, it was easy to override the natural impulse to avoid rather than cause more pain. In short order I pulled my knees toward my chest, wrenched my hips to the side—which dislodged him from his perch above me—and kicked back as hard as I could, sending him tumbling not just off me but onto the floor.

Step four, kill that motherfucker.

Whether it was the pain, or the drug regaining some of its grip on me, but my brain shorted out about the time I came vaulting off the bed and after Darius where he was lying on the ground, like an oversized beetle. I punched. I kicked. I used my elbows when only my left fist was capable of doing any damage. I used my teeth to go for his jugular when I couldn't find a knife, welcoming the hot liquid hitting my parched mouth and throat. And when he kept on struggling, I used the chain of the handcuff still dangling from my left wrist to get him into a chokehold—and didn't let go until all I could hear were my own ragged breaths.

Feeling no resistance from my opponent whatsoever, I let go and staggered back, barely managing to keep upright. There was blood everywhere. A lot of blood. For good measure, I kicked the asshole one last time, waiting for a reaction and getting none. Good. I needed to get out of here, and having him come after me wasn't part of that plan. I paused for a second—also to steady myself against the bed frame—listening to the telltale sounds of boots pounding on the ground as someone came to investigate.

There was none.

Oh, there were plenty of sounds going on that I really didn't need to hear, but they made me doubt anyone had become privy to our struggle, brief as it had been. And even if they did, they likely presumed that was Darius giving me a good work-over. I waited for the impulse to try to save one of the other women to come up inside of me, or at least draw the attention to myself and away from them, but found that part of my emotional landscape thoroughly empty.

Escape—right. And if I could manage to find Nate and sneak him out with me as well, all the better.

I realized my plan was doomed to fail from the moment I more fell than climbed out of the window into the darkness—and found myself in the middle of a camp that looked closer to a city than just a few tents haphazardly strung together, at least judging from the many flickering torches I could see that were blinding my sensitive retinas and searing my brain to the core.

I had no fucking clue where I was, and even less so where I needed to go. What I needed was water, food, clothes—above all else, boots—and weapons. What I had was an ebbing amount of adrenaline in my blood that was likely responsible for the drug about to pull me under once more. So what I actually needed was to keep my body pumping out chemicals to keep that shit at bay. If almost getting raped didn't do that, there was only one thing I could rely on to keep myself going, and that was pain. Looking down at my yet-again mangled hand, I couldn't help but smirk. Pain? That was one thing I could easily provide.

Gritting my teeth, I did my best to steel myself before I forced my fingers to close into a fist—as much as they would, which wasn't impressive—before I slammed it into the sturdy, weathered wood of the barn at my back, succumbing to the haze of red-hot lava running through my brain once and for all.

Chapter 4

I came to in what must have been the early hours of dawn of the next day, finding myself sitting on a huge bough of an oak tree with a rope tying me tightly to the tree's trunk. I was shivering hard enough that my teeth were chattering while my body felt more like a furnace than an icicle, covered in blood. Way, way more blood than I remembered sticking to me when I'd left the barn. Some of it was probably mine, particularly on my face and right hand. Most of it was visible because all I was wearing were combat boots that were ridiculously large on my dangling feet, and a checkered flannel shirt that I'd tied closed across my upper stomach because it felt huge enough that it would have slipped from my shoulders otherwise. No underwear or pants, but considering where I'd likely found the clothes, that was probably a sanitary blessing. The handcuffs were gone, and there was minimal bruising on my wrists—underneath lots of dried blood.

The fact that it vaguely bothered me that my privates must have been exposed to thousands of insects living on this tree for what might have been hours let me know that, for the most part, I was back in the driver's seat of this not-quite perfectly functioning meat suit.

Shit.

What should I do first? And how the fuck would I manage to pull it off?

First things first—I needed some water, and not just to wash away the blood. I tried to remember more details of my escape, but after I'd slammed my broken hand into the side of the barn, everything was kind of fuzzy. Some things that swam up in my mind seemed way too insane to be true, even for my track record. That was likely the drugs speaking. I could still feel them raging in my system, making my motions sluggish if I didn't pay a lot of attention to what I was doing as I started unknotting the rope that kept me securely off the ground. I forced myself to stop and looked around, trying to orient myself. Knowing where east was thanks to the rising sun didn't help me at all as I didn't have a single point of reference. The only thing that I could tell was that I was a good seven feet off the ground, tied to a lone oak tree sitting in a gently sloping meadow with a lot of flat ground all around and not a distinct, recognizable landmark anywhere in sight. No rivers, no roads, not even a fucking dirt track that I could have followed to get to the tree. At least that made it unlikely that anyone would find me here any time soon, if they were even looking for me. I doubted anyone would miss me since they hadn't even bothered asking me for my name. Oh, I was sure that Darius's buddies—and the friends of whoever else's blood I was covered in—were out to hunt me down, but what was one lone woman gone from an entire city-sized camp?

Staring off into the rising sun didn't help—including my head that was still pounding like crazy—so I went about getting rid of the rope before I carefully made my way down from that branch. My descent was more of a controlled fall but I managed not to damage myself further, which was a plus in my book. The motion was enough to make me both woozy and nauseated, so I spent another ten minutes or so leaning against the tree, staring off across the unfamiliar landscape. Water, food, clothes. Then I would start scouting the territory to find out where the fuck I'd ended up. And then—

Something deep inside my chest seized up when my thoughts drifted to Nate. No one would have given him the benefit of not taking him and his tats seriously. No one would serve him an opportunity to escape on a silver platter. They'd make sure that he couldn't escape.

Maybe he wasn't even alive anymore.

That thought cut through the fog of complacency so temptingly caressing my thoughts, forcing my attention to snap back to the here and now. No, that wasn't an option I'd consider, at all. I knew he was still alive. There was no doubt about that in my mind. If only for the fact that, unlike me, they'd find him useful. Even if whoever these fucking assholes were didn't know who he was, they'd recognize the potential of a trained soldier and survivor with three marks across the back of his neck. I had no clue what their organization was up to—besides keeping women as prisoners to be raped as they saw fit—but someone like Nate must be valuable, either to sell off or trade with whoever might have some use for him, as a forced laborer, or maybe to recruit him for their cause. The way they'd hit our home spoke of training and coordination, and that fit with what little I remembered of the conversations I'd overheard. Plus they hadn't hit just us; the other prisoners must have come from somewhere as well.

What the fuck had we stumbled into, and without knowing that it was even existing out there?

Shit, but we should have moved over to the lake house weeks ago, damn that fucking salad.

Exhaling forcefully, I made myself focus on the important things. Water, food, clothes. Since no direction seemed better than the others, I decided to head south since that was downhill the way the meadow sloped gently, and I didn't particularly feel like doing extraneous work when a slow, staggering walk was fucking exhausting as shit already. Maybe I should make that food, water, clothes instead? Not that I had much of a choice, except if I wanted to switch my diet to full-on herbivore and gorge myself on grass. Since that wasn't a sustainable option, all I could do was walk.

Water turned out to be the easiest to find once I happened on some plants with leaves large enough for dew to gather on them. It wasn't much that I could lick up, but when you're so dehydrated that ripping someone's throat open and drinking their blood suddenly seems like a legit option, you can't be picky. Before the rising sun could burn it all away, I found a few shallow pools of water that had gathered in the ruts of an overgrown road. If I didn't disturb them too much, I could actually suck up some water before my mouth got full of grit and loam—not that I gave much of a shit about the latter. It was still water, and to my feverish brain that was enough. That I couldn't taste it helped, too.

Next stop: food.

And clothes. Even though the unknotted shirt came down to my thighs, I didn't much care for having my ass hang out like that.

Food turned out to be problematic. In the back of my mind I'd known this from the second I dropped from that branch, but it had been years since scarcity of food had been part of my life. When Nate and I had set out inland from the Georgia coast, we'd had weapons to hunt, and more so, to clear houses of any squatters that had declared them their dens. Sure, it wasn't fun to live off rice, pasta, and beans for weeks at a time, but we'd never had issues procuring either. More often, eating what remained of our last kill or preserving the meat before it could spoil had been the issue, and once we stopped being nomads exclusively, neither had mattered anymore.

Now, I had no weapons—not even a knife—and while the proximity to the camp city had the advantage of keeping the land free of apex predators, I soon realized just how much of a good job they'd done establishing themselves here. Car wrecks had been pulled off the roads and stripped of anything useful, and the first three houses I found—and crept through very, very carefully—didn't even have a hammer or screwdriver left that I could turn into a makeshift weapon. Also no food whatsoever, or clothes; they'd even ripped the sheets off the beds and dragged the mattresses off. As much as I could applaud their craftiness and level of organization, it was a living nightmare for me now. The only loot I found was a cracked plastic measuring cup that had been discarded because it was broken. I took it with me to make drinking water easier.

It was after leaving that third house—reluctantly, because the sun was baking down on the land and my body was still fighting the drugs, and what water I'd found wasn't enough to make up for yesterday's dehydration—that I happened upon the first patrol, thankfully far enough in the distance that I had plenty of time to hide. Within the hour, three more followed, always in teams of two or three vehicles, carrying up to ten men, armed to the teeth. I still had no clue in what direction the camp was but must have wandered into their exit corridor. While I kept on foraging, a larger group blasted down a road about a mile from where I was hiding, looking a lot like the raiding party that had been our introduction to this illustrious group. I noted in what direction they were heading but cut down on the impulse to follow. Without weapons or provisions, this was a recipe for disaster, and getting those fucking drugs finally out of my system would be great, too.

I still hadn't found anything useful by nightfall, which forced me to reconsider my plan. I wasn't even sure if I'd managed to keep heading in the same direction as my senses were somewhat addled, the pounding headache not helping. There wasn't any good shelter to be found so I kept on wandering into the darkness, trusting my freak eyes to do their thing better than during the day. A flock of birds taking flight finally led me to a small stream, which felt like a gift from the universe by that time. Sweat during the day had done away with some of the grime sticking to my body but it was an amazing feeling to not just drink until I started puking up water, but to cool my blistered feet and clean up what signs of last night remained that I could. My body had taken more of a beating than I'd realized, and without proper nutrition, healing was as much a curse as a blessing. I didn't give a shit about my nose but my fingers were still bothering me, mending crookedly if at all.

I spent about an hour at the stream before I got dressed again, shivering in the frigid night air. With no other option in sight, I ended up crawling into an abandoned car's backseat; at least the closed-off space kept some of the night's cold at bay, even if there was no blanket to wrap myself up in.

I returned to the stream in the morning to make sure I got enough water to last me through the next day before I set out once more after crossing it. It wasn't much of a natural border as it was barely reaching to my knees as I waded through, but humans had, for a long time, used mountain ranges and bodies of water as demarcation lines of their territory. Maybe if I went south a little farther, I'd hit pay dirt.

I almost couldn't believe it when, late afternoon, I found a small cabin in the middle of nowhere that, while ransacked, hadn't been stripped of absolutely everything. Bingo. I managed to get some water from the well that didn't smell rotten; while the box of ramen noodles I found in the back of a cupboard soaked in it, I put together a small arsenal of tools and kitchen knives that were better than my bare hands. An old, threadbare blanket and the ratty sofa would make for a great bed, and the oversized, torn shorts would be wearable tomorrow morning after they'd dried from my efforts to scrub them clean. I ignored what little else there was left in here—mostly pots, smashed plates, and old books—in favor of wolfing down the food as soon as it was chewable. Since I found some more rope, I set out a few snares but doubted I'd catch anything overnight.

And then all that was left to do was curl up on the sofa—for once not either ice-cold or stewing-hot—and feel the weight of the world come crashing down on my spirit.

Two days. That's how much I had wasted, and I hadn't even managed to properly feed myself. If nothing changed tomorrow, I'd have to resort to eating bugs to keep my strength up. I still needed more water—and containers to carry it with me—clothes, gear, and a fucking brilliant idea of how to get Nate out of that camp. Two days was a fucking long time in which a lot could happen and go wrong. I didn't even need my inherent paranoia to come up with options to know that; I'd seen and experienced enough of it firsthand.

Being afraid for his life was one thing—and not something I was used to. But feeling so utterly useless? That was a much harder pill to swallow. In the end, Nate was very capable of taking care of himself, even under bad conditions. Me? I was rapidly failing all the tests that fate had started throwing my way.

I woke up as early dawn light brightened the world outside the dirty window by my makeshift bed, feeling just a little less glum than the day before. Keeping the blanket wrapped around my shoulders, I gathered up my little pile of loot and stashed it in a pillow case before I set out once more, this time heading east. That's the direction the raiding party had gone in.

My guess about the stream being a natural boundary turned out to be at least passably right as I happened upon a few more houses over the next hours. As with the one I'd slept in, all of them had been looted, but there was enough left that was useful to someone who had literally nothing. My best weapons remained a long kitchen knife and a hammer, but at least I could stock up on clothes that, for the most part, covered my body and fit well enough not to be a hindrance. I hesitated to switch the boots out for running shoes, but since I'd much more likely run for my life than kick someone's face in, I went with the better-fitting, light option. Food was still scarce, but I now had a small backpack and enough mismatched water bottles to last me two days, if I didn't spend the hottest hours of the day sweating out in the sun. Days of walking had helped make my body work normally for the most part, although I still got the shakes when I remained immobile for too long.

With little additional food to be found but shelter aplenty, I decided to go hunt for the camp now that darkness was falling, and try to learn what I could in the hours when guards would be tired and cranky from having to pull graveyard shifts. With all the torches lighting the camp, it would also be easier to find than in broad daylight.

It turned out, finding the camp was the least of my problems; getting close to it was a different matter. Lacking binoculars or weapons with optics, I had to rely on my eyes to get the information I required, and since those were still attached to my head, that came with drawbacks. Even at what must have been close to midnight, they had patrols out aplenty, and after the second close call I realized they weren't just using night vision goggles but some thermal vision imaging shit that made me feel lucky I hadn't tried in earnest to sneak closer. Even from a distance, I managed to get some information, and it wasn't looking good, I had to admit, when my nightly suspicions turned all too true once the sun rose.

What I'd thought was the main part of the camp turned out to be just the part near the entrance—one of three entrances that I found. I could have been wrong, but once I realized what the weirdly shaped slopes behind it were, my stomach sank. It was built right in front of a coal mine, and they would have been stupid not to colonize the tunnels as well. That meant I would likely have to drastically increase my idea of how many people lived there—and that also explained why nobody I watched from afar seemed to be in high alert status after I had killed at least one of them. A town of two hundred people would mourn one of their own. In a settlement of several thousand, what was one asshole that had likely had it coming?

The fact that only parts of the camp were aboveground also meant that I couldn't really do much with what little intel I managed to gather. Before I withdrew toward the nearest shelter to wait out the heat of the day—and get some much-needed sleep—I realized that another of my first assessments had been wrong, besides the size of this operation: while the raiding parties seemed to exclusively consist of male soldiers, there were plenty of women going about tasks, from guarding to vehicle maintenance and more domestic chores. Most of them seemed to give the barn—the one landmark I could pick out without problems even from a distance—a wide berth, but the same was true for a lot of the men as well.

It was on my second return trip, close to sundown, that I noticed another complex of buildings outside of the flux of people moving around. I would likely have ignored them like I did before if not for the string of people that were shooed into them, coming down over a sequence of ramps from what must have been the top of the mine at the north side of the camp. Without any means of magnification, I couldn't be sure, but they seemed to be walking willingly enough in single file, but that on its own made my hackles rise. Farm workers, maybe? I didn't expect the mine to be operational still as there likely was no need for that, but food? Food was always vital.

Or maybe that was just my cramping stomach speaking.

True enough, the next morning just after sunrise, the procession started in the opposite direction, mostly ignored by the waking population. I quickly lost count, but that must have been a good thousand people mindlessly slogging up that hill, guarded by only a handful. It was such a bizarre undertaking that I couldn't help but watch in fascination—and the sinking feeling that no human being, however desperate, would let themselves be led like sheep to the slaughter like this just because they were hungry. Something weird was going on there—well, weirder than drugging people and kidnapping them—but none of that helped me to locate Nate.

I tried a few times to get closer to the camp, but they had their perimeter set up well, and even toward noon it was an impossible task. With no other option, I decided to go the long way around, heading back toward that oak tree, and try to find out what the labor force was up to in the north. Half a day of dashing from cover to cover—and long stretches of walking once I was away from what I'd figured out were their patrol routes—I finally veered toward my destination. My guess had been right—north of the mine, an area about as large as the territory Nate and I had patrolled just a week ago was set up as fields, including irrigation channels and connective roads to make them accessible with smaller machines. Not that I saw any as most of the labor seemed to be back-breaking, hands-only kind of shit. They were growing a lot of vegetables and grain, at least from what I could tell enough to feed their camp several times over. Guards were much scarcer up here than around the camp entrances, and taking my time, I managed to sneak as close as a hundred feet to where the workers did their thing in the baking-hot midday sun. It was close enough that I could have alerted them by shouting, which I, of course, didn't do. It was also close enough to see that several of the lean-going-on-emaciated figures had dark marks across their sun-burnt necks—and not all of them just a single X but three.

I spent hours looking for a familiar face—or tats; it wasn't like Nate would have been hard to spot if he'd been shirtless like most of them—but came up empty.

They worked through the entire day without taking a break—the guards went through one more rotation that I could track. None of them slacked off when the guards weren't looking, and none of them seemed particularly enthusiastic about what they were doing—not a stretch of the imagination there but they looked more like robots than human beings. And once the workday ended and they were shooed back toward the mine, they all went without a single scuffle or fight breaking out.

What I knew was happening at that barn might disgust me on a cellular level, but this? This freaked me the fuck out.

There were no guards posted on the fields once the last worker had trudged away, but I still waited until after full dark before I sneaked into the agricultural space. Why, I couldn't say—it wasn't like any of the crops would be ready for harvest any time soon; from what I could tell, they'd been busy with plucking weeds, and in one corner planting more seedlings.

That was until I traipsed across a small connective trek into another field and realized what the bushels coming out of the ground belonged to: carrots! That they weren't much longer than my palm yet and barely thicker than my fingers, I didn't care as I tore into them, pulling as many of them out of the ground as I could hold in my grubby little hands. Then I ran, already munching on the first one, swallowing it as soon as I'd chewed it into manageable chunks. I'd never figured I'd be so damn happy to have vegetables back on the menu.

After finishing the carrots—and getting seconds—I waited another hour, sitting in the high grass, before I tried to get closer to the mine complex from this side, but like before, I soon got too close to the perimeter guards and had to backtrack. I tried several more times, wandering south again, but once morning broke, I had to admit one devastating fact to myself: no way was I going to get in there unless it was tied up at the back of a truck or ATV again. With no weapons, and no backup to create a diversion or overwhelm one of the guard teams, my cards couldn't have been worse. Until then I hadn't realized how lucky I had been to get away, but the same wouldn't be true a second time.

With a heavy heart I realized that there was only one thing I could do: I had to get help. As much as I hated leaving Nate behind, lingering out here wouldn't help him at all, and every hour I remained increased the chances that I would be caught—and that wasn't an option I could risk. So I did the only thing I could do, and left.

Chapter 5

It took me a good two days to leave the zone of heavy looting and chance upon a house that hadn't been breached yet, a good forty miles away from the camp, roughly north to northeast of the fields. It wasn't completely pristine—something had burst through the screen door in the back and left it open to invasion by smaller critters, but I didn't mind the raccoon feces all over the kitchen floor. The little assholes had made it into the pantry, but I found an entire shelf full of cans and preserves still undisturbed. One of the former inhabitants had been close enough to my size that I could finally grab some underwear that fit and update my gear to something that would help me survive out there. I also found containers useful for travel, and maps. I'd done my best trying to find out in which state I had ended up in over the past day, and that finally confirmed it— much to my heavy swearing. Fucking Alabama. The camp was a good hundred and fifty miles away from our tree house base, which left me with several options, none of which I liked.

Option one: backtrack to our home and check if they'd left anything useful behind. With luck, the buggies would still be charging at their station, and a usable vehicle would take days, if not weeks, off my trek back to civilization. There was a small chance that they'd left guards behind, but until I got there, well over a week would have passed, which made that more than implausible. Yet considering how well they had been equipped and how thoroughly they had raided the land around their camp, I doubted I'd find anything left behind except one or two of the hidden caches.

Option two: directly make for the nearest settlement that I was aware of and hope I didn't doom myself in turn.

Scrutinizing the maps spread out on the kitchen table, I couldn't help but clench my barely mended fingers into as much of a fist as they would go. I was smack in the middle of Alabama now, which was about as no-man's-land as the southern states went. We hadn't exactly kept up with the establishment of settlements around the territories we roamed, only making sure we weren't getting too close to any of the established trade routes. I knew two towns I could be heading for, both over three hundred miles from my current position, and about as far away from the tree house as well. None of our temporary hideouts were en route, but if I took a two-day detour I could make it to one of our oldest caches in four to five days from now. I didn't remember what exactly we'd left there, but I'd finally be armed again and have some basic survival gear.

Either way, that meant I would spend at least a week out there, on my own, without backup.

For just a moment, I allowed myself to let despair come up from the depth of my soul and envelop me like a weighted-down blanket. Fuck, but I really missed him. For years now, Nate had been a constant in my life, and for the past two of those, the only human being I'd had any contact with. Sure, I'd often been close to murdering him in his sleep, but that didn't give anyone on this planet the right to just take him from me!

Exhaling slowly, I forced myself to let go of the frustration and anger, but also the latent fear licking up my spine. I could do this. I would do this, no question. I would find help, I would get him out of there, and then I would get bona fide gloating rights for the rest of my life that I'd been the heroine that came to his rescue. I was sure that Nate would graciously accept being the damsel in distress in this scenario.

The very idea—and the grimace he'd offer me when I laid that all out to him—made me crack a smile for a moment. Yeah, that's exactly what I would do.

As much as I hated having to leave everything behind, there was no sense in returning to the tree house. Everything could be replaced. Getting to the weapons cache was more important, and then connecting to the rest of the world. That came with its own host of issues that I chose to ignore for the moment. First, I had to make it to that settlement; the rest I would deal with as it slapped me in the face. And, who knew? Maybe this would all be over soon in a month from now and we could slink away into the sunset just like we'd done once before already.

I didn't buy my own bullshit for a second, but that didn't change anything about the plan. Taking one last look around, I gathered my pack, stowed away the maps, grabbed my hammer, and off into the wilderness I went.

Being all on my own out on the road wasn't a pleasant experience, but it wasn't that different from how Nate and I had spent the time since the Georgia coast drop-off from the destroyer. Sure, two people with firearms could deal a lot more damage than I could on my own, but for the most part, we'd relied on stealth rather than firepower. Being on foot had a lot of drawbacks, but it also meant that I was almost silent even if I didn't try to be stealthy, and it was easy to get sensory input from my surroundings. I often smelled shamblers miles ahead of encountering them—or in those cases, avoiding said encounters— and most larger predators of the four-legged persuasion left humans the fuck alone if they could help it. Loneliness and my own mind were by far the biggest problem, although I did my best to keep the frustration at bay. Walking from early dawn to well into dusk each day helped; there is only so much emotional turmoil you're capable of when the largest part of your mind is in constant crisis and survival mode. Except for a few brief detours, I made good time and reached the location of the cache a day sooner than I'd estimated.

I still remembered the lone farmhouse in the middle of nowhere. We'd stayed there for a few days, as long as the provisions we'd found in the pantry held up. We'd found a storm cellar out back that had remained sealed throughout the first two years of the apocalypse, and it had made a lot of sense to keep some of our meager belongings and gear there, should we ever need a fallback location. Coming here now on my own made my latent misery return in full force, but I swallowed as much of it as I could and went down the rusty stairs to check on our stash.

Everything was still where it was supposed to be, and I let out a breath of relief I hadn't realized I'd been holding when my fingers closed around the cool metal of the assault rifle. There were two shotguns and several handguns there as well, but since I had no intentions of letting anything come close enough to me that I'd need a slug to put it down, the M16 it was. Dumping the sparse contents of my pack on the floor, I grabbed one of the stashed backpacks— larger and sturdier than the one I'd picked up earlier—and started repacking it, making sure to grab enough ammo for the rifle and the two handguns I took as well. I hesitated with my—shaking—hand hovering over the first-aid kit but took it, same as the small stash of meds. None of them would do me much good, but it might come in handy for trading. The sleeping bag and spare clothes were tempting but I forewent them, only grabbing two sets of tinted shooting glasses and the modified gloves from the shelf. It was an early pair, barely better than the prototype I'd used in France; this one had all fingers attached, making me look less like a freak, but the chafing inside annoyed me as soon as I put them on. I'd had much better-fitting ones at the tree house base, but there was no use in crying over their loss now. A solid pair of boots, sturdy cargo pants, and a lightweight jacket were quickly exchanged—and then all that was left for me to do was decide whether to set out now or spend the night. Since there was no food left—an oversight that I only now realized was a fucking stupid one—I decided to hit the road. Now that I had firepower again, I could make for a better target than abandoned cabins that had, at best, slim pickings.

I ended up sleeping in another car that night, a broken-down pickup at the side of the road that had seen better days at the end of the last century—but came with mechanical locks on the doors and spare keys under the sun visor, making it one of the most secure hiding places I'd had in a while. Just for kicks and giggles, I tried to start the engine the next morning, but of course it was as much of a useless hunk of metal as all the other cars. Martinez could maybe have gotten it working again but what little skills I'd picked up along the way had become useless by the time any freely available fuel spoiled for good. That had been one of the reasons why we'd built the electric engines of the buggies from scratch—necessity. I idly wondered for a moment if someone with enough manpower had already raided the Tesla factory. That, in turn, made me realize that I had absolutely no clue what was going on all over the country right now—which I had the nagging feeling would come to bite me in the ass very, very soon, if it hadn't already. I really didn't care for the glum feeling that spread through me as I realized that maybe it had been simple complacency that had gotten us kidnapped because we hadn't paid attention to a rising threat outside our borders.

With that positive outlook on life, I hit the road once more, doing my very best to ignore my own thoughts.

Finally being armed again certainly gave me better chances of survival, but it didn't mitigate the fact that I was just one woman, on her own, against the whole wide world. I'd been lucky so far not to encounter a lot of shamblers, but that changed later that day when I caught a whiff of decay coming from up ahead where I couldn't see what lay beyond the small rise in the road. I halted and tried to decide what to do, but ended up moving forward after all; walking cross-country was only an option if it helped my immediate survival, but in the long run it would slow me down too much. I heard them long before I saw them, and eventually retreated into the trees to the south as I inched closer.

And there it was—an entire streak of zombies, the horde a good thousand individuals strong. I'd seen way worse in the past, but usually with backup and cars that made flight much, much easier. They weren't bothering with the road but the terrain evened out once the road left the sparsely growing trees, giving them room to roam in all directions—and already, a few had halted from their vaguely northeast course and were turning to face me, making me guess that they'd picked up my scent.

Not good. So not good.

I didn't even think for a second about confirming my suspicion but instead started backing away as quickly as I could do so quietly. As soon as I was back on the road, I started to run, ignoring the alarm going off in my mind about the thunder of my boots on the cracked tarmac. A chorus of angry, hungry screams started up behind me.

Crap. At least I didn't need to waste any time on checking over my shoulder—that I'd just rung the dinner bell was obvious.

My first impulse was to head for one of the car wrecks littering the road but none of them looked like it would be able to withstand an entire swarm of hungry shamblers. My next best option would have been the trees thinning out all around me, but none looked large enough to support me, and I wasn't too keen on finding out exactly how bad my already less-than-stellar grip was due to my right hand still needing days, if not weeks, to mend. I had no illusions about winning an endurance race against creatures that were no longer governed by things like exhaustion and energy expenditure calculations. My best bet was to find refuge in a house and pray that it either had a storm cellar or attic.

Too bad the closest building I could make out was a good five miles to the south, cross-country.

To make sure that really was an option, I did look back, finding a good hundred shamblers hot on my heels, a lot closer than I liked. I didn't bother with waiting for the trees to be replaced by open grassland and took off toward the house, hoping that some of them would get confused. I considered dropping some of the load I was carrying, but I direly needed both my weapons and my pack, and there was no telling in what condition I'd be able to reclaim them later, if at all. So I ran, and ran, and hoped for the best.

A few of the zombies got awfully close, but I managed to stay ahead of them the entire race to the small cluster of buildings that got bigger and bigger way too slowly. I was huffing and puffing by the time I threw myself through the rickety screen door, more falling into the house than stepping inside. I had a split second to orient myself before two shamblers came for me—from behind the couch in the den. With no time to waste and little room to maneuver, I ignored them in favor of sprinting for the stairs I saw up ahead, taking them two at a time. The squatters collided with my entourage, the resulting snarls spurning me on further. Not all of them remained behind, though, their pounding feet on the squeaking stairs a reminder that I wasn't in the green yet.

There were five doors on the upper level, all ajar and two torn off the hinges, making me guess the squatters might just be the original residents of the house. None of the rooms looked inviting—or a good place to make a stand—so I ran on to the other end of the landing, frantically searching the ceiling. There it was, the trapdoor leading up into the attic—but it was closed, with no cord conveniently hanging down to be pulled open.

Not that I would have had time to pull it right now, anyway.

The first of the shamblers slammed into me, doing a good job screwing with my balance and trapping my rifle between my body and the wall. It was stupid enough to latch onto my pack rather than me, giving me the second I needed to pull my gun. It even did me the favor of wrenching me around so that I could fire the three follow-up nuisances in their partly decomposed faces, felling them all with eight bullets. The zombie still clinging to me let go, either to make another grab for me or because the scent of blood and gore distracted it; two bullets into the back of its skull and I was free to go hunt for the pole that would open the attic hatch—provided I found it in under ten seconds flat. To buy myself a little more time, I leaned over the bannister and emptied the rest of the magazine into the mass of shamblers tearing into each other all over the stairs.

Light came in through four of the doors so I discarded them as bedrooms or bathrooms, and instead kicked at the last door, making the light plywood bang against the wall inside. The free space in the room beyond was barely large enough for me and my pack to fit inside, which would have made it a good alternate hiding space if I didn't have other options. Shelves full of cleaning supplies and crap nobody needed anymore greeted me—and the pole, leaning against the wall just inside the door. I grabbed it with one hand while holstering the gun with the other, and swung it around just in time for the next shambler to get hit in the leg by it. The pole didn't make for a good weapon but I still stabbed the end of it not intended to open the latch of the hatch at the shambler's face, hoping for the best. It didn't do much damage, but it distracted the blasted thing long enough that a good kick to its abdomen sent it toward the top of the stairs, where those storming up grabbed it and tore it down to the floor. Whipping around, I stabbed at the latch with the pole, needing agonizing seconds to make the parts connect—and finally, the trap door opened, spilling the folded-up ladder down on top of me.

Too slow to sidestep, it hit me in the shoulder, but I wouldn't be deterred by the brief spark of pain radiating down my arm. It was made of aluminum, sturdy enough to hold my weight well as I scrambled up, vaulting into the attic. As soon as I was through, I whipped around and grabbed the upper rung of the ladder to pull it up. Two zombies made a run for it but got tangled in the bodies littering the floor. The ladder folded with a satisfying "snap" just as the hatch fell closed.

Panting heavily, I allowed myself to sag into a half-crouch as I pulled the rifle around and pointed it at the closed hatch. Below, I could still hear them howl and scream and tear into each other, but unless they got really ambitious and built a stack of bodies big enough to reach the ceiling, I was safe—or as safe as I was going to get inside a stifling hot attic that reeked of decay, badly enough to make me cough now that I'd inhaled enough of the tainted air.

I almost expected another shambler to come launching itself at me, but quickly realized that the source of the stench had long since stopped being a potential menace. Flies were swarming over the mummified lumps of bones with parchment-like skin stretched over them. My heart seized up when I realized that the human one was too small to be a woman, at least not a grown one. Folded in on top of the other, I figured it had been the family's child and dog—and judging from the fact that the trap door pole had been neatly stored away, someone must have locked them in here. Not to die, presumably, but to buy them a little more time, maybe to be rescued by someone—until they'd run out of food and water, or, more likely, the child had succumbed to the fever but never reanimated. Sealed to the outside elements and baking away in the heat of hot summers, the corpses had been well-enough preserved rather than decomposing completely.

I stared at the mummies for a while before lowering my rifle and sitting down next to the hatch, my heart heavy with someone else's loss. I remembered all too well how bad those first few months had been, how many tragedies like this one we'd happened upon. If the shamblers had one thing going for them, it was that they were great about disposing of easy prey, and they didn't mind if it was more decomposed than they themselves if fresh meat wasn't available. At least the smart ones had learned along the way that, sometimes, houses and cars held precious protein still available to them. If they didn't turn into squatters, that usually made raiding a house all the more easier as we didn't even need to smash in windows or kick in doors as they'd already done it for us. I generally didn't like to consider how much of a natural selection advantage that must have been, letting the smart ones survive as they feasted on the dumb and the dead.

But most of that easy food was gone now, making me their option for prime rib—a consideration that I was more comfortable with than continuing to imagine how the last days of that child must have been. I had water for a little over three days with me that I could possibly extend to five if I was crafty, or seven if I got really desperate. I hoped that by nightfall, the shamblers would walk off, letting me slink away quietly like I should have done at the first whiff of decay in the air. A rookie mistake that almost cost me my life, and at the very least an entire day.

Sighing, I stretched out on the floor and closed my eyes, waiting for my body to calm down completely. What was a single day to me? Nothing. But to Nate? I didn't want to consider that, but unbidden images swam up before my mind's eye. Would they torture him? Try to break his spirit to turn him into a mindless worker drone? Or did they have fucked-up drugs for that as well? I'd never forget what that shit Bucky had shot him up with had turned him into, and while they'd told us we were immune to that now, I didn't believe that for a second. But it had been a very different kind of mind control than with the workers on the fields—and besides, I didn't think that anyone still had resources left to waste on a labor force. Some naturally occurring compound that regrew or could be bred made more sense—not that any of it made any sense at all.

It took forever for the screams to die down, and longer still until the wet sounds of feasting dropped off. The attic felt like it was at least a thousand degrees, and since I would be fucked if anything got in here whether I was all geared up or not, I peeled myself out of my clothes before I lay down next to them once more. The attic had two windows but both were impossible to pry open, and I didn't dare smash them; somehow, disturbing the peace up here with my presence was bad enough; I didn't need to add to that. It wouldn't bring me any relief as long as the sun was up, anyway.

I dozed off eventually, even though I wasn't accustomed to sleeping under these conditions anymore. As much time Nate and I had spent preparing for worst-case scenarios over the past months, we'd gotten fucking complacent and pampered as well. Not for the first—or hundredth—time I regretted that we hadn't gone straight up to Alaska after leaving the bunker. Sure, spending half the year buried in ice and snow wasn't fun, but I didn't mind hardships if they came with a good overall chance of survival. With the entire summer to prep, hunt, and gather, we could have easily established an enclave for fifteen to twenty people. Hell, why had Nate been so stupid and let Emma pretty much run us out of the bunker that was ours as much as hers? Why did we have to play heroes? Wouldn't it have been enough to survive?

I never voiced those thoughts around him, but now, on my own, all alone in the world, it was hard not to be a little resentful. I'd lost so much that year—and I didn't even mean physically, although I sure missed my fingers and toes an awful lot. We'd been a family, a rag-tag band of survivors and all that shit. In fact, that first winter I'd felt more like I had a place in the world than ever before, and, if I was honest, ever since. I'd belonged. Of course it hadn't been perfect, but

I'd had food to eat, water to drink, and people to annoy—what more could anyone ask for?

And what had I traded that in for? A stinking sauna of an attic, and no one being the wiser if I ended up locked in here, dying of thirst.

That idea—that for whatever reason the hatch was permanently shut, locking me in here—made a bout of paranoia surge through me, but I forced myself to relax before I could bolt for the trap door and increase my problem tenfold. No, I would get out of here, and if I had to shoot a new way for me to get out through the floor, wall, or roof, so be it.

The day kept dragging on forever. Once the sky outside started to darken, I decided that I'd had about enough of this and tried the hatch. A little fumbling got the latch to disengage and I managed to push the door open just far enough to peer outside without letting the ladder down. I didn't remember how many shamblers I'd put down before, but there were enough torn-apart body parts for at least twice that many, the feasting still going strong. Even though I had barely made a sound, two heads snapped up and turned in my direction immediately, intelligent, bright eyes zeroing in on the gap in the ceiling. I quickly pulled the door back up, stepping away to err on the side of caution. I wasn't going to get down there tonight, that much was sure. Maybe not even tomorrow. I liked the odds about as much as the stink in the attic, which wasn't better now that the acrid scent of my sweat and urine added to it. Time to go look for option B.

The attic wasn't exactly spacious but had been rudimentarily furbished, mostly for storage. I ignored the spare duvets and boxes full of old clothes in favor of looking for something more useful... like the toolbox I eventually found near some electrical wiring supplies. It was old and rusty, squeaking somewhat awfully as I opened it—obviously the backup box—but I didn't mind. Fuck fancy new drills that had, years ago, run out of batteries. I'd take an old-fashioned screwdriver any day, thank you very much.

I found not just one but an entire set of them—and, just as I was about to set to work on the recalcitrant windows, there was the attachable handle for the windows. Feeling slightly stupid that I hadn't looked for that first, I tried my luck—and, seconds later, got my first free and unencumbered breath in fucking forever. The window was high up and small, but thanks to boxes full of old books and a discarded lawn chair, I managed to build enough of a ramp to first check, then push my pack up and out through the window, with me following closely behind. I didn't much care for the height of the roof, but it only took me ten minutes to gather my courage, tie a makeshift climbing harness of the rope I'd liberated from a house the day before, and set about getting down to the ground. As if to make up for my blunders earlier in the day, it all went without a hitch or much noise, and I managed to slink away without disturbing the shamblers still busy inside the house. Those that must have lingered outside had long since wandered off to greener pastures, and that was exactly what I set to do as well. The next time I'd catch a whiff of death, I'd be long gone before it could try to catch up with me.

Chapter 6

Two more nights of sleeping in cars, and two more days of walking as long as my legs would carry me, and I had about enough of traipsing through the wilderness on my own. So, when I got close to another small town and noticed a rusty, dirty sign advertising a bike shop, it made me halt in my tracks. I would normally have passed it up, but there'd been an abundance of old signs praising the beauty of the recreational areas around, and the "bike" in question seemed to be a bicycle rather than something that relied on fossil fuels. I still had over a hundred miles to go, maybe farther if my intel was old and the settlement didn't exist anymore, so finding an alternate mode of transportation wasn't the worst idea I'd had that week. In my head, I could hear Nate's voice taunting me about little girl bikes, pink with unicorns on them, but rather than annoy me, that idea made me smile. Now all I could do was hope this idiocy wouldn't get me eaten.

The town wasn't large—the sign near the outskirts declared that Willis Springs had been home to 4,795 souls—and thanks to the resorts in the hills outside rich enough that there were lots of spaces between the houses, once well-kept and loved. I'd have lots of exit routes, even if the center proved to be overrun. Just to make sure I could spare myself an unnecessary series of potentially-fatal jump scares, I got off the road leading through town and walked around it, hoping to find the bike shop with the inevitable Mattress Kings and car dealerships. Nope—another sign told me that it was smack in the middle of town, along the quaint main street and its many shops selling fake art and overpriced outdoor gear. My trek around town hadn't yielded any run-ins but I had heard the odd scrape or moan that made me guess it wasn't completely deserted. I longingly looked down the road leaving town, the sheer endless miles of straight tarmac making me shudder. It had been more than a day since I'd last had to run away from anything—I at least owed it to myself to try.

With the sun beating down on me, I decided to disregard every single instinct I had as I ventured into the town—and continued walking, slowly and softly but steadily, in the very center of the road. The squatters would be inside the houses, and I had yet to see one of them pick up a habit of staring out of windows. The more open the space, the more distance to the houses, the more warning I'd get, I figured.

I was about ten blocks into town when I realized I could have tried one of the resorts as well.

There went nothing.

Like most towns, the center of this one was just as clogged with damaged cars left behind by the people who'd tried to get out a little too late. It was too small—and too far away from larger cities—for the remains of FEMA camp tarps. They didn't even have a hospital from what I could tell, and the apocalypse must have hit them late enough that the residents must have known that the shit had hit the fan, judging from virtually no storefront having remained untouched—or the last citizens had had some anger management issues. The signs of looting didn't deter me; at least I wouldn't have to be the one to bust the locks or break the glass, creating unnecessary amounts of noise. It was still nerve-wracking to slowly weave my way through the cars, eyes wide open, stopping every so often to listen.

I realized I'd reached the shop before I'd had a chance to look at the sign; the fact that the sidewalk was littered with twisted metal frames was a dead giveaway. Apparently, I hadn't been the first to get inspired to go hunt for a different mode of transportation. I considered for a moment if it was still worth checking out but figured, since I was like already in mortal danger, I might as well go forward. I was very thankful for my boots as I crunched my way through what remained of the storefront's glass facade, stepping into the shadowy interior of the shop.

The bicycles that had landed on the road outside must have once been lined up by the windows as that space had obviously been cleared. Someone had been in here to loot as plenty of empty racks that must have held clothes one time proved. Since I had all the gear I needed, I ignored what little they'd left behind and sneaked deeper into the store, toward where the remainder of the bikes stood, mostly undisturbed. A few had fallen over, and none that I could see at a first glance still had air in the tires, but that was something I was sure I could remedy—I was, after all, in a bike shop, where there must be pumps and spare parts aplenty.

It took me a few minutes to decide on which one to go for and ended up choosing a bright purple-framed mountain bike. It had been years since I'd owned anything with splashes of color, and I figured that me being a moving target would make me more so in the first place than the bike's frame could. The front tire held the air I sneakily pumped into it well, but the rear one needed patching—or replacing, seeing as I had a good thirty more to choose from. Since I was still on my own and the town around me remained quiet, I took the time to get some extra water bottles—and screw bottle holders to the frame. I considered some kind of saddle bag contraption abomination as well but decided that my pack on my back was as much as I wanted to lug with me. There was just enough room left to cram a tire-mending set in there, and I was ready to leave.

On my way back to the store's front, I paused when my gaze snagged on a bright pink pair of bike shorts. I had absolutely no fondness for the color but I did remember what a vacation's lazy bike excursion had done to my ass and thighs a few years ago all too well. Sure, back then I didn't yet have abs and glutes of steel, but there was something to be said about mitigating likely discomfort. And it wasn't like anyone would see them until I got to the settlement.

For once, I hit the jackpot and wasn't accosted by zombies with the pink bike shorts around my ankles, and made it back out onto the road all dressed and ready to roll. I caught some movement further down the road, the way I had come, and decided to take one of the smaller side streets to circle the town once more. Getting on the bike was easy—and I had, smartly enough, chosen one with a frame fitting my size—but balancing on it was a little harder. In short order I realized that it was kind of a blessing that my right hand was the more busted one, seeing as a hasty, hard brake ended up relatively smoothly with only the rear tire's brake catching—from where my left hand was clawing at the brake handle. Thankfully, there was no one to watch my first shaky mile, and by the time I hit the grassy stretches to get from someone's garden back to the road leading out of town, I was handling myself pretty decently. The heat of the day was just as bad on the bike—and with extra strain on my thighs now maybe even worse, thanks to the additional layer of the shorts—but as

I gathered velocity, I couldn't help but grin at the wind streaking across my face and hair.

I decided that, yes, indeed—this would do.

I pedaled until nightfall and ended up crashing in the hayloft of a barn half a mile from the road. I still had water and the last pack of extra-protein nuts—or so I kept telling myself as I wolfed down the contents of the pack that hadn't been in pristine condition when I'd picked it up. That was enough to get me through the night, and in the morning I decided to risk it and go for the settlement straight away rather than try to find more food elsewhere. I'd lost some weight since that fateful night at the tree house, but not enough to concern me too much. With luck, I'd get a chance to eat—and clean myself up—before the sun set again. I didn't know what I looked forward to more—probably the cleaning supplies. I wondered if I should try picking up something else to barter with, but I couldn't exactly transport it. Maybe trading in the bike would be worth something. Quite frankly, that was one bridge I wasn't too scared of crossing—but found myself oddly apprehensive as I swung back onto the bike and aimed for the road.

And the bike pants turned out to be a saving grace for sure.

I had sixty more miles to go, and while that was better than staying in an attic with two mummified corpses while more lively ones ate each other below, it still was that endless kind of drag that wore me down mentally as much as physically. I did my best to keep the glum thoughts at bay, but I didn't really look forward to reentering civilization once more. Sure, all the amenities of a settlement were nice, but as far as I knew, the world at large wasn't exactly on speaking terms with me. Then again, with over two years since anyone had last seen me, I was probably presumed dead. I likely didn't look anything like what people expected, either—the last sheen of red had long since left my hair, and I'd likely cut off what had once been dyed the last time I'd trimmed it. Unwashed for weeks—and haphazardly braided thanks to my lack of fingers to do so well—my hair was a dark blondish mess that was, if anything, very unremarkable. I still had the marks, of course—and the tattoo down on my back proudly proclaiming my affiliation—but not many would get to see that, or even know about the significance. My memories about what had happened at the camp were more than a little fuzzy but I still remembered that, upon seeing them, they'd all thought of me as an imposter. What had been up with that still left me curious, but I was sure that I would be able to make it work in my favor.

But to worry about all of that, I needed to get into the settlement first without anyone shooting me on sight; I could only hope that this wouldn't be the hard part.

By midday, I saw the first signs that I was getting somewhere close to where the living still roamed freely, after switching from my straight, single-lane road onto a somewhat broader two-lane highway. There was a dust cloud in the sky toward the west, and most of the cars that had broken down on the road had been pushed to the shoulders on either side, creating space enough for larger vehicles to pass at decent speeds. Seeing that gave me a brief pang deep in my chest—damn, but I still missed my Rover. From what I could tell, that dust belonged to a caravan, likely heading to the same settlement or coming from there. I was still miles away from being able to see anything, but already I felt my paranoia come alive.

Maybe this wasn't such a good idea after all. So many things that I didn't know anything about were waiting for me. So many things that could go wrong… but unless I wanted to hoof it north to Dispatch or traverse the hottest states in the country all by my lonesome self—which would take me months at this rate—I was out of options.

Fuck this shit.

And fuck those fucking idiots with their fucking camp and—

This was getting me nowhere, but the settlement was something, somewhere. At the very least I could ask them to get someone on the radio for me—or if worse came to worst, I could always try to track down that caravan. At this point, stealing a car in the middle of the night wasn't beyond me. I considered that option for a moment but since the dust was already settling, I figured I'd have a hard time catching up to them.

Settlement first. If that failed, I'd look for a different solution.

It took me the remainder of the afternoon to get to the first sign proclaiming "10 miles to Sweet Water, Alabama"—my ultimate destination. On the maps I'd picked up, it didn't look like much more than two roads crossing in the middle of nowhere, but that was the same for most modern settlements. They had roads, access to water, and woods around aplenty to build fortifications and new buildings, if needed. They were also far enough away from larger towns that people could have survived there, although I wasn't sure when this settlement had been established as such. I hadn't paid much attention to that besides the few places we'd decided to visit—which had been farther north and west of here. For all I knew, it could have sprung up the summer after we'd dropped off the side of the earth; the intel we had about it was from the year after that—last year—and nothing more than a name and vague location.

I figured it was a good sign that, as I drew closer, I reached the end of the forest to where trees had been felled only days ago, the scent of freshly cut wood still heavy in the air, and nature hadn't had time to grow over the drag marks of where the logs had been pulled closer to the road to be transported off. I didn't see any guards out on patrol but with the sun about to set in an hour or so, they'd probably returned to the town already—or were stealthy enough not to let themselves be seen. I couldn't help but feel watched as I continued to pedal down the road to where, ever so slowly, the settlement came into view.

They hadn't bothered digging ditches or erecting flimsy metal fences like some communities but relied on a double wall of heavy log palisades, easily spanning several miles in circumference from what I could tell. Directly around the palisades and close to the road, the ground was barren, even the grass whacked to below the height where anything larger than a cat or rabbit could have been hiding. Beyond that, I saw the setup for fields large enough to support a community several hundreds strong but nowhere near what I'd seen at the camp. Along the road, I could still see what remained of the old village; the new settlement lay to the north and west of where my road met a similar one coming down from the north. Remained, because they'd done a good job deconstructing everything that could be carried off, further adding to the large, open space that kept hiding spots to a minimum. People had known what they were doing as they established this settlement; good for them, but it made me a little wary. I hadn't forgotten who had been all too ready to volunteer their help, expertise, and manpower for guards to all those who had survived the first winter. Hell, this far south, it probably didn't even snow during the colder months; they might very well be one of the earliest established settlements as far as I knew.

The lack of guards was easily explained once I got a better look at the palisade as I drew closer. It was manned with several people walking the perimeter between three established guard houses that I could see, and several more that I could guess at, plus two right and left of the—right now securely barred—gate. A few continued their circuit but several stopped to keep track of my progress. I could only guess at how bemused they must have been to see anyone come down that road on a bicycle.

None of them shot at me, so that felt like a win.

I sure as hell was glad to stagger off that damn contraption of a vehicle, trying not to fall flat on my face. My back and legs were aching but none too happy to have to support my weight now that I was back on earth where I belonged. My body was in dire need of sustenance, and still way too hot. All that mixed with more than just a hint of trepidation—not the most ideal circumstances. I still did my humanly best to appear confident yet calm as I looked up at the guards and waved. Nobody guns down whimsically funny girls, right?

"Hey there!"

"Hey there, yourself," one of the men called down, a bemused look on his face. He seemed friendly enough. "It's been a while since anyone chose to show up on a bike."

"But that did happen before?" I would have been lying if I'd said I wasn't surprised.

"Now that you mention it, no," the guard confessed, chuckling softly to himself. "Looks like you got lost out there?"

Never one to dissuade people from jumping to conclusions that worked in my favor, I shrugged. "You could say that. Would be awfully nice if I could use your radio to call someone to pick me up?" Better to start humble and let them be generous, I figured. Even if they didn't let me in, that guy sounded like he'd drop me some blankets to get cozy by the palisade overnight.

"I can do you one better," he suggested. "How about you come in before some enterprising undead bites you in the ass? We sure have enough food to feed one more mouth."

I waited for further instructions, but the gate was already opening, so I took my bewildered self—including the bicycle— through it. They didn't even activate their kill chute but raised both parts at the same time. Not that I felt much like protesting, but it sure struck me as gullible.

The twenty armed guards out of sight of the gate that I only saw once I was through, not so much, but that put my mind at ease more than on edge. I stopped, waiting, not surprised when the guy I'd been talking to before came clumping down the stairs on the inside of the inner palisade.

"Nice to meet ya. I'm Steven, and this is our welcome committee in this fine town of Sweet Water."

"Anna," I said confidently, shaking his offered hand. He must have noticed that something was weird about my grip but didn't comment on it, instead offering a small nod. He seemed to be waiting for something, so I turned around to let him see the back of my neck, free as my hair was all gathered up under the ball cap I was wearing. "Three, as you can see, but no current affiliation." Turning back to face him, I offered a wry smile. "Hope that's not an issue."

"Not unless you make it one," Steven offered, sounding sincere. "Does help explain why you've been out there, on your own."

"You mean because I'm a woman?"

He shrugged, chuckling again. "As a living, breathing human being. Lots of things can kill you out there if you're not careful. Must help to be a tough bitch."

I took that compliment for what it was but hoped that he wouldn't elaborate on it. Since he wasn't asking, I didn't go into details, but I had to tell him something; there was a certain edge in the air, and I didn't want to bring things to a head by appearing too silent or hostile.

"That's true. Still, not something I'm overly fond of, that being out there on my own thing. I got separated from my people and figured it would be easiest to call in and have them pick me up either here or further along the road. They're likely a state or two away by now." That should take care of any delays in responses—at least for a reasonable time span. I didn't intend to stick around longer than a week if nothing happened.

Steven nodded wisely. "Yeah, things used to be so much easier when the cell towers were still working." He gave me a quick up-and-down before he jerked his head toward the building right next to the gate. "Tell you what? We'll give them a call and see what comes of it. Might be a while until we get a response. In the meantime, we can get you cleaned up and fed. How about that?"

"Sounds great, chief," I offered as jovially as possible. I didn't miss the mistrust in most of the guards' eyes, but there was nothing I could do about that right now. Actually, things were going pretty well as of yet.

I followed Steven into his radio station, not surprised to see a rather basic—but likely indestructible—setup. It took him a bit to get the right frequency, and he filled the time with idle chatter that was really anything but.

"So what's your story, Anna? Where're you from?"

I realized just how sketchy my backstory really was when I didn't immediately think of a good response. I had figured simply going with the same as I'd used before in that blasted town after the incident with Taggard was good enough. I might have been fooling myself with that.

Steven's brows rose when I still hadn't replied ten seconds later, making me shrug and spill more beans than I had intended. "You mean before the shit hit the fan? Medium-sized town on the east coast. But that's hardly who I am anymore. We've spent the last few years touring the south, mostly Arkansas, Kentucky, and Louisiana, my husband and me. Then things got a little too exciting, and, well, here I am."

"Your husband, eh?" Steven muttered under his breath, sounding, if not disappointed, a little suspicious. Gee, the one thing I didn't lie about, and that's where he smelled a ruse? Yet before he could ask, static squawked and the radio came alive. Steven prattled off a few codes I didn't get—and really didn't like how that made me feel—before he raised his brows at me. "Dispatch, I presume?"

"Would be awesome," I agreed.

Somehow, I'd hoped to hear a familiar voice, but whoever was manning the radio wasn't anyone I knew. Steven came to the point quickly after exchanging minimal niceties. "Listen, we have a girl here who got lost in the woods." He grinned at his own joke. "Name's—"

"Anna Hawthorne," I dutifully supplied.

He repeated that without missing a beat. "She's looking for her group, close family and such. Thinks they're likely en route to—"

Again he eyed me askance. "California," I offered succinctly, letting him jump to conclusions. His answering smile was actually a real one, alleviating some of my concerns. "The Coast." He said it with implied capital C. "Got anyone on the move, or someone who could give her a ride? And send them the updated travel schedules as well."

The guy on the other end of the line grumbled about knowing how to do his job and promised to report back as soon as he knew more—tomorrow. Steven looked quite chipper at the chance of having annoyed him. Somehow, that endeared him a little more to me.

Once he'd turned off the radio, he leaned back in his chair and studied me a little more shrewdly. "You got friends in the big city in the west?"

I shook my head—and it wasn't even a lie. "Friends of a friend of a friend whose brother met someone once," I explained. "No deep, profound connections." I'd never consider Gabriel Greene a friend, and after losing Tanner, I wasn't sure if Gita would ever forgive me— if she was still alive. If any of them were still alive, the nasty voice at the back of my mind supplied. That wasn't anything I would concern myself with right now, either.

"Uh-uh," came his response, which could have meant anything.

More to distract him than because I was actually curious, I looked around, noting a few yellowed papers that looked like those damn bounty posters that had once existed of Nate and me when Bucky and his people had—passingly—tried to accost us before we could become more than a nuisance—which had proven to be all lies, anyway. They looked more like trophies, or what you'd see in a teenager's bedroom. "What's up with that? Sorry if I sound clueless, but it's really been a while since I was in a larger settlement."

"Still holding a grudge?" he mused. When I didn't react—also because I didn't have a clue what he was talking about—he explained. "I know that, for a while, things were pretty much us against them against everyone, but as you likely know yourself, politics in reality are never what they are over the propaganda radio waves. Hell, half of our guards are former scavengers, and we're damn happy to have them." He actually looked taken aback for a second. "Pardon my French—"

My laughter cut him off. "It's okay. I've been running with some rough types for a while. Nothing I haven't heard before."

"Just don't tell my wife," he said, actually winking at me. "Anyways. As I said—if you don't stir up any shit, no shit will be flung your way. Like most settlements, we do our thing, and that includes being on talking terms with all kinds of folks. Besides, you can't trust half the sh… stuff some people tell you. Everything gets exaggerated times two when it gets retold. Easily takes twenty people from where it happened until it arrives here—it's anyone's guess if there's any truth to the tale at all anymore. Besides, we've all made mistakes. What counts is that we're still living and breathing, right?"

"Right." It wasn't hard to agree with that. I idly wondered if he'd been waiting for a different reply but Steven nodded and got up before I could think of one.

"Anyway, some things don't change. Marks or no marks, you understand that we'll have to check you out before we let you into the settlement proper?"

"I was wondering when you'd ask for the customary striptease."

He actually looked uncomfortable at my worst impression of innuendo but didn't let himself get deterred. "My wife and two armed guards will check you in private. Female guards. And my wife's our resident doctor. Also, if you need anything checked, just tell her. She's used to it. We'll go through your pack with you now so we can make sure you're not carrying any contraband, and we'd be much obliged if you kept your assault rifle or larger weapons than those handguns with us here at the armory. You'll get them back when you leave."

That was too tantalizing to pass up. "Contraband?"

"Bombs," he said with suddenly icy calm. When he caught my frown, he backed up a little. "As I said, it's been a tumultuous time for a bit. If you have no clue what I'm talking about, be happy you spent those months lazing around in, where was it you said you were?"

"Arkansas, for the most part," I repeated.

"Right. Follow me, please."

My things were exactly where I'd left them, untouched as far as I could tell. I'd expected they'd ask for my rifle and was surprised when they didn't take the magazines as well. My few belongings raised a few questioning looks, particularly as it was obvious that I was running very low on everything, and what few things I'd gathered were recent acquisitions—except for the weapons and survival gear. No one asked, so I didn't volunteer information that might get me in trouble. While they were busy checking my things, I snuck a few peeks myself, and, true enough, several of the guards had marks across their necks, but only two had all three. I watched them a little more closely but, if anything, they seemed to ignore me more than the others—either pretending to be ignorant, or really not wanting to know about my background. Considering what I knew about pretty much every one of the former soldiers who had gotten all three marks, I couldn't hold that against them. Or it was a trap, but nothing I could do about that now.

Satisfied that I wasn't about to suicide-bomb their settlement, Steven shooed me off to one of the adjacent buildings where large kettles sat over fire pits, one of them ablaze at the moment. Three women were waiting for me there, the two guards and the doctor. She seemed less than pleased to be here and told me with a clipped tone to get naked and state my business quickly should I have any. I didn't, and was more than happy to peel myself out of my sweaty, grimy clothes, even though I dreaded the usual reactions ahead.

And, oh boy, they didn't disappoint.

The first of the guards turned away after I peeled off the second glove; the other managed until I shook my boots off. Even the doctor herself stopped acting like a royal bitch and continued to watch me undress with a stony expression only. I did my best to ignore them until I was as naked as a babe, and did the obligatory whirl as quickly as possible without looking like I was trying to hide something. They still all caught the tat on my lower back, and their reactions were comically identical: pity quickly turning to derision. I wondered if someone would finally explain to me now what that was all about.

"See something you like?" I quipped, not really trying to be nice. I'd never liked this being-stared-at-while-naked business, and that had only gotten worse since Canada.

Before either of them could answer, the doctor signaled the guards to leave, and they beat a hasty retreat. She remained but rather than reply, she handed me a bucket full of steaming water, some washcloths, and soap. I didn't hesitate, telling myself that if she wanted to talk, she would.

Turned out, she did. "Most of those scars look like the work of a professional," she pointed out.

"Guess so," was all I was willing to volunteer, trying to both shield as much of my body from her imploring gaze and not let her see my back at the same time.

"Some are real hack jobs."

That assessment made me laugh. "Also true." When she kept staring at me, I shrugged. "Sometimes when you're out there, all you have is someone with a steady hand. Sometimes they don't really have a clue what they're doing, except keeping you alive."

She didn't respond, but I could tell that she agreed. I almost asked her if she was a real doctor, or maybe had some basic knowledge and that had been enough to get that title bestowed on her, but kept my trap shut. No need to antagonize the woman who, quite possibly, got to decide whether they'd throw me out in a minute or two, or let me stay.

"You've seen war. That much is obvious," she finally went on while I got busy scrubbing what was left of my toes. I stiffened, not sure if I should correct her—or whether there was a need to—but she went on before I could come to any conclusions. "I know what those three marks really mean. I don't mean the walking-bomb part—nobody's that superstitious here. Most of us are alive only because of someone with high endurance and immunity, and we are grateful for that. But I know what you very likely did to get them."

Anger wanted to flicker up my spine and make me spew something stupid, but for once asking myself what Nate would have told her helped me keep a moderately calm demeanor. The irony of that wasn't lost on me. "And your point is?"

She actually laughed at my cool tone, irritating me further, until I realized that I'd, somehow, broken the ice. "I'm not passing judgment," she assured me, although her tone was laced with too much sarcasm to be completely honest. "But, after all that, why would you mark yourself up like some imposter fangirl? You can't seriously believe in all the crap people tell themselves when they think those in charge aren't watching."

And that's where she lost me. Not even my cool stare could get me out of that situation, and I got the sense that letting her know I was oblivious was not a good idea. So I left it at a tart, "It's often hard to know all the sides to what went down. And sometimes the simple truth is that even good people make stupid decisions." I hoped to hell that this statement was confusing and vague enough to work as an answer.

I was surprised that it did, although it made the doctor shake her head. "That's true." She paused before she got up, but didn't leave quite yet. "Don't make us regret letting you in. We really don't care about people's ideologies as long as they don't force them upon us. I hope you can hold yourself to that standard as well?"

"I have no idea what you're talking about." And that wasn't even a lie.

She smiled, if tightly. "Exactly." She then gestured in the vague direction of the center of the settlement. "Once you're refreshed, come find me in the village square. We'll get you a place to sleep and make sure you're well fed. You can wash your clothes here and hang them up over there. Nobody will touch them."

That was a strange reassurance if I'd ever heard one but I thanked her nevertheless, happy to finally be on my own again. Damn, but people could be draining sometimes.

Even though I only got half of what was going on, I couldn't really complain. So far everything seemed to proceed splendidly. What could possibly go wrong?

Judging from history, I was minutes away from a full-blown disaster—but I hoped disaster would wait until I got some stew into my stomach. I figured I deserved at least that much.

Chapter 7

The shit didn't hit the fan before I got some stew—beef, which was a very welcome change to my usual diet—and freshly-baked bread into my stomach. Also not before I got some time to socialize with the natives, who turned out to be pretty relaxed about my presence, used to traders and mercenaries as they were. I was downright antsy by the time most people got ready to hit the sack, and still the other shoe hadn't dropped. It was downright frightening how boring and uneventful my time in the settlement started out.

There were no poisonous spiders hiding in the sheets on the mattress in the otherwise empty guest dormitory. No one sneaked in to strangle me in my sleep. By the time the doctor dropped in to fetch me for breakfast, I was ready to jump at shadows. This was beyond weird. How dare people be actually honest and nice to someone who didn't even have a chance to become a nuisance to them? The gall!

I didn't let my guard down, and that was probably the reason why no one tried to mess with me. Even to me it was obvious that I acted like a caged animal—and that was ignoring the shakes and spasms that still plagued me, particularly in the morning after hours of inactivity. The doctor kept watching me closely, and eventually, I asked her to check on my nose and right hand, telling her I'd broken both months ago. If she really knew as much about the serum project as she claimed, she probably saw right through my lie but didn't comment on it. The nose she declared as slightly crooked but okay if I didn't mind the optics; I didn't, quite happy not to have bloody sniffles for days again. I could tell that my hand in its general state upset her—she couldn't hide her discomfort once I took the gloves off again, but valiantly tried nevertheless—but after carefully prodding every inch of my fingers declared she couldn't really do much without an X-ray machine—and didn't think there still existed an operating one of those. I didn't correct her about it and instead listened to her verdict.

"You will very likely regain full functionality once everything is healed completely. But such things take time." The pause that followed was a pregnant one. "What you're really wanting to know is how long the withdrawal will last, right?"

My confusion must have been quite plain, but for whatever reason, that made her fleeting compassion turn to vexation once more. "I don't know what you're talking about," I insisted. She gave me a rather hard, "Yeah, right," look. "I really don't. Lady, if you know as much about us as you say, you know that it takes a damn potent drug to even affect us. Trust me when I say that I really, really wished at one point in my life that painkillers were still doing a thing for me, but they don't. And correct me if I'm wrong, most of the recreational shit is chemically pretty close to that." I almost got into the structural specifics but stopped myself before I could out myself as someone I pretended not to be. Plus, the cursing seemed to throw her off as well.

"Right. And that tells me that whatever you've been abusing must have been some darn potent stuff," she snarled, badly imitating my voice. "When did you take your last hit? Just before coming here? Or is the reason you ended up here because your people cut you off? That would explain why we haven't gotten any news yet."

My mouth was already open in protest but then something occurred to me. "You know something you're not telling me."

"Oh, I know a lot of things," she huffed, narrowing her eyes at me.

"I'm not lying," I insisted again, then looked around to make sure no one was close enough to eavesdrop. "And I think you know that. But you have seen similar things before. That's why you don't trust me. Tell me, what was it?"

"I will do no such thing," she protested, but some of her ire had already transformed to curiosity. "Why should I, if you're just a lying junkie?"

"What if I'm not?" Leaning closer, I made sure to catch her gaze and hold it, which made her mighty uncomfortable all of a sudden. "What if it wasn't my choice to be drugged? What if I'm actually a victim and survivor? What do you think I'd do to someone who I suspected knew something about the people who victimized me?"

I didn't get off on scaring people, and seeing her blanch like that didn't give me any satisfaction. But if it got me answers—or even mere suspicions, which was more than I had at the moment—I really didn't give a shit what I'd have to do.

"I—" she stuttered, blinking rapidly. "I don't know anything." The "know" she stressed hard enough that it only took a sharp look from me for her to spill the beans. "But there have been rumors.

Mostly friend of a friend stuff. About recreational drugs that someone manufactures that actually do work on your kind. Tales of smuggling, and some more unsavory stuff."

"You mean like forced prostitution and slave labor?"

"Lord, no!" she gasped, at first offended by perceived implications, until a possible alternative to the meaning of my words occurred to her. I knew the moment she came to the right conclusion—well, mostly right—when pity took over her face once more.

Before she could speak up, I quickly shook my head. "Not me, but—" I really didn't know how much to tell her, and it wasn't just a matter of trust. I didn't know how far this thing reached, and the last thing I needed was to get someone killed just because I'd confided in them. "Someone close to me," I settled on saying. "But believe me when I tell you, I didn't take that shit willingly."

She nodded, although I could tell that she didn't quite believe me. Right now, that was something I could live with. "I don't know anything about the compound. Just that it exists." She weighed her options carefully before offering, "Maybe your friends in the west know more about that."

I was shaking my head before I realized I was doing it, making myself stop. True, there weren't many things I didn't think Greene capable of, but this was too much even for him. "As I told your husband already, I don't have any friends in New Angeles."

"I didn't say—"

"Is there anything else but that godforsaken town in California?" I griped—doing my best to throw her off again.

She gave me another one of those offended looks but appeared calmer once she opened her mouth to reply. "I wouldn't know as I don't lead a nomadic life. But what I do know is that nothing good comes of this. If one of your friends is caught up in this, I'm sorry. We've heard a few reports about people disappearing. It's not safe to the east."

That sounded about right. Too bad I only now heard of this apparently being common knowledge.

But didn't that raise another question? "Why isn't anyone doing anything about this?"

My question seemed to actually stun her. "Why indeed?" she offered as if that was answer enough. Huh. I was still mulling this over long after she'd gotten up and left me to my own devices. Somehow I got the sense I was missing a big part of the picture, and I doubted I'd find the answers here.

I was still thinking about this when Steven signaled me to join him. "Good news! We got some of your friends on the line."

That was quick, although I did my best not to show my surprise. "That's great! What did they say?"

"They will be here later today to pick you up." Now that I hadn't expected, and this time I was too slow to hide my reaction. "Something wrong?" he inquired, suddenly suspicious.

"It's probably nothing," I tried to assure him. "I just didn't expect anyone to get here this quickly."

He was still squinting, but in a less hostile way. "They said about the same. Dispatch confirmed that they were already signed in for the trip to California for the past couple of days. Must have gotten turned around. Or they were still looking for you."

I absolutely hoped that wasn't the case but I couldn't very well explain that now since it perfectly matched the bullshit I'd dished out yesterday. Oh well—as they said, only one way to find out? But why, oh why, did I feel like, finally, that other shoe was dangling right above my head?

I tried to rest some more—which was a different way of saying that I was hiding from the people in the settlement, feeling a little overwhelmed after so much time on my own. I could sure use some sleep, but my mind wouldn't shut up now that my alertness was triggered. I was also missing Nate like crazy, which seemed idiosyncratic at first since out there not having him around had been way more inconvenient than now, but that was probably the reason why—now that I'd let down my guard, even if only a little, the events of the past days were catching up with me. I almost laughed at how alone I could feel with hundreds of people around, while out on the road I'd been mostly okay.

Way too soon—or not soon enough for my agitated paranoia—Steven sent someone to tell me to get ready. I met him at the gate a few minutes later, busy stowing the last provisions away that I'd been handed—food for two days, and I'd refilled all my water bottles, even those scavenged from the bike shop. I got my rifle back, and Steven watched with a bemused look as I checked it over, then made sure that I had a round in the chamber. "Expecting trouble?"

I left it at a simple shrug. "So many things out there that can kill you. I didn't survive this long by being stupid."

Someone called down from the palisade that the caravan was arriving—apparently, my taxi had been hitching a ride with them, providing additional protection. I couldn't help but hope that I wouldn't have to shoot anyone in the face as soon as that gate was open. Guards all over were getting ready, but their generally relaxed state made me guess it was more for show and to help with hauling cargo from and to the vehicles than to make sure the settlement wasn't invaded.

I couldn't wait to be out of here and find someone who could—finally!—explain to me what was going on.

Steven and five other guards joined me at the gate to wait for the inner part to open. Apparently with more strangers outside they went through the usual procedures, locking us in for a good minute between the doors before the outer one creaked open. I forced myself to relax and clear my mind, prepared to do whatever would help my survival. If I recognized anyone from that damn camp, I'd try to alert the good people of Sweet Water; if it was anyone else gunning for me, I'd make a break for the next available cover and then get the hell out of here, hopefully avoiding civilian casualties. But, who knew? Maybe I really was just paranoid. Maybe those would be familiar faces waiting for me that I'd yearned to see, with all my heart, for months and months on end? That would cut down my calculated timeframes as well.

Convenient indeed, and highly unlikely, I told myself. Keep calm and roll with the punches.

Then the gate was finally out of the way and let me get a glimpse at my transport. I couldn't hold in a short bark of laughter when I saw it—and who was waiting in front of it. "You got to be fucking kidding me," I muttered to myself—but with the hint of a smile. I wasn't quite ready to put away my rifle yet, but it could have been worse.

"Not quite who you were expecting?" Steven asked, studying what had caught my attention himself.

"Not really," I admitted.

"You expecting any problems?" he went on.

I shook my head, if after a moment of deliberation. "Probably not. Nothing I can't deal with."

The guards around us had all snapped to attention upon seeing who the additional guard for the caravan was, and one of them gave me a weird look. "Who the fuck are you that they play pick-up service for you?"

"Wouldn't you like to know?" I quipped in his direction, but since Steven seemed to wonder about that himself—and I didn't want anyone to shoot me in the back once I started walking over there—I answered, leaning conspiratorially closer to Steven. "I really don't have a clue what happened to this country over the past couple of years, but you can tell your wife that she knows who I am. She's seen my tats. There are only two women in the entire world entitled to that tattoo, and nobody would ever confuse me with her. Tell her I'm the real deal."

That said, I nodded to all of them, and started walking toward the Humvee idling at the side of the road.

Chapter 8

I might not have been afraid for my life as I approached the vehicle, but a million different reasons zoomed through my head why they, of all people, were here. The most likely was that I was seconds away from hearing some kind of ultimatum or other that I absolutely didn't like—but I had to admit, if it got me help with getting Nate back, my threshold for what I was okay with was rather high.

It could have been worse. Honestly, when I'd seen the Humvee, my immediate fear had been that I'd have to deal with Hamilton again—although that would have made hunting him down so I could eviscerate him much, much easier.

Still, I much preferred to see Richards, Cole, and Hill standing by the armored vehicle.

There was also some other guy I didn't know hovering beside them. If he was much older than eighteen, I'd be damned. He also obviously had no idea who I was since he kept eyeing me with amusement and the other three with something akin to confusion. So they must have told him something, but not everything.

That begged the question—what on earth were they doing here?

"Don't tell me it's coincidence for you to show up here," I offered instead of a conventional greeting. Just because I might have been willing to cooperate with them didn't mean I had to show it.

I got a tight grin from Cole and a snort from Hill, while Richards crossed his arms over his chest. "Nice to see you, too," Red shot back, calm as always.

I hated to admit it, but seeing the three of them here made me realize that, on some level, I'd missed them, too.

"I'm sure it is," I drawled back. "Cut the crap. Why are you here? And before we have to dance through an entirely necessary conversation, yes, I'm still paranoid as hell, and no, I still won't trust you if your answer involves the term 'classified.'"

Richards considered—which meant he knew exactly what information he was ready to divulge but was letting me stew without admitting as much—before he pushed away from the Humvee, still the picture of lack of concern. Sure, I didn't have my rifle at the ready anymore, and it was unlikely I'd try anything with the caravan and settlement guards close by, but he knew what I was capable of—probably more so than any of the others. The new guy sure seemed to be bursting with curiosity but didn't dare speak up. Sheesh, how was I going to survive that? He'd probably start "ma'am"ing me in under ten seconds flat.

"You missed a drop-off date so I figured I should come investigate why," Richards explained, confusing me both because it did sound honest, and I had no clue what he was talking about—but I could guess.

My answering smile couldn't have been very warm—or friendly. "Come again?"

Red didn't even grimace as he kept staring at me, unmoved. "He didn't tell you."

"Who?"

"Guess."

Really not that hard to do, but it rankled to have to realize that, once again, I'd been in the dark about something. "My husband."

None of the others reacted, although when I glanced his way, Cole gave me a look that spoke plainly that he'd expected me to be smarter. Oh well. Story of my life to keep disappointing people. I took a few seconds trying to remember how Nate had sprung the idea on me to disappear off the side of the earth, and how we'd gone about it. I vaguely remembered him letting me choose what to do and where to go for a long time—until he'd started making suggestions again that had, eventually, turned into him making the decisions. Ah. Smart move, outsmarting me by playing me against my ego. It didn't even hurt. I even knew exactly what he would have said had I confronted him about it now: "What did you expect? For me not to have a backup plan?"

That explained parts of it, but not all the details—particularly those that still had my paranoia raging inside of me. "That explains why, maybe, you should be looking around northern Arkansas, or maybe the border to Alabama. Not here."

Richards seemed a little surprised I took all this in stride, but not devastated by it. "We checked on your last two known locations and the nearest bug-out cache. I presume you know that your tree house is completely destroyed?"

I shook my head. "No, but I figured there was no use wasting time checking on it." I was tempted to say more—wasn't that one of my fatal flaws?—but didn't. Two could play this game, and if Red wanted me to dish, he'd better go along himself as well.

He went on explaining after a curt nod. "After we'd confirmed that there were no other instructions left behind, all we could do was wait. I presume your gear is from the storm cellar?"

Now he was starting to freak me out. "Who says—"

He cut me off before I could get any further. "No offense, but you're not looking your A-game right now. That makes me guess you had to fall back on what you could find on short notice and had to rely on an old cache. The only one between your last confirmed hideout and here is the storm cellar cache. Just continue to blink in irritation if I'm right."

I forced my eyes to stop doing exactly that, going completely still. Sadly, that had no effect whatsoever on Richards, although Cole and Hill seemed a breath away from laughing in my face. Great. Exhaling slowly, I did my best to keep my vexation under tight control. "To sum this up, you know all this because, somehow, Nate managed to relay the information back to you. Coordinates, I presume?" I got a nod for my guess. "How did he get to you in the first place? Because I don't remember leaving him alone for long enough to accost you, and I distinctly remember Hamilton scrutinizing him like a hawk all the damn time on the way back to the States."

Red's grin wasn't a fond one. "That's because he didn't do it himself."

"Burns." It wasn't a hard guess—and it also explained why Nate hadn't considered it necessary to inform Burns of his plans. He'd already known. That made me feel vaguely stupid, and it didn't take away from my own guilt of having disappeared without a word. That still didn't change one fact: I was married to one deceptive asshole.

And, shit, I missed him.

Richards didn't seem bored of this game yet, but Cole and Hill decidedly were. It fell to the latter to speak up. "Long story short, either you're hitching a ride with us, or it's going to be a long, lone walk for you. What's it gonna be?"

It wasn't that I was opposed to either idea, but there were too many questions left unanswered.

"To keep piling non-coincidences on top of each other, you're already en route to New Angeles?"

Richards shrugged. "It wasn't hard to guess that you'd want to head in that direction. And, who would have thought—we have actual tasks to complete besides babysitting you."

"Like what?"

I knew what was coming at his bright, fake smile alone. "You know what I'm going to say, right?"

"Yeah, yeah, it's classified," I grumbled, but the ire ran only skin-deep. "Aren't you going to ask me how exactly I ended up here?"

"That's rather obvious, wouldn't you say?" When all he got from me was a blank stare, Red was only too happy to fill in the blanks. "I could be wrong, but going on what we know, you got some visitors you didn't plan for and ended up in their camp. Since you're on your own and in a hurry to get backup, my guess is that your husband is still there because with him, they knew what precautions to take. You, they underestimated, so you managed to get away, grabbed some provisions from your cache, and hit the next settlement you knew of in the area. Did I miss anything?"

It wasn't that hard to guess right, but sounded too well informed for my likings.

"How would you know that they underestimated me?"

Cole chuckled—asshole—while Hill left it at a grin. Red jovially offered, "Because, isn't that the story of your life?"

"Touché." I had to give him that. "You know about the camp?"

Richards was good about cutting the visual clues of his reaction short but I'd spent enough time around him in the past to read him well to catch them nevertheless. He must have realized that; my glare was enough to get him talking.

"Yes, we know of them. We didn't expect them to get so aggressive about their raiding this soon or else we would have warned you. Looks like they are recruiting again."

That told me more than he'd probably intended.

"You have spies in that camp?"

I half expected to be shut down once more but after a moment's hesitation, Richards inclined his head. "We do, which is why we know that there has been some sort of altercation around the time you missed your schedule. It's not a stretch of the imagination to figure out that must have been you."

"But you don't know."

Another shrug. "It's taken us long enough to establish some moles in there that didn't end up tortured and skinned alive. I'm not going to risk them just to get confirmation for something quintessentially unimportant."

It rankled to hear my well-being described as such, but I got where he came from.

"If you know about them, and they've killed some of your people, why do they still exist? Even the people here at the settlement know of them; why haven't you smoked them out yet?"

"Good question," Cole supplied, getting a harsh glare from Richards that went ignored.

"We missed our opportunity," Richards admitted, surprisingly candid. "With everything else that's been going on over the past two years, nobody paid attention to a group that wasn't out there for blood but pretty much doing their own thing. And, whoops, suddenly they were too many people, too well equipped, to just send in a team and be done with them."

"You didn't even try?" That sounded ridiculously far-fetched.

Red smirked. "Oh, we did. Not just once, but three times, with some additional support from the less-well-adjusted elements of your former ranks. That's how we sent their numbers into the four digits for the first time."

I couldn't help but laugh. It was a harsh sound. "What, just because they were scavengers, they must have been untrustworthy scum?"

Richards had the grace to look at least a little appalled. "No. From what we could figure out, they did a great job doing what they could, and holding out when they couldn't, but there's only so much any man can take. Around half of the force we sent in survived, and overall a third converted. All we accomplished was give them better vehicles and weapons. Command decided to cut the losses, set an embargo zone, and leave the problem to take care of itself."

Why wasn't I surprised? Actually, that wasn't true. I did feel surprise, because I couldn't quite see how they'd let a thorn in their side fester like that, considering how they'd come after us scavengers in the first year after the shit had hit the fan. Not even me drumming up support for my little crusade came close to the issue this must have turned into in the meantime.

"You do realize that the camp must have grown several times over since then?"

Red's expression turned rather stony at my accusation.

"We know. That's part of the reason why we were in the region in the first place."

Ah. And just like that, something else occurred to me. "You're going to use me to get another chance at eradicating them, aren't you? That's why you're so damn happy to drive me across the country on a moment's notice."

The new guy was the only one who looked vaguely surprised at my guess. Damn it!

Richards went for a slight smile as he leaned back against the Humvee's grill. "I wouldn't call what happened a stroke of luck, but it has occurred to us that worse could have happened."

The anger in the pit of my stomach was back, but I managed to keep a lid on it, at least trying to appear as calm as he was. "It really doesn't paint a nice picture that you didn't warn us, but now want me to clean up your mess. Again."

Red sighed, and while not exactly exasperated, it held a certain note of… was that regret that I detected?

"Look, I understand where you're coming from. And I get that there's nothing I can say or do to convince you that we didn't deliberately let you traipse into the lion's den, so I'm not going to try."

"You could tell me the details of what exactly the deal was between you and my husband," I proposed. "That might help."

I got a look of surprise, and after a few seconds' consideration Richards inclined his head. "Very well. He didn't deceive you, if that's what you're trying to get at. His plan was to disappear without a trace and by taking you both out of the equation, keep other forces from thinking they might get too interested in you." I couldn't help but smirk myself that even now he wouldn't call the devil by his name—Decker—but didn't interrupt him. "But I don't need to tell you that your husband is a man who's paranoid enough to always have a contingency plan. In the event of said forces changing their mind and making a grab at other people near and dear to your heart, he wanted my oath that I'd make sure that information got back to him so he could do something about it—or maybe even prevent it from happening if I learned anything early enough. In turn, he was ready to share your whereabouts with me that in the case of a true emergency, we could reactivate you both. I promised to run interference in the meantime, making sure no one got too interested in the areas you were squatting in, or warning you ahead of time so there would be not a trace to be found. That hasn't happened, if you are curious. It seems that your plan has worked so far. In the official records, you're both presumed dead."

Now that was something you didn't hear every day—and under different circumstances I would have very much applauded the fact. "Do my people believe that as well?"

"That's anyone's guess. You know them far better than any of us do. Do you think they believe it?"

It would explain why the radio had been silent although I hadn't exactly been sneaky about the code name I'd used. Then again... "Not unless they see my half-rotted corpse."

"There you have it," Red agreed with me—and I didn't miss the self-satisfied note in his voice.

"Wait. What am I missing?" I also didn't miss how Cole and Hill traded glances, at least until they caught the warning look from Red. "Spill it. You want my cooperation, you better dish out the dirt—particularly if it might as well become an issue for me very soon. If I don't get any support, I'm no use to you, remember?" Still not knowing what they had in mind didn't help, but that much was a given. New Guy was so clueless he followed our back-and-forth with morbid interest.

"Presumably, a lot," Richards admitted. "Too much to explain now. But there won't be anyone else offering you a ride to the coast. Either you come with us, or you risk adding months to the tour—and that's just one way. You should ask yourself—does Miller have that time for you to waste?"

And there it was—the stick I had been waiting for. It never was all carrot with these people. But I probably would have trusted Red less if he'd continued to be agreeable.

"I wonder about a lot of things these days," I grumbled, mostly under my breath. "Like what the fuck you let happen to my country in our absence!" That was maybe a little overdone but no less true. What little hints I'd gotten didn't paint a pretty picture. It also made me dread learning more as I wasn't sure it wouldn't make me feel terribly selfish and conceited for thinking about us hanging out in isolation while we could have done something to prevent what had happened... whatever the fuck that was—

But I knew that led nowhere, so before any of them could answer, I let out a loud sigh and straightened my shoulders.

"Whatever. It's all water under the bridge. I'm coming with you. And I would be much obliged if you would bring me up to speed. It's in your best interest, too, as I can't very well work on making a plan to undo the damage if I don't have a clue what said damage is. So, shall we?" I jerked my chin in the direction of the Humvee.

Red graciously inclined his head as if there'd never been a debate about the matter. There really hadn't been. He'd known the outcome all along, as had I.

"After you," he offered with a grand, sweeping gesture.

"I'm calling shotgun," I quipped, then paused. "Actually, can I drive? It would show how non-threatening, non-coercing, and selfless your motives are."

Red allowed himself a small laugh at my acerbic remark. "Be my guest. But have you even driven a car since you totaled the last two in quick succession?"

I was tempted to point out that there had been months between the incidents—and crumbling bridges were beyond my control—but offered a sweet smile when I realized that he knew far less than he thought he did.

"How do you think I got here?"

A hint of doubt cut through his gloating. "On foot, presumably. I know you can manage forty miles a day." I hadn't, not with my body still healing and necessary pauses. It kind of turned into a moot point as I had to admit the truth.

"On a mountain bike, actually. But you didn't know about the buggies? Too bad. We built the engines up from scratch. Unlike what you probably did. Are those solar panels on the roof?"

"Makes crossing the country in a week feasible," Red shot back, still a little annoyed. "And yes, we did liberate what electrical engines we could find. Not that it's any of your business, but part of the reason for our visit to New Angeles is to continue to keep relations strong with the powers that sit on most of the available technology. Or did you really think that Gabriel Greene managed to stay neutral because he chose to go his own way? He's got his hands in so many pots that I doubt anyone but him can keep track of it. That means he's just as agreeable with us as he is with your lot. Surprised?"

"With him? Never." It wasn't hard to put an extra bit of derision into my voice—that did a good job hiding the actual relief flooding through me. No, Greene and I would never become friends, but good for him—and my people—if he'd managed to stay not just relevant but ahead of the game. Considering the alternatives, I'd much rather throw my lot in with him.

Pulling the driver's side door of the Humvee open, I peeked inside, whistling softly. "Damn, that thing's huge!" There wasn't just room for my rifle in the middle compartment, but easily for my pack as well, wedged between whoever the other gear belonged to—and there was still room aplenty.

Richards cast a surprised look at me from the passenger side. "You've never actually been inside one?"

"Only to liberate some women your less-savory compatriots were about to drag off to do with what nobody wants to talk about," I offered succinctly. "And another for maybe five minutes in the back, but I don't remember too much of that day. Why should we have bothered with these huge gas guzzlers? Would have been a waste of fuel. We did well enough with our cars."

"That you ended up trashing," Cole supplied from behind my back. Clearly, he'd won the battle of who got to be demoted to the elevated jump seat crammed in between the packs. I figured it was still better than riding in the back—not that there was too much room there from what little I could see of it.

"And still I wasn't the one who would have left all of his men to die in a fucking death trap of a laboratory," I snapped back as I settled into the seat. Damn, but this thing really was huge and came with a lot to fiddle with. All it was lacking was a popcorn machine to make it a full entertainment center. I didn't miss how Richards deliberately didn't react, which made me smack my lips. "Speaking of which, I'm a little surprised not to see that asshole here. Where is Bucky Hamilton? You'd think he wouldn't miss a chance to rub in my face that I need anyone's help for anything."

"He won't be a problem for you," Richards offered, still for the most part ignoring me.

"Why?" I asked with a hint of glee. "Is this shit important enough that someone put a leash and muzzle on him so he wouldn't get in my way?"

Red hesitated, leaving the opportunity wide open for Cole to jump into the breach.

"He won't become an issue for you because he's dead."

Now that was disappointing, and I couldn't quite keep a frown off my face as I looked back over my shoulder. "Seriously? Who did he piss off more than me?"

"KIA," Cole explained. "Killed in action, if you don't—"

"Sheesh, I'm not an imbecile," I snapped, facing forward again. "Whatever. So how do I start this thing?"

For the first time, Babyface spoke up after clearing his throat. "LT, do you really think it's smart to let her drive?"

Richards cast an amused look back before he turned to me. "I'm sure she'll figure it out since she's such a know-it-all, right?"

He got a sweet smile back—and cursed when I managed to start the ignition, make the vehicle surge forward, and kill the engine, all within five seconds of each other. The collective cursing made me grin in earnest. "Oops, my bad," I simpered, then went through the proper sequence with a few smooth moves. The Humvee came alive smoothly this time, and peeled back onto the road and away from the settlement without another hitch. Hill seemed to be the only one besides me to find that funny. Well, I wasn't here to be entertaining.

As I'd said, it could have been worse. As it was, I was determined to make the best of the cards fate had dealt me—once someone finally filled me in on what I'd missed. And damn, it was good to sit in a proper car again!

Chapter 9

Nobody protested when I brought the Humvee up to what seemed like a reasonable speed to me—fast enough to eat up miles in minutes, but not too fast that I couldn't avoid any possible obstacles on the road ahead. This close to the settlement it was cleared, but we'd had enough jump scares over the years that I didn't trust the open terrain one bit. Part of me was tempted to send it off-road and give it a little test-drive there, but I was afraid that would cost me my driving privileges. I was still a little surprised that Red had let me take over the wheel—but then, wasn't apparent agreeability his thing? As much as it didn't surprise me that Nate had decided to establish an additional layer of contingency plans, I hadn't expected him to trust Richards with that. But who would have been the alternative?

And now that bastard was apparently dead, and the most I could do was piss on his unmarked grave. Damn it!

"You know, as much as I appreciate not having a corps of backseat drivers, it would be great if anyone could tell me where exactly we're going," I remarked a short while later. "I'm good with directions, but I presume we're on some kind of schedule? And might be preferable not to end up in the next cannibal hideout, or something."

"From what we know, they have pigs," Cole wisely informed me. "They don't need to eat each other. Also great for disposing of bodies."

I ignored him, instead glancing at Richards. He leaned over the bulk in the middle of the vehicle and tapped one of the screens between us, making it come alive. I gave an audible gasp. "You have Satnav! And air conditioning! No wonder your recruitment efforts are running so well! Wait. Are they actually?" But it was kind of neat to let that thing tell me where to go, and I sure appreciated the fact that, in zipped-up jacket and sturdy pants, I didn't feel like I was about to be fried alive. Maybe we really had cut things back a little too far…

"Har har," Hill provided from the back. "I'd forgotten how absolutely not funny you are."

"And still you've missed me," I replied as sweetly as I could.

"Surprisingly, yes," Hill professed. "It can get so boring when you don't have anyone constantly jonesing to usurp control and wisecrack at every single thing."

I couldn't help but bark a brief laugh. "I never had any intention of leading you bunch of assholes. Still don't. I'll just never get how anyone can have such a 'follow the leader' mindset." Hill snorted his derision at me. "I mean, seriously, weren't you Delta? Don't you train your operators to be independent thinkers?"

Sadly, he didn't bite. "And when's the last time you went against your husband's 'directions'?" He went as far as raising his hands to do air quotes. "Just because we don't need it all spoon-fed and rolled up in a nice package with 'independence' scrawled all over doesn't mean we're that different."

I would have loved to say something acerbic back, but sadly, nothing came to mind. The sad truth was that he was right—kind of. But not enough to let me keep my trap shut.

"That's because usually his plans are better than what I can come up with. And he's smart enough to explain things to me in a way that makes me see reason." That was more of a concession than I'd been willing to give, but, whatever.

Hill's laugh made me grip the steering wheel tighter. "That's because he's thoroughly brainwashed you."

I was tempted to send the Humvee off the road to shut him up, but instead chuckled softly. "Hey, if telling yourself that helps you sleep easier, be my guest. I don't have anything to prove to you, or anyone. We all know that I'm a homicidal bitch, no additional manipulation required."

Hill and Cole laughed, and even Richards allowed himself a smile. Only Babyface piped up, "I don't."

"Shut it, Gallager," Hill ordered.

Not another sound came from the back, making me snort. "What's up with Private Numbnuts? No explanation needed why anyone thought I'd favorably react to some familiar faces, but what did he do to deserve this shit job?"

Richards responded right over Cole's suppressed laughter. "Corporal Gallager is one of our most promising recruits. Leave him alone."

"Aw, Babyface can't take the heat yet?"

I would have left it at that—and, really, I'd said worse to Martinez as far as terms of endearments went—but apparently that was a touchy subject. "Can anyone finally tell me who this fucking bitch is? And tell her to shut it before—"

"Before you what?" I challenged. "Put me in my place? Far better men than you have tried. All of them have failed. I'm a lost cause. Get used to it." The others' amusement must have annoyed him more than my words. Too bad, really. I decided to play nice, though, since there was no reason to antagonize him besides boredom. Shit, but I really was turning into Burns… "I'm Bree Lewis."

"Who?" And that wasn't even feigned ignorance, far as I could tell.

"Ouch," I muttered, snorting when Richards sent me a grin that was bordering on a smirk. "Co-leader of the Lucky Thirteen? Nate Miller's wife?" I kind of hated designating myself as that; I'd by far gained enough notoriety on my own not to need a sentiment of attachment. Still nothing. "The bitch that rallied the scavengers in the year after the zombie apocalypse and kicked your collective asses at that base in Colorado, forcing a truce for the coming winter? Any of that ring a bell?" Now he was starting to annoy me for real. "The expert virologist these yahoos here needed to come with so they'd get the damn cure—and who knows what other weaponized versions of the serum—from a hidden laboratory in fucking France? Come on. Now you're just playing dumb."

Since nobody threatened my life, I figured the last wasn't exactly a secret—and, even if it was, I didn't give a flying fuck about that.

"Wait, are you the one because of whom the assassinations and suicide bombings started?"

That wasn't what I'd expected. It didn't help when Richards responded with a succinct, "She is."

I waited for anyone to elaborate—and react, but Babyface seemed to have lost all interest in communicating. He may even have looked a little pale, but I couldn't glance back at him long enough to make sure. Eventually, I caved, turning to Richards. "Spill."

If not reluctant, he didn't seem happy to oblige me. "Remember that part about where we propagandized you helping us?"

That was one way of putting it. "Let me guess. That backfired?"

"It did." I was surprised at his admission, but he didn't give me time to gloat. "Turns out, come spring there were some people who weren't happy about the news. They threatened actions against us if we didn't hand you over. Since we couldn't produce you to do so, we had to call their bluff. Turns out, it wasn't a bluff. At least nobody thought so anymore when they blew up the docks of New Angeles."

"They did what?" No need to feign incredulity there. That made absolutely no sense.

Red kept his voice even as he responded, but I could still hear some latent anger in there. "We'd struck a truce with Greene to help us keep the pretense up. He of course knew what had happened, and since we'd in good faith let your people go—as promised—our hands were tied. In exchange for information, he was happy to help establish our false claims by forging evidence. Turns out, his security is less tight than he thinks it is. Those that were already angry and felt betrayed now had a new target to be even angrier at. I don't have to explain to you that this didn't help. Greene himself survived but hundreds were killed, and it set back the progress of the city for months. He consequently enforced much tighter rules, and further alienated others. Tales and resentment spread like wildfire, and come fall, things looked worse than the year before."

"Who would have thought," I grumbled, but wasn't sure exactly who to be angry at. Everyone, pretty much.

"Hindsight is always easy," Richards pointed out. "Be that as it may, some of the larger established settlements like the Silo and Dispatch used the changing socio-political climate to cement their independence, pretty much declaring martial law. Some applauded and flocked there because of it; others left and went elsewhere. A lot of people disappeared. Many of the settlements skipped out of the network we'd tried to establish over the first two years because they felt we didn't do enough to support them and had caused too much trouble."

"They weren't wrong, from what you just told me," I interjected.

Red ignored me. "Another harsh winter, and heads had cooled off, but as spring turned into summer, things further deteriorated. I know you think we and the settlements that joined the network were fascist assholes to force you scavengers to identify and hold yourselves to an established set of rules, but without that nobody was better off; on the contrary. Those with power now had more people, more food, more resources, and more weapons. Those lacking all those things were pretty much doomed to starve—and starving people never seek the blame by themselves. So they blamed everyone else—the settlements for being greedy; us for forsaking them; you for being a dead figurehead without a cause. You wanted to know what I meant with, 'we're your only option'? That's because we are. I'm sure that more people recognized the name, but nobody in their right mind would be foolish enough to openly offer support to you, should it turn out that you're not dead yet. We're making an exception because we have little to lose and a lot to gain. That about satisfy your curiosity?"

I shook my head, mulling what he'd just dropped in my lap over. "Why didn't you tell us? You could have prevented some, if not all, of it if you would have thrown me to the wolves, from what it sounds like."

"It wouldn't have made a difference," Richards confessed. "Besides, I gave your husband my word that I'd only contact you if your people were under attack, or we needed you for the survival of the human race."

"So things weren't quite bad enough yet?"

"Not quite," he agreed.

That still didn't paint a pretty picture—and it made me regret my last words to Steven at the settlement. He probably wouldn't believe it, anyway, but still. Had I known about what Richards just told me, I'd have been a little more cautious.

"That's why you didn't do anything about that camp," I mused. "You really didn't have the resources."

"And lots of other fires to put out." Which left the question of where that left us now. When I pointed that out, he shrugged. "Let's hope your people are the free-thinking, independent folks you always made them out to be. My guess is, your husband still owes enough people favors that you can pull enough strings to get the support you need to spring him. That will take time. By then, we'll see what new and exciting waves of violence this summer will bring. You've established quite the tradition there, I must say."

"We didn't start it," I pressed out. "You forced our hands. All we did on our own was find out how to better kill the super-juiced zombies, liberate innocents from cannibals, and offer our help. Your people had to up and try to kidnap me. If you'd taken Taggard and his boys out like you should have in the first place, and made sure that whatever that madman kept cooking up inside NORAD never saw the light of day and poisoned hundreds of your soldiers, none of this would have happened." I waited for reactions from the back row but was only met with stony expressions. "But, let me guess? It's still all the scavengers' fault. And my fault, because not being around, or even dead, isn't enough to not put the blame on me."

The silence that followed was all kinds of awkward, and I couldn't help but feel like, maybe, that last part hadn't needed to be said. I didn't like how whiny it made me sound. I didn't like any of it, truth be told, but until I could verify it with someone I trusted—well, trusted more than the prime examples of manhood gathered in this car—I had to assume that it was true. They had no reasons for lying to me, and I even got the sense that Richards had been very forthcoming with dishing out information.

"Why are you helping me?" I figured it was a valid question.

More silence, until Richards cleared his throat noisily. "It's not my place to say. I'm just the messenger, and the one who had what counts for your contact information these days."

"That's not cryptic at all," I snarked—but not even my tone got him to spill the beans. Too bad, really. I wondered if I should harangue him about it but dropped the point.

"So Greene knows we're coming?"

Richards inclined his head. "By now he likely knows that we picked you up as well, but I trust that he'll try to keep it pretty low-key. But it's vital that we don't miss our window."

"What window would that be, exactly?"

He made a big show of checking his watch. "We have exactly six days and three hours to get to the port for pickup. If we miss the boat, we'll have to wait another week, and by then someone will be on the way to make sure you'll never reach New Angeles, or your people. They're still on the coast north of the city, although they've upgraded, from what I hear." He didn't elaborate, and when I didn't inquire, he went on. "Provided we make good pace, it shouldn't be hard to make it. It's only a little over sixteen hundred miles."

"Easy peasy," I muttered, but couldn't quite quell the flicker of excitement. That was a lot of driving to be done. "Does this thing run in the dark as well?"

Cole snorted behind me. "You do know the definition of solar power, right?"

"I also know the definition of a battery," I snapped back. "We always kept spares in our buggies. Don't tell me your amazing engineers didn't."

Before things could escalate, Red interjected, "Yes, we have three spare batteries that are sequentially charged after the main one, but we need some extra power for the first hours of the morning as well until we're recharging more than we're spending. I hate to break it to you, but we won't go beyond fourteen-hour days."

"Slackers," I muttered. "No wonder things got out of hand with that sort of discipline."

Red grinned, as did Hill, while Gallager murmured to Cole, "Is she for real?"

Cole guffawed in answer. "Hate to break it to you, but she's worse. Just this once, I need to give her some credit—it took her two weeks to go from barely being able to hobble down a corridor with support to almost eviscerating our commanding officer in a sparring match, and three more to go toe-to-toe with some really fucked-up zombies. Try not to get on her bad side. Not sure if there's still room there, and I don't think you've stuck around us long enough to know how you'd go about trying, but it will be easier on you if you just don't."

"You know that I can hear you?" I quipped, although I needed to keep my eyes on the road now. We were far enough away from the settlement that here the cars were still obstacles, if easily circumnavigated ones. Apparently, the other roads or directions were the more frequented ones.

Hill laughed from the other side of the back row. "That may have been part of his reasoning."

"You're all so fucking funny."

Nobody protested.

It was only a while later that I realized that talking so much—and with several people—had exhausted me just a little. That was hilarious on so many levels, if mostly compared to what I'd been through recently. I didn't protest when after around two hours, Richards told me to stop by the side of the road for a quick break, and took over the wheel from me once we moved on again. I busied myself for a bit checking on the paper maps that were stashed under the seat, scanning for the marks of settlement and other points of interest. Some I was already familiar with, but a lot were new to me, even in areas I'd spent some quality time in. Wyoming had two other larger settlements now—good for them, I hoped. The one in Utah was still there as well, if with a large circle that made me guess marked the territory roughly taken over by it. Looked like Minerva had been a busy, busy woman building up her already-flourishing community. I couldn't help but ask myself if all these were people who'd hate me once they learned I was still alive. Not exactly something to look forward to—but until I had Nate back, it also wasn't something I felt like concerning myself with. But, damn—if what Red had told me was true, we'd missed out on some deeply fucked-up things.

Maybe my latent paranoia was simple overreaction. Maybe this really didn't have anything to do with the ghosts of Nate's past. Maybe it really was coincidence.

I just didn't buy it.

Chapter 10

We drove until the sun was about to set, when Richards sent the Humvee rocking cross-country toward a small thicket of trees—not really enough to be called a forest—to stop for the night. I couldn't help but grin when I realized how easily I fell back into the routines of helping set up camp, even if it was just prepping a fire pit and setting everything up for a possible quick exit. I didn't protest when Cole dropped a mat and well-insolated sleeping bag in my lap, both things I'd dearly missed over the past days but hadn't bothered with picking up. It got downright domestic when he held up two MRE packs for me to choose from.

"This is getting awfully domestic, you know?" I remarked. "Give me the one you like least."

"Not used to getting wined and dined?" Cole joked, handing me the pack in his right hand. I didn't even check what it was before tearing it open. Oh, such abundance of... whatever that stuff was.

Red hunkered down on my other side, getting his own MRE ready. "The least we can do is feed you, considering our ulterior motives. And you are taking over a guard shift, I presume?"

I gave him a quick, fake grin as I nodded. "Graveyard shift, I presume? I doubt you've forgotten just how well I see in the dark."

"It's also the one no one else wants," Cole offered jovially. "And we already have our rookie digging latrine pits and having to wait for his chow."

I ignored him, and instead angled for the hot water steaming away over the fire. "I'm also surprised you haven't run out of these yet."

Cole shrugged as he tore into his own meal, setting the bread and other stuff away for later. "Still plenty left, and plenty more to pick up along the way if you just know where to look. But I suppose I don't have to tell that to the queen of looters."

They were so fucking funny tonight—and judging from how Hill grinned into his own stew or whatever, they knew it. "I haven't touched one of these since France. Not before that, either. I know we had some at the bunker but kept them for when absolutely necessary. Never happened, so I was spared."

"Oh, come on," Cole offered around a mouthful of food. "They aren't that bad. And you could have chosen the other one. It's your own fault if you don't like the chicken curry."

That was what this was supposed to be? I briefly considered the texture of my next bite. Maybe, maybe not. "It smells edible," I admitted.

"That bad, huh?" Cole still wouldn't shut up. "What did you eat in the meantime? Obviously, you of all people could subsist on irritation and the steam you blow up your own ass, but you look moderately well-fed for someone who's been slumming it in the woods for ages."

"Well-groomed, too," I offered back. "Venison, for the most part. Boar, if we had to kill some to drive them out of our territory. Rabbits and fowl, if they were stupid enough to end up in the traps or happened to traipse across our path. Lots and lots of fish. You know, all the good stuff that's high in fat and protein and didn't make us consider literally eating one another. Can't really afford to lose another piece of me, you know?"

Richards kept a straight face at that last bit but Cole and Hill laughed. Babyface, set to guard the perimeter, missed out on all the jokes he wouldn't understand. Too bad.

"So you pretty much went full-on live-off-the-land carnivores?" Cole surmised.

"If we happened on some tubers or other produce growing somewhere, we'd take it with us, of course, but we didn't stay anywhere long enough to set up our own produce. Although I almost got to where I could have harvested that salad if those idiots hadn't rained on our parade a few weeks ago," I explained wistfully.

Hill gave me a curious look. "Really, that's the part you're mourning? Salad?"

"It would have been a mighty fine salad," I pointed out, my beginning smile swallowed up by real grief, because obviously, it wasn't the salad I needed to be sitting here, beside me, right now.

"Hunting is a good choice," Hill agreed with me. "Just sucks if you don't have anything to season the meat with."

"Salt, pepper, is all you need," Cole interjected. "You don't need a fancy gourmet kitchen for that."

When he looked at me for agreement, all I had was a shrug for him. "I'm the wrong one to ask. Even before that shit happened, I lived an entire summer on kibble and Fancy Feast. The taste of food's the last thing I've been concerned with in the past years. If it's edible, I'm down for it."

Cole visibly shook himself while Hill guffawed. I really couldn't remember if I'd told them the tale of the great cat food cache before. "Still sure you made the right decision not joining up with us? The very least they do is keep us fed."

I didn't justify that with a response and instead fished around in the extra small packages that were part of the MRE and started dumping everything else into the main bag, much to Hill and Cole's horror. Watching them watch me spoon it all out and devour it without batting an eyelash was so worth it.

"And there they say women are dainty creatures," Cole muttered once I was done.

That made me laugh. "Nobody has accused me of that… ever, I think."

Hill chuckled softly. "I can't imagine why."

As much as it was fun teasing them like this, I decided it was only fair that I let them in on the secret of my culinary ambivalence. "I can't taste any of this shit, so it's literally all the same to me."

Hill and Cole traded glances. "Seriously?" Hill sounded both incredulous and filled with pity—a first, if I remembered correctly.

"When I got infected, the virus must have fried my taste buds. Explains why the shamblers really don't discriminate what they subsist on. Good for them, I guess, but it sometimes does suck for me. Not with the MREs, though."

Cole shook his head, muttering something to himself that I was sure I didn't need to hear. Richards seemed to be the only one interested in this topic. "Guess that fits with the analysis of your saliva. Even when we were already on the way to France on the destroyer, Emily was still bitching that she still hadn't managed to completely decontaminate the operating room equipment."

I pursed my lips, considering what I should quip at first, but Cole was quicker. "Well, that explains why in our briefing they told us to make sure not to get bitten by you."

"Very funny." At least I presumed that had been a joke. Cole's grin about confirmed that. Turning back to Richards, I figured I might as well try to get more out of him since he was already so talkative. "Speaking of which, what else is in that file you have on me?"

Richards took his time chewing and swallowing—the only one here still showing manners, which I really wasn't accustomed to—before giving me a startlingly white smile. "That's classified."

"Oh, come on! It's my file! I should know what's in there!"

"That's kind of the point," he drawled.

"Well, maybe one of these days you'll realize that if you gave a little, you'd get a lot."

His amused grin looked surprisingly real. "You wouldn't trust me if I handed you the entire tome of a manila folder, so what are you even complaining about?"

He kind of had a point. My right hand, currently wrapped around my mug full of cool water, gave a painful spasm, reminding me that I had way more important things to consider.

"I'm going to hit the sack, if you gentlemen don't mind. I have some sleep to catch up on and several more days in your company to look forward to. If I'm expected to survive that, I need some rest."

Red wished me a good night—which I found rather sarcastic since it would end two watch shifts from now—while Hill nudged Cole's knee. "See, you even put the girls who don't want to screw you to sleep. You really need to up your game."

I hid my grin at the retching sound Cole made while I unfurled my sleeping bag. Well, at least not every single person in the world hated me. That was something, right? Yet as I lay there, trying to fall asleep while listening to the dying-down flames and the soft murmur of conversation, I couldn't help but feel even more alone than the previous nights out in the wild.

Waking up at two in the morning was never fun, but at least Richards had a steaming mug of coffee ready for me as I took over from him. Nothing happened during my watch, and while I tried going back to sleep once it was time for Cole to take the last shift, my mind wouldn't clock out once more. So I got up again and got a fire and some water for coffee going. Since that took only so much of my attention, I went over to the Humvee and retrieved one of the weapon maintenance kits I'd seen in the back, and set about undoing the damage of a week of dust from the road on my trusty firearms. Because I didn't want weapon oil all over my gloves, I took them off, which also helped with fiddling with the smaller parts. I was so focused on my task—and knowing that someone else had my back helped lull me into a false sense of complacency—that I didn't realize that Gallager was already up and moving toward the canteen full of coffee, until he let out a partly horrified, "What the fuck?" as he stopped, staring at me.

I looked up at him, puzzled and just a little annoyed at myself for letting him startle me, then down at what he was staring at. "Sheesh, I almost forgot I was missing three of my fingers," I muttered, then grinned up at him with somewhat feral intent. "Make sure you never see me naked, Babyface. The damage doesn't stop at my wrists."

Cole, coming from behind him, gave Gallager a push that made the young soldier come out of his trance. "Nobody wants to see you naked, Lewis," he called down to me. "Stop traumatizing the rookie. We still need him, and he'll be useless if he spends the next days trying to figure out how you look in your skivvies."

"Hell, I don't want to see me naked," I muttered. When that hit a little too close to home, I did my best to aim for a real grin. "I'll do my best not to accidentally flash him. It's so hard to keep all my million layers of clothes on around such fine specimens as yourself."

Cole, still grinning, gave a brief bow over his M4. "Much obliged, ma'am."

"If you keep this up, I will drop my pants right here and now, I swear."

Gallager looked still a little shell-shocked as he got his coffee. I decided to take pity on him and finished up quickly so I could clean up and pull the gloves back on. "Better now? You really need to toughen up a little if you want to run with those guys."

He didn't even react to that barb, and instead burped out the next thing that must have been on his mind. "How did it happen? IED?"

It was only then that I realized just how little he knew about me. Normally, that might have maybe been a relief, but my ego just wouldn't let me shut up. "What, you think I got blown up? Nope. And to clear up something else: I've never been part of any military organization, least of all the army."

Now he seemed even more confused. "But you were part of the serum program. That's what the three marks mean—that you're a deserter."

"Excuse me?" Leaning forward so I could look around Gallager to Cole, I quipped, "You really have to educate your young better, or else someone will shoot them in the face out of spite." I went on addressing Gallager when Cole just grinned back. "Seriously, get some perspective. Medical personnel were inoculated as well, particularly those part of the program. Which I never was. I got infected when I was shot and savaged by zombies, and only survived because of a partly conferred immunity that I got from doing the dirty with my husband apparently often enough that his immunity rubbed off on me. The only reason I eventually got shot up with the serum was that I was rotting from the inside out as it wasn't the full bandwidth of protection as my body was just producing antibodies, not the serum virus itself. I'm sure there's a line of people truly regretful that they had to waste that dose on me." I paused for a second. "Anything else you wanna know? Now's your chance."

Gallager wisely kept his trap shut, although I didn't miss that the previously incredulous looks he'd shot me had turned a little more cautious. I briefly considered apologizing to him, but I really wasn't in the mood. I wasn't all that surprised when, as soon as the rookie disappeared to take care of business, Richards hunkered down next to me, presumably to get some coffee—but that obviously wasn't everything.

"Something you wanna talk about?" he asked.

I cast him the most caustic look I could manage, which was likely medusa-level strength. "Do I look like I have something on my mind?"

"Besides murder and bloody mayhem," he joked. At least I thought he was joking. I hoped he'd drop it if I didn't respond, but that had only worked with Gallager. "It might surprise you, but you don't constantly need to convince everyone that you're a badass. It's okay to simply be yourself."

"Does that mean you don't think I'm naturally a badass?" I teased, but went on before he could respond—better this way. "You're wrong. All I have left is to be strong. To look forward, and never, ever slack off. This world eats you as soon as you let up. But even if it wasn't a tough choice between zombies or civil war, I still couldn't ease up on myself. I did that twice in my life, and it almost destroyed me. Thanks, but no thanks. And you can stop trying to shrink me now."

Never that easily deterred, Richards tried again. "Let me guess— after the factory, and Canada?"

I blinked for a moment, irritation warring with surprise—that he was so far off. Normally, he was much better at reading me. I was tempted to let him stew in his misconceptions, but then decided to set him straight after all. "After I was recruited to work with the man I had nothing short of hero worship for, and then he died the weekend before I started on the job. And after my new boss poisoned me so I'd have a breakdown and lose my BSL-4 security clearance so she wouldn't have to kill me, but I read that as utter failure of myself. Everything that came after the shit hit the fan? Sure, there were some setbacks I wish I didn't have to work my way through. And it was hard more times than not. But do you seriously think I'd still be alive if I let any of that drag me down?"

Red didn't look disappointed that he'd been wrong. I wasn't quite sure, but that could have been a self-satisfied look in his eyes. Damnit. When would I ever learn to keep my trap shut?

"When do we leave?" I asked, mostly to turn the conversation in a different direction. "Camp life is nice and all, but the sooner we get to the coast, the better. No offense, but I don't need a shrink, and I need a shoulder to cry on even less, if that's your next move. If spending the last two years alone with my husband has taught me anything, it's to work through my own issues—on my own. You wouldn't believe how much time there is for self-reflection between hunting deer and chasing rabbits."

"Half an hour," Red told me nonchalantly—and ignored the rest. "Be ready by then. I presume you'll want to drive again?"

"I'd love to."

And that was that, as they said.

Either Red had gotten the message, or he was trying to go for the silent treatment to get me talking. Fat chance on the latter—nothing beat Nate in a bad mood only communicating with grunting sounds and vexed glares for three days straight. Cole kept making fun of me whenever he could, with Hill sometimes running interference. Gallager continued to have a hard time dealing with me, flip-flopping between pissing me off and being pitifully green behind the ears. Since we had a lot of miles to make in just enough time not to force us to drive into the night, every new day was mostly the repetition of the previous one. We only needed to stop to stretch our legs and refill the water tanks in the back of the Humvee, no additional stops at any settlements required. We saw few caravans on the move, and even less shamblers, which surprised me, but we were headed into the hotter states now that already made driving with the AC on full an annoyance. Any shambler smart enough to make it through several winters in a row would have learned that summers weren't any less lethal in the southern states.

And then, finally, what would be our last day on the road dawned, bright and early. Richards had informed us the night before that, should we catch the boat, we'd get to New Angeles tomorrow morning, and if nobody shot me in the head, further up the California coast later that same day. Before his little diatribe about what had happened in the meantime, I would have considered the chance of that happening slim, but now? I had one more reason not to want to cross paths with Gabriel Greene. On some level that annoyed me; I may never have liked the man himself, but knowing that we had New Angeles as a possible safe haven to fall back to was always nice. With that option now, presumably, gone, I felt oddly displaced once more—and that wasn't anything I'd expected.

Our schedule said that we needed to reach the dock by three in the afternoon; the boat would be gone by four at the latest to make a few miles before stopping at an undisclosed location before moving on in the morning. I would have figured that a little paranoid, but I could see how losing their docks once made them cautious; and, after all, they were the people hiding behind a gigantic maze of a destroyed city, full of traps and kill chutes. At least coming from the sea would spare me having to traverse that ever-shifting maze of beacons—or so I thought, until suddenly, I felt a pulse coming from somewhere to the south, making me step on the brakes hard enough to draw a few choice curse words from the others.

"What's wrong?" Richards asked, eyes darting across the horizon. We were in the middle of nowhere on a dusty road in a dusty landscape pretty much abandoned by all life except for some recalcitrant shrubbery that I felt could have been my spirit plants.

The pulse hadn't been a strong one, just unexpected, but it still left my stomach upset. "Fuck. I'd kind of hoped they wouldn't be using those down here, too," I mostly muttered to myself. When no one got my meaning, I sighed, reaching for the belt buckle to free myself of the driver's seat. "The zombie deterrent beacons? I can feel them, too. Did I ever mention how much fun it was for us the first time we got into New Angeles?"

Richards still looked moderately alarmed, while Cole asked, nasty laugh included, "Do you ever ask yourself how much human you still are, Lewis?"

I shot him a sharp look back. "What, you accusing my husband of necrophilia?"

Cole grimaced, but the stricken expression on Gallager's face was so worth it. Ignoring them both, I turned to Richards. "I can drive through that but I probably shouldn't. Switch early?"

"Move on over," he told me, reaching for his own belt.

The next pulse hit what I figured was five minutes later, and they remained at that interval. It was all deterrent beacons, which made me feel like crap but I much preferred that to the beckoning ones that had almost made me walk into the midst of a gigantic zombie streak once. I'd take puking over that any day. Thankfully, it didn't seem like it would come to that, at least if I just kept my eyes trained on the horizon and the coastline that got closer and closer—

Until a cloud of dust, a few miles to the north, caught my attention.

"Does that look like trouble to you, or someone catching the same boat as us?"

Hill already had his binoculars out, checking on where I was pointing. "Impossible to say from a distance, but probably a bit of both," he surmised.

"Are we expecting a little bit of both?" I felt like it was a valid question.

Red gave a mirthless grin. "With you along? Always."

"Gee, thanks for the vote of confidence. I can behave myself, you know?"

Cole chuckled softly. "That I need to see."

Three more pulses, and the dust cloud turned into a group of cars—three if I wasn't mistaken. They looked like two gigantic SUVs and a pickup truck, the truck with not one but two mounted machine guns on the flatbed. Since Richards didn't act tense, I told myself to relax, but I didn't exactly like what I saw through the binoculars—and soon enough by just squinting over there through the bright sunshine. While not as bad as before, my eyes still didn't like sunshine, and the heat mirages going on didn't help it.

"Please tell me I'm wrong when I assume someone tried to dose them with some calming meds and ended up driving them insane,"

I muttered as I kept studying the getup of the cars. All three were painted black—which wasn't that out of the ordinary—but had acquired interesting hood and door ornaments. When nobody answered me, I glanced into the back row, meeting three sets of stoic—and clueless—eyes. "Babyface is excused in favor of that likely happening before his time, but, seriously? Doesn't ring a bell?"

Cole snorted. "That no one knows your obscure pop culture references? Not really our loss."

"Oh, it is," I grumbled, but dropped the point. "Exactly how crazy have things gotten in the months since you picked us up and carted us to France?"

Red's expression was slightly bemused. "Did you listen to anything I told you?"

"Listen, yes. But if that's the new normal now, it didn't sink in yet."

He didn't gloat; Cole didn't have the same qualms. "Still that upset we picked you up? Or that anyone would associate you with us rather than them?"

I had to admit, if this was what the scavengers had ended up turning into, I wasn't so sure about my allegiances anymore. All we'd tried to do was carve out a niche to exist in; even Burns and Bates in their most raucous moments wouldn't have gotten it into their heads to create hood ornaments out of shamblers—and I wasn't quite sure if they were dead for good and that was only the velocity of the moving vehicle that made it look as if they were moving.

"I think I may need another refresher on some of the finer points of what happened. But I'm not sure you're the right people to give that."

Now Richards seemed rather amused. "And you think your people will tell you something less biased?"

"No, but their bias might be more in line with my own," I offered— but with less conviction than I would have preferred. "Who knows? More than half of them have been part of your more clandestine operations for quite a while. If you'd never come after me and tried to kidnap me several times, they might even have agreed with you in the first place."

I didn't miss the hint of ire in Red's expression, although he evened out his features almost immediately. "How long are you going to keep beating that dead horse? Is what a few bad eggs on our side did really worse than what the same misguided elements on yours have done?"

I hated it when he made sense about something that had become pretty much pure illogical loathing deep inside my soul. My following silence seemed to be answer enough, although I wondered if it was the right message received. I couldn't wait to sit down with the Ice Queen—and Burns, and Martinez, and Andrej, and all the others, but foremost her because she was the closest to an uncompromisable straight shooter among my people—and ask her opinion. And hopefully, it would come right on the back of a stellar plan of how to get Nate back.

If only I'd be able to keep them from gunning down these four fine specimens I was traveling with...

I had to admit, I felt foolish that now was the first time I'd actively considered how that meeting would go down—for anyone besides me. While I expected to get some flak for what I'd done—and where I'd been after that—I knew, deep down, that my people would forgive me, if there was even anything to forgive. But they'd seen Richards at the Colorado base, and might know Hill and Cole as well, and I didn't hold it above Burns to simply keep his trap shut as a potential character witness and let someone else take care of that problem. I really didn't like that idea. I may not see eye to eye with them, but they had volunteered to help, and I might very well need them before we were done with all this. Considering how much blood there was already on my hands, I didn't need to add that of people I at least somewhat cared about—and maybe a little more than I should.

"Any pointers you want to give me how to act around them if we'll spend an entire day on the same boat? I presume Greene has some rules in place, or else he wouldn't have given you the go-ahead to use this route," I mused.

Cole, again, proved to be a real charmer as he responded. "How about you don't act like a vapid bitch?"

"That's my winning personality you're talking about," I harped back, waiting for Richards to give his two cents.

"He's not entirely wrong," Red stated with more conviction than my ego felt was necessary. "If I thought it would help, I'd tell you to keep your mouth shut and avoid eye contact, but we all know that you never back away from a pissing contest. So maybe just try to be a little less like you. Remember how you bristled at Gallager calling you a deserter? They might think the exact same thing since you're hitching a ride with us. Deescalating any arising situation might be a good idea."

I almost bit out whether he thought I was even capable of that and left it at a curt nod. I could do that, no problem. Just because I kind of got off on flying off the handle didn't mean I had to.

But looking over at those cars—and seeing a few of their passengers eye us with what I presumed was equal consideration and disdain as we had going on—really made me want to. Somehow, I didn't think they'd give me a choice. Maybe that was a good thing.

Chapter 11

The scavengers drew ahead of us eventually, mostly because Red let them. At first glance, that seemed very reasonable, and also turned out to come with the added benefit of us being the last vehicle to arrive. I'd expected some kind of dock structure or an old, abandoned marina. What we found was what I realized must have been a wharf or dry dock, and a small tanker-like ship idling at the very end of it. There was a huge retractable ramp extended toward land, but the concrete structure that led up to it was barely wide enough to let a truck—or Humvee—traverse it. There were already ten other vehicles waiting, not counting the scavengers who'd beaten us there. None of them were military vehicles, and at a first glance I would have shelved all the others as traders, if rather heavily armed ones. It was only as we drew to a halt and a few of them turned to face us that I realized that several of them also had three marks, not just one. They looked at the Humvee with the same disdain as they had for the scavengers, making me wonder if they belonged to the faction that was the most neutral in this newly shifted power struggle.

I really needed a cheat sheet for this, and stat!

I would have loved to remain inside the Humvee, but as soon as he'd turned off the engine, Red got out, the others following. I did my best to appear as uninteresting as possible but I could tell that, to all of them, I must have stuck out like a sore thumb. My gear was nowhere near as good as that of the not-traders and a very far shot from the top-notch quality the scavengers sported—although that was easy to miss at a first glance because of the paint they'd put all over it; simulated blood and gore, I figured. I obviously didn't belong to the soldiers, which was still something I prided myself on, but since it drew curious looks, it wasn't that convenient. I tried my very best not to look anyone in the eye but also not mime the cowed, beat-down refugee that I kind of was. That, at least, should have put me a long shot from who I was—or had been, more precisely—acting as a good cover.

That still left a lot of room for improvement.

Richards didn't show any hint of concern as he walked by scavengers and traders alike to talk to the cargo officer of the ship and his loading personnel. The other three soldiers remained clustered together by the Humvee but did a good job pretending they were simply hanging around rather than guarding each other's back. In all fairness, they drew more attention than I did, even when I joined them, looking around the desolate coastal wasteland for any kind of trouble. Nothing moved out there, the beacons having permanently cleared the entire area. Their low thrumming still set my teeth on edge when the next sequence hummed toward the coast from inland, the last three of them strong enough I could feel them in my very bones. That's why I almost missed one of the scavengers—a woman, judging by her wild, long hair—sneering a low, "Whore!" in my direction.

None of the soldiers responded, but Cole wasn't the least bit stealthy about turning around so he could see how I'd react. A few of the traders cast glances our way as well but, like before, they didn't seem impressed by the bunch of spray-painted idiots. I knew I shouldn't say anything, but after a few seconds passed and I heard the bitch chuckle, I just couldn't let it pass. So I muttered, just loud enough that she'd hear it, "And your father smelt of elderberries."

Cole cracked a smile, making me guess he wasn't completely immune to my pop culture references after all, and two of the traders grinned outright. I kept a straight face and my back turned to the scavengers, waiting to see what would happen.

I didn't have to wait long; five seconds later, strong fingers wrapped around my shoulder and jerked me around. From up close, the ridiculous face paint—more black and red, with some white over it—looked even worse, and I was tempted to ask her how early she had to get up to have all that ready and set for the day. One of the reasons why I kept my hair braided up was because I couldn't be bothered to brush it most mornings.

"What did you just say, bitch?"

I gave her one slow, deliberate blink, but neither tried to pull away or give any indication I was intimidated by her—which I wasn't. Under all that garish getup, we were pretty much evenly matched physically, which meant I could wipe the floor with her in my sleep. Feeling that superior helped keep my voice perfectly even and pleasant as I drawled, "Nothing." Shit, but I was turning into Nate.

Her fingers tightened, and she raised her other hand in a fist. The gesture was so overdone it was easy not to react—if she fought like that, all obvious moves, it would be child's play indeed to best her. It was only then that I noticed exactly how wide her eyes were, the pupils dilated far beyond what the bright sun overhead should have made possible. I quickly reversed my assessment of her—I had no idea what she was on, but people could get freakishly strong if they rocked the wrong chemicals.

But the same was true for me.

"Guess I called your mother a hamster," I responded, still calm but now watching her every reaction closely. She blinked twice as she worked through my words, another sign that her mind wasn't as sharp as it should—or could—have been. Confusion crossed her expression before turning into yet more rage. Her fingers digging into my shoulder hurt, and her entire body seemed to vibrate with tension. Someone was really looking for a fight.

Well, she'd definitely met her match there, because so was I.

It was that very thought that made me back down, unease gripping me that had nothing to do with possibly losing, or losing face.

"It's a joke," I explained, making sure my voice was as calm as if I was talking to a dangerous animal. In a sense, I figured I was. "A bad one. From a movie. Entirely inappropriate. My bad. Please forgive me, I meant no insult. I thought you were the kind of people who'd find that funny."

Again, that same fight raged behind those eyes as she tried to make sense of my words—and like I'd led her to, she jumped to the conclusion that I wasn't worth it. She snarled in my face as she pushed me away and let go before stalking off back to her people. All of them were watching me now, one of the guys swaying ever so slightly from side to side. If I had to take a guess, I'd say none of them were sober, clean, or not under the influence of whatever made them trigger-happy lunatics. Or more trigger-happy, and way past where they should have been locked up in the loonie bin. My attention roamed to their vehicles; yes, those were definitely bones, but with strips of cloth wrapped around them rather than flesh. Still weird as fuck but somewhat less of a health hazard.

Turning back to the soldiers, I found Richards had rejoined the group. He gave me a vexed look for my trouble but didn't say anything, instead turned to the Humvee and got back behind the wheel. We watched in silence as he got it over the ramp and onto the ship. The trader cars were next, piling them on according to what group they belonged to. Last, the scavengers got their turn not sending a vehicle down into the surf below. Whoever was driving knew what they were doing, but I couldn't help but feel uneasy around them—and none of that was due to their behavior and get-up anymore.

I must have been a little too obvious in my studying as one of the traders sidled over, joining me in my perusal. "Been a while since you've got to deal with the finer elements of modern society, huh?"

I gave him a calculating look—that should have dissuaded him from wanting to further talk to me—but toned it down to a grunt. "What makes you think so?"

His bright grin was a startling surprise to how guarded he'd seemed a moment ago. "No offense, but your gear is crap—except for your weapons. That makes me think you spent time out there, far away from all the shit that's been going on. Can't say I blame anyone for going for that option. Missed some nuances, probably. Then shit caught up with you, and you had to cash in some favors, look up some old contacts." His gaze briefly flitted to the side of my neck where the collar of my jacket was turned down just enough to show my marks. It made sense he'd assume I was former army to have gotten them, and that's how I'd ended up with Richards and his men.

"Maybe, maybe not," I offered, but with a smile that should have told him I had my reasons not to spill my life's story. Hell, if I'd learned anything over the last few years from the people I hung out with, it was that everyone had skeletons in the closet. Except for those scavengers, who used them as hood ornaments. I shuddered again as I watched the last vehicle go past us and up the ramp. "Just makes me wonder where that went wrong."

He laughed softly under his breath. "Yeah, don't we all? Listen, I don't know you and you don't know me, but if you need help, we'll get you some up in the city. You may trust those guys, but they have a habit of not letting people off the hook once they get too tight once more. Happened to a buddy of mine. Good guy, and way too trusting."

Considering what Red had told me, I was surprised by the offer, but maybe shouldn't have been. "Trust me, I'd love nothing more," I professed, maybe a little too freely. "But fact is, I may need them longer than I want to hang out around them."

The trader nodded wisely, not pissed off that I wasn't dishing any details. "You got someone else to rely on out there? Because if not, get your ass back to New Angeles somehow and ask for Hernandez. He's my contact there at the armory. At the very least he'll set you up with some good folk who'll give you some good gear and let you do honest work for a living. Doesn't have to be those idiot junkies and their senseless war."

The nameless trader walked back to his people then, and I found Cole looking at me, bemused. "What?"

He shrugged. "Didn't take you long to get comfy with the natives."

"Afraid I'll take my first chance not to spend so much quality time with you?" I quipped.

"Life does get more interesting when you're around," he joked. "Come on, let's get on the ship before they decide they're better off without you. Wouldn't be the first time, eh?"

I left it at a snort as I followed him, walking over the retractable ramp after the scavengers had joined their vehicles near the bow. It was only then that the meaning of the trader's words sunk in; he'd called them junkies—just like the doc at the settlement had figured I was on the tail end of a really bad trip. Her latent resentment—also for what counted for my life choices these days—suddenly made a lot more sense. I would have snarled at that, too. And I could see how she'd jumped to the conclusion, all the other details considered, like that I was obviously someone who'd seen conflict and not always gotten away clear. That still didn't explain what the hell was going on with these people, but it was something. Part of me was tempted to go over to them and ask—what's the worst that could happen? But I knew that was a stupid idea, and not just because my brief encounter with one of them had gone so exceptionally well. Maybe I could bother that trader for a few more details? We had a good twenty hours on that ship—lots of time for talking. As much as I appreciated Red's update, I didn't trust him not to have a heavy bias—and add more to manipulate me. Looked like some things really hadn't changed. As much as it wouldn't help me right now, I got the sense that, eventually, I should find out what had.

As soon as everyone and their packs were on board, the crew got everything ready and moving, and we cast off without much fanfare. I couldn't remember the last time I'd been on a boat—over two years ago, the destroyer to France and back being the exception, and that had been a very different experience—but this one was heavy and low enough in the water to be surprisingly stable, only minimal rocking going on. The vehicles took up maybe a third of the deck; most of the rest was jam-packed with all sorts of containers and odds and ends, as if someone had gotten really busy collecting all the things people might have a use for later—provided they were not on the road and could simply pick up new items somewhere. It made sense that the boat would haul stuff for the city—or other settlements—along, and I didn't doubt that below deck there would be more still, probably the things they didn't trust us with. The crew seemed to consist of fifteen people, all of them well-armed, and they eyed all of us with equal disdain. I was immensely curious to find out what fuel the ship was running on, but curbed my enthusiasm in favor of not attracting too much attention.

We were maybe fifteen minutes into our journey when a man in his late forties appeared on deck, the fact that several of the crewmen stood a little straighter giving away that he must have been someone important. The captain, it turned out, as he introduced himself with a loud, sure voice not unaccustomed to shouting at people around him.

"You've been warned before, but let me remind you of the rules on my ship," he told us in no uncertain terms. Nobody had told me anything, but I figured Red had, for once, expected me not to behave like an imbecile. I wisely didn't point out how negligent that had been. "You've been allowed to keep your weapons, but draw them on any one of the crew, and you go overboard. Attack each other, and you go overboard. Cause any undue trouble—overboard. Instigate any kind of shit—you've guessed it: overboard. And there's a very good chance we'll add whoever you belong to, and your vehicles, so don't tempt me. Don't fuck with us. You all got clearance from New Angeles, and you better make sure you earned that trust, or we will take matters into our own hands. Understand?"

A chorus of murmurs rose—including from the scavengers—making me guess that was part of the deal. The traders looked bored rather than alarmed so I figured it wasn't out of the ordinary. It sounded fair enough. The soldiers took it all with their usual stoic lack of emotion. The scavengers were grumbling among themselves but went mostly ignored.

The captain went on after he must have felt his message had sunk in. "In the unlikely event that we encounter pirates, we'd be much obliged if you'd help us defend our vessel. Since you'll end up just as dead as we will, it's in your best interest. Any questions? Keep them to yourselves and don't cause any trouble for us, and this will all be over soon."

He disappeared with about the same amount of aplomb as he'd shown upon his arrival, leaving us to do whatever we wanted to. I waited for Red to give any orders—I'd at least consider his suggestions—but the others had already retreated to various places around the Humvee, Hill and Cole starting a game of cards. I kind of appreciated it that he didn't warn me not to do anything stupid but missed the opportunity to tell him to fuck off. With nothing else to do, I strolled around the Humvee and over to the railing, looking out over the ocean beyond. There was a light breeze going, invigorating in the blazing heat, and watching the coast in the distance was something to do. I wondered if I should ask the traders if anyone was willing to lend me a book—if they had any along; the soldiers didn't—but since they seemed to keep to themselves as well, I didn't bother. I wasn't that bored yet.

Maybe now I'd come up with what to say to my people once we got to their settlement? Because, try as I might, I didn't have a clue how to start that conversation—and that wasn't anything I was accustomed to. Under different circumstances, I would have laughed at myself, and at the low-key feeling of dread that the idea of coming face to face with them once more made appear in my stomach. I'd never had any doubt about seeing them again, and that I'd be welcome—

But that was before I'd learned what had happened over the past two and a half years.

As homesick as I was feeling right now—and had been the entire time we'd been gone, that much I could admit to myself—that unease was stronger. What had I ever done to deserve their loyalty and friendship? But I could think of a few things I'd done to jeopardize it.

Only time would tell, I guessed—and time was something Nate didn't have. Tomorrow it would be twenty-three days since I'd last seen him as they'd dragged him off. Three weeks felt like nothing, sometimes, and considering the distance I'd had to traverse to get to my destination, three weeks were a very short timeframe—but I bet that, to him, they were well past an eternity.

Meeting my people again was only the first step in getting him back; who knew how many more until we arrived at the perimeter of the camp, and how long it would take us to breach it? A month? Three? That idea made me sick to my stomach, but it came with a single advantage: I suddenly didn't care any longer about the reception I'd get tomorrow. Fuck the grief they might want to air and the beef they had with me—all I cared about was Nate. If they were really my friends—ours, really—they'd help. If not, then not. It was that easy—and that was all I cared about. So fuck those weirdo, drugged-up scavengers; fuck the traders; fuck fucking Gabriel Greene and the horse he rode in on.

There was comfort in that knowledge, but it came with a new bout of paranoia. Nate had once joked that I was his single vulnerability, and also his greatest strength. What did it say about me if getting him back made me ready to go to war all over again? That the same was true for me. Romantic as that notion may have been, it came with a huge drawback: it turned me into a tool, and one that was very easily controlled at that. That very idea made me want to do the polar opposite of what I felt pressured to do, but that was, of course, impossible. So where did that leave me?

I had a feeling I would find out soon enough—and likely after it was already too late.

Chapter 12

Considering the scavenger's posturing at the shore, they were surprisingly subdued during the rest of the day, and also the following night. They didn't miss a few chances to harass the traders—who ignored them—and Gallager—who was too afraid of them to do anything but hide by the Humvee. Smart boy. There was some gloating and name-calling going on toward me but I chose to ignore it as best I could; it simply wasn't worth the trouble, and I'd heard worse coming from people I harbored more resentment for. Richards took it in stride as if he hadn't expected anything else from me, but Cole seemed downright puzzled as he stopped next to where I sat on the Humvee's grill, gazing out onto the ocean, trying to munch my morning jerky with as much meditative deliberation as possible.

"You know, I would have expected at least a small tussle, a few broken bones," he commented. "Not you going all Mother Teresa on them."

I stared at him long and hard—willing him to lose interest and just leave—but no such luck. "Has it maybe occurred to you that some of what you've perceived as my normal behavior was me actually acting like a stressed-out, caged version of myself, mostly due to some fucktard doing everything in his might to put me down? I know, surprise, surprise. I can act like a normal human being when I'm not constantly being threatened and disparaged. Who would have thought?"

He considered that for a second but shook his head, grinning. "Nah, not buying it. Either you're pretending to be all meek and calm because you lack backup, or you're half of a mind you might need their support later."

I hated that he kind of had a point—in both cases—but not entirely. "Would that be so bad? I still don't get why you're helping me, but I know someone has ulterior motives in this game and I'm not going to like that. I know I won't manage to get anything done with just the four of you along. Those weirdos over there might just be insane enough that I can hurl them at that camp and use them as a distraction. Can you say the same for your people? For all I know, nobody in the army has a clue that you're here, with me tagging along."

I knew I was right when I didn't get any gloating back. It was both a relief and a disappointment—because in the end, I needed someone's help, and as things were shaping up right now, "anyone" would soon sound good if they only volunteered.

"But you know why we are doing it," Cole stressed. "With them, can you even trust them not to deliver you on a silver platter to demand special treatment from whoever runs that camp? Because I'd be very worried about that." He did some gazing out over the ocean of his own, ignoring my baleful glare. "LT said to tell you that we'll be in New Angeles in about two hours from now. Should be showing on the horizon any moment. You know that they know you're coming? Better get your speech ready."

I laughed softly as I shook my head. "Not intending to give any kind of speech. And there's nobody in New Angeles I feel the need to convince of anything."

"Well, they might disagree," he prompted and turned to finally leave me in peace—but not quite yet. "You are aware that your usual MO won't work? People are tired of fighting for causes. Of dying for causes. You may have rallied hundreds by pointing at the next best scapegoat and letting them loose, but nobody gives a shit about you or your husband anymore. Or about the fact that we've rediscovered the greatest achievements of our civilization—slavery and indentured servitude. Trying to pander to their finer sensibilities will only get you one thing: shot. You'll have to be smarter than that."

All I had for him was a slow smile. "And there I almost thought you had a clue who I really am. So glad to know that's not the case."

Cole finally turned away with a snort, amused by what he probably thought was me deflecting. While completely wrong about my warmongering nature, I appreciated the warning he'd inadvertently given me. I hadn't planned to do any kind of rallying call, but my knee-jerk reaction about that camp and what was going on there was to get into everyone's face and ask them how they could let something like this simply happen, and continue to exist. Good to know that I needn't bother.

As Cole had predicted, soon New Angeles came into view to the northwest as we kept hugging the coast. Even from afar, the ruins of the gigantic old city made my skin crawl, while the industrial bustle of the new core reaching from the beach further inland than I remembered sat in clear defiance to everything that common sense dictated nowadays. In the middle of the day, the entire bay was busy with fishing boats, and off to the deeper waters I could see several groups of tied-together ships still—their last-resort, ready-for-action navy that had already been around back when I'd first come here, remnants of how they'd taken back the city—and, from what I could tell, it had grown substantially. That made me wonder if they'd taken over the many islands yet—there had been talk about it back in the day, but since I'd never actively belonged to the community, nobody had shared any details with me. Fat chance they'd do so now. I couldn't even say why that rankled, except that having an island to oneself sounded like a pretty neat bug-out plan—except that I was lacking someone to bug out with.

The captain came on deck once more, this time not to threaten us but to declare that we'd gotten clearance to dock, and that everyone was to get off as soon as we landed, except for "those who have business elsewhere." The traders cast a few glances in Red's direction since the captain practically glared at him, but no questions were asked, so none got answered. The trader who'd been pretty friendly with me yesterday gave me a look that I couldn't quite place; it wasn't entirely hostile but also not friendly. I had a certain feeling that he knew who was squatting a few hours up the coast from the city, and what that might say about my identity. I didn't need anyone to warn me not to open my mouth and doom myself.

That last few miles ended up rather tense, and things got even more interesting as the ship prepared for docking, aiming for a suddenly completely abandoned part of the dock, with no other boat around for at least a mile's radius. The dock itself was far from empty, quickly filling with all kinds of people, all of them heavily armed and in protective gear.

I couldn't say I was surprised about that welcome committee, but I was far from happy about it.

And, wouldn't you know it, at the head of the group stood none other than Gabriel Greene—a little older than I remembered, a little more grizzled—a look that suited him, I had to admit. That sleek trust fund-baby-turned-CEO thing he'd had going on before the shit hit the fan hadn't survived well into the year after. Now he sure looked the part of spymaster and brain of one of the world's last surviving cities.

The ship came to a halt and lines were cast to moor it to the dock; the ramp was extended once more, and once the guards at the dock made room, the scavengers were the first to disembark, gathering on the dock once they were out of the way to let the traders follow. I had a strong inclination to go hide in the Humvee, but I was sure that Greene had already spotted me where I'd watched near the stern earlier, so I remained standing, a little apart but close to Richards and his men to watch the proceedings in silence.

The sooner we were done here, the sooner we'd be able to go further north, the better.

Of course, Greene had other plans—yet before he could make any declarations or grand gestures, one of the scavengers sauntered across the dock toward him. I'd vaguely flagged the tall, muscular guy as their leader, but from what I could tell, they had some weird kind of consensus thing going on—weird for me as, either way, I was used to someone being in charge, even though they might or might not have asked others for their opinion. The female scavenger who'd tried to start shit with me was still glaring at the ship, roughly in my direction, making me guess that she hadn't forgotten about me yet.

The scavenger stopped when two of the guards close to Greene stepped forward, a silent reminder to keep a distance. The scavenger raised his hands placatingly—appearing anything but—as he rocked to a halt. "Gabriel! What a surprise!" he hollered. "Such a lovely procession you have here, and all in our honor? You shouldn't have."

Greene had been looking at the ship, deliberately not paying any attention to the scavengers, but upon being approached, he scrutinized the man walking toward him. "Amos," he acknowledged with a dry tone that made me smirk for a second. So much derision and boredom in just one word—I hated to admit it, but I'd kind of missed Greene's all-around assholery. That probably said a lot about how entertaining my social life had been since our return to the States. "Much as it pains me to have to open my doors to you and yours, but the procession isn't for you at all. You can go right on over to the barracks; I'm sure someone will have some hot chow and cool booze ready for you."

What had been a rather triumphant grin on Amos's face froze, his eyes narrowing as he took a step forward. Greene remained unfazed but his guards closed ranks, building a wall of bodies and weapons between him and the scavengers. The bitch who'd come after me joined him, cocking her head to the side as if she had problems making sense of the situation—or not. "Why would you bring so much manpower for a whore and four lapdogs?" she asked.

I thought it was Cole who chortled behind me but it could have been Hill as well. I didn't turn to check. I was more interested in Greene's reaction—and he didn't disappoint.

Greene's brows rose at that statement, his gaze remaining focused on the scavenger for a moment before zooming right up to where I was hovering, apparently not as out of sight as I'd figured, a slow smile spreading across his face. He focused on the scavenger again, giving her one of those infuriating politician smiles. "Eden, Eden. When will you learn?" he more muttered than said, making both scavengers frown, but Greene didn't seem to care about antagonizing them. Louder, he asked, "Did you call her that to her face as well? Of course you did. And you're still breathing, which tells me what I needed to know. As always, a pleasure." I was sure that most onlookers were as confused about that statement as Eden and Amos seemed, but Greene has apparently lost all interest in them.

I figured, since he seemed so keen on a conversation, I might as well step up to the top of the ramp so I could look down at him unhindered. If he really wanted to have me gunned down, a sniper could have done so minutes ago. Greene and I stared at each other, him still wearing that slightly triumphant smirk, my expression hopefully as cold and hard as I felt inside. Maybe I was wrong—and I'd be very, very happy to find out I was—but somehow I got the sense that the general goodwill that Greene had harbored toward me in the past was all gone.

Yet before either of us could spew venom in the other's face, Eden had to rain on our posturing parade. "Who exactly are you, whore?"

I cut down on my impulse to tell her to fucking stop calling me that, but Greene, rather unexpectedly, came to my rescue. "As much as I may share the sentiment, I'm sure the insult is wasted on this one. Very likely unfounded as well as her dedication to her husband seems to be the only virtue she has left."

I couldn't very well let that sit on me. "My disdain for you is a close second," I called down, offering up a smile.

One thing Greene had always had going for him—he wasn't actually insulted by my insults, and that hadn't changed. His grin at my statement was real, if short-lived. "That's true. I almost forgot how unforgiving and vindictive you are."

"Hardly."

His grin broadened. "You mean, you're not?"

"That you'd be able to forget that I am," I corrected.

Ever the showman, Greene bowed, his arms stretched out to the sides. "My bad, indeed. Well, let me welcome you back to our fine city. Or as one could also say, the prodigal daughter returns."

I didn't even try to suppress a shudder as I crossed my arms over my chest. "Way to make things even more creepy between us as they already were. I kind of miss the days when I was still deciding whether you just wanted to bash my face in to scare me, to actually kill me, or were really incompetent at raping me."

Greene's grin never faltered but it did turn wry at that. "And, as always, your arguments are delivered like a bucket full of shit—not very effectively."

Oddly enough, if there hadn't been a ramp and a dock filled with armed guards between us, I might have offered him my hand to shake. Or tried to clap him hard enough on the back to make him stagger. As it was, I had to leave it at a satisfied smile, hoping that I wasn't reading his banter wrong. "Well, what can I say. That's me in a nutshell."

Greene was the only one who laughed, but since I didn't see a single familiar face down there besides his, I didn't much care about the rest. Deep down I'd expected to see Gita there with him, but for now I had to hope that she was still alive and doing well. Maybe Burns would know—provided he was still alive and doing well, also, but I wouldn't allow myself to consider that not being the case.

"Where's your worse half?" Greene asked, drawing my attention back to him.

"Don't you mean, better half?" I groused, just for the sake of it.

"Nope," Green told me succinctly. "Myths and old wives tales aside, I'll never believe that you're capable of outdoing the shit he'd already had sticking to him long before you even met."

I shrugged. "Apparently, I now cause civil wars without being present, or actually while being dead. I'd call that quite a feat, wouldn't you say?" The two scavengers perked up at that, and a few of the traders—still lingering not to miss the show—looked downright disconcerted. I did my best to ignore all of them, keeping my attention on Greene.

He begrudgingly inclined his head. "You do seem to have a skill to inspire people who have never met you to believe the worst of you. I can see it in those who have crossed your path but will always marvel at the rest." He added a dramatic pause there but went on when no curious questions came from anyone. "I see you're avoiding answering my question. I completely understand why. I should probably extend my condolences to you. Your husband may have deserved the reputation he had, but not the end he has likely met in the meantime. It's been, what? Three weeks now?"

I had to fight for composure for a second, the urge to come down that ramp and punch the answers right out of Greene so strong it almost overwhelmed me. It took me a few deep breaths to steady my voice to the point where I could ask instead. "What the fuck do you know?"

Greene remained calm, but the always-present teasing quality disappeared from his tone. "Less than you do, presumably, but enough to draw the conclusions that you would have come to already if you weren't, well, you. Nobody has ever gotten away from that camp after they got caught."

"I got away," I pointed out.

Greene cocked his head to the side, considering me for a moment. "I can guess why, going on your unusual combination of physical shortcomings and compensatory strengths. Consider yourself the one lucky exception. Nobody would have underestimated your husband like that. It pains me to say that, but I will miss him. In his own way, he was someone I always considered good to know he was still around, if maybe not for my personal health. If you're here looking for support to go on another crusade, I have to disappoint you. We don't have anyone to spare for fool's errands."

"I'm not here to ask anything of you," I clarified, pretending like his words didn't make my heart sink. I didn't allow myself to believe him—I simply couldn't. "Except information, maybe, but since you already confirmed that you know nothing, I'm happy to take my leave. I'm just passing through."

"Not quite yet," Greene offered, his attention skipping from me to something to my right—Richards, if I wasn't completely oblivious. "You weren't the one bargaining for passage, and you're not the one who's here on a mission."

I found Richards his usual calm self as he pulled something from his jacket pocket—a flash drive, I realized, surprised to see that one still existed, but probably shouldn't have been. At Greene's nod, one of his guards lowered his weapon and started up the ramp, accepting the device from Richards to hand to Greene once he was back on the dock. Greene didn't even look at the drive before letting it

.disappear. He gave Richards a curt nod, and took a dramatic step to the side. "Must be something important you've got planned if you're pulling some of your moles out," he noted as he turned his head to look further down the dock, where a group of three men stood surrounded by the guards, looking none too happy—and neither did the people around them. I wouldn't have picked out any of them as spies, and I didn't seem to be the only one as one of the guards—a woman in her late twenties—visibly stiffened as they passed by her on their way to the ship.

"You lying asshole!" she hissed after one of them—the rightmost, who was doing a shit job avoiding looking at her, his shoulders tense enough to make him look a bit like a turtle yearning to disappear into its shell.

"Trish, it's not what you think—" he tried to explain, halting momentarily, but one of the other guards quickly pushed him forward.

The woman would have nothing of that. "It's pretty obvious, wouldn't you say? You're dead to me! Don't bother ever coming back!"

He stopped again, briefly wrestling with the guard to get a few more seconds, but they pushed him forward—and a moment later, the woman had disappeared into the crowd of onlookers. The scavengers looked tempted to come after the small group, but thought better of it considering the guards were giving them pretty much the same looks as the apparent spies in their midst. I couldn't help a wry smile as I turned to glance at Richards. "Must be a pretty good reason for you to play home-wrecker like that."

His expression didn't give me much, but there was a brief spark of anger in his eyes. Interesting. "As I said before, we didn't come here just to play taxi for you." I knew that was all I was going to get out of him, so I didn't ask. It was enough to see all the newcomers glare at me with enough venom to know they blamed me for having to leave their cozy little hideout here. They toned it down for Richards, but made no attempt to mingle with the other three soldiers, much to Hill's amusement.

"I presume that concludes our business here?" Richards called down to the docks, but that might have been addressed to anyone.

Greene nodded, but rather than retreat himself, he started up the ramp, followed by a cluster of guards. I didn't miss the obvious limp, his right leg not quite working as well as the left—a reminder of past conflicts, maybe? When he saw my surprise, he gave me a dazzling smile. "Oh, you thought I'd miss out on that happy reunion you have planned? Fat chance. That I need to see."

Since it wasn't up to me—and I doubted anyone would ask for my opinion—I kept my mouth shut, stepping aside to let them all onto the ship. The guards fanned out except for two refrigerator-sized guys who remained glued to Greene, who seemed happy to remain right there next to Richards and me.

"You shouldn't have come," Greene told me, his attention at the dock—and scavengers—below. "Things would have been so much easier if you'd remained gone."

"Easier for you?" I presumed, hard-pressed not to sound full of glee to have, once more, made a nuisance of myself.

"For you," Greene corrected, turning his attention to me. "The best thing you ever did was drop off the face of the earth after the rumors started that winter. I thought you'd gotten that message."

"We did. But seeing as I'm short a husband, I couldn't very well continue to skulk around the very edges of nowhere. Don't bother telling me again he's dead; we both know he's tougher than that. He will survive, and I will get him back."

Greene's smile wasn't a nice one. "You say that like it's a fate you'd wish on anyone you profess to love." Before I could respond to that, he turned to Richards. "What's so important that you uncover your moles? Bad choice, by the way. I would have gone with Connelly and Shanks instead. We've known for years they're your people. Too stupid to get a single coded message out without tripping all of our warning systems."

Richards didn't take the bait. "Why should I have pulled out our top recruiters? Would be a bad move, wouldn't you say?" He gave a curt nod—to me only—and left to join his men, and after a few words to Cole went on to the sulking extractees.

Business here concluded, the ship cast off once more, slowly gaining speed as it got further away from the docks. I would have loved to take my previous place at the railing once more to run a few more great lines through my head that I might offer once I stepped off the boat again—somehow, "Sorry I disappeared, now help me," didn't quite feel sufficient—but Greene seemed to have other plans, remaining plastered to my side. The remaining guards at the dock dispersed quickly, as did the traders, until only the scavengers were glaring after us. Lovely. I kind of had a feeling that might, eventually, catch up with me. And there I'd tried to be so nice and diplomatic. But first, I had to pull off and survive the impossible—and after that, get my husband back.

"Are you going to spend the entire time north standing there, staring at me?" I asked Greene when, ten minutes later, he still hadn't found something other than me to entertain himself with.

"Thanks, I quite enjoy looking at ghosts," Greene offered, his usual inanely annoying, constantly goading tone back. "But as you seem so conversational, how is it that I had no clue whatsoever where you were hiding, but they managed to pick you up within days? Doesn't really paint a pretty picture for you, considering you will be running the 'I didn't do anything with them' narrative, I presume?"

"I'm not using a script, if that's what you're asking." The very idea made me chortle—until I realized what he was really asking. "No, I don't suspect that Richards had anything to do with what happened. But thanks for confirming that we actually did manage to pull a complete disappearing act."

"And still, those asshole slavers found you—as did your buddies with a penchant for all shades of drab green," he noted, sounding very self-satisfied.

"Bad luck," I shot back. "And no such thing as coincidence on the second count."

Greene looked properly disturbed, which made all this worth it—at least for a second. "I can't believe you set up a safety call with them but not your people. And I know you didn't because they learned that you're in trouble through the grapevine, which in and of itself will get you shit."

All I could do was shrug at that. "Then our plan worked. Nothing I can do about the consequences."

Greene kept studying me for a while, either waiting for me to elaborate or change topics. When neither happened, he heaved a theatrical sigh. "Please, have it your way. Which reminds me, I have been thinking—"

"Never a good idea. Did you hurt your pretty head?"

Greene flashed me a brief grin at my taunt but otherwise ignored me—which didn't bode well. "You mentioned a name on our brief talk when you were in France. Since you never do anything like that casually, it piqued my interest quite a bit. In this case, I figured you were just mining for dirt you could get on any number of your associates, but ever since, it never quite left my mind. Do you remember who you were asking about?"

Any levity I'd felt before was gone in under a second flat. "I'd hardly forget the reason why we decided to disappear."

For once, Greene didn't look pleased at having guessed right, but he also seemed annoyed with me. "The thing is, I tried to find out something—anything, really—but there is nothing to find. He's dead, just like millions of other grumpy old bastards who had no chance whatsoever to survive the apocalypse. I didn't think you'd be someone who believes in ghost stories."

Maybe not me. "Nate does. And that was enough for me."

A frown crossed Greene's expression, making him look downright pinched. "You sure your husband didn't just want to shirk some responsibility? Endless guard duty and diaper runs aren't all that entertaining if you do it for years. Could it be possible that he sold you on the idea because he wanted to spend some quality time doing whatever you weirdos do when you're out there, all on your own?"

I couldn't help myself; even knowing he was baiting me, that one I had to take. "You mean, fuck like animals? Of course we did lots of that, but being near people has never really stopped us."

Suppressed laughter coming from further down the boat made it obvious that our conversation wasn't staying between us. Greene gave me an exasperated sigh, but he had been asking for it. Literally.

"Don't you think that, four years into this shit that we call civilization at the moment, we'd know if there was such a big, bad wolf hiding in our middle? I guarantee you—I'd know. I may not have been able to pinpoint your exact location, but you haven't been that completely off the map that I haven't been able to narrow it down to a few select regions. If I'd wanted to, I could have sent someone to fetch and drag you back to us anytime."

That got the derisive smirk it deserved. "You had the right people on your doorstep who we'd gladly come with if needed. You didn't send anyone because you had your reasons not to. Don't play the saint and protector now; that's never worked with me, and never will."

If anything, Greene seemed challenged rather than annoyed—good. I needed any help I could get, and I wasn't that choosy where it came from anymore. That lesson I'd had to learn the hard way.

"You both really think Decker's still alive? And not just that, but behind everything that's going on? I hate to break it to you, but the main issue we've faced has always been chaos rather than fascist order. We must have lost a good five to ten thousand people to faction after faction doing their thing which ended up undermining themselves and costing even more lives. You can't really negotiate for a truce when there is no one to negotiate it with."

That sounded quite a bit different from what Richards had told me—and I gave it the same amount of credit. I didn't expect any one of them not to lie to me. "Is that what happened? To your docks, I mean."

"And my leg," Greene griped, but didn't offer up any further details. "Make fun of me all you will, but New Angeles has become one of the stabilizing powers. All that we got for that was making ourselves a target. That's why we're closed now to anyone we don't have a very good reason to trust."

"And I'm the exception again, right?" I guessed.

He took way too long to reply not to confirm my guess. "Let's just put it this way: nobody in the city would spill a tear if anything was to happen to you."

"Even though I didn't commit any of the atrocities that everyone seems to be pinning on me now?"

Greene looked confused for a second before a nasty, enlightened expression took over his face. "Ah. You don't know."

"What don't I know?" That I didn't was obvious—as was the part about not really wanting to hear this, but what else was new?

Greene turned around so he could look over to the soldiers, studying them for a moment. "I'm not going to waste my breath on asking what tall tale they dished out. Let me set all this in perspective for you. What everyone knows is that your people turned up in the spring in the first year after the world went to shit, well-fed, trained as a team, bustling with weapons, ammo, and gear. You hung out just long enough to establish yourself as power players, and the next thing we knew, we had open war on the roads. Lo and behold, it was you who rallied the scavengers to fight back, which you did with lots of ease and surprisingly few dead—including enemy numbers. It was such a shining victory for freedom and self-empowerment—are we on the same page so far?"

"If you completely ignore the loss of lives and why we did what we did, sure," I snarked, not liking where this was going.

"Collateral damage, as we soon found out," Greene offered succinctly. "Next thing, you both disappear, leaving some semi-believable tale with just enough evidence to make it sound real for a while. Add confirmation about your forced cooperation—which, really, was a great move, abusing my gullibility to establish the different fronts there—and then you simply disappear, presumably to spend the next years lazing away at some base or other, to watch the world burn. And burn it does, because what your crusade really did was highlight the players who might be strong enough to fight, and happy to dissent. How am I doing so far?"

"Talking a lot of BS, if you ask me." I didn't have to feign annoyance. That was all real.

"Is it?" Greene asked, striking a musing pose. "It makes so much more sense than any other explanation. You weren't the only one who disappeared that winter. We don't have exact numbers, but estimates are that more than half of the scavengers who went to Colorado with you vanished without a trace, including two entire settlements."

"It was a hard winter," I objected. "Besides, we know the army was recruiting. Maybe people just changed their minds?" Those were feeble protests at best. I hated how doubtful my voice sounded.

Greene pretty much agreed with me on that. "A few, maybe, but not people who had families in settlements and were just out there to make living a little less like hell. It's not like we have official numbers, because come spring, Dispatch was the first city that quit working with the network, and after that it quickly turned into a free-for-all out there. Must have been coincidence that, just like your husband, Dispatch is led by a woman who has direct, and very close, ties to the powers that you claimed to fight against."

This was getting better and better. "What do I know about what Rita does? I've met her two times in my life. Maybe three. If anything, her and my husband's shared past seemed to have been a probable cause for issues, not agreement. And no, not because they were screwing around for a while, if that's your guess. I'm not the jealous type."

It was funny to see how much my deviation from the topic annoyed Greene, but it didn't stop him from continuing to unfurl his fairy tale. "It doesn't matter what I know, or what I believe—this is what the world believes. You served them up on a silver platter and betrayed them—and, if anything, getting caught up in the hell that you caused and left behind serves you just right."

"You can't be serious." It was a rhetorical question, but one I had to ask—because this was magnitudes worse than what Richards had alluded to. Maybe even worse than the scenario from which we'd been hiding from.

Greene's smile was surprisingly sad. "Figured they hadn't told you about that. Else, you wouldn't have so freely admitted at the docks who you are."

"You pretty much made me," I groused.

He shrugged, not denying it. "It was the quickest way to get you out of my city, and make sure you couldn't come back. Also, not linger for long in our vicinity, because you know what those savages will do come morning? They'll be at your people's doorstep by noon, and chances are, if you're still there they'll kick you out the door, shared history or not, just to be rid of them."

The anger was back, but nothing I could do about that—and I could kind of see where Greene was coming from with the reasoning for wanting me gone. "How come my people are still living on your doorstep then if we're all persona non grata?"

"Just you and your husband," Greene was quick to explain. "Consensus has it that your disappearance sealed your fate. You used the others and discarded them like rags after you'd gotten your use out of them."

"Is any of that actually supposed to make sense?" I'd managed to keep a lid on my anger until this, but enough was enough. "And you, personally, don't believe that shit, right?"

His smile was a little sad but mostly neutral—not very easing on my nerves. "It doesn't matter what I personally believe when I have twenty thousand people close by who say otherwise. Of course, I got to meet you face-to-face on several occasions, and I may know a few details that the rabble out there isn't aware of. It doesn't really matter. It's the fallout you have to deal with, whether you caused it or not."

My, wasn't that just perfect? At least Greene had had the common decency to warn me—which Richards hadn't, and I didn't believe for a second that he and his soldiers didn't know this version of the story. Of course, if I'd known all that, I may not have simply come along with them—although, I hated to admit, they still were my only option, unless I'd wanted to add weeks or months to my journey.

It sure added a new layer of unease to what was already churning deep in my stomach.

"Guess returning from the dead is never without a hitch," I finally offered when Greene was still waiting for something a good few minutes later. He had no wise words to offer in return. Maybe it was better this way.

Chapter 13

Three hours later, and the time for feeling sorry for myself was up. I hadn't been to New Angeles often by boat, but even so, I could see how much growth and progress there had been along the coast. Gone were the few overrun towns, fire and looting having reduced a lot to bare bones, with no shambler moving in sight. A few times I'd thought I felt the light thrumming of a beacon coming from the distance—a good explanation why, after the cleanup, the coast had remained abandoned. Twice, we passed working docks that were in much better condition, if empty of people at the moment—leading to settlements further inland, I figured. Once in a while I thought I saw movement on the coast but couldn't be sure; we passed our fair share of small fishing vessels, going up and down the shoreline, a few also hauling cargo. It all seemed so normal, like nothing had happened after we had to learn not to rely on fossil fuels and electricity any longer, although to a point they obviously still did. I had lost all interest in inquiring what the ship was running on. Who cared if they'd managed to get a refinery running again or not? I had much bigger fish to fry—or get fried myself, which seemed all the more likely.

We passed the old cliff that we'd used in the first months of the budding settlement to get to the boats, and consequently, the city, now abandoned, the pier destroyed for good. Since the ship was already slowing down, I figured they must have established a different docking site.

Or beach-front town, as it turned out, I realized a few minutes later when the ship went around more cliffs jutting out into the ocean, with sandy beaches opening up behind—and a well-established marina, complete with a dozen anchored vessels of different sizes, and the accompanying town behind it coming into view. At first glance, there were a good hundred houses near the water, with more further inland. Palisades, watchtowers, and several rows of fences and trenches, making the town easily defensible toward land, and very hard to breach, while leaving the waterway somewhat more open. Someone had known what they were doing as they'd dug in here. I really fucking hoped that I was right about my guess on who that had been.

It turned out, I didn't need to guess much longer. As the boat drew into the marina and toward the farthest-extending part of the free dock, I saw that the square beyond was packed with people— and quite a few familiar faces were among them. Under different circumstances, I would have laughed at the trepidation and joy, twisted around each other as they were, that arose from deep inside my chest—and the wave of homesickness that was overwhelming me, strong for a few moments, choking me up.

Right then, I felt like our decision to disappear had been short-sighted and stupid. Why spend months living off the land as nomads, then slowly start rebuilding everything we needed when we could have had it all here? Without months of bad diets, months without enough sleep because one of us always had to be awake, or at least easy to rouse at the first hint of danger? And just look what it had gotten us into with the slavers from the camp—none of that would have happened if we'd been part of a larger group. So many familiar strong, capable people living here—Andrej, Pia, Burns, Martinez; Moore, Collins, Clark, and Santos. A handful more who I still recognized from when we'd started the settlement at the coast—before I'd left. Lots more that I didn't know but who looked equally competent.

But then my gaze snapped to the tall, blonde woman in their midst with the child half wrapped around her left leg, half hiding behind it, and right there I had my answer. I'd left because I'd known, deep down, even before I got confirmation, that I was a danger to both Sadie and her unborn kid, and considering how much of a target Nate and I had both painted on us at the time, leaving had been the right idea—and nothing whatsoever had changed about that. And that wasn't the only child I saw, or new face next to a familiar one. Life had moved on, and so had they, and deep down in my gut I knew that us staying wouldn't have ended well for any of them.

Still, being the odd one out now sucked. Being the one who came crawling back, on her knees, because she needed help, sucked. Having to admit that I hadn't been strong enough, smart enough, quick enough to make it out there on my own sucked.

And, damn. You'd think that after everything I'd been through, my ego wouldn't be the thing I'd have to fight the most as I stepped from the ship onto the dock, my pack swung over one shoulder, the rifle tied securely to the back of it. I was the only one who left, the rest remaining as a—hopefully silent—mass of onlookers. I really didn't care for all that attention directed at me, but no way around that now. So I straightened my back, squared my shoulders, took a deep breath, and made my way down the dock to the square.

Well, here went nothing.

Halfway across the distance, I considered punching myself in the left thigh to let the pain take away all those nasty emotions warring inside of me. It would be so much easier to get through this keyed up, letting focus and attention override any stupid thing my heart might get up to. I didn't expect I'd need it to fight my way out, but better safe than sorry, right?

Wrong, I told myself as I forced my fingers to relax and spread out from the fist they'd already curled into. I had no clue whatsoever what they all thought of me, but appearing as the emotionless robot wouldn't help me. On the contrary—there was a chance they'd believe the powers that be had actually gotten to me, brainwashed me, turned me into an anathema of what I actually was. Couldn't have that, now, could I? So all Bree, no plan—as usual—it was.

Shit. But I'd really expected this to be easier and less painful by the time I finally got here.

I stopped exactly one step off the pier where sturdy, weathered wood met cracked concrete. That left me close enough to all of them that I wouldn't have to shout, but at a rather obvious distance. Swallowing thickly, I took a moment to check in with those who had once been my closest friends, but got nothing from them. With the Ice Queen, I'd expected no less—I'd know whether she'd try to kill or hug me the moment before either happened—but Andrej and Burns cut me deep. Martinez had been pretty pissed at me the last time we'd .talked and I could tell that he still remembered as well, but I would have preferred that anger now to the neutral hostility I got instead. And Sadie—well, she was seething with rage while trying to appear very elder-stateswoman-esque, but failing horribly. The obvious dissonance between us came at the worst of times.

Walking down the dock had already been awkward. Simply standing there was worse, so I took a last breath and let it rip, hoping that it wouldn't come out as pathetic as it sounded in my head. "I am very aware that you're likely not at all keen on seeing me here. Trust me when I say, I wouldn't be here in the first place if I didn't need your help. Which I do. Please, just hear me out. If none of you feel like supporting me, I'll just go, no hard feelings." Maybe not my most eloquent string of sentences, but at least it came across real—or so I prayed. Shit, but when had this turned so fucking hard?

The silence that followed was oppressive, and thick enough to cut with a knife. It was almost a relief when Sadie let out a derisive snort, although it was obvious I wouldn't like what I had coming.

"Help, huh? That's rich."

I did my best attempt at a nonchalant shrug. "Why don't you just let me have it so that we get this out of the way and can get to the important part?"

Sadie looked ready to explode in my face but something held her back. Her attention briefly skipped from me to the boat at my back, a wry twist coming to her face. "Sure, why not? How about you start with the company you're keeping nowadays?"

"I needed to hitch a ride. They were in the area," I explained. "I trusted them moderately more than the slavers that seem to have become a real pain in the ass. And they were my only option to get here before the summer turns half the country into a desert wasteland."

She seemed to be waiting for more. Nobody else spoke up. "That's it?"

I offered another shrug. "I've spent the last two and a half years hiding in the middle of nowhere. If it was up to me, I wouldn't be here, but, as usual, other assholes had other plans. How about I start where we last saw each other, so we're all on the same page? Because, as things are, I may not blindly trust those yahoos back there, but they are the least of my problems at the moment."

I could tell that there was so much grief she wanted to air, but Sadie left it at a curt, "It's a start." I already had my mouth open to do just that when she added, "And while you're at it, why don't you explain why you and your good-for-nothing husband decided to abandon me, seven months pregnant, and leave us short people we direly needed at the time?"

Looking around pointedly, I raised my brows at her. "You seem to have done well enough for yourselves. But, sure, let's start there. Let's start with that we left because I already had a very strong suspicion that my immunity toward the zombie virus was wearing off, or something similar was very, very wrong with me—and it turned out that I was right. Because of the bites, I'd gotten a nasty secondary infection that made me rot from the inside out—or outside in, depending how you want to view that. I'm sure that, in the meantime, you got confirmation of that from the Silo. While I was waiting for their results, we got an invitation I couldn't refuse, mainly as it was my only chance to survive. And we got to that base in Canada with hours to spare, hours that I had left to live."

Sadie crossed her arms over her chest. I was sure that she'd heard the tale from Burns—or Jason, or Charlie, or anyone who'd talked with them since; maybe even Gita. "What a coincidence, really."

I couldn't help but snort as I looked back over my shoulder. "Richards, how many ATV charging stations did you have out there?"

Red seemed very amused at my question. "Four or five. I can't quite remember anymore. You missed the first two at the very least."

Turning back to Sadie, I did my best to ignore her frown. "Yes, we knew it was a setup when we found an electric ATV at a charging station. It was obvious to Nate and me both that we had this one chance only, and he wouldn't just let me die. So we went. And it went about as well as you'd expect, because while we were waiting there at the fence of the base, with me coughing up blood, none other than Bucky Hamilton himself rolled up to the gate to gloat all over my misfortune. Not that I had much energy to give a shit about that anymore. At the base, they gave me a routine physical, realized just how close to the brink I was, shot me up with the serum so I'd have a fighting chance to survive, and then they fixed me, as much as they were able to."

For the first time, confusion appeared on Sadie's face, making me want to snort. Oh, this was going to be fun. Apparently, Burns had kept his trap shut about my... changes. A quick glance in his direction got me the same stoic look as before, so I turned back to Sadie. "It's easier if I show you." That said, I dropped my pack, and started to strip out of my jacket so I'd have an easier time to drop my pants and get the gloves off that went halfway up my forearms underneath the outer layers. Pausing to look back briefly, I couldn't help a quick grin. "Gallager, you may want to look away for this, if my hands already made you want to hurl." I didn't get a response from the young soldier, loitering somewhere behind Red, but I had something else to focus on, anyway—like the rampant self-loathing that chose just the right time to rear its ugly head once more.

"Not sure if this is necessary," Sadie started when she realized I was about to drop my pants—but she cut off as I shoved them down to my knees, revealing the wasteland that was my left thigh. She turned a little white in the face, even visible through her permanent tan.

"You maybe remember the nice patch of scars I had up here where the zombies got me? Well, good news is, that down there is so much worse that it's almost not noticeably anymore." I prodded at the middle of my thigh. "Part of my femur is a titanium replacement now because necrosis went not just down to the bone but straight through it." I then pulled up my tank top and partly turned around so the mess that was my lower back—worst where my kidney had been but overall bad—was in full view, a nice addition to my abdominal scarring. "Part of that was from where Nate had to open several of the wounds a few times to keep draining pus. I really wouldn't advise letting him do sutures unless you really, absolutely need them. Oh, and this is where, a few weeks later, their medic had to cut me open again to remove a last festering nest of necrosis that they either missed, or more likely was growing anew even after they'd cut out whatever they could reach, including a few of my redundant organs." Leaving the clothes where I'd shoved them for the most effect, I started taking off my gloves last, having to use my lips and teeth to peel them off, talking on when I could. "I'm too lazy to undo my boots, but, suffice it to say, my feet are even worse than my hands. Thankfully, I don't need them to shoot, right?" With that, I dropped both of the gloves and extended my arms in front of me, fingers spread—what was left of them. Sadie looked downright ashen, and a few of the previously silent onlookers started to murmur and fidget—and not all of them leaned away. I let them all get a good look before I put my shirt and pants back where they belonged, but left the gloves off. It was hot as hell, and getting the sweaty leather back on would take ages. Propping my hands up at my hips was a much more reasonable idea.

"I have no clue how long it took them to fix me up, but quite a bit—"

Richards clearing his throat behind me made me pause and look at him.

"Sixteen and a half hours," he offered.

I was tempted to roll my eyes at him but refrained, instead shouting, "I so didn't need to know the exact number. 'A small eternity' totally does it for me."

"You always complain that I never share information with you. Consider it a token of trust."

Just what I needed right now, but I chose to—mostly—ignore him as I turned back to the others. "Well, there you have it. Actually, that sounds like a rather low number, but I may be biased—and they did have an entire team of people, from what I remember."

I was about to skip ahead but Martinez spoke up, his voice a warring mix between anger and barely-contained horror. "You remember."

Holding his gaze, I did my best impression of an "oh, this is nothing" shrug. "I just told you—they shot me up with the serum, then they dragged me into the OR. I don't have to tell you how standard procedure on those who've gotten inoculated works. Shoot 'em up with a paralytic, and then do whatever the hell you want."

I hadn't planned on dropping that bomb—actually, I'd kind of hoped to not have to explain a lot of this—and seeing true horror, mixed with tons of empathy, on my best friend's face slayed me. So much for that stoic look from before—all pretense, with not much behind it. Part of me wanted to spill the remainder of the beans but I wasn't sure Martinez could take it right now, so I went for the very abbreviated version.

"Anyway, what counts is that I survived, but I was barely coherent from pain the next morning, when they told us in no uncertain terms that we would come to France with them on their fucked-up mission. And it wasn't like we could decline, with them being all nice and threatening to kill the rest of our little group that had come all the way to the base in the meantime. Sorry to tell you this, chico, but I didn't bargain myself away so they'd fix your spine; I just took the carrot rather than let them beat Burns, Gita, Tanner, Charlie, and Jason to death with the stick. The latter two remained behind to make sure you weren't alone up there; the rest of us got on a plane with the whole bunch of those idiots over there. I don't really remember much of that flight, or the first few days on the destroyer across the Atlantic. But, sure, once we got to France, I did my very best not to get killed, and that, as always, depended on not getting any of the others killed as well. Enough of us ended up dying, anyway. We got to the lab, we got what we came for, I sadly didn't get to kill Hamilton although he really, absolutely deserved it, and then we headed back home. Only that because of extenuating circumstances, Nate and I decided that it was better for everyone involved if we just disappeared—and that's exactly what we did. Long story short, we spent months on the move before we found a few hideouts that we used for weeks at a time. We missed everything that happened here in the meantime—including that damn slaver camp growing in the southeast. I got away, Nate didn't. I can't get him out of there on my own, and that's why I'm here. I need your help, plain and simple. Maybe you hate us both for various reasons, warranted or not, but I know that a lot of you still owe him. I'm here to ask for your help, and if that's not enough, to cash in any and all favors owed. And that's about it."

After Martinez's outburst, a different kind of quiet had settled over the group, and by the time I was done, you could have heard a pin drop. It took a few moments for murmurs to rise again, and I didn't like how what little I heard was mostly conflicted. Sadie seemed to listen as well, looking torn as she did her best not to appear concerned as she spoke up once more.

"And you expect us to believe you? And that this is all?"

"Of course I hashed over a few details," I admitted, quickly speaking on before murmurs could turn into something more. "Mostly for personal reasons, or because they are inconsequential. We were there at that lab to supposedly retrieve the cure, but Hamilton also took several versions of the weaponized serum—it's anyone's guess what became of those. Yes, I spent the entire way back on the destroyer working on the notes we'd picked up to finish what they'd started on the cure, hoping that, maybe, my contribution would make a difference. I have no illusions that they are still working on their perfect bioweapon, but maybe they can get a working cure out of it as well—either as a vaccine against the virus, or as an antidote for the freshly infected, or just to cut down on some of the side effects of the serum inoculation. Frankly, I don't give a shit because I never want to have anything to do with any of these people, but, alas, fate's a bitch and had a different plan for me. Do you need the details on why exactly I was very sad to hear that Hamilton was killed in action in the meantime and I never got the chance to bash in his gloating grimace with a sledgehammer? You bet. Part of me is tempted that, once this is over, I go out there and try to find his rotting, shambling corpse so I can take it apart limb from limb. He sure deserved worse, not least for the fact that he was ready to let all of us die in that damn lab if he got away with the samples to complete the mission. If you want to be angry with me because of my forced compliance, be my guest. If you think it was wrong of us to disappear, well, I doubt I can convince you otherwise. We did it because we were one hundred percent certain that it was in all of your best interests."

I took a deep breath, trying to gain a few more seconds of deliberation, but decided to simply go in for the kill.

"Don't trust me? Well, trust two of your own. Just watch Zilinsky and Romanoff's reaction to what I'm about to say." I let my attention drift over the lot of them before I settled on the Ice Queen, holding her stare evenly. There was a hint of a frown on her face, as if she was guessing at what might be coming—and praying that she was wrong. Well, I had bad news for her.

"You see, the day after their medic did that hack-job field surgery on me, I woke up and the world had turned into a kaleidoscope of details, my focus sharper than it had ever been before, my body, bruised and beaten as it still was, suddenly working smoothly as it finally started healing for real. The serum had kicked in for good, and my first order of things—well, second, after some other minor details—was to go after Hamilton. He must have realized that, and before I could get any stupid attempts of mutually assured suicide underway, he told my husband to put a muzzle and leash on his wife, or else. Of course he knew us well enough to be aware that would never work—unless Nate had a very good reason to. Turns out, he did." There went nothing, I told myself—and went on. "Decker's still alive, and as it turns out, he changed his mind. He wants his top attack dog back in the fold, and how convenient that now I'm in the game as the perfect way to force Nate's hand. Since I had no intention of either being killed or brainwashed and turned into a mindless killing machine, we decided that, just maybe, we shouldn't put all of you in the crosshairs and instead lay so low that nobody would find us, and nobody had a reason to come after any of you. Only that we got complacent, and someone else jumped the crazy asshole train and came after us. I have no idea whether that's connected, but I know that the powers that be know I'm still alive, and likely, that Nate is, too. I have no illusions that the moment we're back together, we won't get a second chance at hiding. So what I'm really asking is for your help to not just get my husband back, but I'm afraid we'll be back on the warpath after that once more. What do you say? Still mad we tried not to get every single one of you tortured and killed?"

For me, hearing waves of disbelieving murmurs wasn't funny—but seeing them quiet down as people realized that Pia and Andrej were both still staring at me, motionless, was worth it. The Ice Queen was the first to tear herself out of it, exchanging a quick glance with Andrej before she turned back to me. Her voice, usually so matter-of-fact, had a cold, pressed edge to it that I'd rarely heard—fear.

"You did the right thing, if he's still alive. Miller suspected as much a few times but we were never able to find even a trace of evidence. Hamilton would have known as he likely got his orders straight from Decker. He was the one who told you?"

I nodded. "Yes, and that he went against his orders to make sure I was dead because he figured that, in turn, would incentivize Nate not to get involved again. I hate to say this, but there's a good chance the only reason I'm still alive is because Hamilton wanted to remain top dog. All the good that did him in the long run, but I'm not complaining."

"You always complain," Pia muttered, but went on before I could do more than grin. "We will help you. There's no question about that." A few people looked ready to protest but thought better of it even without her glaring at them. Fuck, I'd missed her so much, I was sorely tempted to annoy the shit out of her and give her a long hug right there. Only that she wasn't done talking yet, and what she went on to say made my heart sink again. "But I'm afraid it won't be enough."

I hadn't thought an answer could make me feel both conflicted and glad at the same time, and I was more than happy to focus on the latter only. "I don't intend to wipe that camp off the face of the earth, although we'd probably do the world a favor if we did. I just want Nate back."

Pia nodded solemnly, but the doubt in her eyes didn't dissipate. "I can call in a few favors. Ten, twelve people or so. That would get our numbers up to close to twenty. That won't be enough, even if we had excellent intel—which I presume we don't?"

I shook my head. "I barely remember how I got out, and the patrols were too tight for me to sneak closer again. Plus, there was that small matter of finding food and water first." And clothes, but I didn't think it was time to regale them with the tale of how I'd woken up, tied to that tree, my naked ass exposed to the world.

The Ice Queen nodded again, already turning to Andrej, a rapid-fire conversation in Serbian starting between the two, mentioning names and locations I had no clue about. I felt a little at a loss, not sure what to do now. Rescue came from the woman standing next to Burns—although it didn't feel much like being saved.

"So, that's it? We just up and forgive this bitch everything she did?" She got an amused smile from Burns for that—but no protest.

I hadn't more than glanced at her before, too focused on getting the right words out. She didn't look familiar—definitely a newcomer—but the fact that she was practically plastered to Burns's side gave away that they weren't just friends who happened to be standing next to each other. Bright, intelligent eyes studied me intently, and not very favorably. I could see what Burns saw in her—temper and attitude included; and she was beautiful, no question, the ragged scar across her left jawline adding rather than subtracting from her beauty, standing out slightly against her otherwise flawless, dark skin. I was half tempted to ask her how she kept the skin around it supple, definitely a topic near and dear to my heart. Just maybe not right now as she didn't sound like she was ready to be my best friend forever yet.

Zilinsky broke off mid-sentence, sending her an annoyed look that I was all too familiar with. "Yes, just like that, since there is nothing to forgive. Ask your lover—he can fill you in on the details if you haven't caught up yet."

It was rather funny to see someone else receive the treatment usually reserved for me—and she reacted about as favorably as I would have. "Excuse me? Am I the only one who sees the glaring holes in her story? And you yourself told all of us not an hour ago to be on high alert!"

Andrej gave a soft laugh at that. "But not because of her," he drawled, looking from me to the ship at my back.

The woman would have nothing of that. "You can't just give her a pass just because you knew her years ago."

The Ice Queen gave her a look that screamed, "Watch me!" Burns still appeared highly amused, but he finally gave me a wink that made me relax a little. Apparently, I'd just met my replacement as resident troublemaker.

"I don't need a pass," I offered. "But you shouldn't believe all the BS people say about me. If we have to hash all that out, we'll both be old and gray before we're done."

Her eyes narrowed. Apparently only I found that funny. That wasn't exactly boding well—but not that unusual. Fuck, but I'd missed them all so much!

Glancing briefly at Red, I proposed, "Maybe there's a way we can bolster our numbers to where we do stand a chance at accomplishing our goal. That is, if you let someone else besides me leave this dock?"

Pia didn't look happy about the implications, but before she could say anything, Richards spoke up. "We're not getting off here. We have other business to conclude. But if you agree to work with us, we can get another ten to fifteen people to cooperate with you. Our next stop is the Silo, and I have someone in mind there." As did I, come to think of it, I realized—once this was settled, I should ask about what had happened to the Idiot Brigade that we'd left there on the way to Canada. Probably dug in like ticks, and less than thrilled to leave their comfortable, underground lives.

The Ice Queen looked at me, obviously less than thrilled about the prospect of dealing with the likes of Richards—and whoever he would manage to convince to come along. "Do you trust them?"

It occurred to me that Burns would also make for a great character witness, but I could see why she was asking me—that way, the blame for whatever would go wrong was my burden to bear. I shrugged, not quite sure what to respond. "Right now, the number of people I trust is rather limited; those I trust explicitly, even more so. But Nate trusted Richards enough to make him the one person he kept in contact with, so I guess since this is about rescuing him, why not?" That whole "beggars can't be choosers" thing definitely sucked.

Pia's mouth twisted into an even thinner line but she sounded downright civil as she turned back to Richards. "What's your stake in this? Why would you help her? And why would the people you're planning to coerce into helping her?"

Richards, if anything, was amused by her distrust—but it couldn't have come as a surprise. I was pretty sure he knew who he was dealing with, and it wouldn't have surprised me if the same was true in reverse—at least as far as my involvement with Red was concerned. I really needed an update on the general state of their intel, and stat.

"It's not really coercion if you're triggering a contingency plan," he offered, briefly glancing at me but mostly talking to the Ice Queen. "You're not the only ones who are less than thrilled with the developments of the past years. There are some who have been waiting for a chance at change for quite a while. But for that to happen, we'll need an agent of change."

I could tell that Pia was getting mighty pissed at him beating around the bush. I couldn't help it—I would have paid good money to see them laying into each other, but right now didn't seem the right place or time for that, so I cut right to the chase.

"And you think my husband is said agent."

Red inclined his head after a moment's—likely deliberate—hesitation. "He's a great candidate. More so, he's a name that people know. What might very well get you killed if you walk into the wrong bar has the power to attract followers elsewhere just the same."

Yup, I was with the Ice Queen there—his verbose statements were starting to get on my nerves as well.

"So what you're saying is, you will help, and you have connections for more help, but it all comes at a price."

"Doesn't it always?" Red mused. "But in this case, you might find that the logical consequence of you and him both returning onto the stage coincides with the needs and wants of certain elements. Why not take help freely offered when you would have done what they want you to, anyway?"

I should probably have shut up there but couldn't make myself. And since I'd already quite publicly spit out my suspicions, I might as well seal my fate. Cocking my head to the side, I did my best to judge both Red's reaction, but also those of his men, and Gabriel Greene's as I spoke. "So you suspect that what happened to my husband is indeed connected to Decker, and whatever the fuck he's doing."

Cole and Hill had too much of a pokerface to give me anything. Gallagar obviously knew nothing. Greene seemed way too interested in checking on everyone's reactions himself to give me much. His guards were well-trained, not showing anything, either. I was sure that Red could have completely closed off his face as well, and took it as a show of trust that he gave me the smallest of smirks before his face turned into a stony mask. "Direct connection? No. As you'll see when we get together and share what intel we've gathered in the past, we have lost a lot more skin to those slavers than any other faction currently operating in the country. But you may be less alone with your raging paranoia than you likely think." He added another pause, his focus switching to Pia. "We'll share intel when we meet again. Your choice when and where."

That she knew where we would be going was obvious—another detail I would need to ask about. She briefly looked at Andrej by her side before coming to a decision. "You know the location of the old Ozark settlement in Arkansas? Meet us two miles north of there, exactly thirty days from now."

Red winced but nodded a moment later. "We will be there."

Why did that location ring a bell? I'd never been there myself—and it could have gained significant infamy in the time since whatever I might have remembered had happened—but it definitely didn't come with good impressions. It was only when I saw Greene make a face that I made the connection. I vaguely remembered that, the first time we'd come to New Angeles, I'd talked to some scavengers who had been from that very settlement—and had lost a lot of people when it had been sacked by what had been declared the rogue army faction Taggard's people had belonged to as well.

She likely couldn't have chosen a less neutral ground, unless it had been that blasted base in Colorado.

No one else said anything, prompting Greene to clear his throat. "That's it? You're done here? Very anticlimactic. I would have expected at the very least someone to get shot, if not killed. None of you are living up to your reputations."

Red didn't react beyond ignoring Greene's jibe, and Pia looked equally nonplussed by his accusation. "Don't worry. I'm sure that moment will eventually come. It always does. Too bad you won't be there to witness any of it."

I loved her even more for calling Greene a coward. Not unexpectedly, Greene wasn't fazed by that. "You know I'll eventually hear every little juicy tidbit of it," he told Pia—and turned to the captain of the ship. "I think we're about to overstay our welcome. If you will bring our guests to the next station so they can disembark in peace, without having to negotiate free passage? We'll hitch a ride back to the city." He likely said that for Red and my benefit, because the captain didn't seem surprised at all.

I wondered if I should say goodbye to anyone, but the soldiers were already turning back to their Humvee, leaving me standing there, feeling weirdly out of place. What few belongings I called my own were in the pack next to me, so no need to fetch anything. Greene I gladly ignored. That left me facing the people I would be staying with now—and, damn, that didn't feel half as great as I had imagined it.

Chapter 14

"Guess you're stuck with me, at least for a while," I offered when things turned from awkward to painful. Martinez had the grace to wince, but while he still kept himself in the background, gone was his anger from before. He looked about as uncomfortable as I felt, making me want to give him a hug for that alone—but somehow, taking the first step didn't feel right. The latent unease that crept up my spine and got acid churning in my stomach made me realize how strong my social anxiety had gotten in the meantime—spending the last two years virtually alone in the middle of nowhere could do a number on you, it turned out. I was almost glad Nate wasn't here to see me—he'd have a field day with that realization. Then again, he wasn't exactly Mr. Sociable most days himself, so seeing him squirm might just have been worth it— not that I had that option. And that set my unease into a very stark context.

It was impossible not to notice how a few of them kept staring at my fingers—probably because getting fidgety did a thing or two to draw further attention to them—so I decided I might as well take that out of the equation and started putting on the gloves again, which wasn't much less of a spectacle but would put an end to the stares. When I looked up again, the crowd had started dissipating in earnest, the only people remaining were who I didn't mind so much getting stared at by—plus Burns's plus one, who still scrutinized me as if I'd tried to steal her lunch.

My gaze was inadvertently drawn to Sadie and her kid. I still couldn't tell whether it was a boy or girl, the large, blue eyes and wheat-yellow hair not helping at all. The kid was fascinated with my hands, covered as they were now, but in a curious rather than scared way. At a little under two and a half years, that was likely no surprise, but not scaring the shit out of the little bugger was a bonus. Sadie was momentarily distracted by talking to two women who kept hovering close, but must have caught me watching. I felt a twinge of disappointment when she grabbed the kid and hoisted it up to her shoulder, but rather than turn away, she stepped toward me, briefly checking that the kid wasn't scared.

"This is Chris," she said, looking from the kid to me. "Well, Christine, but I doubt anyone's ever going to use that except for me in full-on wrath-of-mom mode. Since she'll never know her dad, I figured the least I could do was give her his name."

Deep in my chest, I felt the familiar, painful twinge, but it was hard not to smile when the kid gurgled a laugh at me. I stopped fighting it as soon as I realized I was doing so. "Hey, Chris." I addressed the girl herself, speaking softly. Glancing from her to Sadie, I couldn't help but snort. "I know telling you she looks just like him is what people do, but really, she's an adorable little girl, she doesn't look like anything else."

Sadie flashed me a bright smile that reminded me of the girl she used to be, before life had forced a little more responsibility on her than she must have been bargaining for. "I know, right? It's so weird, and I doubt I'll ever get used to it. I mean, sure, there's a very good reason why her dad was her dad, but leave this little cutie pie out of it." The smile dropped away and she inhaled noisily, as if she was steeling herself for something.

I spoke up before she could. "I am really sorry we weren't there for you. And I know I'm speaking for Nate, too, even if he may never say so in those exact words. As things turned out, I wouldn't have been around either way. But for what it's worth, it's one of my biggest regrets."

It was obvious that she was still struggling with letting go of what must have been years of festering anger in minutes, but her shaky exhale as she nodded in agreement as much as acceptance made me relax just a little. "Yeah, looks like you've added a few of those to your list. Regrets, I mean." Her gaze had dropped to my hands briefly, but she did her best to keep a straight face. "Would have been nice if you'd have left a message, but…" She trailed off, looking over at where the Ice Queen and Andrej were still busy talking animatedly with each other. "Guess I can see why you didn't."

I shrugged, not sure what to say. "I figured someone would tell you. Then again, Nate would say your obvious disappointment with us was likely the best he could do to keep you safe."

She chuckled briefly. "Yeah, it's something he'd reason." Her unease visibly flared up, almost making me laugh. "I know you'll get him back," she offered, unintentionally pulling her daughter closer. "If anything, he's too stubborn not to hold out. He wouldn't just die on you like that." She had the grace to wince. I couldn't help but ask myself if she was actually talking about Nate or thinking of Bates.

Neither of them could have expected that when they left the bunker with us, they wouldn't return.

"I know," I offered, trying to chase away the ghosts of the past. "Hey, we've been together going on four years. If he survived that, he's practically invincible."

"That's the spirit!" I heard Burns say behind me. That was all the warning I got before I found myself caught up in a crushing hug—that I reciprocated in turn. Much softer, almost as a murmur, he went on. "Damn, it's good to see you again, girl!"

"You, too. You, too," I replied, then pushed away before the burning in my eyes could turn into more. Chances were, they all still thought my eyes were super sensitive to light so I could have used that for an excuse, but I had the suspicion that once the waterworks started, there would be no holding back.

As I'd expected, the woman whose name I still didn't know was glued to his side, her disapproving glare almost making me laugh since it had gotten even worse. It was only then that I realized the likely cause of it. Grinning broadly, I offered her my right hand. "Bree, as you undoubtedly know. Nice to meet you…"

Her glare was on my hand now, and she obviously had no intention of shaking it. Burns saved the situation—if not without a lot of mirth—by reaching across her shoulders and mashing her into his side, holding her arms captive so she would have had to fight him to be able to reach for me. "This is Sonia," he introduced her. His grin turned feral as he looked her straight in the face. She returned it with an uppity stare that held quite a lot of challenge. Rather than say more—which she obviously demanded—he leaned in and kissed her, and that wasn't a chaste peck on the nose.

I had a hard time not laughing out loud, and mostly to distract myself I glanced at Sadie. She caught my gaze and smiled, but soon rolled her eyes when that kiss was still going on. She playfully held her free hand up to pretend to shield her daughter's eyes. "Guys, either cut it off or take it elsewhere! Nobody wants to see that!"

Burns finally pulled away a little, giving Sonia a private, intimate smile that made my heart seize up for reasons entirely independent of the display in front of me, before he looked back to me, still holding her close. "My wife."

"Good for you!" I punched his arm hard enough to force him to take a step back to steady himself. The action put a confused look on Sonia's face, which was both priceless, and made me want to punch Burns in earnest. "And none of my business," I told her in no uncertain terms. "Just like any other woman who he's ever looked at, or whatnot, which interests me even less! Don't let him get under your skin like that. We're friends—good friends; maybe best friends, but since we're not in kindergarten I hope I don't have to bother with such qualifiers. Good friends who have seen each other naked way more often than they care for, thanks to us living in the glorious times of zombie bites. But he's never been anything but a big brother to me. Seriously, if we were the last two people on earth—and that scenario is problematic on so many levels, including the human gene pool needing thousands of individuals to make it, but that's beside the point—there would be no consideration about repopulating the planet going on. Also ignoring that I couldn't be part in any repopulating, anyway, but that's a different story."

I got a truly shit-eating grin from Burns for that. "You wound me," he drawled, looking around. "Really, the absolute last? What about Martinez?"

Our medic, who'd slowly drawn closer, gave Burns a semi-crazy look. "Leave me the fuck out of this."

Burns obviously had no intention of doing so, turning back to me. "Between him and me, who's last on your list?"

That didn't need any consideration. "Still you. One-hundred percent." Burns gave me a hurt look—which Sonia thankfully missed since she was smiling at the face Martinez was making.

"Why?"

The twinge of annoyance in his tone made me laugh. "Because he's actually nice to me, while you're mostly a jerk. I know that he has less than zero interest in banging me, but I'd do it, as a favor, you know? Would be damn traumatizing to be stuck with you and me as the last people around. He could, I don't know, always close his eyes and pretend it's someone else giving him a blowjob—"

"Stop it!" Martinez shouted, clapping his hands over his ears. "You're traumatizing enough with other people still around as it is!"

Sadie snickered, and it was only then that I realized that, just maybe, I should use different language around a kid in her formative years. She noticed my wince, which made her grin as she spoke to her daughter. "Yeah, you're learning all the interesting words first, aren't you?"

Martinez finally joined us, rocking to a halt between me and Sonia, still plastered against Burns as she was—which couldn't be coincidence. It also gave him the perfect excuse to hug me—no less bone-crushing as Burns—when I smirked at his move. And, fuck, I needed this! So, so much. And judging from how he refused to let go even after we'd gone past the polite five-second mark, I wasn't the only one.

"Yeah, I'm starting to see what you mean," Burns remarked, laughter in his voice. "Should I tell Charlie he has a reason to get jealous? It sounded reasonable at the time that he went north to Utah earlier this week, but now I'm not so sure about your motives."

Martinez kept hugging me for what I was sure were an extra few spiteful seconds before he let go, trying hard to wipe the conflicted look off his face now that I could again see his expression. I stared right back, not quite sure what to say. It was obvious that I wasn't alone with that. Cracking a sarcastic smile, Martinez briefly glanced at Burns. "Asshole didn't tell us anything, you know? Just showed up one day, told us he'd dropped off Gita down in New Angeles, and that you two weren't coming. And that was it. Nothing about what you had been up to in France, or why you'd decided not to tag along."

"It wasn't my story to tell," Burns interjected, sounding not the least bit apologetic. "Didn't take a genius to figure out they had a reason, so not shitting all over that by running my mouth seemed like a plan."

It was obvious that this had in the past led to considerable tension between the two men—and from what I could tell, that wasn't the only thing that had changed. Romanoff and Zilinsky finally joined us as well, and after both hugged me—Andrej a little longer than the Ice Queen, but hers felt warmer, for whatever reason—they stepped away a little, creating some physical space as well as emotional between the others, except for Sadie. That it was all easy for me to pick up on didn't bode well. Collins, Moore, Clark, and Santos also joined us, leaving it at nods and good-natured slaps on the shoulder. I noted the odd guy who, in any other settlement than here, I'd have figured was a guard hang back a little but none came over, and they eventually wandered off.

Sonia had stopped glaring at me, but with the Ice Queen joining us, she seemed to gain a new focus for her ire. Pia ignored her, of course, but she didn't seem as relaxed as I would have thought. "You trust those four you came with?" Pia asked me, but also included Burns in her question.

"I don't know shit about the rookie," I offered. "But the other three, mostly, yeah." Burns seemed pretty amused by my statement.

Pia, less so. "You mean the lieutenant?"

I couldn't help but snort. "Please ask him to his face next time we meet. I think his age is a sore spot for Red." No need explaining that nickname to anyone, or that I of all people was prone to dish them out. "Richards may be young but he's a smart cookie. And the only thing I can hold against him is that he followed his orders a little too closely for my liking." Zilinsky's eyebrows shot up, and I was quick to fill her in. "Hamilton pretty much decided to let the rest of us die down in that fucking maze of a lab if he just got the samples out that he was tasked to get. Richards helped him with that. If not for Nate and Tanner making a stand, we all would have died in there. He did come with us after the fact when we went back to get Nate out, but it was too late for Tanner by then. I know, I have issues with officers who let their people die and prioritize the mission objective, so I'm the wrong one to ask for a character assessment, but even if Hamilton is asshole enough to do so, there was no reason for Richards to follow along."

Burns, for once, objected. "Hate to be the one to rain on your righteous parade, but if we had died, Hamilton would have needed backup to get back to the coast."

It was obvious that the Ice Queen was still trying to get the whole picture from my remarks—Burns seemed to have included her in the no-talk policy, which would explain why she was distant toward him—but she seemed to agree with him. "Miller more than once complained that it was the norm that the mission parameters forced his hands where the objective was valued higher than any of his people's lives. That was cause for a few altercations before he decided to take his leave. It's also the reason why he still has people ready to do what he says even though they could be doing whatever the fuck they want to."

I'd known there was a reason why Nate, even as persona non grata of the nation, had had a pull when we'd established our little scavenger group officially, but everyone had forgotten to mention that to me.

"Does this mean I'm really the only one who thinks Hamilton deserved to get his teeth kicked in for acting as he did?"

"He generally does," Andrej offered, sharing a grim smile with me. I knew why I'd missed him.

"Yeah, that," Burns said, but changed the topic. "What happened to your epic grudge of the ages? How come he's not number one on your list? Any list, really."

I was irritated at first but this absolutely bore repeating. "Richards told me he was killed a while ago. I know, ruined the moment for me, too, when I learned of that. Wanna tag along to find and desecrate his corpse? I'd be up for it."

Zilinsky, as usual, ignored my joking, although this time I was half serious. "What did he do? The short list; I know you—and him—well enough to know that sticking you in the same group with him in command must have caused lots of strain."

Another thing Burns seemed to have neglected to mention—and I couldn't remember how much he even knew. I vaguely remembered him noting the strangulation marks on my neck on the destroyer, but couldn't remember much from the early days—except for the pain. It seemed unlikely that Nate had spilled the beans, though.

"He's dead—what does it matter?" I pointed out. The Ice Queen would have none of that, but before she could do more than breathe in to better chew me out, I gave her a blank stare that I hoped was a good imitation of Nate's. From the way she visibly drew up short, I did okay. "And even if he was still alive, that's between him, Nate, and me. Really, mostly between the two of them." It was a little too close to home—and probably answered her question though I tried to avoid it—but there was another detail she needed to know. "Which reminds me—they've developed a new version of the serum; probably more than one, but when we got up to Canada, they shot me and Nate up with the new one. They've managed to get some mind control shit working that the version you all are inoculated with is useless against. We're presumably immune to that."

Several of our group looked alarmed at the news—and I didn't miss how Burns narrowed his eyes at me, but I chose to ignore him— yet Zilinsky thankfully refrained from badgering me for details. "I'm more surprised they didn't use that back in my day," she grumbled, although she kept watching my reactions closely. "But none of that has anything to do with our problem."

"No, it doesn't," I agreed with her. "And I sincerely hope I'm not getting you all killed with this. I don't think Nate would appreciate that any more than I would." Although rescue would sound wonderful to him—after weeks. Just thinking how long it would be until we could launch a rescue attempt made my stomach flip.

Zilinsky's hand on my shoulder made me jump. Her expression was surprisingly gentle. "He knows that you're doing everything in your power to get him back—because that's exactly what he would be doing for you."

"But that doesn't change anything in the meantime, now, does it?" I harped. "We're both equally to blame for it, but I'm the one gallivanting all over the country, doing what feels like nothing. He doesn't have that same luxury."

Now her expression turned that very typical kind of pinched that I'd missed so much, although it still made me feel guilty. "Stop being so stupid. If he had the choice, he would always choose you to be free. Don't make me regret saying that, but I think I prefer it, too, because he was one miserable fucker to be around back when you got captured by Taggard and his men. You got through that, too. He will, as well."

I knew she'd said that to make me stop in my whining, but in many ways, thinking back only increased my latent anxiety and frustration. Those days had taken a lot out of me and they'd left scars—and that had been days; I'd been separated from my people for less than two weeks, and a consequential part of that I'd spent running through the countryside or hiding in that damn settlement, afraid but mostly safe. Nate had been gone for almost a month now—and who knew how long it would take us to set our plan in motion and execute it?

I knew that thinking about that didn't do anyone any good, least of all Nate, so I forced myself to focus on the things that mattered. "How many people do you think you can reach? And how many do we need to stand a chance for it to work?"

Pia glanced at Andrej for support, but ended up responding after Romanoff just shrugged. "Twenty at full fighting strength. And that won't include a few who will volunteer."

She didn't even need to look at Martinez—or Romanoff. Or Clark, for that matter—for our medic to speak up. "Like hell I'll remain behind just because I can't run a mile in under ten minutes! The bloodier you expect the fighting to be, the more you'll depend on support that hasn't just dragged themselves out of the hot zone in need of being sewn together themselves. I'm coming along. Don't even try me to tell me not to."

Andrej agreed with him, but I noticed that Clark seemed less enthusiastic. From what I could tell, they all looked fully functional—and a lot better than the last time I'd seen them, although I was pretty sure that Romanoff had gone blind in his injured eye—but I'd only been here for half an hour and hadn't seen them do more than a few steps of walking. Zilinsky looked ready to put up a fight but dropped the point after a few seconds of glaring at everyone. "I'll get on the radio and see who I can reach. But don't keep your hopes up for more. And that's hoping that your new friends won't kill us all when we meet them, and whoever they dragged along for support."

I really didn't need that reminder. "They are not my friends," I insisted—and realized only then how wrong that statement sat with myself. Zilinsky gave me a smirk that told me she'd noticed as well but didn't comment. Andrej followed her after telling me that it was nice to have me back—and that left the rest of us standing there, quite uselessly. Sonia didn't hesitate another second before she wrapped one hand around Burns's arm, pulling him away. He went willingly enough, a huge smile plastered on his face.

Martinez stared after them, silently shaking his head before he turned to me. "Let's get you settled then. Guess I'll give you the grand tour, since everyone else is busy. As usual." That last bit came out a little bitter but I didn't ask; he'd let me know in time if it was something he felt like chatting about.

"Do you have some kind of barracks, or guest quarters?" I had to admit, the idea of a bunk bed sounded mighty fine after the last few weeks I'd had.

Martinez gave me a scandalized look. "You're staying with me. Unless you start up that talk about that list of yours again, that is."

Grinning, I bent down to grab my pack. "There's no list. Just needed to make Sonia stop glaring daggers at me."

He snorted, nodding deeper into the settlement so we could get going. "Yeah, she's quite a handful. Reminds me of someone I know." I gave him wide eyes and my best "who, moi?" gesture as I followed along. "But she's good for him," Martinez admitted, if grudgingly. "Just way too insecure sometimes. Also like someone I know."

I flipped him off, glad that I'd donned the gloves already so it was a nice, two-handed thing. "Won't Charlie mind if he comes back and finds me crashing on your couch?"

I didn't know what to make of the considering look Martinez gave me but he sounded certain enough when he proclaimed, "No worries. He's not the jealous type. Although, he still has a beef with you for abandoning him and Jason in Canada in the middle of the winter to fend for themselves."

I felt a hint of unease creep up my spine until I realized that he was joking. "Speaking of which—did they give you or the guys any trouble leaving the base again? Because part of the reason why Nate and I skipped out early was because I had a certain feeling that Emily Raynor wouldn't just let me walk away a second time if she got her claws into me again."

It was obvious that, like me, Martinez wasn't full of fond memories of the army surgeon, but he answered with a dismissive shrug. "I deeply disappointed her when I refused her repeat offer to shoot me up with the serum, but once she'd accepted that, she was pleasant enough—as much as that woman is capable of that. Particularly after the video call with you she was oozing what she thought was charm all over me. I don't think she ever got the message that not everyone is as fond as she is of cutting-edge technology."

It was such a bad joke that he got a loud groan from me. His answering smile was worth it, though.

Chapter 15

A s we wove through the settlement, I got my first good look around. The docks were only a small part of it, with a few warehouses and other buildings easily isolated by portable barriers now shoved to the side. There was a huge gap between them and the settlement itself, and I saw machine guns on the first row of houses toward the docks, two of them manned by lookouts. The settlement itself consisted of roughly two hundred houses, two larger, barn-like structures, and several more warehouses. It was bustling with activity, making it obvious that only a fraction of the residents had been at the docks before, most others ignoring what was going on. At a first guess, I would have estimated that it held over a thousand residents—quite a lot more than the old camp I'd helped establish before my declining health had forced us back on the road.

Martinez kept pointing out things of medium interest to me, like the assembly hall—one of the barns—and the mess hall, right next to the armory—occupying two of the low, single-story warehouse buildings. They had a few stalls set up as a marketplace for nomadic traders, although that was abandoned at the moment. From what I could tell, the commune worked well with shared food and common goods for everyone, in exchange for which everyone did the tasks that needed to be done or they were best at. People around seemed to know each other, and I got my share of stares—and glares—but no one approached me directly.

We ended up at a small wooden building—very rustic, cabin-style—built close to the wooden palisades that ran in a semi-circle along the land-facing side of the settlement, turning it into a peninsula with the docks at the southwestern point. As we stepped onto the porch, Martinez picked up two cloth-wrapped bundles someone must have dropped off there earlier and carried them inside. The cabin was a one-room affair centered around a couple of sofas and chairs, with a bed in one corner, and a rudimentary triage station in another. From what I could tell, the settlement had electricity, but not for everyday use in the individual houses—and the same was true for indoor plumbing.

"We have a proper doctor as well," Martinez explained when he saw me eye the cabinets and supplies in the corner. "But she has enough on her hands as it is. Rudimentary stuff like stitches and setting broken bones is what I do."

"That happen often?"

He snorted at my question. "Probably more often now that you're back with us." He dropped the bundles on a chair in the triage station and shooed me over to the couches. "Are you hungry? We still have two hours until the cantina opens but I think I have some fruit and bread left over from earlier in the week."

His question made me hesitate mid-motion of dropping my pack, a fist closing around my heart for a moment. He noticed, eyeing me curiously for a moment before a frown replaced it. "Right. Still no hunger, and no sense of taste?"

I shook my head, finally kicking my few possessions under a side table. "The serum did a lot of weird shit to my body, but it didn't change that. Probably for the best—it also didn't turn me into a great cook, and this way, only one person had to suffer through my culinary disasters."

I got a weird look for that. "Don't tell me you got all weirdly domestic on each other and shit. You know he's a more than decent cook himself? If he pushed cooking at you, that was because he was too lazy, not because he doesn't know how to."

Snorting, I shook my head. "Oh, no. He did most of that. I'm a bit of a spectacle cutting onions, you see? And I'm gifted enough to burn water for tea, so once we settled in a place for more than a few days, Nate took over meal prep. Not that there was much to prep, really."

Martinez chuckled. "Didn't take him long to go all carnivore on you, eh?"

"It was easier in the winter," I offered. "We ate preserves and dug up tubers when we found some, but not that much around anymore if you don't tend to them. Damn herbivores, eating all our veggies! Served them right to become food themselves. I had some salad growing at our last base, but that will be all eaten or dried-up by now. Damn shame. I was really looking forward to eating it."

"Salad trauma, huh?" Martinez joked. "Well, you'll get plenty here if you want it. We have two greenhouses by the docks and they produce year-round in this climate, so no chance that there's no greens on any plate handed out. Meat's mostly chicken because they're easy to keep, and you get the eggs as well."

"You'd think a settlement this large would have cows and pigs, too," I mused as I kept looking around. It took me a few moments to realize he hadn't answered yet. When I finally looked back at him, Martinez had gone still.

"We had some," he offered once he pulled himself back together. "But they all died in the fire. Ever heard pigs scream as they get cooked alive? Nobody felt much like starting up new stock after that."

It was only then that I made the connection. "That's why you're here now? The old settlement burned down?"

He nodded. "We already had some structures built by the docks, so we didn't have to start from scratch, but that was rough. Gave us some ideas for improvements the second time around, but not everyone did well with losing everything they owned a second—or tenth—time around."

"Casualties?"

"A handful," he explained. "Thankfully, we saw it coming ahead of time. Or rather, the few native Californians did, so rather than die in the fire trying to fight it, we withdrew early and tried to rescue what we could. We got the chickens out early because the pens were on the other side of town. The cattle and pigs, not so much."

"Shit." Fire was one of the few things Nate and I hadn't been forced to deal with, but our nomadic first few months had brought us through a few swaths of land that had been completely devastated.

Having gotten a jug of water and some cups to deposit on the table, Martinez dropped onto the couch opposite the one I'd staked out for myself, getting comfortable.

"Had some issues with earthquakes, too, but the upside of not owning shit is that it can't break," he joked. "Things may look very domestic to someone who's been roughing it on the road, but we're a long shot from where we used to be. Not too many people felt like putting that much effort into it when we don't know how things will be down the road."

That confused me a little. "You don't expect to stay here?"

He looked at me as if I'd said something crazy but then relaxed, chuckling. "Right, you probably don't know. Half of the settlements on the coast got destroyed by the fire. And half of those that made it then got razed by the scavengers. There's nothing between New Angeles and Salt Lake City left that's not either a smoking ruin or openly declared support for them. The only reason we're still standing is because Zilinsky killed not one, not two, but five of their leaders, finally making them give up and declaring us a dead zone. Since they took over New Vegas, things have quieted down in the region. People weren't happy with Greene when he opened up the docks to them last year again, but it's done a lot to stop the raids."

"Shit." There wasn't much else I could say to that. "We had a bunch of them come to the city with us on the transfer ship. Took about five minutes for one of them to get in my face."

Martinez offered a mirthless grin that was pretty close to a smirk. "Why am I not surprised?" He paused, chuckling. "Actually, I am. You'd think they'd recognize their prophet. So much for that."

"Prophet?" I didn't need to tell him that he wasn't making any sense—and I was still missing so many parts of the picture. "Didn't they start the new civil war because they felt I had betrayed them?"

He shrugged, leaning back into the couch. "Don't ask me to explain their logic. The prophet thing might have started up later, once they were convinced you were dead. What do I know? They do worship you as the harbinger of doom. But don't get your hopes up—you won't get any support from them. You're much more useful as a dead sinner-saint than anything else."

That reminded me of something. "Zilinsky's your head of security, I presume?" Who else, really? "I should probably tell her about those idiots. Greene pretty much forced me to reveal my identity, and they looked mighty pissed that they couldn't get back onto the boat once they got dropped off on the docks. He said he expects that they will show up here tomorrow."

"Don't bother," he grumbled. "She's never not got the guards primed for defense. We'll see if they wise up in the meantime. Else, someone's gonna get some extra workout tomorrow. Sit back and relax. It's likely the last respite you'll get for a while."

Our banter turned to other things, and got diverted again when an hour later, Sadie dropped by, happy to hand off the kid to Martinez. Chris obviously knew him well, happy to get a chance to play with her funny uncle—one of many, I imagined. Sadie watched them goof around for a bit from where she had taken a seat on a chair next to the couch—close, but not close enough to be intimate. Or maybe the difference was all in my head and I was simply imagining things. Conversation remained light, mostly centered around our shared memories of the winter in the bunker, and Sadie fast-tracked me on what I'd missed with Christine growing up.

Part of me could have spent endless hours like this, for what felt like the first time in forever relaxed and without having to watch my back. But underneath that, I was restless enough that it took a lot of effort to keep sitting on the couch instead of pacing up and down, or hunting down Zilinsky and having her order me to do something— anything, really—to get going.

When dinnertime rolled around, we took our little party to the cantina for some chow and yet more mingling. Sitting in a barn full of people, all talking over each other, set my teeth on edge. Having Sonia sitting opposite me, staring me down whenever she wasn't engaged in conversation, didn't help. There was no sign of Pia or Andrej, a very unwelcome lack of distraction. At least I got to catch up with a few of the others, although conversation was usually borderline painful, with stops whenever it turned to Nate, or us disappearing.

It was well past sundown by the time we made it back to the cabin, me feeling borderline overwhelmed from too much interaction going on at once. Martinez must have noticed but didn't comment on it, naturally gravitating away from me once it was just the two of us to give me some much-needed space. I was still in my stinking clothes from the road, but upon our return, we found another bundle sitting on the porch. It had the Ice Queen's hand written all over it. No surprise that she'd remembered my size, and calculated for how it had decreased over time in some areas. Martinez gave me instructions where to drop off what I would have otherwise thrown away, and where I could get cleaned up. As I entered the bath house, the line of tubs ready to be filled was tempting, but I got a washcloth and a bucket filled with steaming water instead, keeping it to the basics. At shy of midnight, the building was empty and abandoned, and since I didn't need much light, I was happy to do my business in the calming dark.

Martinez was still up as I returned, if down to shorts and a T-shirt. "I hope you don't mind?" he playfully teased me as I gave him the obligatory wolf whistle.

"Your home, your rules. Can't stop you if you decide to sleep in the nude."

He seemed split between cracking up and being scandalized but settled on the former.

"Perks of living in a community with gates and guards," he remarked. "But I always keep my gear and weapons ready. You should, too."

I hadn't planned on undressing further than my sturdy pants, but it was hot in the cabin, even with the windows open, and seeing him in his skivvies made me feel terribly overdressed. Hesitating now seemed ludicrous since I'd already—and quite literally—dropped my pants at the docks before, but leave it to my weird mind to feel conflicted now. Martinez made a big show of turning his back on me where he sat on the bed, making me chuckle softly as I started to peel myself out of the layers I'd only just donned. "Your fault if you get nightmares if you peek," I warned him as I got down to a similar state of undress, ditching everything except for my sports bra and underwear.

Martinez hesitated but then turned around, watching me quietly as I did my best to work stiff muscles and hardened scars. "Anything still giving you trouble?"

I was tempted to hold my hands out to him and laugh in his face, but decided to take him seriously for once. "Leg's a bit annoying in winter, in the cold. Also because I never got the full range of motion back—too much scar tissue there, although it all healed well from what I can tell. My hip gets stiff if I sit around for too long. Most of the rest is just cosmetic. If I don't get it into my head to participate in a bikini contest, I'm fine."

I had been so occupied with working my leg—and no more than glancing at my fingers while they dug into the thick muscles underneath the pebbled skin—that I hadn't realized Martinez was up until he materialized next to my elbow. His gaze was focused on my thigh as well, but unlike the look of horror that had taken over his expression at the docks, curiosity and professional calm was all I could see there now.

"May I?"

I hesitated but then gave him a quick nod. "I'll show you mine if you'll show me yours."

In typical Martinez fashion, he wasn't all over my leg—or hands—but instead turned around, pulling up the hem of his shirt. In the flickering light of the candles, the white lines of the scars all over his back along the spinal column were easily visible, although I was a little envious of how smooth the surface of the skin was compared to the topographical map that was my hip and thigh. He explained what Raynor and her team had done—as far as he knew himself—and ended it with, "As you already got to see, I can walk without any problems, but running's hard, and worse over longer distances. Zilinsky's not entirely wrong when she says I should stay here."

"But you won't," I assumed.

"Like hell." He barked a brief laugh, mischief twinkling in his eyes. "Knowing you, you'll need someone to put you back together after you're done getting rent apart. Now turn over. It's only fair that I get to gloat, too."

"Knock yourself out." I likely would have shied away if someone else had touched me, but with Martinez it was different. His fingers didn't linger, mostly probing and stretching rather than anything else. He concentrated on my thigh for a while, and again my stomach with the multiple butcher lines there. He didn't ask so I didn't prattle off the list of internal parts I was lacking but it was hard not to remember. He rolled his eyes at me when I wriggled what remained of my toes—and stubs—at him, and ended up at my hands at last.

"You wear the gloves because you hide," he muttered under his breath as he turned my hands over to study my palms, and how the partly atrophied muscles moved under my skin as he made me curl my fingers into a fist.

"Wouldn't you?" I asked, hating how hollow my voice sounded. "It's all people see when they stare at me. Great as a distraction in a pinch, but since that part's not just cosmetic, I can really do without."

Martinez nodded, finally letting go of me so I could partly hide my hands as I crossed my arms over my chest.

"How's Nate dealing with all this?"

I was a little surprised about the question, present tense and all that. "It's not exactly his problem when I randomly drop something, or have to learn the hard way that I can't knit a hat anymore."

Martinez frowned slightly. "They sliced and diced up his woman. Don't tell me he simply took that in stride."

"Well, he had other things to worry about at the time," I snapped— too late realizing that I bungled right into the trap he'd set for me.

"Like what?"

Martinez got the venomous glare he deserved for that question, but after a few moments I decided to spill the beans. This wasn't something I'd felt comfortable talking to anyone about, including Burns, and while I'd had enough time to learn to deal with it, maybe a little bit of oversharing would do some good. Plus, Martinez was a prime contender for who Nate might confide in as well, once he got the chance again. Him and Zilinsky, although I wasn't sure if, this once, he'd forgo the Ice Queen. She'd never shared anything of her past with me except how she'd lost her two children, but I'd more than once gotten the sense that she hadn't gotten away as clean as she'd made it sound. Back then I had been too upset with Nate's lies to be able to ask, and since the moment had passed, no other opportunity had presented itself—and thank fuck for that.

Leaning back into the sofa cushions—and probably looking defensive as hell as I was now actively hiding my hands in my armpits—I did my best to look as evenly at Martinez as I could, where he was perched on the sofa opposite mine. "When we got to that damn base, I was barely alive—coughing blood, needing the last of my energy to stay upright. I knew things would come to a head when Bucky Hamilton of all people came marching out to get us. I knew I should have made Nate leave me there and run, but of course he didn't."

"He never would," Martinez insisted—needlessly, since I knew he was right. "Not even if you'd have been in a better state, but even less so if you needed all the support he could give."

"Well, much support that turned out to be when they shot him up with some mind-control shit and Hamilton ordered Nate to hold me down so Hamilton could rape me."

I shouldn't have felt so spitefully satisfied when Martinez went completely still, swallowing thickly as he continued holding my gaze. I only let that go on for a couple of seconds, long enough for the message to sink in but maybe not yet send him on a crazy train of speculation.

"Hamilton didn't do it," I went on. "But whatever that shit was, it worked all right, and Nate didn't snap out of it when I tried to get him to. Burns saw the bruises on my neck that were still there a few days later, and considering what they did to me in the meantime, that's saying a lot. My body likely didn't have the energy to deal with a few hematomas when it had to heal, well, all the rest of it. When they dragged what was left of me back, he was his usual chipper self, but I can tell you, I had a much easier time dealing with it than he did. Guess those sixteen hours or however fucking long it took couldn't have been easy for him, and he doesn't deal well with me being in so much pain, that's true. And then he had to cut me open a few times and drain the pus that my body kept producing. That's why some of the scars look so wonky. Gita did a much better job with the sutures than he did, but it's still nasty business."

I got the feeling that Martinez had expected that I wasn't telling him everything, but that didn't diminish the impact of getting confirmation for that. "Sounds like you had a lot of fun."

I shrugged. "It wasn't boring, if you mean that. Never thought I'd say that, but I was glad you weren't along."

"My sutures are way better than that," he quipped.

"Yeah, but their good-for-nothing medic had to cut me up once more in the middle of the French countryside. The stumpy left middle finger is thanks to him as well. The only saving grace of that was it wasn't you who had to do it." I paused, remembering all too well—but also what had come next. "But when I woke up in the morning, the serum had finally kicked in and since then it's been one fun romp of hilarity and bloodlust. You're really missing out on so much."

Martinez took my words with a somber nod, but grimaced at the last part. "Thanks, but no thanks. It's hard work keeping my soul pure and light around the likes of you imbeciles. I'm not deliberately desecrating my body."

I couldn't help but glance at the small, wooden cross fixed to the wall by the left side of the bed—Martinez's side, judging from where he'd plonked down earlier before joining me in the living area. I'd noticed it as soon as I'd entered the cabin, but it wasn't like I had the right to remark on it—or had felt so until now.

"Does it help? Having faith, when the world around you turns into a living nightmare?" I more mused than asked, only on the last words looking back to him, just in time to catch his grimace "I'm serious. I'm not being a bitch, or trying to knock you down. Just…" I exhaled slowly, flexing my fingers before I finally dropped my hands in my lap, briefly staring at them. "That winter, I had a few moments when suicide sounded really damn good to me. Less of an active action but just being a little too slow in the next defense, or missing a step when I knew I had to take one to keep my balance. I sure as fuck was mad enough at Hamilton to have a reason to keep living, but, you know. There was a dark abyss there and I did a lot of staring straight into it. Does it help you to believe in something beyond our mortal coil? Or is it worse because you can have the whole 'God, why me?' thing going on?"

He gradually relaxed as I explained, wincing at my obvious pain but no longer looking ready to get in my face.

"God didn't do any of this," he said, briefly reaching behind his back to touch the scars there. "That was our fault for being stupid enough to run straight into that trap. And the fault of whoever placed the charges and detonated them. That I can walk again is partly your fault, I guess. Faith isn't that easy. There's no quick fix. You don't just pretend to be pious one day and ramble off two Hail Marys, and bam! You're saved. Everything you do, and have done, and will do, counts. That's what I like to focus on. That my actions count, because I have faith. Because I believe. That I have very good reasons not to be the most petty fucker on earth just because I can." He sighed, his fingers idly drumming on his drawn-up knee. "Doesn't mean that I didn't rail against it all a time or two. Being tested is part of the deal. It's always easy to be good when the world is perfect and everyone treats you right." He cracked a brief smile then. "I do get extra credit for hanging around you bunch of raging heathens, though. Pretty sure of that."

"So we make you look good, huh? Isn't that cheating?"

He ignored my jibe, instead getting back on topic. "I can't tell you if it's easier to have faith. You believe in things, too. Doesn't always have to be religion. And you don't seem to need faith to get the concept of a crusade."

"Yeah, don't remind me of that," I grumbled. "All the good that did us."

"It's not all bad, what came from it," he pointed out. "Plus, I doubt that all, if any, of it is actually your fault. People using people is way older than the Bible. You can be a terrible person in the name of God, and a good egg without. Not that you're a good egg. But your shoulders are way too scrawny to carry the entire weight of the world."

Staring into the air between us, I took my time formulating my reply. "I just want him back, you know? Very much unscathed, pretty please, but I can deal with a little bit of tarnish. I never wanted to incite rebellion. And I sure as hell never wanted to kill anyone. But they seem to get in my way, one way or another."

"That's life," Martinez succinctly let me know. When I raised my brows in surprise at him, he laughed. "Oh, come on. You married one of the biggest warmongers around. You didn't expect you could just disappear and pretend like nothing happened, or the past wouldn't catch up with you? He sure didn't; I know that for a fact."

I hadn't expected the conversation to go there, but it was too good an opening to miss. "What's your take on Decker? You must have heard of him. Known someone who knew of him, at least." I hesitated, but then went for it. "Didn't Smith ever talk about him?" That would have been his boyfriend—who was one of the first to turn, thanks to some contaminated syrup at a coffee shop, even before that wave of zombies had chased us out of the city. Who I'd killed, with a cake knife. Thinking back, I once again marveled at how Martinez had never held that against me. He was likely the only truly good guy left on the planet.

His expression turned sad for a second as he must have thought along the same lines but quickly snapped back to animatedly neutral. "He didn't, but then he was an NCO." When I just looked at him blankly, he snickered. "You remember that he was a staff sergeant? Will you ever learn to understand military ranks?"

"Never tried," I offered with a grin. "I know, how terrible of me."

"You sure keep pissing people off with ignoring them," he muttered but got serious again. "As far as I know, Decker only got to the officers. Apparently, built up his own little cadre of homicidal nut jobs. He's a ghost story to most." He paused, suddenly conflicted.

"What aren't you telling me?" Now things had suddenly gone from idle reminiscing to interesting.

Martinez shook his head, if somewhat apologetically. "It's personal. And it has nothing do with him, or Miller. Who never breathed a word to me, just saying, which isn't that unusual. But I heard from another medic who was stationed at the hospital back when they discharged Rita—you know, Dispatch's Rita?"

I'd figured he'd meant her since I didn't know anyone else by that name, or who might have caused emotions to run high among our people. One of these days I would have to find out why the Ice Queen hated her almost with as much animosity as I had toward Hamilton. Had had. Whatever. "Sure, her. She was discharged because of the injuries she sustained when Nate's attempt of dropping out didn't quite go as planned." Also due to Hamilton—yet another reason to hate his guts.

"Word is, she tried to hang herself in her hospital room first thing after they told her that she was out. I know the official story goes, it was because she lost her purpose, not being able to be out in the field anymore. But the medic told me that she'd heard it was because she was afraid where she'd end up, now that she was officially useless."

I had a pretty good idea where that would have been, after our visit to Canada and France. That almost made me feel for her—almost.

"How come she didn't?"

Martinez snorted at what I felt was a valid question. "Because maybe some tales are taller than the people they are told about," he offered. "Or maybe she just got lucky. Who knows? Maybe someone figured she might be handy at a later date and she'd be wasted as a lab rat? Your guess is as good as mine. But if you ask me about her real motive? If what Nate was running from is true, she probably decided to end her own life because she was afraid of what Decker would do to her again now that whatever she went through the first time had gotten useless. Then again, nobody has a clue where she's been between then and showing up in Dispatch, so, who knows?"

Now didn't that paint a pretty picture? And one I absolutely didn't care for.

"You think she's compromised?"

Martinez shook his head. "Not saying it's true. But when you and Nate didn't return from France, she immediately upped her security, and word is, she made damn sure that Dispatch was a veritable fortress come spring. That's why it's pretty much the only place where the scavengers never managed to do any damage—she kicked out anyone who even looked at her the wrong way. But before you get your hopes up, she won't help you. She might as well be one of them for how she deals with the rest of us—either you're with her, or you're about to get shot."

Hearing that made me wonder if, maybe, Nate had gotten a message to her—or Bucky had decided that, just like Nate, Rita might get in his way after all and he'd warned her just like he'd warned us. The usual anger was right there, familiar and comforting, not diminished by hearing that the bastard was dead.

"Is anything still the same from before?" I harped, not caring for how grumpy I sounded.

Martinez smiled briefly, likely at my tone rather than the question. "They still won't let you into the Silo," he offered. "And I'm sure Emma will be about as friendly if you get too close to her kingdom of Wyoming. Since most of the country didn't much care for you before, I'd say things are pretty much the same. It's for the rest of us that things changed drastically." He paused, as if to gather his thoughts. "That spring, after you disappeared, we all started fresh into a new year, into the world you'd promised us—and for a lot of people, that ended way too soon, way too bloody, with more violence than they could handle. I guess you've been wondering about the scavengers—the new breed of them? They got to call themselves that because none of us old dogs are left, pretty much."

I really didn't like hearing that. "They killed that many people? How?"

"Not killed, at least for the most part," he explained. "Oh, they got a few shots in before people realized what was going on. Hit some of our strongest and hardest—like Jason's guys."

"Shit."

He was ready to agree with me. "They'd stocked up to thirty people. Seven of them returned. Jason himself survived; Charlie, obviously, too. The rest, all new guys you've likely never met. Other groups met about the same fate. Remember that ranking list they had up in Dispatch when we dropped by? Of the top fifty, only four got away unscathed, mostly because they'd been hunkered down in colder regions at the time and were late to hit the roads. Everyone else either sustained heavy losses, or immediately disbanded when people decided that it wasn't worth it. Before the heat of summer forced the entire country to its knees, most scavengers had decided that settling down sounded mighty reasonable. And they could pick and choose from several settlements, as they were next to be hit, after they did away with the roaming defenders that might have come to anyone's help out there. I don't have the official stats, but I think I remember someone telling us that only one in three settlements had made it until the next winter. Those that are still standing mostly did so because they had already semi-settled former scavengers calling their town their new home, or welcomed the freshly disillusioned road warriors with open arms."

I listened to his grim tale with as little emotion as I could manage, but I felt my heart seize up nevertheless. Somehow, that was worse than what Red and Greene had told me. At least nobody could blame me for that.

"And the army? And everyone else—they're not alone out there, I know that. Wilkes and the Silo can't be the only ones who have marines among their ranks—and whatever navy personnel that weren't mere paper pushers. Air force, coast guard, national guard—I know we've met a few on the road and heard about small groups at various settlements, but this must have gotten someone worried."

Martinez nodded, not looking particularly happy. "The three major players—the Silo, Dispatch, and New Angeles—found themselves with a lot of support they hadn't expected. I'm sure that some were spies, but I think after the shit we pulled at the Colorado base and everything that came with it, a lot of those who'd been sticking it out on their own for the first two years decided that civilization came with some perks, like strength in numbers, so they went where strength was already on the fence, and in numbers. We heard from a few bases that they were attacked as well but for the most part, we thought they were just watching. Turns out, they got hit just as hard, if mostly from the inside. When they vetted the former scavengers who wanted to flock to them, they were very thorough—but they missed those that had come before the wave of violence swept over the country. There are no official numbers, but I know Zilinsky did some snooping. We think that the army lost at least a third of its installations and bases. You weren't the scourge of their existence, after all. The rest—no idea, but I doubt they fared better."

It suddenly made a lot more sense that Bucky had bit it—and that Red had been so quick to respond when we'd gone silent. Even if he hadn't told anyone who he was in contact with, he likely must have dropped hints that he still had an ace up his sleeve, hiding in the middle of nowhere. But that in turn posed a question—why hadn't Red dropped by and told us about this? And not just him.

"Did any of you try to reach us?" I felt like it was a valid question. "We wouldn't have been easy to find, but we might have found you if you'd shown up in the region."

Martinez shook his head. "I think we all kind of agreed that if you'd managed to get away for real, you deserved to live your quiet life all on your own. I'm surprised you didn't know anything about what went down."

"We were pretty insistent on that stay-away-from-everyone doctrine," I admitted, not particularly liking how that had turned out. "But we wouldn't have stayed away if we'd known that it got that bad."

"It was likely for the best," Martinez offered. "They did what they did whether they had you to blame or not. If you'd been around, someone would have delivered you to them—and the only difference would have been that you'd both be dead."

"Does anyone know why they did this?" I tried to remember the specifics of what Richards had told me. "Resources? Power? Anything?"

Martinez shook his head. "That's the thing—they never asked for anything. Well, except your head on a pike, but that's it. After they slaughtered people and burned down settlements, there was a lot of grand talk about equalizing things, but from what we know, they didn't bother trying to trade or live off the land. They're also not one coordinated faction that strikes with distinction. It's as if suddenly, a percentage of people went insane and started going after everything they perceived as 'other,' no explanation needed. And no, far as I know there was no calming agent experiment involved."

I couldn't help but grin at him making the exact same reference as I had before, but that was a very brief moment of respite.

"And then there's the slaver camp on the other end of the country that chose to 'nap the wrong people," I concluded.

"There's them," Martinez agreed. "Like everyone else, we've heard stories, but with over a thousand miles of distance between here and there, we never really considered them a serious threat. Until now."

I stared at him for a few seconds flat before I leaned forward, placing my elbows on my knees so I could let my head rest on my hands and still look at him. "We're so fucking screwed."

Martinez laughed softly. "Pretty much. But what else is new?"

I kept staring at him, as if that would yield any answers. "How did it come to this? Why didn't anyone do anything to stop it before it turned into... well, this?"

All he had for me is a shrug. "And who, exactly, should have done it? You saw yourself what you got for taking a stand, and the very same is true for the other side. We still have no government, and if the last years have yielded one fundamental truth, it's that nobody gives a shit on a global level. It's a dog-eat-dog world out there, often more literally than most of us feel comfortable with. You want an answer to the question you actually want to ask—whether you or Miller could have made a difference? I doubt it. Those who blame you as a traitor and a spy, who say that all you did was tag the people who might become a problem in the long run, weren't completely wrong, because rising up did end up getting a lot of people killed. But so did hunkering down on their own and trying to isolate themselves from the rest."

I couldn't help but shake my head, less in avoidance or disagreement but simply because it all went miles over my head. "And there I was about to complain that I sometimes spent days not talking to anyone because Nate was in one of his moods again."

Despite the grim topic, Martinez flashed me a quick grin. "I know how hard that must have been for you."

"Terrible," I emphasized.

"Without a doubt."

"The worst, actually," I insisted.

He chuckled, and I could see the exact moment when he was ready to throw the curveball he'd been holding for the past several minutes. Ah, how I'd missed that as well. "I figure with everything that happened to you up in Canada, it must have taken Nate some time to get over it. But he did, right?"

I considered my answer carefully, wishing for a beer—more to have something to hold than because the booze would do anything for me, which it wouldn't. "I'm not going to lie. It did a number on him. That I was way too occupied with myself, my pain, my anger—none of that helped. But as things between us do, eventually they came to a head and we had to pull through, together. I didn't realize it at the time, but I think this more than anything that Hamilton said was what made Nate decide to be cautious and disappear. But neither of us did well in isolation, that's for sure. I may be the one who's been more vocal about it, but I know we both felt it. We weren't so much being smart and cautious but had simply stopped the clock for a while—but eventually, it would start ticking again. I know this sounds insane, but I'm almost glad the slavers got to us, because now this diffuse sense of being suspended in weightlessness is finally gone. Now, I can act again. I have things to do and people to meet, plans to think up, and actions to set. We weren't doing the smart thing, we were just avoiding the inevitable. That's over now. I just hope like hell that we'll both survive this so we can face what's coming next head-on."

Martinez listened in silence, not trying to interrupt me or add anything. By the end of my little speech, his expression had turned pensive. "Maybe you're wrong."

"Oh, you don't say," I griped—but then inclined my head. "About what?"

"That your withdrawing yourselves from the equation put a hold on things, and nothing further. What if you're wrong? Because, correct me if I'm wrong, but if you'd returned with Burns and Gita, if you'd been here when New Angeles was attacked and when Jason lost so many of his people, and then demands had risen up for your head—what would you have done?"

"I really don't want to think about that," I admitted.

"Nobody who cares about you does," he said, snorting softly. "You would have given yourself up, that's what would have happened. After you tried, and failed, to rally people under a common banner once more. Nothing would have changed, except that you'd be dead. Or..." He stared off into space, considering.

"Or what?" I wasn't even being pesky, or anxious for his answer. I really didn't understand.

His eyes found mine, an almost unfamiliar intensity burning in his gaze. "Okay, this is coming from way out there, and likely heavily influenced by the fact that I had a little too much to drink earlier, and you've been all up in my business with conspiracy theories all night…" He paused to let me protest, and seemed surprised when none came from me, so he went on. "I didn't see it as such at the time when it was happening, but what if a lot of what happened did happen to draw you out? Yes, you going on the crusade tagged the troublemakers, but even more so, it tagged the people who you were close with. People who you formed bonds with on the road, if for no other reason because they were in the same boat with you. I mean, take Chino Torres and his Raiders. If we hadn't gotten caught up in the factory ambush with them, you never would have thought about checking up on Gussy, Taggard's guys could never have sprung the trap on you, and you never would have led Torres and his people to NORAD and slaughter that bad impression of a mad scientist. Just like with Jason and the Chargers, who would never have worked with us again and again if we hadn't shown up that morning to join them to free Harristown of the zombie siege."

"What exactly are you getting at?"

He visibly deflated as he let the air rush out of his lungs. "I have no fucking clue? Made more sense in my head than out loud." A quick grin followed. "Sound like someone you know?"

I was very tempted to roll my eyes at him. "Very funny." Even so, I mulled over what he'd said. "There's just one flaw in this theory, or non-theory, or whatever it is."

"Which is?" he wanted to know.

"That's all connected to me. Or us, as the Lucky Thirteen. Wouldn't shit that's planned to flush out Nate cut closer to his heart?"

Now, Martinez's smile almost got belligerent. "Don't you see? That's exactly my point. You are his heart, and his soul. His greatest strength and vulnerability. Which is why it makes sense, kinda." I must have looked rather doubtful because he went on explaining. "Just think. Sure, you're concerned about his health and well-being right now, but deep down, you know he will be all right—why is that?"

"Because he's a damn mean motherfucker himself and virtually impossible to break?" I suggested, awfully tempted to add, "Duh."

Animated as he had gotten, Martinez leaned forward, staring straight into my eyes. "And, what, five minutes ago you told me that all it took to throw him off-kilter was to make him complicit in roughing you up a little? Come on. I know you like to think of him as invulnerable with almost saint-level endurance, but that sounds like a huge fucking flaw to me." I could tell that he wasn't done yet when he rocked back to lean into the couch, staring up at the ceiling. I sure didn't like the paranoia his words got creeping up my spine. "Which makes me wonder…" he went on, his eyes snapping back to me. "Did Hamilton tell you why exactly he pulled that stunt? He could have simply told you about the mind-control drug. Or made Nate jump on one leg for a minute. No, he sent you a message, and he reinforced it when he told you about Decker later." Once more his gaze flipped up to the ceiling, and he looked almost impressed by his powers of deduction.

"Or, you know, Bucky Hamilton is a gigantic ass wipe who deserved to have his balls cut off by me and shoved down his throat," I suggested, smiling sweetly.

Martinez snorted, shaking his head. "Yeah, maybe you're right. I mean, you did spend some quality time with him. Way more than I did. But they were friends once, you know? And you've seen how keen Nate's instincts are for who to trust, and to see through people's bullshit. Even now, his name is enough to make people abandon what lives they built to come help us get him out of that hellhole. Do you really think he could have been that dead wrong about a guy?"

I did not like where this was going—but in the end, it didn't matter. "He's dead now, so who cares?"

"Right." Martinez even added a nod for emphasis. "Sorry that you didn't get to cut off his balls and feed them to him. I'm sure that would have undone all the damage he did that you are still lamenting about."

"Now you're sounding an awful lot like my husband," I let him know.

"Doesn't mean it isn't true," he insisted, taking some of the sting from his words with his grin. "But, seriously—I don't have to tell you that people in your line of work should work harder on their anger management issues. Whatever he did, or almost did—is it worth you losing your humanity? I'm not even going to start with things like your soul or compromising your moral compass because I know that will only get me mocked, but let's face it. If you lose it completely, you're gone, forever, just as if someone had put a gun to your head and pulled the trigger." He paused for effect, his intense gaze holding mine captive. "Just a thought—if what Hamilton warned you about is true. If Decker is still alive, and he's pulling the strings—has it occurred to you that you may be playing straight into his hands? Your anger, particularly as volatile as it is, centered on Hamilton, is a ticking time bomb. What if that was planted deliberately? Someone only has to spend an hour around you to understand that part of your personality. Inoculating you with the serum added a layer of security for Nate, a way to keep you alive that would make him worry less about you—but it also opened that one huge flaw in your defenses."

Speaking of flaws—

"Hamilton insisted that he had orders to kill me first, and then watch me die a slow, painful death when they realized I'd started rotting from the inside out," I insisted. "He actually went against those orders when he let me live so I could get shot up with the serum."

Martinez gave me a tight, toothless smile. "What if he lied?"

It sounded very stupid, but I hadn't considered that possibility until now. Of all the things that asshole had said or done, this had been the least suspicious. And he had even explained it—that I'd looked so fucking miserable, weak as I'd been, but still managed to hold on and pull through that he'd felt I deserved that one break—or something like that.

But what if that had been the plan all along? Like Nate, I knew that Hamilton was an accomplished liar who could go toe-to-toe with the best—or at least, I presumed so, since they were so damn similar in way too many traits. Looking back, if he had tried to trigger me, or just see how far he could push me, or indoctrinate me into having a hard time keeping a lid on my rage—his constant being all over my business, doing his very best to set my teeth on edge and make my blood boil, made a lot of sense.

Too much sense.

"That fucking bastard—" I muttered under my breath, not quite sure how to give word to what I was actually feeling—besides the rage, once again churning in my stomach. Focusing on Martinez, I did my best to keep at least a calm exterior, if not actually relax inside. "You think that's really it?"

Martinez shrugged, looking less certain than moments ago. "Only one person alive who could give a valid guess, right? Since you can't beat the answer out of Hamilton anymore, that is."

"Well, perfect that we're already planning to spring him from the slaver colony," I said, more chipper than I felt.

He had nothing to say to that, and neither did I. Since it was well past midnight now—and our talk had done its own to further exhaust both of us—I didn't think that would change any time soon.

"Let's call it a night, shall we?" I suggested, hard-pressed to avoid a yawn.

"Sounds like a plan," Martinez responded, getting up slowly, his body obviously protesting. Seeing him wince as he turned around and walked—slowly and deliberately—over to the bed made my heart seize up. So much had changed. So much we had lost. Was it really worth it?

I was just about to plonk down on the sheets on my sofa when Martinez cleared his throat, making me look up at him once more. He looked just as serious as before, all his usual smiles gone. "Promise me something, Bree. Whether our theories are right or wrong—don't let them win. Don't ever give up, don't ever give in to the anger that's constantly raging deep down inside of you. Keep on living. Keep on laughing. Keep on loving with all your heart."

"You say that like it's that easy," I griped. When he kept staring at me, I eventually inclined my head. "I swear, I won't let them win."

He flashed me another grin, if a small, private one. I must have looked rather confused because he explained as he sat down on the bed with a sigh. "You asked me earlier if it's easier to deal with shit if you have faith. Well, you tell me—is it?"

I hated it when he pulled a stunt like that on me—and that wasn't even the tenth time since we'd become thick as thieves that he'd done it. I just shook my head and turned my back on him, refusing to answer—but deep down, I knew that he was right. Faith may be a shield to some, a crutch to others—but as long as we refused to give up, there was always one thing: hope.

And if hope was all I had left, I'd ride that bitch until kingdom come.

Chapter 16

"Any idea how long this will take?" I wanted to know, hard-pressed to keep the frustration out of my voice.

Eight days. I'd spent eight entire days in the settlement at the California coast already, and still we were biding our time, with no real progress made. The first day or two had been a nice respite, and a much needed one at that—also to catch up with the rest of my friends—but now every hour that passed without us hitting the road grated on my nerves. Consequently, my annoyed pacing grated on the Ice Queen's nerves, which was never a good idea.

Like the four times before that we'd had this conversation, her emotional range ran from annoyed to vexed, and a slightly homicidal edge had started leaking into the mix. "As I told you before, we cannot rush into this, unless you want us all to end up dead? Missions take preparation!" she reminded me, none too patiently, I might add. "And we're still waiting for more detailed intel, and without enough ammo and suitable vehicles we won't get very far, either."

I raised both my hands in a mute show that I wasn't blaming her for any of this, but that didn't change anything. That she shared my torment only made it worse, not better. At least we'd heard back from a few of her contacts, adding eight more people to our not-so-merry band of misfits—providing the last four made it to us, but at least they were en route. Me included, that made eighteen—which wasn't that bad a number, but came with its own issues.

"How is it possible that you can only allocate three cars?" I asked, also not for the first time. "We had over fifteen working vehicles when we left for the Silo that late fall! Nate and I fucking built our buggies almost from scratch! And now you tell me we, what? Have to walk almost two thousand miles across the country?"

Pia's eyes narrowed, and I knew I'd gone that one step too far—but somehow she managed not to come after me and punch me in the face. Her glare almost accomplished the feat but I did my best to steel my spine and not let her intimidate me. That had, for sure, changed over the past years—feeling like I was actually Nate's equal had put an end to my already sketchy view on accepting anyone else's authority. I had no intention of going toe-to-toe with her—and she was, by far, the most capable XO and logistics officer I'd ever met, and that wasn't anything I was going to contend with her for—but all this stalling and "can't do" attitude was slowly getting the best of me.

"We have vehicles," she informed me, her tone biting but less aggressive than I'd expected. "But only three that will make it two thousand miles without needing maintenance or other kinds of fuel we will not find on the road, or that would be sorely missed here." Her eyes narrowed, and I fully expected her to chew me out next, but instead she looked actually chagrined. "I planned for a lot of contingencies. I fully expected the two of you to show up on our doorstep sooner or later, probably in need of help. But I did not plan for something like this. I'm sorry. My primary concern was about moving as many people out of the camp and to a safe location, not to go on the warpath instead."

To say I was gawking at her was probably an understatement, and I forced myself to stop when I saw that most of her self-directed anger was about to acquire a new target.

"You couldn't have anticipated everything," I offered up quickly—and it was true. Biting my lip, I was at a loss for how to navigate this unexpected, new minefield. Should I apologize as well? Would that make her even angrier? In the end, I went with the truth—usually the best with her. "I'm just so fucking frustrated! It took me a small eternity to finally get here, and now it takes even longer in the other direction? I'd laugh if it wasn't kind of a time-sensitive thing."

Pia shared a quick, true smile with me that was gone as soon as I'd caught it. "I know. And it's not without mirth to see how similar to him you've become. No wonder, being stuck together day in, day out, for years, but—" She paused, considering me for a bit. "You have changed, no doubt there."

I couldn't help but laugh softly under my breath. "You mean because I no longer let you boss me around, unchallenged?"

She gave me a vexed look for that, but followed it up with a shrug. "That, too. But you're no longer the woman who left the camp at the coast in fall to find out what was wrong with her. I'm not quite sure what to make of the woman who came back to us, yet."

Her statement confused me, and I would have been lying if I'd said that it didn't set my teeth on edge—but no way around this, I figured. "A lot happened since then. I can't change any of it, so why dwell on whether the change was for the better or not?"

"That's not what I meant," she insisted, the way she kept studying me remaining critical. "I guess just like I didn't think we'd meet again to launch a rescue mission, I didn't expect that you'd lose all remaining will to bow to authority—although I should have expected that, particularly if Miller was convinced that Decker is still in the game. In that case, the last thing he'd want was to make you susceptible to following anyone's orders ever again."

"Or, you know, it could be a side effect of being married for three years and spending most of that time just with each other," I suggested, playing for levity that I didn't necessarily feel. "I honestly don't think we would have survived if we'd continued to take each other too seriously."

"There's that," she agreed, snorting.

Looking around—as if that would, miraculously, make more vehicles appear—I realized that a young man, in his early twenties at most, came sprinting toward us, eyes fixed on Zilinsky. She visibly drew herself up into a commanding posture as he came into shouting distance.

"We got news from the others," he called out to her as soon as he came to a skidding stop. "They called ahead to say one of their vehicles broke down, and if maybe you'd want to head out and fetch them?"

Her brows drew together as she looked less than happy. "Where are they now? Are they in any danger, or just too lazy to pile into a single car?"

The boy shook his head. "They said they secured the location but you'd want to head out with spare parts and a mechanic. They got stuck west of Yosemite. I have the coordinates right here, and the parts they were asking for."

Pia took the paper he offered, giving me a slightly exasperated look—that I could now see for what it was: the same frustration I felt at yet another delay.

"I'm coming with you," I insisted more than offered. I was useless in the settlement as it was, unlike everyone else she could have asked for. She didn't protest, likely having expected as much already. "We'll take Romanoff, Martinez, and three of the local guards," Pia declared. "You wanna drive?"

This time, I didn't have to force a smile. "You bet I do."

And, just like that, twenty minutes later, we were off, heading north with two solar-powered pickup trucks and enough weapons and ammo for a small army.

With two hundred miles to go, it was obvious that this would turn into a longer field trip that didn't end with us back in the settlement by sunset. I didn't mind, although I had gotten rather fond of the couch in Martinez's cabin, to say the least. Even though it was a reason for further delays, driving north gave me something to do, and distracted me from what was going on—at least for the first few miles, until we cut through a swath of land that, while lush green now, showed signs of terrible devastation everywhere. The heat of the summer hadn't started yet so the vegetation that had reclaimed the burnt ground was still here, but it wasn't enough to hide the destruction that the fires had left behind. Even with no personal loss and connection to what had happened, it put quite the damper on my mood.

It was in the middle of the afternoon that I realized why the landscape, here a little better off, was familiar—we'd been here before on the way to the Silo, with a settlement up ahead that hadn't let us in for the night, making Nate, Burns, Tanner, Gita, and me camp outside. Oddly enough, I felt myself looking forward to at least catching a glimpse of the assholes again—until I realized why there were no signs erected anywhere pointing the way to the settlement.

"What happened there?" I asked when we topped another rise and saw the smashed ruins of what had once been the flourishing town off to the side. The landscape looked like the fires hadn't reached this far, so that couldn't have been the cause.

Zilinsky gave me a weird look before she explained. "Scavengers, raiders—you can piece together the rest, I'm sure."

I hadn't forgotten what Martinez had told me, but seeing this firsthand somehow made it more real. "They refused help?" I guessed—not a hard one, since they hadn't let us in back then, either.

Zilinsky gave a brief nod. "We weren't keen on spreading our forces thin, but we could have been here in hours. We offered—they told us to get lost. That was a few weeks after they blew up the docks in New Angeles. Before that, we thought we were all safe down here. Turns out, we weren't."

The former settlement dropped out of view as the road kept angling toward the hills. "Is that the reason why we only have three working cars to take with us on the road? Because everyone thought there was a world of resources out there waiting for them, until there suddenly wasn't?"

"Something like that," the guard—Kepler, I remembered—grumbled. "I'm not saying he knew, but Greene sent us out to raid what we could weeks before. Then shit went down, and suddenly, nobody dared stick their noses outside of their fences. Been like this the entire time since."

Zilinsky glared over her shoulder at him before she turned to me. "He's not wrong—including Greene's great timing. We hit a factory full of electric car motors hours before a convoy of Humvees arrived."

"No coincidence there," I mused.

"Exactly. We had just enough time to load everything we could carry onto the trucks and be gone before anyone got close enough to shoot at us. Because there was still more to loot there than to get from us, they didn't come after us, but that's why we only have eight cars retrofitted. The other seventeen are in New Angeles." The look on her face turned sour. "Before you ask, I already tried to get more of them, but they won't hand them over. Turns out, the doors your name used to open are now firmly shut."

I had to admit that stung, but wasn't a surprise—not since I'd had a brief chance to talk to Greene himself. We kept driving on in silence, Pia only breaking it to let me know when to turn off the road and onto something that resembled a deer trail at best. The only positive thing I could say was that the entire region seemed as devoid of zombies as it did of still-living humans.

That changed once we drew near a lone house close to the foothills of the mountains—and thankfully only on the living part. Two cars were next to the building, with four armed and armored humans waiting for us—two men and two women, three of them looking well into their fifties, except for one of the women who was roughly my age. The site looked well secured and neither of the cars seemed in bad shape, making me instantly suspicious. Zilinsky was frowning as well but not in a paranoid way.

As we got out, she introduced the newcomers as Rozen, Cohn, Calveras, and Neeson. The first three were apparently retired army personnel, Joelle Rozen having served with Bert Hughes, Sadie's father, and the two men friends of hers. Marleen Neeson, the younger woman, got the very brief moniker of "casual acquaintance," which made her grin and me guess that there was a story behind that I really needed to hear. Before I could ask, she sized me up with a curious expression on her face. "So you're the woman who's mad enough to marry Miller? I kind of pictured you differently."

"Don't say 'taller,' or I might have to hit you," I offered, hoping she'd get the joke—at half a head shorter than I was. Put her in a yellow sundress, and she wouldn't have looked weird as a spunky kindergarten teacher.

Her smile, bright yet a little crooked, let me know that she was used to people underestimating her because of her diminutive size as well. "More crazy, but maybe you're just good at hiding it?" Her brows drew together as she studied me more intently—and quite comically so. "I guess you'd have to be. Else, you would have killed each other by now."

"You sound like you know my husband quite well," I observed, not quite sure what to make of that.

Her smile got a little too knowing for her own good, but she didn't beat around the bush. "If you mean, did we fuck? Yeah, we kind of had a thing going for a while, but very casual. I honestly didn't think he could get more attached to a piece of ass than that, and neither did I want to. So, no worries, I'm not going to fish in your pond. Not that I'd dare, present company and likely affiliation considered." She turned her head and stared straight at Pia, who calmly stared back. It wasn't amiable on either woman's side, and still, I got the sense that they liked each other. There must have been a story about that as well.

"I'm not really worried about that right now," I said, doing my best to sound like I meant it, too. "We'd have to get him back first, too."

Breaking off the staring match—and obviously not considering herself defeated—Marleen caught my gaze once more. "Never thought I'd be part of a rescue mission to spring him of all people, but when Zilinsky called, I couldn't not get in on the fun. You see, I owe these three buckaroos, and I will repay that debt."

She made no move to explain herself further, prompting the Ice Queen to do so for her. "We crossed paths with her on a mission once. That should have ended with her brains going splat all over the wall. Miller decided she was more valuable alive than as a tapestry ornament, and she's helped with some wetwork during his time working as a free agent. She has a big mouth—and an even bigger ego—but does come in handy in a tight spot." The way she glanced at the other woman sideways made me think she meant like someone else she knew. Huh. Reevaluating Marleen, I tried to do the obvious, superficial judging thing but came up blank; we had nothing in common except for less-than-giant height. With olive skin, dark hair, and slightly tilted eyes she was impossible to place heritage-wise, but still had a more wholesome than exotic thing going on. Must have been the homicidal tendencies underneath the nice exterior.

"Valuable how?" I asked the obvious question.

Marleen perfectly preened. "Contract work."

"Let me guess. Not as an event planner," I proposed, smirking.

Her bright yet cold grin pretty much confirmed that. "Assassin. Not that keen of a sniper, particularly when I have to lug a rifle around that's as long as I am tall, but I'm pretty good with poisons and knives. Great infiltrator, because even in plain sight, they never see me coming. So, no worries. I won't shank you in the back. If I ever come for you, it will be mano a mano."

"I'll make sure to remember that!" It was hard not to laugh despite—or maybe because—of that not-even-veiled threat she'd just uttered. Turning to Pia, I snorted. "I think we'll get along great."

The Ice Queen offered another rare smile. "I knew you would." She then turned to the others. "So what's with the BS you sold us about a broken-down car?"

Calveras jerked his head toward the house. "Never said it was one of ours. Check the garage. When we stopped for a break and stumbled on that, we figured you might want to take a look."

The house looked unremarkable enough that his comment further confused me, but it took Martinez only a step into the carport to let out a succinct, "You gotta be fucking kidding me!" before he disappeared inside, soon followed by the sounds of human banging around car parts. Curious, I went to check on him, finding him pretty much hanging over the popped hood of a dusty SUV inside. It wasn't a make or model I was familiar with, and it took me looking at the steering wheel to realize that it was a Ford. Judging from the lack of a conventional engine, it must have been an electric car. When I mentioned as much—proving once again how far my immense automotive knowledge ranged—Martinez halted in his gawking for a moment to flash me a boyish grin. "That must be a prototype! I've never seen one like it!"

"Don't those usually have some kind of dazzle pattern wrapping, or something?" I mused. It was something he'd told me on one of our long hours of me helping with rebuilding the cars in the bunker.

While the matte, dark gray paint job of the car looked unusual, it wasn't that out of the ordinary.

Martinez paused for a moment, as if that hadn't even occurred to him. Boy and his car, obviously. "Probably to make it look less like a prototype," he offered, turning back to the hood. "At least we won't have to repaint it. And if this isn't obvious, I'm calling dibs."

Pia and Rozen had followed me, the Ice Queen not quite caught up in Martinez's enthusiasm yet. "Can you get it working? Or do we take it apart?"

He looked perfectly scandalized at the latter proposition. "Oh, I will get this baby purring smoothly in no time! Battery's likely shot, but we brought spares. Give me a few hours and we're good to go." Glancing at the reddening sky outside, he shrugged. "Let's make that tomorrow morning. I should have it running before midnight."

Rozen spoke up as Pia considered. "We've secured the area as well as four people can. It's safe enough, just needed a little housekeeping a few miles to the north. Nothing remarkable inside the house, and it looks looted several times," she professed. "Still good enough for a hideout for the night. I'll tell Cohn to get some chow started?"

All she got—and needed—was a nod from Zilinsky. Just as she stepped back outside, Andrej and the guard who'd been riding with Pia and me—Kepler, I reminded myself; he looked like he might stick with us, so I might as well try to remember his name—came in, immediately joining Martinez in slobbering all over the vehicle. I quickly followed Pia when she left, lest someone rope me into handing them tools I once again didn't remember the designations of. It happened. Spending months working on the buggies with Nate had had one advantage: we'd both done our thing, without much talking except what we were planning on doing. Who needed to know what kind that wrench was, anyway?

After spending the day driving, I was quite happy to loosen my cramping, hard muscles with some bona fide perimeter watch, happy that, for once, I didn't get the graveyard shift. It was when Pia joined me two hours later that I realized she'd done so for a reason. I half expected her to offer a more in-depth analysis of Marleen's character or past, but instead she went for something else entirely as we kept strolling through the foothills.

"I didn't want to have this talk in town where anyone might overhear us," she muttered, gaze roaming the countryside for predators we'd already established were long gone. I felt myself perk up, not sure whether this was going to be good or really, really bad. Her attention briefly flitting to check on my face made me guess that it wasn't anything that would make me feel warm and fluffy.

"What's so important nobody overhear that we have to go all countryside clandestine on the topic?"

She obviously found my joke less than funny—and so did I, as soon as she said, "I know that what actually happened to you while you were gone that first winter wasn't fun, but it was for the best that you weren't around when Sadie had the baby."

Talk about a gut punch. "Why? Think I would have made a terrible godmother? Not being present is pretty much the definition of that." It couldn't have been because of the smear campaign the army had started, because that must have only just started around the time Chris was born.

Pia sent me a vexed glare but didn't deny my assessment. "For Sadie and the baby, maybe. But while I generally don't play favorites, in this, my concern is with you rather than her."

Ah. That. I looked away before I could catch more than a hint of sympathy in her gaze—not something I was used to from Pia, and in this case not necessarily something I appreciated. Calling her a hypocrite was much easier.

"It couldn't have been much easier for you, either," I prompted, forcing myself to look her straight in the face. "You lost two children that you watched grow from toddlers to little humans. All I had was a bad aftertaste of a lot of what-ifs and regret."

Normally, I would have expected her to get annoyed with me, but seeing her oddly calm and gentle freaked me out on a deeper level. "It's okay to hurt, you know?" she stressed. "And you would have hurt. I know you did a good job ignoring her while she waddled around, seven months pregnant, huge as a whale. But once she went into labor, once the baby let out her first cry, once the world stopped for all of us and focused on the new life in our midst, you wouldn't have escaped the knowledge that it could—maybe even should—have been you. You would have likely had your child within a few weeks of her. And you would have hated her, and the child, and Nate for putting you in this situation, and all of us for being happy for her. But most of all yourself, for being human and feeling like that, even if you understood where it came from. That's why I was glad that you weren't around. And why I never sent anyone to track you both down. I figured he'd reasoned the same way as I did and took you both out of the equation that would put strain on friendships that wasn't necessary. I thought he was doing it for you."

I knew she was serious not just because of how guilty—downright gutted—she sounded, but also because she used Nate's given name. Sometimes I felt like they'd both forgotten each other's, easily. And it was much easier to mull about that than what she actually said—and what was expected from me in return.

"I'm not that petty. Or small," I stressed, quickly speaking on when her mouth snapped open to interrupt me—or contradict me, more likely. Fuck, but I really had missed her! "Yes, that's a rather accurate guess of my mental landscape, I'm not denying that. But I would have found a way to deal with it, likely involving lots of physical exertion, and not necessarily of the horizontal kind." The brief smile I offered must have been more of a grimace because she didn't respond, so I went on quickly. "But what I meant is that I don't hold it against you that you never came looking for us. My guess? He must have reasoned that would be your expectation and used that to his—and your—advantage. When I dropped by here I was kind of surprised that Burns hadn't breathed a word of what he must have figured was Nate's true motive, but it makes sense. You're great about keeping your emotions under wraps, no shit. But I doubt you would have reacted the same way if you'd figured we were hiding from the big, bad wolf rather than our messed-up feelings."

Pia let out a sigh that sounded like the weight of the world had lifted from her shoulders. "Makes sense, doesn't it? And it's true. If I had even the slightest hint to go on that Decker might still be alive and coming for you, I would have been a lot more defensive in my actions and paranoid in building up our town. Someone would have noticed, and I'd have inadvertently painted a target on all of us. You might have been safe from the slavers, but it stands to reason whether any of us would still be alive—if you are right, and he is still out there."

I couldn't help but shake my head in wonder once more. "Who the fuck is that guy? And why hasn't anyone taken him out yet?"

That her face closed down was yet another piece of the puzzle, but at least she answered me. "How does that quote go? 'The greatest trick the Devil ever pulled was convincing the world he didn't exist'? That sums him up in a nutshell. He's a dangerous man. Ruthless and manipulating—"

My grimace made her pause. "Nate told me about Bucky's sister."

Pia's eyes widened—clearly she'd been in the know as well. That she seemed surprised, if only for a second, that I knew hurt a little, but maybe shouldn't have. Considering how secretive—and generally closed-mouthed—Nate was about his past, it only made sense. She seemed to come to the same conclusion.

"Of course he did," she muttered. "Which means that you know exactly as much as I do. Which is more than either of us want to know, that much is for sure. It shows how serious he thinks the threat is, or else he would have kept his trap shut. Your husband is not someone who likes to admit that there is actually one person in the world who he's afraid of."

"Sounds about right," I agreed with her. "But that doesn't give me much to go on, particularly if he is still alive, and somehow connected to this. How can I prepare for something I don't know anything about?"

"You can't. And it's how you react to something you can't predict that might just let you get out ahead in the end."

That statement sounded a lot like what Nate had told me about our plans for where to go once we'd gotten back to the US—only that it had been a lie, as the fact that Red knew where to go look for us had proven.

"I really don't like this," I hissed after thinking this through once more, still not getting to a different conclusion.

"Let's take this one step at a time," Pia offered, sounding weirdly relaxed. "We have a few aces up our sleeves—like you, like Neeson; like so many others we have picked up along the way who have never had a chance to learn from the same rulebook as our opponents are playing by."

"Like the slavers," I pointed out.

A thread of contempt was back in Pia's eyes, making me feel much more at home. "We will find a way to deal with them as well," she said, confident enough that there was no contradicting her. "Nobody took them seriously as a threat until now, that's why nobody bested them. We won't make the same mistake, and we will get Miller back. And, who knows? Maybe we'll pick up a few more wildcards along the way."

That last sentence made me uncomfortably paranoid. "Do you think he actually let himself be caught?"

She didn't hesitate as she shook her head. "From what you've told us, no way. But he didn't expect to have an insider scientist with him when he went to avenge his brother. Who knows what will come of this? Don't underestimate your husband, either. He's a crafty fucker when he needs to be."

I had a few choice words to say to that but opted to keep them to myself. Instead, I looked back toward the house, visible on the lower rise about half a mile south of where we were standing. "What about the four newcomers? Can I trust them? Do you?"

The Ice Queen gave a rather neutral shrug. "As I said earlier, Rozen came on recommendation from Bert. And before you ask, no, Emma isn't aware that we're still in contact. Rozen knows Sadie, too, so that's a character reference if you don't trust my instincts."

"I always do. That's why I'm asking you," I let her know.

She gave something between a chuff and a snort. "Cohn and Calveras are friends of hers. Beggars can't be choosers, right?"

"No suspicion because none of them has the marks?"

Pia shook her head. "No. They'd been part of one of the first settlements. That's why they got around it at the time. They stayed because all of them had family. Things change—and now they have their own reasons to come along. You can ask them. I'm not at liberty to tell without their permission. But yes, I do trust them."

"And Marleen? What's up with her?"

"There is no woman named Marleen Neeson who looks like that," she offered with a slight smile. "Or any of her other three aliases that I know of. She was a ghost before the world went to shit. I'd say it's lucky coincidence that I was able to track her down, except it's not. She tracked me down last year, wanted to get the details on you and Miller. She left some contact details, so that's what I did when I knew you were showing up."

"Wait—you called her before I even got to your town? And how's none of this suspicious?"

I got a knowing look for that—sprinkled with a hint of pride. "With anyone but her, I would have shot her on sight. But she's different."

"Why? How?" I felt like those were valid questions, and her evasive answers didn't help one bit.

I almost expected her to tell me the same as with the others—go ask them directly if I really wanted to know—but at the last moment she decided against it. I knew this was going to be good. "Let's put it this way—if I was going to assemble a crew that was going to hunt down Decker, she would always be in my top five. With shitty intel about the slaver camp, we need an infiltrator, and she's good at that as well. The possible combination of our task ahead made her the perfect candidate."

"What's up with her and Decker? And does every fucking person in this whole country know about him except me?"

The Ice Queen gave me a condescending look for my outburst. "You might be personally acquainted with half of those still alive," she said before answering my other question. "That contract that should have ended badly for her—and had her facing us at the wrong end of too many guns for her comfort—was connected to one of Decker's pet projects. She knew who she'd been pitted against, and chose to become a ghost rather than get a bullet between the eyes. She continued to work with us both out of obligation and need for money, but, looking back, she more than once pointed out a few flaws in the system that seemed obvious to her but our contacts always explained away. Maybe things would have turned out differently if we'd listened to her. Maybe not. My point is, as much as you can trust anyone, she's on top of that list. And I wouldn't be surprised if the two of you'd hit it off right from the start. She's special. So are you."

"How nice of you to say," I grumbled, but couldn't hold it against her. "Mighty convenient that they found the car here."

The Ice Queen shrugged. "I told them from the start that transportation is our main issue at the moment, so they knew what to look for. I wouldn't be surprised if one of them had found the car months or maybe even years before and just happened to remember it now. Who knows? Quite frankly, I don't give a shit. I need room for eighteen people and their gear, and with six cars, we now have that. Even five would have worked but I prefer one spare, considering that we will bring one additional man back with us. If the last few years have taught me something, it's not to ask questions when something is convenient and to just roll with the punches once they land. We're still short on provisions, and we don't have sufficient ammo should we decide to storm the camp."

I shook my head, not because she'd said anything stupid, but because I already had an answer to that. "We can't storm it. Even if Richards brings more people to that gathering than we expect, we will still be outnumbered over one hundred to one. I know you're good, but not that good. I'm not even talking avoiding bloodshed, but simple survival. If we have a chance to go in, find Nate, and get him out without anyone the wiser, that's our best plan by a long shot. With luck, we won't even need any weapons for that."

"Let's not hope it comes to that," Pia said, rather cryptically. When she saw the confusion on my face, she looked toward the house once more, but it seemed like she wasn't really seeing it. "Easy plans like that never work. Plans without bloodshed usually never work, either. I'd rather calculate a thirty percent casualty rate and be surprised if only one or two bite it, rather than hope for less and end up with too much blood on my hands." She paused, focusing back on me. "Or who would you pick should give their lives so your husband is freed? Martinez? Burns? Romanoff? Exactly. But we still have a while, so we'll deal with that once we get to the Ozarks. If we survive that, we can always draw straws."

I didn't like her pessimism, but it closely matched the latent unease that had been riding shotgun ever since I'd realized how fucking huge that camp was. I still didn't give up hope that Richards would show up with something more important than manpower or weapons—information.

Whether I could trust said information was a different thing.

I couldn't help but smile for a second when I realized that I really missed the good old days when it was just us against the zombies and no care for anything else in the world. Of course, that had been my perception only, while the others had many more things to guess at and worry about—including how to keep me alive. Maybe those days hadn't been that much better to begin with, just different.

But, damn, different sounded pretty good to me right now.

Chapter 17

Ten days after I'd gotten to the California coastal town, the miracle finally happened—we hit the road. After more lamenting, much pleading, lots of plotting, and even threats being thrown around, we were finally ready to go. I still only knew half the people who were tagging along, but that was the least of my worries. Five weeks since I'd last seen Nate—and five weeks were a damn long time. Back when the shit had hit the fan, our journey had taken less than twice that long, and we weren't about to bust down doors soon and be done with it. We were only just beginning to start our rescue mission. Five fucking weeks.

It would be closer to eight by the time we got to the final stage.

Marleen turned out to be a more welcome distraction than I could have expected. That first night at the house with the prototype car, she'd started laughing maniacally when she'd caught a glimpse of my hands, finding it incredibly funny that not only wasn't I former military, but I was a cripple to boot. I wasn't even offended since she went right on to crowing about how much more fun it would be to stick it to the man seeing a cripple was doing said sticking. She also found it incredibly endearing how I fondled the sniper rifle Pia had found somewhere for me before we got ready to set out. When it took her all of five minutes to meet Sonia, piss off Sonia, and laugh in Sonia's face, I knew we'd be friends for as long as fate would let us be. Sonia wasn't exactly ecstatic to see her not-quite favorite person—me—pair off with her new even-less-favorite person—Marleen. Burns found it all incredibly amusing but did a good job placating his missus. I knew I'd hit gold when, seconds after those two disappeared, Marleen crowed a loud and carrying, "Well, at least someone is getting laid tonight!" after them, making Martinez choke on his laughter.

Sadly, Marleen was the only one with a sense of humor. The three old soldiers—Rozen, Cohn, and Calveras—took everything with a grain of salt, including my less than-standard military MO, but the four new recruits were oh so serious. Kepler I'd already gotten to hang out with on our two-day sortie to fetch the new car, and unremarkable was the best term I could come up with for him. Sarood, Brook, and Halecki were, like Kepler, very eager to prove to Zilinsky that they were young yet capable, but they had their issues getting over me pretty much running outside the hierarchy the Ice Queen had established. I could kind of understand why— she was running a tight ship, and even after years of being on my own, I was still surprised when she accepted me disagreeing with her on something. But I was the exception and they were the rule, and I could understand where my special status didn't sit well with them. That Marleen equally did what she pleased, and Sonia, at best, listened to advice that she chose to follow, didn't seem to count.

And what I really wanted to do was to punch some sense into them and yell at them to stop being such babies—which reminded me awfully of how Zilinsky had sometimes glared at me when I'd been a little too stupid and goofy with the guys. The irony wasn't lost on me. That Nate wasn't here to see it and laugh in my face, either. But none of that mattered, I told myself, if only I'd get him back in good time.

With twenty days left and around two thousand miles to go, our trek to what used to be the Ozark settlement should have been a breeze, or so I'd thought—until we left the vicinity of New Angeles and its radius of influence, and things got interesting quickly. Either Red had had intel that we were sorely missing, or we'd just had a lot of luck on the way to California, but the state of the roads was bad. At least once a day, we had to backtrack and find a new route because the old one ended in a minefield or landslide or destroyed bridge or other obstacle that hadn't been there the last time anyone had passed by. Three days into this, I complained that Dispatch was really slacking off where road safety reports were concerned, only to be met with seventeen disbelieving pairs of eyes. It took me a while to figure out that I was wrong, or rather, because we were trying to fly under the radar, we couldn't rely on the official trade routes that were open, well-guarded, and heavily populated at times. Well, my bad.

More than being stealthy, keeping the cars running was the real problem. In theory, driving around with solar panels hooked to spare batteries to power the cars was a great idea—particularly in the more arid states where the sun was beating down mercilessly now that spring had turned into summer for good. Because Marleen and I were riding with Martinez in his snazzy Ford, we even had A/C most of the time—when the newly hooked-up solar panels were doing their job. Every single day, one of the cars had some issue or other, forcing a stop to switch batteries, tinker and repair, or plain wait out the noon heat until we could resume driving after six in the afternoon—only to have to stop at around nine because we couldn't risk lights, and we had to preserve batteries for night vision gear for the mission itself, not lumbering cross-country.

A week into this, and I was ready to walk, sure that we wouldn't have been much slower if we'd done things the old-fashioned way. It soon became obvious to me why the slavers could do what they did— it was damn hard to get twenty people from one place to another, let alone a group large enough to make a difference. Nate and I had been oblivious to this as we'd either travelled light, or spent, at the most, a few days on the road going from one base to another, with lots of detours for hunting and scavenging. What did it matter that for every three hours driving we'd had to let the buggies charge for another hour, if we'd wanted to go for a swim or crash in the shade of the trees, anyway? What angered me the most was that, as such things go, I hadn't realized just how close to living free in paradise our days had been—until they hadn't.

At least I had my friends back, and I appreciated that more than I'd expected every morning when we sat around the fire, meditatively drinking coffee and tea, and every evening, between grabbing some chow and getting ready for bed. Even with so many strangers—and only two of them slowly becoming friends, even if they couldn't stand each other—it felt like home. Way more like home than where Nate and I had been living for the past two years. That once again reminded me that home didn't necessarily have to be a building but could be great company just as well—but that also made me afraid of what lay ahead, once we had Nate back. But that was one punch I'd roll with once it hit, as the Ice Queen had stated so perfectly earlier.

Even if the going was slow and tedious, we made good progress, and ended up at our destination with three entire days to spare— only to find that we weren't the first to arrive. Or second, or third, as it turned out. Pia had expected Richards and his people to come from the north or west, so she'd plotted a course that got us closing in on the ruins of the settlement from the southeast, pretty much the direction we would be leaving in after whatever would happen here had happened. That gave us a few glimpses of the old settlement, burnt to the ground and already surprisingly overgrown, but nobody focused on that once the small city of tents and vehicles came into view roughly a mile north of the ruins, well in sight of the road. Rozen reported in that she'd counted fifteen vehicles and at least three different factions—army, marines, and one she couldn't place. And while we were still debating how to proceed—well aware that they must have seen us just as we'd seen them—another convoy came down from the northeast, only the front three vehicles veering toward the tents after the rest remained at pretty much the distance we'd assumed.

After handing her binoculars to Marleen, the Ice Queen gave our little six-vehicle group a once-over and started calling out names. "We're taking two cars over there with us. Romanoff, you hold down the fort here. Two snipers at the very least, three would be better." She then glanced at me—no need to tell me I was tagging along. "Martinez, Burns, you're with us."

Before she could say more, Sonia stepped up to her man. "I'm coming with."

Pia gave her a pained smile. "Wouldn't have it any other way." She kept considering the rest. "Kepler, Halecki, you provide backup. Stick to the vehicles while the rest of us do our thing."

Marleen was still studying the group, and when Pia didn't call her name she chimed in. "I'm coming with, too. Mostly for the funny commentary, but might be good to have an extra liaison in the field." When Pia kept staring flatly at her, Marleen shrugged as she handed the binoculars back. "I know at least three of the guys pretending to be stone cold killers over there. I presume she"—she nodded at me—"can do the army, but who do you have for the marines?" She got a nod, if a hesitant one. I could tell that Pia would have preferred keeping Marleen's presence a secret for a while longer.

That set, we piled back into the vehicles, Pia hopping into the car with us, and the extra guards sharing with Burns and Sonia. I was surprised that she didn't leave our gear and provisions with the others, but clearly, she didn't expect a trap as much as minor altercations that might warrant a third time reloading. And she wasn't done yet being all mysterious, as the moment Martinez started the car, she got out a walkie-talkie I hadn't seen in all the days we'd been on the road together. I had no clue who had its twin, but after minimal static, her demand for an update got a gruff, male voice offering, "En route." What that was all about got resolved several seconds later when two vehicles peeled out of the ruins of the settlement and headed straight for us, drawing up alongside us about a third of the way to the tents. I was more than a little surprised to find them splattered with paint and streaming rags and chains made of bones behind them. "Something you care to explain?" I asked her, not sure what to make of this at all.

Pia gave me a rather amused snort. "We need a diversion to get into the camp, right? How about sending a hooting horde of raiders right at them that makes the guards ignore everything else and open up their backdoors to us?"

"And how in the world will you get them to comply and do that? And not turn on us first?" I asked, feeling like that point was a valid one. Marleen looked a little disturbed herself, but the fact that Martinez wasn't reacting to any of this made me guess that my dear friends had kept a few secrets they might not have wanted to broadcast to their fellow townspeople. "Let me guess—you have contacts to the new scavengers as well?"

The Ice Queen gave me a look that made it obvious that I needn't have asked—and it made sense, kind of. Their territory had bordered on what had apparently become scavenger central. What I hadn't expected was her response. "As do you."

Up ahead, the people already gathered didn't seem too enthusiastic to see their numbers suddenly double with three new groups arriving pretty much at the same time. Orders were shouted and weapons readied, but at least nobody went into complete defensive mode. After yearning for this day to finally arrive—even ahead of schedule, as it seemed—I suddenly didn't know how to approach this. Great.

The tents turned out to belong to four groups, with enough room left to let both our two convoys come to a halt and form a wonky circle, large enough to leave lots of cover around the vehicles—not that I figured we'd need it. The scavengers ended up to our right, with most of the remaining free space on their other side since nobody except us seemed to want to come too close to them. Then there was the unidentifiable group, the newcomers from the north, and—closer together—the three more easily identifiable camps, comprised of marines, army, and marines again, closing the circle with Burns's car once more. That obvious room left between the tents spoke of clear segregation, making me wonder what that was all about. Looked like I would find out soon.

One question answered itself the moment I got out of the car and watched the larger of the two scavenger vehicles drop its passengers on the ground—and found myself face to face with someone I hadn't expected. "Is that you, Dan Harris?"

The leader of the New Vegas group—or at least that's what he had been when we'd rallied to attack the Colorado installation back in the day—gave me a mock bow, but just like back in the day, his grin was real as he responded. "Fancy meeting you here, Ms. Bree! So good of you not to do anyone a favor and turn out dead for real!" Yup, that was definitely the guy I remembered, if a little more ragged and worn-out than before, and, if not quite sober, not as tweaked out as his compatriots. The two younger scavengers taking position next to him were the ones I remembered from the ship up to New Angeles—Amos and Eden, if I remembered correctly. Actually, I vaguely remembered seeing most of them there, with Harris the single exception.

"Always a pleasure," I responded, not quite lying. Harris had turned out to be one of the good ones, and had helped us with our cover story once I'd fallen ill and decided to do that fateful trip up to the Silo. I'd assumed he had died in the altercations with the scavengers everyone had told me about, but that was obviously not the case.

"I must say, I'm almost offended that you didn't drop by for a visit," Harris went on, still using that soft drawl of his but now with a slight edge to his tone. "Almost like you didn't want to associate with us."

I briefly glanced at the Ice Queen to get a clue from her, but she was busy staring down the other present parties while everyone got ready for the upcoming parley, so I was on my own. Marleen sure seemed interested in what was going on here but since she wasn't a California native, she probably had no clue about any of this, either.

"Ah, you know how it goes," I offered to Harris, doing my best to appear way more relaxed than I felt. "After being on the road for so long, all I wanted was some chow and a soft bed, so I went to my folks first. Kinda relied on them to relay the good news, you know? After all, if you know someone competent to do the task, why not let them handle this?" No need to nod at the Ice Queen but I still did, since she must have been the one to get Harris involved.

Rather than more scowls, I got a downright jovial laugh from Harris. "Smart thinking, Ms. Bree. No surprise there since that has always been your strong suit. Letting others do the work for you, never a bad idea. But you'll have to come visit our splendid city, you and your husband, once we got him back. It's the place to be these days!"

And that was definitely a veiled threat—and I wasn't stupid enough to antagonize him now since we might as well depend on him later. "Sure thing," I offered as friendly as I managed, with his people still glaring daggers at me. Oh, that would be a visit for the ages. Suddenly, jumping over all the hurdles yet ahead of us didn't seem so bad as falling might come with some advantages, too—like avoiding that visit.

Harris took that with a nod and turned to his people, whispering what were likely commands, hopefully not to kidnap me. When I turned to the others, I found Marleen staring straight at me. "You know people," she surmised, more neutral than I would have expected, present company considered.

Glancing out at the bunch gathered for this not exactly clandestine meeting, I had to agree with her. "I do know people." Way more than I had expected, to be true.

Richards, clearly heading the army group, wasn't a surprise, and neither were Cole and Hill behind him. I even spotted Gallager in the background. I didn't know any of the other seven soldiers— all men—but the tall, bald guy next to Red looked both ready to chew through steel and quite unhappy to be here, and like he was someone who had an opinion as well. Since they usually were big about keeping their traps shut when their officers got up to shit, I presumed he was someone semi important—a sergeant maybe? At least that was my guess.

To their left, the marines were definitely from the Silo, and I knew five of the people gathered there, still more intent on glaring at the group on Red's other side than us, their not-quite fellow marines. It took me a few moments to remember his name, but Sgt. Blake hadn't really changed from when he'd been my silent shadow at my last stay at the Silo, before we'd decided that facing the music at the base in Canada was better than watching me rot away piece by piece. Sgt. Buehler next to him I remembered more favorably, since she'd helped Nate and me hide on the destroyer after coming back from France. I made a mental note to ask her what had become of the ship itself since I wasn't sure it could still be operational. My guess was that she and her people must have joined the other marines already at the Silo. And, lo and behold, I knew the three otherwise unremarkable guys lurking behind them as well, although the way they fit perfectly in with the entire bunch made me do a double take at first. True enough, those were Francis and his two friends who I'd not-so lovingly dubbed the Idiot Brigade who we'd met on that trek up to the Silo. Glancing briefly at Harris, I wondered if he'd recognized them as well but if so, he gave no indication. My plan had been to implant them at the Silo as possible moles for New Angeles. It stood to reason they hadn't been captured and kicked out if they were here now, but I had no idea if they'd changed their minds about me. Back then, they'd been pretty stoked to meet us, after I hadn't killed them for getting a little too close and personal with me. I had a feeling I'd soon know either way. As not to blow their cover, should it still be intact, I decided on letting them approach me—I had enough on my plate already as it was. The other five men I didn't recognize, neither from the Silo nor the destroyer.

That left the newcomers from the north—who Pia was mostly focused on—as the last remaining bunch I knew someone of, in this case their leader, who turned out to be none other than Rita herself. That also answered the question whether Dispatch was going to get involved. I'd wondered about that since she and Nate had been tight—a little too tight for my preference—and she had helped us, or at least Nate, on a few occasions. That she had no love lost for me wasn't a secret, but back when we'd been gunning for Colorado, she had seemed to at least respect me. Now, I had no clue. The same went for the woman by her side—Tamara, one of Dispatch's communications specialists and frequent radio hosts. I'd gotten drunk with her and her sister the one time we'd hit Dispatch. The next time we'd seen each other, they'd been less friendly. Now, she didn't even glance at me so I figured nothing much had changed—at least not for the better. With them were two men; the rest stayed in the cars, looking ready to bolt. Interesting.

Next to them, the seven people—two women and five men—were likely traders, judging from their mismatched outfits that ranged from worn-out fatigues to outdoor and hunting gear. They were well armed and alert but didn't seem to need to broadcast either. They'd kept farthest away from the posers, which further made me guess that they weren't too keen on associating with them. They had visibly perked up when Rita and her people had arrived, and took equal notice of us. Harris and his people they seemed to want to avoid, inching closer to the Dispatch group as they were.

Last were the glaring marines between us and Richards, who screamed "operator" to me to a "T"—from their uniform, dark fatigues to their behavior. I wouldn't have been surprised if we'd missed a good bit of chest pounding with our ahead-of-schedule but still-late arrival. Theirs was the smallest group with only five men, but they looked ready to rumble at any moment. They also kept glancing our way with disdain, so that boded well. I had a feeling that, should they join us for real, I'd get into some trouble with them within the first hour at a campfire. Too bad that Nate was going to miss this.

We all spent a good five minutes getting out of the cars, getting in prime posing positions, and staring at each other before everyone seemed ready to get this underway. Pia caught my eye, quietly raising her brows at me in question—how did I want to play this? Not at all, if I'd had that choice, but since that wasn't an option, I gave her a small nod to proceed. After all, she'd been the one who'd contacted the most groups from what I could tell, and while I doubted I would leave this meeting without putting my foot in my mouth, it was a good idea to let her start things off.

Taking a step forward from our haphazard bunch to both draw attention to herself and be able to look at everyone unhindered, the Ice Queen raised her voice. "Thank you all for coming here today. I presume nobody is still missing? Good. As you all know, the matter is time sensitive, so not wasting another couple of days waiting is a welcome change of pace for once."

There came some quiet murmurs from the traders, but everyone else was either too tense or too well trained to mess around. I couldn't help but crack a smile when I felt myself very tempted to turn to either Martinez or Marleen, between whom I'd ended up standing. When had Martinez sneakily positioned himself between me and Harris and his bunch? Our two guards had appeared there as well, while Sonia and Burns stood behind Pia.

"Should we do introductions first?" the Ice Queen proposed. "I assume most of you know who I am. I'm rather certain all of you know who she is." She paused to glance my way, which I rewarded with a big grin. I could have waved as well but there was already so much glaring going on that I didn't want to accidentally trigger anyone. Sheesh, this was going to get messy soon.

I'd expected Richards to speak up now, but one of the marines did, a wiry, bearded guy in his late forties. "We've already wasted enough time as it is, so let's get this underway quickly. MARSOC sent us, our qualification is none of your damn business." He then went nodding at each of the groups. "Army. Silo navy boot hill lickers." That drew scowls and near-silent sneering from both Buehler and Blake. "Dispatch." Which Rita accepted with a small nod. "Traders." He didn't wait for acknowledgement there before looking straight at Harris. "No fucking clue why anyone would invite you." And last, Pia. "And New Angeles." He said that with barely less belligerence than when he'd talked about Harris's bunch.

Keeping my eyes on him but leaning toward Martinez, I mouthed, "Do I need to know what MARSOC is?"

His snort was telling me he hadn't expected more of me—he knew me too well—but dutifully replied. "Marine Corps Forces Special Operations Command—their special forces branch. Don't garble the acronym or you'll make someone cry."

That, in turn, made me chuff with suppressed laughter, drawing a little too much attention from all around. Pia ignored me, although from the way she stiffened further, she wasn't happy we weren't as well-behaved as some of the others.

"I invited them because we need strength in numbers, and from what I can tell, neither of you is ready to provide anywhere near what we will need if we have to create a distraction. And you are mistaken—we are on our own, and have never acted as representatives of any city or faction except our own." Disdain was dripping from her clipped words, and she didn't leave time for him to respond. "To clear any further misunderstandings up ahead of time, you can and will refer to me as Zilinsky, no rank required. I am in active command of the rescue mission we have gathered here to plan. Please state your names for the record so every negotiator knows who they are to address."

Scowl Beard narrowed his eyes at Pia but ground out, without protest, "Scott."

Red went next with a rather neutral, "Richards," and Blake bit the bullet for the Silo people. I was a little surprised that Rita offered up, "Connel," only then realizing I'd completely spazzed out on her surname when someone must have told me before. The traders didn't offer a peep and Harris just grinned maniacally at everyone, which the Ice Queen ignored after a momentary glance in his direction. Marleen waved at Richards and Rita both, and only Richards seemed aware of it, quickly averting his eyes. I didn't ask; she still volunteered, "You know Rob, right? Such a cutie pie when you forget that he's probably constantly psychoanalyzing you. Not half bad in the sack, either. A bit of a slut, though."

I had to bite down hard on my tongue not to offer a candid, "Oh, you don't say?"—that probably wasn't needed judging from her brief, bright grin. I wondered if I should warn her not to get too comfy with him in front of Buehler, or maybe any number of other women. Or maybe it didn't seem necessary, considering that list pretty much boiled down to the Ice Queen, Sonia, me, and Rita— who was a mystery on that count but probably hadn't bumped uglies with Richards as he was likely too young to have been around before she'd dropped off the map.

Marleen wasn't done yet, still whispering in my ear. "That was a while ago, while he was ROTC in college. Do you need dirt on him?

Because I can tell you a few things that will make him go as red in the face as his hair is." She grinned and answered her question before I could. "Of course you do. Remind me later." Pia glaring at her made her shut up.

Turning to the gathered groups at large, the Ice Queen acknowledged, "Perfect. Who is actually here to fight? Because if anyone was wondering, those fine individuals over there are our support to bring additional provisions for us, and not part of our actual fighting strength." That explained why the traders hadn't even nominated a speaker. Scott looked downright offended at her insinuation as he raised a hand; Richards and Blake followed suit with no hesitation. Rita kept her arms crossed over her chest, making no move to volunteer anything. Harris kept on grinning, which nobody could have mistaken for disagreement. Pia did her best to ignore Rita, but I didn't need Marleen to lean over and stage-whisper, "Oh, trouble's a-brewin'," to know that this was the case.

Pia got ready for the next question, but halted when Buehler stepped up next to Blake, glaring toward Scott. As far as I could tell, she hadn't stopped since Scott had called them Wilkes's boot lickers. "Just to clarify for anyone who is stupid enough to listen to that clown, we are part of the over four hundred proud members of the US Marine Corps currently stationed at the Silo, and we cooperate with the less than fifty US Navy personnel who are running the day-to-day affairs but are in no way our command staff. In fact, we have been the ones who have worked diligently to keep up relations with both the army and the free agents in this country, often lending support or neutral ground for negotiations, while this is the first time since the shit hit the fan that I hear that, supposedly, there are still Marine special forces in the field. What exactly have you been doing that makes you puff up your chests like that while we've been on the ground, doing our jobs?"

Scott looked less than impressed with her tirade but voiced little of that. "We've been guarding the president," he offered. A round of murmurs rose, almost drowning out his much smaller amendment to, "Presidents."

I hated taking the reins out of Pia's hands but that one was too good not to jump on it. "We actually have a president? Or several, if I heard you right?"

One of the hulking figures next to Scott grumbled, "Hard to keep them alive if they keep dying on us." I must have let out a snort, or otherwise looked amused because his eyes narrowed. "Not that you'd know anything about that."

"Learning how to survive and kick ass? No, absolutely not," I offered, but chose to ignore him in favor of Scott. "What happened? I know I've been out of the loop for a while but I have a pretty good idea of what went down the summer of the apocalypse and the first year afterward. Why did we never hear anything about surviving politicians? And since when do the marines guard the president?"

I should maybe have dropped the last point unasked since more than one military member from our happy circle scowled my way, but the rest were valid questions—not that anyone seemed to care that I kept asking those.

Scott scratched his beard, not happy that I was—intentionally or not—questioning his competence. "The why is easy to explain—right place at the right time. I formed my team from competent members that I found through several steps of the evacuation process, and we ended up guarding one of the bunkers where then-vice president Thompson was waiting for further news from his family. The only news we ever got was that the secret service had gotten overwhelmed and lost fifty members of congress and the White House, including his three predecessors, so we took over from there. To you, the numbers may look like incompetence, but we've been battling assassination attempts since the first hour. We are right now on our Commander in Chief number fifteen."

I couldn't hold back a whistle. "That's quite a lot. Any idea where your leak is?"

His expression darkened further as he ground out, "We have suspicions. Danvers here is convinced that we've had attacks from several interested parties over the years."

Much to my surprise—but I probably should have seen this coming on some level—Marleen next to me spoke up. "You actually do, and on so many levels. Not to trash your conspiracy theories, but number twelve, Evans, was me. Very likely unrelated, so better disregard that entire fracas."

Scott looked ready to chew through stone—and several of the members of the other factions drew up short—but the fact that he didn't point any guns at Marleen or even tried to come after her told me a thing or two. Again, this was too good to drop.

"You killed a president?" I asked, not quite sure whether to settle on awe or derision.

She shrugged both emotions mingling in my tone off as if I'd accused her of double-dipping into our morning coffee reserves. "Trust me, I did the world a favor. I accepted that contract the week before everything went to shit, just before your husband contacted me and let me know that, just maybe, he'd need me on standby should that thing he had going on go south. Since there was no time bonus on the contract, I postponed it—and the rest is history."

Scott wasn't satisfied with that explanation. "He died three fucking months ago! Why do it now? Why do it at all, after everything that's happened?"

She gave him a look as if he'd just insulted her honor—which was probably true. "I was tempted to let bygones be bygones, but then I heard of his surprise nomination and figured, if he was going to make a grab for power, he had this coming. I don't have proof for it but my inside source gave me some good hints that he was likely to blame for number ten, eleven, and his two main competitors biting the dust. So, cry me a river." Marleen then turned to me, still chipper and very much unconcerned by the topic. "I took the hit because I got presented with evidence that he was an absolute bag of shit. Ick-factor level child molester, corrupt to the bone, and well-enough connected that he has been untouchable for over a decade. Don't spill a single tear for him."

That was easy to respond to, even with curiosity—and a latent sense of horror—still riding shotgun. "Not really tempted. I'm not known for being very compassionate with anyone, least of all assholes."

Marleen grinned and glanced back to Scott. "As I said, you have multiple moles and leaks in your operation, and your good man Danvers here is on to a few of them. You should listen to him more closely. If you play nice, I might even confirm a few of them later. Play your cards right, and you may hold on to number seventeen a little longer."

"What's with fifteen and sixteen?" Burns wanted to know.

Marleen made a throw-away gesture. "Already pretty much dead, unless we cause way more of a fuss than is good for us. Probably even if we do. Not our concern at the moment, trust me."

The guy who'd been hulking next to Scott—presumably the Danvers in question—turned around and stalked back to one of their two Humvees, presumably to radio the new information in. A few people looked after him, and Scott's glare made me guess that as soon as he could get his hands on Marleen's neck, he'd try to wring some answers out of her, but didn't speak up further—in her direction. Instead, he turned to fix Red with his glare. "Explain to me again why I let you talk me into coming here? Because so far, all I see are posers and madmen, and I have something better to do with my life than waste it like this."

I waited for Richards to say something. When he didn't, I waited for Pia to speak up, but she was studying the army bunch the same as I was. I even waited for Rita to offer her opinion but she in turn was glaring at us and Harris's scavengers.

Looked like I would have to be the one to do the deed—oh joy.

Taking a step forward so I was right next to the Ice Queen, I cleared my throat, getting way more attention than I felt comfortable with, and not just because I got the sense that nobody wanted to be here. Last time I'd done something like this had gone so phenomenally well—what could possibly go wrong?

"The way I see it, we all have a common problem. And if we leave all the bullshit behind, we can all admit that yes, that problem exists, and yes, somebody needs to do something about it. That's why we're here, even if some of our motives may be different. So why don't we tackle that first and maybe we won't have to go into detail on the crap that really doesn't concern anyone else who isn't neck-deep in it?"

Rita let out a derisive snort. "So you're the voice of reason now?"

I smiled briefly. "Trust me, the irony of that isn't lost on me. And, like most of you, I don't want to be here and I have very little reason to trust any of you or want to cooperate with you, but why don't we at least pretend to be adults and talk about it?"

Blake and Richards looked close to agreeing with me, but Scott obviously didn't. "I couldn't give less of a shit about what happens to your husband, and I will not let any of my men get killed to rescue a traitor."

I was a little surprised that I wasn't even mad at him; dealing with Bucky Hamilton for weeks had apparently turned me into a better person. Who would have thought?

"But you clearly give a shit about something, and just maybe, you'll need my husband to take out the trash? And me, and our people, because believe it or not, we're a package deal. Just had a good reason not to get too tied up with each other over the past years." I made a point to look at each group before addressing all of them. "None of you brought anywhere near enough people for what I need, and you know that—and still, you are here. Let's hear it. What's your why?"

Rita was the first to speak up, again surprising me, but then nothing here seemed to go according to plan. "A word of advice? Tuck your tail between your legs, turn around, and go back to wherever you've been hiding from the world for the past years," she offered, her eyes zeroed in on my face. "With luck, it's not too late to save yourself. Right now, you're just a blip on someone's radar. Don't become a signal."

Ah, and there it was—the hint I had been waiting for. And not just me, judging from how Scott perked up. Since he didn't demand clarification, I spoke up instead.

"That's cold, even for your standards. I mean, I'd have expected you to feed me to the wolves if it was my ass grounded in that slaver camp, but Miller's? And here I thought he was one of the few people you still cared about, and one of only two who could actually understand you. Guess since Hamilton—the other one so lucky—bit it, you're all about letting others clean up after you?"

Her mouth twisted into a thin line, and she definitely didn't like being called out like that, but also didn't refute my accusation. I would have considered that interesting except that this was the one thing I didn't want confirmation for. Fucking Decker…

But maybe I was wrong. Maybe this was about something else entirely, like her being afraid Nate would try to usurp her standing in Dispatch, or become more of a nuisance than I had been when I'd called for a crusade, or whatnot. I didn't know her well enough to take a guess.

As it turned out, I didn't need to, since she was all too happy to explain. "Don't be so fucking dense, Bree. It's no coincidence that they found you, and that you got away. It's a last warning. Heed it. You don't want to bear the consequences, trust me."

If she really thought that would deter me, she knew me even less well than I knew her. I didn't bother with checking in with Pia, but instead cocked my head to the side, striking a considering pose. "If that's true—and I'm not convinced it is, but let's pretend you're right—that would mean that Decker already has his claws in his favorite pet. That's not something I want to consider and still be able to sleep well. Shouldn't you be calling for us to go hunt him down and kill him if there's a chance that someone brainwashed my husband?"

While I had addressed her directly, I watched the others for reactions. I got none from the scavengers nor the traders, and Richards and his people hadn't given me anything back in France, either, but several of the Silo marines gave a little jerk—as did Scott. It was he who finally asked the relevant question.

"Who the fuck is this Decker guy?"

His mistake was that he asked me rather than Rita, so all I could do was shrug. "Wish I knew? It's kind of funny to collect all the rumors of rumors people tell each other, but not very satisfying. It's almost as if he wasn't real."

"Oh, he is real," Rita ground out, taking my bait hook, line, and sinker, which in itself told me just how much the topic was a trigger for her. I still had no clue how she had been involved in all this, but what Martinez had told me about her trying to commit suicide made it pretty obvious that Nate's reaction to hearing that Decker was still alive wasn't a fluke, or something that had come out of nowhere.

Since she didn't offer up more, I had to goad her on further. "And you really think that he's behind that slaver camp? Sounds a little far-fetched to me."

Rita looked less than amused by my dismissal. "You think? Guess again. Just look around, at what the world has become. Do you think that if he was just a ghost story, the world would have turned into a free-for-all, real-life death match?"

As easy as it was for me to dismiss her first guess, hearing that made my blood run cold. Scott reacted a little more irreverently, cursing under his breath before adding, louder, "Yeah, right. Because one single guy, however well-connected, has that much influence, and in a world where you can easily go weeks without meeting another human soul."

"He doesn't need that much direct influence," I pointed out, deciding to run with it. When Scott's glare turned to me, I shrugged. "I still don't buy that the slaver camp is connected to him, or at least not the part that they got to us. That's a hundred percent on us, rookie-level mistake, I hate to admit." When Rita looked ready to tell me I was full of shit, I laughed softly. "They caught me while taking a shit, at night, in the woods. I'd love to say it's the only time anyone caught me with my pants around my ankles but it's not. Not my point—they clearly expected heavy opposition, and they came packing for that. We gave them a good fight, but there's only so much two people can do. But that's exactly my point—they expected someone, not us. They had no clue who we were, and they made it disturbingly easy for me to get away. When we were in France, I was stupid enough to give Hamilton, Richards, and their soldiers a good look at what I'm capable of, and I'm pretty sure that had anyone in that camp known it was me, they wouldn't have been stupid enough to pretty much leave the door unlocked for me to walk out."

Buehler, across the ring of mostly silent onlookers, cleared her throat. "That's what they did?" She sounded appropriately doubtful.

"Well, not exactly," I offered, hard-pressed not to massage my right hand. "But they drugged me, cuffed me to a bed, and tried to beat the shit out of me. Do you have any idea how fucking stupid you need to be to do that to someone who already has serious anger management issues when she has her full mental capacity? I'd love to entertain you with all the gory details, but I pretty much ran on autopilot after that first punch hit, and woke up the next day covered in blood from head to toe, up on a branch in a tree. Even those of you who don't think I'm a homicidal bitch wouldn't have been that negligent." No protests came up, and a few of the soldiers behind Richards looked impressed. Apparently, someone had already updated the file they had on me—just as I'd predicted. Scott looked less impressed, but I had a feeling I'd have to pull weirder stunts to accomplish a change there.

Turning back to Rita, I paused for a moment, considering. "I do think you're right that it was a warning. A warning I'm not going to heed, because I'll be damned to let the man I love rot away in a deep, dark hole. If by doing this I'm turning the blip I am into a steady signal on anyone's radar, so be it. Maybe that's exactly what the world needs—a signal."

Rita continued to glare at me, and I thought I recognized Cole's voice that murmured from over there, "And here we go again."

I forced my focus to remain with Rita instead. "Is that the only reason you came? To warn me? Message received. You can go now." That dismissal must have grated, and I could tell that she was itching to physically fling herself at me and punch me in the face, but she had considerably more self-control than I could have mustered. That realization also gave me pause—and part of me was tempted to ask how she managed that feat—but only for so long.

Turning back to the others, I spread my arms wide so my following shrug was oddly exaggerated. "Do I love making myself into a martyr, again? Fuck, no! But someone has to do something, and from what I can tell, the only thing you or the factions you represent have done is stick your heads in the sand and slam your doors shut to ignore that everyone else out there is dying. And there I thought the zombies would be our real problem going forward, naive that I am sometimes. Great job you've done serving the greatest country in the world, like most of you probably swore at one time or another." I sure as hell deserved the hostility I got for that from all sides—including Sonia and Burns—but since the highway wasn't an option, I had to do it my way. "Don't like hearing that? Well, I don't see anyone protest that it's true nevertheless. How about we change something about that before it's too late?"

Glances were exchanged and a few murmurs rose, but dropped away as soon as Rita offered a cold, hard laugh. "You think we're selfishly ignorant?" she said, taking a look around but mostly focusing on me. "Let me tell you something, Bree." She spit my name out as if it was a slur. Maybe to her, it was. "The only reason why Dispatch still stands is because I did exactly that—at the first sign of danger, we closed ranks, we sealed everything tightly, and made sure that we minded our own fucking business. Wilkes did the exact same thing with the Silo, only that he was smart enough to use that—and the influx of able people—to increase his offensive strength to achieve true independence once more." I didn't miss that her gaze briefly dropped to Red, underlining whose influence the silo's commander had greatly limited. "Think I'm lying? Look what Greene got for trying to be a middle ground. And look how he and everyone else in New Angeles scurried when they got their docks blown up. Not a day later, the city's security was as tight as a virgin's asshole, and has remained like that ever since. All of us got the message, loud and clear. Only you're too optimistic to see it for what it really is. I warned them, and they listened. What do you have to say to that?"

All I had for her was a tight smile. "Well, you knew Decker personally, back in the day. You'd know his MO."

No audible gasps went through the gathered ranks, but I could tell that a few of the people—like Scott—suddenly got a lot more interested in what Rita had to say. Her eyes narrowed, and it was quite obvious that any goodwill she'd ever had toward me was gone now. Too bad—I really felt like bawling my eyes out over the loss.

"You fucking conniving little bitch," she spit out, not quite taking a step toward me but looking like she really wanted to. "You think you can throw me under the bus like that? Well, guess again. Everyone here knows how much power I have—as in, actual manpower. If I don't make it home, there will be hell to pay, and no one here wants to risk that. You know what? Not everyone will be as lenient as Hamilton was when he had the perfect chance to kill you without even getting his own hands dirty. Someone, and likely very soon, will get you, and that will be a great day indeed."

I didn't miss the "I know what you did that winter" threat in her words, but didn't give two shits about it. Knowing where she stood was worth the price my ego had to pay for that. So much for counting on Dispatch on being our backbone—or at least our eyes and ears—once more.

"Well, good for you," I offered as jovially as I could—which was likely pretty close to a growl—before I pulled myself up to my full height, addressing the others, mostly the marines and army soldiers between them. "I'm not saying to go and get her so we can beat the answers out of her. She knows something, but nothing that we need for this mission—or whatever else will come after it. Because, let's cut to the chase. You're all here because you know exactly who my husband is, and what he's capable of. You also know that there's something very, very wrong with how this formerly great nation is developing. You want to help me free my husband because you know you will benefit from him being an active asset in the field. None of you have a pure heart and do it out of good will without ulterior motives—but, quite frankly, I don't give a shit about any of that. You want our cooperation, and you will get it, provided I get Nate Miller back first. It doesn't really matter why everything is going to shit, and if we start blaming each other, we won't be done until hell freezes over with still no resolution in sight, so let's just not go there. State your business and your requirements, and then we can negotiate a deal. Otherwise…" I made a great deal out of turning to face Harris, smiling sweetly at him. "Harris, can you give me two hundred men and women mad enough to follow my lead, quite possibly to watch the world burn?"

The way his people looked back at me, eyes too wide and too bright, gave me the creeps, but so did his answer. "Thought you'd never ask," he drawled, giving me a very fatherly nod. "Of course, Ms. Bree. Your wish is my command."

I couldn't help the triumphant grin that wanted to plaster itself onto my face. Not the ideal solution, but I'd take it. "How soon can you get them ready so we can go after that slaver camp?"

Harris's enthusiasm didn't so much falter as fold. Uh-oh. "That may be a problem."

I didn't miss the smirk on Scott's face, but I'd be damned if I let this bring me down. "Why, is that where you're getting your drugs from?"

Harris didn't respond, obviously not happy with my accusation, but Marleen took that moment to pipe up. "Actually, that's good news."

"How so?"

My question—or the doubt in my voice—made her chortle. "Oh, you're all the same. Always flinging massive numbers at massive numbers for maximum casualties. No offense, I like a good bloodshed, but not necessarily when I'm involved. And since we've already established that we lack numbers, it would be foolish to try. Infiltration's the way to go, baby!"

That was something that seemed to work much better for Harris. "They won't be suspicious if we come with more than two or three cars," he offered, grinning. The tobacco stains on his crooked teeth didn't make it a pretty picture. "We sometimes drop by for some R&R. Can't get all of you mighty warriors in at once, but a couple? No problem."

It wouldn't have surprised me to see Marleen jumping up and down from how giddy she suddenly appeared. "It's the perfect solution, don't you see? Get ten people in, who can in turn leave gates unlocked and distract guards. And finally get the recon done that you have neglected to do yourself."

I felt like pointing out that just staying alive—and getting out— had been a true feat, but there really was no point to this. The more I considered, the better the plan sounded. It stood to reason that this had really been the Ice Queen's reason for calling on Harris, rather than having to deal with more of his people. Now I just had to convince the others.

Looking around, I asked, "A show of hands please—who here has spies in that slaver camp?"

At first, nobody wanted to admit it, but then Richards raised a hand, followed by Blake, and soon Scott as well. Rita, too, but I ignored her. Pia's arms remained crossed in front of her chest, and I could tell that annoyed the fuck out of her. Smiling pleasantly at the other three cooperative groups, I gave a curt nod. "Sounds about right to me. So it's a solid plan."

Scott gave me a look as if I'd finally gone insane. "There's no plan whatsoever, and even less a solid one," he spat.

I shrugged off his criticism. "Sure, we need to work out the details, but the framework is set. Someone from each group comes in with the scavengers. We do recon, we touch base with the spies who will know all the details we need to know. We send someone back out to alert the others and let them in. We find our objective, and we leave. Unless I'm missing something here, it's a pretty solid, straight-forward mission." And so very unlike anything I'd ever been a part of. I was well aware of that, and I was sure that, as soon as we were among ourselves once more, Pia would lay out all the many, many things that could—and therefore would—go wrong. But that didn't change the fact that, suddenly, the future looked a lot less glum than this morning.

"That's the shittiest plan I've ever heard," Scott grated, only to be interrupted by Harris.

"It's a great idea," he insisted. "And never you soil your panties over their strength in numbers. If you disregard all the working personnel, and the civilians, there are less than four hundred guards and fighters in that camp. They are dug in like ticks and could mobilize a good thousand strong for assault defenses, but nobody will give a shit if a few people come or go. We never had any issues with them, unlike with other fine examples of civilized folks." The way he glared at Rita made it obvious who he was talking about—which surprised me a little, considering I'd have expected that animosity toward the bunch from the army.

Sheesh, even my grudges had become outdated!

Blake and Buehler exchanged a few hushed words before Blake gave me a nod. "It's not a solid plan, but it's less hare-brained than what we've dreaded someone might propose." The way he glared in Scott's direction made it obvious who he was referring to.

Scott, of course, couldn't let that slide. "Because you've offered up so many useful suggestions? Oh, right—that would be none."

As amusing as their bickering was, it didn't exactly help the general climate of our negotiations. Richards seemed to think along the same lines, physically stepping forward to break the line of sight between the two groups. "Can you keep your personal animosities out of this for the time being? We get it—you're a house divided. But for this, we need unity."

Blake appeared borderline chastised, but Scott wasn't ready to let go yet. "Yeah, you're one to talk. Your own bullshit ended in not one but several waves of civil war."

Richards didn't even look at me—or Harris—as he fixed Scott with a hard stare. "Whatever the nature of the ensuing issues has been, we've always been one united front."

That made me perk up—and not just me, judging from Martinez muttering under his breath, "Wrong move." Of course I couldn't let that one pass.

"You sure about that, Richards?" I called across the wide open space between them and the rest of us. Suddenly, it made a lot of sense to have us, the scavengers, traders, and Rita's bunch on one side of the circle, and the others over there. "Because last time I checked, a few things happened that might make me rather disinclined to work with you. Or has your narrative changed in the meantime? Does the US Army now support raping and killing women for the sake of science and some asshole's personal amusement?"

Only when I saw Scott chuckle did I realize it had been a trap— and I got the well-deserved condescension from Richards for it, if only in the form of a bland look. "I thought you'd finally buried that hatchet?" he rasped.

I answered that with a shrug. "It's a rather shallow grave." The Ice Queen seemed rather amused by my admission, but I didn't miss the hint of exasperation crossing her expression. Message received—I couldn't call the others to order and misbehave myself. So I did what nobody likely expected of me—and dropped the point. "But you are right—our shared, common goal has been to support the people whichever way we can manage it. Yes, there have been setbacks, and we've had the odd bad egg to deal with. I've worked with you in the past, and I'm ready to do so again, provided you are here to turn things around. As I said before, that should be our goal. Any objections? Because if we keep running in circles, nothing will change, least of all for the better."

I got a lot of grim, haughty looks back, but no objections. That boded well.

"This is my signal to go," Rita offered. "I've tried to warn you. You won't listen. My hands are clean." She glanced over to the trader group. "If you want to, you can hitch a ride with us. I know you think you're safe with those four vehicles of yours, but once you get rid of most of your weapons and ammo, you're just another target like any other out there. And we all know that just because some people hold grandiose speeches of unity and peace doesn't mean others will listen." Harris ignored the side-eye she gave him and his people.

The leader of the traders looked conflicted enough that I wondered if my previous alignment with Harris was clouding my judgment whether we could trust him, but decided to trust Pia instead. She wouldn't have pulled strings to make this happen if she didn't think we'd need it, and come out on top. She didn't look happy with Rita's declaration, but left the traders all of a second to waver in their conviction.

"You should go with them," she pointed out. "We owe you for bringing provisions. We won't demand you risk your lives on top of that." She turned to the two guards next to her. "Kepler, Halecki, coordinate with them so that they can leave as soon as possible."

As if that had been a signal, our neat circle started to disperse, leaving the marines and Richards as they had already settled down with tents and all. Turning to Marleen, I found her grinning at me with anticipation. "Oh, this is going to be fun!" she enthused. "I just know it!"

Somehow I doubted that—but nothing I could do about that now. Time would tell.

Chapter 18

Prep work ate up another astounding five days, most of which I spent either sitting around, bored out of my mind, or bickering with one uncooperative faction or another. And once everyone was ready with all potential backup about to arrive and contingency plans laid out, it turned out we weren't as united as I liked to believe as well when it got to selecting who would be among the first wave of infiltrators to hitch a ride with Harris. That I would be going was obvious—but that left a few open spaces in the car, red, white, and black paint all over it drying at the moment. And it wasn't like it was an easy decision.

Before the accident that had seriously threatened his health, my first choice would have been Andrej. He was one of Nate's closest friends, he was one of our heavy bruisers, his accent and behavior didn't scream Army Boy from ten miles away, and I had a certain feeling this wasn't even the hundredth time he'd done something like this. Problem was, Zilinsky had barely let him come along, and the fact that he had a permanent limp and severely hampered depth perception because of losing an eye wasn't making him a perfect candidate.

Pretty much the same was true for Martinez, although he was in somewhat better physical shape. He also insisted that it was highly likely Nate might need his expertise. I agreed, but Zilinsky was right when she tartly told him that he'd be of much more use back in our forward position where he could set up a triage station and help others who might get injured as well. I was surprised that she didn't call out his physical shortcomings, but then I was likely benefitting of the same somewhat softer approach she seemed to have adopted.

Marleen was another point of contention. "I'm coming with you," she said in a tone that left no room for doubt. And far was it from me to protest, but Pia had other ideas.

"I need you for analysis of the recon intel we get," she let the spunky assassin know.

Marleen wasn't impressed hearing that. "Anyone can analyze intel. But I'm your best infiltrator," she insisted. "And I'm a free agent. Who says I let you boss me around?"

Both then looked at me, seeking support. I threw my hands up, taking a step back. "Woah, hold your horses! I'm not getting into this. You decide this on your own."

Now the Ice Queen looked pissed at me, which wasn't lost on Marleen. Rather than further antagonize her, Marleen switched tracks. "You have no spies in there. And just because I go with the first group doesn't mean I can't be around after we've collected all the information we can get. Finding a quick, secure exit route is part of my plan. I'm quite happy to test-drive it as well. And this way, I won't have to rely on anyone's recount but I can see things firsthand." The look she cast the Ice Queen turned considering. "Actually, I'd go as far as to say you need me inside that camp. Who are you going to rely on, huh? Her?" I pointedly raised my brows when Marleen looked at me. She gave me a quick smile but otherwise ignored me. "Her one and only concern is to find her husband. Which is great because she has the most motivation to get him out, so she will be best-suited to find him and get him to safety. But that means she will miss a ton of clues and other things. Also, last time I looked, she was a scientist and semi-proficient fighter, not an intel gatherer. You need someone who knows what to look for, not bumble her way through it. I'm all for using a drunken monk-style in hand-to-hand combat if it will give me an edge over my opponent, but you wouldn't send an actual drunk monk into a death match."

Pia considered her words, which gave me time to speak up. "Are you done insulting me yet?"

Marleen gave me a curious look, as if she didn't get what I was referring to. "I'm not insulting you. I'm stating facts. Wouldn't be an insult if I said you're not my first choice for a rock-climbing expedition, either. Check your ego, bitch. It's showing—and it will get you killed if you let it dictate your every action," she wisely advised. "We already have far too many assholes around who are solely motivated by the next chance to compare dick sizes. If nothing else, it's your responsibility to use your brain instead."

I almost missed the grin that crossed Pia's expression, and my venomous glare seemed close to provoking a repeat incident. She finally nodded, which was all Marleen needed to accept her victory with a similar gesture. "Great, that's two of us. Who gets the other two seats?"

Pia cast a look around but quickly returned her attention to me. "Burns is a good option. I'm surprised you haven't suggested him yet." It was obvious that she left out the accusation that came with the question.

I felt a tad defensive as I crossed my arms over my chest. "If you're insinuating that I'm passing him over because of Sonia, it's not that. But I presume they are a package deal, and they will be much more useful as backup for the second wave. Burns isn't exactly the most incongruous guy. People know him. People remember and recognize him. I'll be very happy to have him at my back when I need someone to have it, but for sneaking around, he might not be my number one option."

"Number two," Marleen offered. "I'm your number one."

I felt like rolling my eyes at her—hadn't she just accused me of making everything into a popularity contest?—but instead looked around for other options. "What's with your old guard? Rozen, Cohn, and Calveras all look like they know what they're doing."

Pia shook her head. "They do, but I want them as backup."

"Care to explain why?"

Her glare told me I shouldn't need to ask, but when I didn't back down, she let out an exasperated sigh. "I need someone committed to the cause. Committed enough that if they get caught, they can and will hold out long enough that backup can arrive."

"You mean, withstand torture?" My, wasn't that a great consideration, warming my heart and soul.

Pia didn't bat an eyelash. "I'm not exactly planning for it, but it's a possibility. I'm surprised you haven't done so yet."

I had, on some level—but not this in-your-face. "Santos and Clark," I said, not needing to give it much more thought. "They are both fit enough, and they have skin in the game where Nate is concerned. I've heard Santos on more than one occasion boast that if Nate hadn't approached him at the barricade at the bridge in Lexington, he'd have been dead minutes later. And Clark is one tenacious mofo." That reminded me of something I hadn't gotten around to asking yet. "What became of his flirting with that one-legged dog trainer from that town where we traipsed into Taggard's trap? I'm kind of surprised I didn't see her in California." That had been one tough broad—and nice, too, not a combination found too often.

Pia's hint of a smile alleviated some of my latent fears. "She's taken up residence in Utah," she explained. "Minerva made her an offer too good to refuse. She's now training others to train more dogs. And wolves, too, from what Clark has told me. They use them for hunting and as guard dogs outside the settlement. Dogs are way better than humans at smelling decay, and they can't get infected. He came down to us when he heard you were about to show up. Good choice. Santos, too. I'll let them know."

It was only then that I realized she'd actually let me decide. Now that she was confirmed on the team, Marleen made herself scarce again, leaving me to follow the Ice Queen on her trek across our haphazard basecamp. "Care to explain what that was all about?" I asked when I was sure Marleen was out of earshot.

Pia didn't miss a step but took a moment to judge my reaction as she stalked on. "It's about time you're in command for real, not just in name," she tartly responded. "Either step down, or take responsibility. You can't pick and choose forever. I'll always be there to help you make decisions, but you have the final word."

Her words almost made me stumble, and I had to run a few steps to catch up with her again. "I don't get it. Why now? Not that I'm protesting. You've all had opportunity enough for five lifetimes to chase me around. I'm more than ready for some payback."

She came to a halt, both so I could catch up, and to fix me with a quite potent glare. "Bree, you are aware that even if Miller is still alive, and even if we get him out, there's a good chance that he's in no condition to do anything but recover for a while? Who do you think will be running this shit-show then?"

That was a sobering thought. Again, nothing exactly new, but somehow it had taken her statement for the reality of it to really sink in. "You think it's going to be that bad?"

She hesitated, which made me stomach sink further. "What I think is of no consequence," she finally supplied. "My job is to plan for any and all eventualities. Do I hope he's his usual chipper and capable self? Yes. Do I expect it? More likely is a somewhat tarnished-around-the-edges version of it. We both know he's a tough bastard, and he's easily motivated by revenge and redemption. And, just like you, he can't show weakness unless he absolutely has to. But even so, his job will be easier if he can rely on you to not just be a rambunctious sidekick but his equal partner in crime. Whatever you like to tell people, you were barely more than a figurehead when we went after the assholes in Colorado. This time around, be the leader you were meant to be."

Trust it to her to give me both an inspirational pep-talk and knock me down a few notches. Her confidence in me did a few things for my ego, but I'd heard enough caution from Nate—and acquired first-hand experience—to know this being-a-leader gig didn't come with positives only.

Our established camp was still a good three hundred miles from our destination—far enough away that no random patrols should stumble over us, but close enough that we could get there within two days. It had been Richards who had suggested that the first wave of infiltrators head straight to the slaver camp rather than help establish our forward base—that way, they could only torture directions out of us, and not the actual location. I really didn't care for the implication, but it was smart thinking. It also meant that today was the last time I'd be surrounded by people I trusted with my life—later this afternoon, once we hit the road, things would be very different.

I couldn't wait to get started.

We ended up settling on eight cars—one from us, one with Richard's people, and one from the marines each, leaving four vehicles full of scavengers. Pia had offered the remainder of Harris's people to stay with them since none of the other groups seemed ready to put up with them. It wasn't hard to see why—or hear, or smell, or guess in general. If not for how much time we'd lost already, I would have called for more planning to maybe find another way. But as it was, we had no time, and no one had miraculously thought of something else, so pretending to be a bunch of unwashed savages it was.

We took our leave in the afternoon, with time aplenty to get the first hundred miles down. We had enough provisions since we only had to plan for a maximum of three days on the road. A lot of our real gear was left with the base camp, same as weapons and surplus ammo. Since we had no idea how much of what we brought would remain with us, it was better to go in reasonably light, if packing enough that we could defend ourselves. Scott and the two operators he'd brought with him had protested vehemently, but they, more than I myself at least, should have seen that this made sense. Even with trying to dress down, they still stood out the most; Richards and his guys weren't much behind, though. Cole, Hill, and Gallager had remained behind so the three men he'd brought instead were as much a mystery to me as Scott, but they behaved about as stupid as the marines. Their antics had made me borderline apprehensive of stopping for the night, but Buehler and her people were a welcome surprise, blending in just as well as Santos, Clark, and Marleen. Thankfully, Harris turned out to have more command over his rabble than I'd been afraid of from what I'd heard about them so far, but that wasn't saying much. I instantly missed Pia as we made camp, and it took all of five minutes for the first fight to start.

Well, at least we didn't look like a group of highly trained professionals.

Getting some hot food helped establish peace eventually, and the two bottles of moonshine making the rounds further quieted dissatisfied voices. I was just about to relax when Richards dropped down next to me on the log that I was abusing for a bench, not even waiting for an invitation.

"You know that they'll sniff us out if we stay segregated like this?" he stated, pointedly looking at the—clearly kept-apart—groups around our two small fireplaces.

"Why? Miss hitching a ride with me?" I asked, well aware that we'd never actually been part of anything, not even a fire team, except for when he'd helped me drag Nate's lifeless body out of the lab.

Richards inclined his head nevertheless. "Actually, I'm here because of that. You and me, we should stick together. One of my men will establish contact with our people on-site, so I'm free to lend a hand if you need it."

"Hardly."

If my immediate rebuke surprised him, he didn't show it. "You can't waltz in there with your people," he pointed out. "They will jump to the right conclusions if they find the same tats on all three of you. Her?" He glanced over at where Marleen was busy joking around with Buehler and her marines, next to Santos and Clark. How had I managed to end up on my own, I wondered? I'd obviously set myself up for this. Richards going on drew my attention back to him. "We can take her along, but I think she works best on her own. But you and me, we're a team."

I was about to protest, but then thought better of it. "That part of my husband's contingency plans as well?"

Red shrugged, not quite denying my accusation. "Not outright, but I think he would prefer you to have someone around who may very well keep unwanted attention at bay."

That very idea made me guffaw. "Really? You're volunteering to be my knight in shining armor?"

"More like meat shield, if you need one, but you make it sound a lot more valiant," Richards joked. At least I hoped he was joking.

Did I want to stick with my people? Yes, but he had a point. He was also a head taller than either Clark or Santos, and that might come in handy in a crowd. Santos and Clark were a well-oiled machine working together, and there was a chance I might throw them off as a third wheel. Maybe I should have thought of that first. I realized the only reason I was protesting was because Red had been the one to approach me, not the other way round, and even on my worst day I could admit that this wasn't a good enough reason to decline his offer.

"Very well, you and me as a team it is. Your people are going to be okay with that, I presume?"

I grinned at the hint of condescension leaking into his expression. "That's what orders are for," he observed succinctly.

I was just about to ask how we would do that with the cars when Harris came sauntering over, followed by my two favorite scavengers, Amos and Eden. They still had yet to speak a single word to me since the docks at New Angeles, but I'd caught them staring at me on more than one occasion. It seemed suspicious to have them trailing him now. At least their open hostility had decreased somewhat.

"Mighty fine to find the two people I need to talk to already involved in conversation," Harris drawled as he rocked to a halt in front of us.

"What's up?" I hoped that sounded sunny enough. I still didn't quite know what to make of all of them, and now was not the time to add dissent to the already volatile mix.

Harris's smile broadened—not very assuring. "We need to make sure that you don't all stick out like sore thumbs. Nobody would want to get caught right at the gate."

I didn't try to hide my confusion. "We've painted the cars and downgraded our gear wherever possible. Feel free to try to get that stick out of Scott's ass that keeps him from behaving like a normal person. I've tried. I won't try again."

Chuckling softly, Harris shook his head. "Your gear is fine. We'll sell them some bull about having gotten our grubby hands on some prime merch a few weeks ago. That's not the problem. But you're the problem."

Not the first time someone told me that. Cocking my head to the side, I squinted at him. "Me specifically, or me as a general entity?"

That did a thing or two to confuse him, but Harris shook that off a moment later. "You as in your entire bunch of stuck-up, look-down-your-noses, yessiree do-gooders."

"You're not making any sense whatsoever," I told him rather emphatically.

Red, ever the smart cookie, answered before Harris could. "He means we're too sober to blend in."

Just that moment, Buehler let out a shriek of laughter that told a different story, but I got the sense he wasn't talking about the booze making the rounds. "Not really much we can do about that, for at least half of us," I pointed out.

I really didn't like how Harris was grinning now. "And this is where you're wrong, Ms. Bree," he was happy to inform me. "The truly good stuff cuts through that mighty fine serum you're all so proud of. We might have to tweak the dosage a little, but double the whammy should even send one of you fine specimens to your knees."

"And we want that?" I tried to keep my hands still, but I felt my left one tremble ever so slightly. Yup, still rocking the after-effects of that shit—I had no intention whatsoever to get any chemicals into my system, even if they weren't designed to knock me out or leave me helpless, presumably.

Harris sure looked very gleeful about his proposition. "If you want to get into the camp, and not get picked out right at the gate, you will want to fit in perfectly with us. No worries. I've told my fine fighters a week ago to lay off the high doses so that you'll only need to take a small hit to blend in."

"And by that you mean all of us?" I asked.

He nodded. "Sure thing."

I really didn't like this, but I doubted he'd suggest this just to spite us. After all, they were losing out on whatever we were consuming. "One dose only," I agreed.

"No can do," Harris was quick to inform me. When I frowned, he raised his hands in defense. "I'm sure that a woman of such keen senses as you, Ms. Bree, has noticed that unless we've hit up very recently, most of our fine warriors display certain signs of…" He trailed off, casting around for the right word.

"Withdrawal symptoms?" I suggested sweetly.

"Close enough," Harris admitted. "Although you'll soon see that's not quite it. You will also do well with some extra time to get accustomed to the sensation. I say you hit up now, and again tomorrow before we get going. No worries, my folks know how to drive under the influence well so we'll take over driving the vehicles. I've wanted to talk to you about splitting your groups up, as well. Didn't sound like a smart move when we were still in the camp, but it will help a lot."

Richards had remained mostly mute next to me. He only offered up a shrug when I turned to look at him now. "Do I like the idea of being high with my men split up over several vehicles, hitching rides with people whose affiliations I'm somewhat dubious about? Not exactly. But he's right. We need to fit in, and it's the easiest way to reach the camp. What's the worst that can happen? We lose a day or two in there before we're sober enough to operate."

"Or we get caught at the gate, and executed on the spot because of who we really are," I suggested. "And that's the best-case scenario."

Surprisingly, Amos found his voice to interject. "Won't happen. Just like you, they tolerate us, but they never completely trust us. So they leave us the fuck alone once they've made sure we're legit. Eden here has tangled with the guards a few times, and never turned out to be a problem. They'd likely get suspicious if you're all too meek and well-behaved. That'll get you killed."

I still wasn't convinced. "I don't exactly have a history of doing well on stimulants." I caught Richards grinning faintly to himself, making me guess that, one way or another, he was already privy to this information that I was about to share. "Ever heard of my grand stand that ended in the truce with these idiots at the Colorado base? I was fucking tripping balls, and that was just the damn booster that should have let me run a little longer and lift a little easier. It's been weeks since I got away from this damn camp, and I still get the tremors. I'm less concerned that I will make an ass of myself and more with turning into a homicidal maniac hell-bent on cutting a literal swath through the masses until I find what I'm looking for."

Amos actually seemed impressed while Harris did his best to alleviate my concerns. "The Glimmer, it works differently, no worries. You may feel a slight sense of euphoria, and some impressions are, well, way more impressive than without, but it's not going to turn you into a hyperactive killer squirrel. Might actually mellow you out, going on what I've seen you do in the past. And if you take the first hit now, you'll have the entire night to see how you react. Trust me when I tell you that I've thought of everything."

There was so much about this that I felt like objecting to. That Harris's suggestion didn't really surprise me that much didn't help. At all. But that didn't change the fact that I kind of agreed with them.

"Looks like we should go over the plan once more before we do this," I said when nothing else came to mind to prevent it. Richards nodded his agreement. Harris grinned.

This was so going to turn into a shit storm, I just knew it.

Chapter 19

It turned out, I had been wrong—the Glimmer, whatever it was, didn't completely turn me into a psychopath, and the marines didn't wholeheartedly threaten me with mutiny, but both were a closer call than I liked to admit. It took a good two hours of heated debating until everyone had agreed to take the drugs, and as soon as the shit hit my lungs and thus got into my blood, things got really weird. It definitely wasn't like what they'd tried to subdue me with at the camp before—and nothing like weed, which had been my first guess since the application worked about the same. But the fine powder didn't look like it came from dried and ground-up plants. My guess was that someone had gotten their grubby hands on a chemistry textbook and started cooking up their own versions of whatever cool stuff they'd seen on TV once. I vaguely remembered the organic chemistry lab I'd had to take in college, and the weird shit we'd produced there. What baffled me was how potent it was, and that the single dose I got seemed to cut right through all the defenses the damn serum should have given me. The reason seemed obvious—the serum did a great job screwing up pain receptors, which went hand in hand with why specific painkillers didn't work anymore, but this compound must be working on a different system.

It made me feel pretty good, and if not for the killer headache, dry mouth, and general sense that I needed to punch the next person in the face who looked at me the wrong way, I wouldn't have minded partaking so much. But withdrawal set in swift and brutal, and that seemed to be something that affected me way worse than our marines—and at least with Buehler I was sure she wasn't kidding when she offered that she felt a little groggy but otherwise fine. So it probably was some downstream metabolite of the drug, not the drug itself, that screwed with my brain—and faster metabolism meant more broken-down poison at a much quicker rate. Just as if someone had engineered it to sucker-punch those who normally got up and ran where others could only drag themselves forward. I kept that thought to myself, not sure if heightened paranoia wasn't just another side effect, but it sure didn't make me happy to get another hit in the morning.

That was, until that really set in and the world turned bright yet mellow once more.

Since switching up the driving and seating order required some redistribution of gear and packs, I used the time to limber up a little and try to stretch the various kinks out of my body. I missed not having Nate around to help—for some reason, helping me bend over until my spine cracked and cut-apart-and-reknitted muscles did once more what they were supposed to had always seemed like fun to him—but I managed well enough on my own. That was, until I noticed I had not one or two, but closer to ten salivating bystanders as I did my very best—in a near-split—to get my damn thigh muscles to loosen up. Rather than getting in their faces, I found myself grinning stupidly to myself. Huh. Yeah, those drugs were packing more of a punch than I'd thought last night. I was sorely tempted to drop my pants and show them the scars in all their horrifying glory so they actually got something to ogle, but restrained myself. Leader, and all that shit.

Damn, but I needed Nate back, because I so wasn't going to do this shit, on my own, for long.

"Okay, everyone know what they are supposed to be doing when we get to our destination?" I asked when everyone was as ready as they were going to get. Thanks to Harris and his people we had a somewhat reliable overview of buildings and troop strength, but only for the areas visitors were allowed in—almost exclusively concerning entertainment and food. It wasn't much, but it was a start.

I got way more stupid grins than nods, which didn't bode well. Actually, the scavengers were the ones best responding to questions. We were so fucking screwed.

I would have felt better riding with Harris but he insisted that Eden and Amos made a much better match, so it was them I shared the car with, besides a rather doped-out Richards. Since we were driving crap cars running on all kinds of fuels—only three had electric motors, one even had its own extra huge tank of vegetable oil—there was no AC, and as the midday sun beat down on us, I started to regret pretty much every single decision of my life. More to distract myself than because I was burning to know, I started a conversation with Eden and Amos, who'd been mostly quiet in the front row of the car.

"How many times have you been to the camp?" It was as neutral a question as I could come up with.

Eden considered as she glanced back to me from the passenger seat. "Five or six times? Something like that. You, Big A?"

"Six, I think," Amos offered, mostly ignoring us in favor of following the cars driving ahead of ours.

I knew I should have kept it at that but couldn't stop myself. "Why go there? I mean, I get it. You've all told me repeatedly they treat you as guests. But you must realize what's going on there."

I thought I caught a weary sigh from Amos, but Eden wasn't so curt with her response. "Why don't you get off your high horse, bitch?" she suggested, ignoring her friend's warning glance when he briefly looked over to her. "It's true! It's so damn easy for her to be so fucking ignorant. After all, we're not doing this because she has anyone's best interest at heart other than her own." Another warning glance went ignored, but when Eden fully turned back to face me, she'd calmed down a little.

"Never said I was trying to make the world a better place," I offered.

"Not this time, you didn't," she admitted, frowning. "But rather than call us hypocrites, maybe check yourself first. We go there because it's fun. Because it's easy to ignore the shit that's going on in favor of letting down our guard. It's not like we can do that anywhere else. And if you have getting eaten by zombies or wolves as the alternative, you fucking learn to not see what else they get up to. They don't even want much from us in return, just some junk we pick up on the road. They treat us much better than the settlements ever did, and they don't sneer down at us like Dispatch does. So what if we want to party a little too hard? Who said this had to be fucking Puritania just because the world went to hell? I dig this way more than what I've been up to before."

"Which was?" I had a hard time gauging her. For all I knew, she could have been a software engineer or something boring like that.

Eden looked surprised at the question but dutifully supplied an answer. "I was a woman of many trades. Guess I should say waitress because that's the single one constant. I was the queen of side hustles. You name it, I tried it. Selling shit online, selling shit door-to-door, blogging, being an influencer, lots of temp work. Always tried to make it all look so great and free and glamorous. The reality was, I was neck-deep in student loan debt, nobody understood how many hours of work went into a fucking ten-minute video, and I didn't even get health coverage. Now I can live life to the fullest and never give a shit about anyone's fucking opinion of me. Tell me that's not a million times better."

I hadn't expected that response, and there wasn't much in it that I could use, so I dropped it. "Never had any issues at the camp?" I asked instead. "Nobody disappearing? Particularly the girls?"

Amos was quick to break his silence. "We take care of our own," he told me in no uncertain terms. "And they know not to mess with us. They don't need to, as is. They know we could mess them up good if they gave us a reason to. That's why they like to play nice, and let us trade merch for Glimmer and other drugs. And it's not just us they trade with, you know? Last year several settlements closed up and moved because they didn't have enough food. No scavenger has gone hungry in a long, long time."

"You do know that the food they produce comes from slave labor," I pointed out.

"Is it really?" Amos shot back.

"I've seen it myself. Pretty obvious. And you yourselves told us that the barracks where the workers live are lovingly called 'sheep pens.'"

He chuckled under his breath, as if I'd said something funny. I really didn't get why. "You'll see when you get there," Amos promised.

Probably not in the sense he likely thought I would. "Why help us, then? If you like it there so much?" I asked.

Eden shrugged, her previous ire seeming to have dissipated completely. "We don't mind some of their practices, but what they did to you and your husband was wrong. So we'll do the right thing and help, easy as that." The grin she sent me was a little too bright. "You're not someone who easily forgets who helped her. Might come in handy down the line."

"You supposedly started a civil war because I cooperated with the enemy," I stated, hard-pressed not to glance at Richards still dozing next to me.

Eden's smile took on an edge, but remained surprisingly real. "Or did we? It's so hard to coordinate bullshit when it involves so many people and you never have any direct lines of communication. I'm not going to say some people weren't out for your blood, but that's the narrative he and his people want you to believe. It's not ours."

"And what, pray tell, is yours?"

Eden considered, but contrary to Amos before she didn't leave it at a cryptic remark. "Let's put it this way. I'm not sure I have a narrative. Sure, many people were angry because of the continuing divide, and famine didn't help. I'm sure you know how cranky a person can get without enough food for weeks at a time. And you yourself were never happy with the settlements and how they treated us. Is it that much of a leap that when you take all that and add desperation and fear, that something eventually blows? You heard what that cunt from Dispatch told you—they don't want anyone else but their own, exactly like the settlements. They used us that first year, before your crusade, so they'd become just another heap of maggots that burrow through enough bread to sustain them several lifetimes. As soon as shit started to get nasty, they slammed the doors shut in our faces. All of a sudden, we had nowhere to hide, nowhere to resupply. Something had to give. And it gave. Only now, we're the assholes and they are the saints, which suits them just fine as they continue to gorge themselves while we need to watch out for ourselves." She paused for a moment as if to weigh her words before she caught my gaze again and continued. "Just think about it. Would your people really cooperate with us if we were as bad as everyone says? Sure, they can't do it openly because they still depend on Greene and his maggots, but they'd be the first to slay us rather than work with us if we really were the worst."

"But you still have Vegas, right?" At least I thought someone had mentioned the city, and since Harris was alive I presumed his base was still operational.

Eden shrugged. "The old settlement, New Vegas, is no more, but we've rebuilt what we needed. But it's mostly just a forward base, nothing sustainable."

"Why not build your own towns then?" I suggested. "Or is logging and farming beneath you?"

My tone, more than my words, seemed to make her chuckle. "Me as a farm girl? Can't say that sounds like fun, but I'd do it, if I wasn't certain someone else would come and take it all away as soon as I had enough to make it worth it for them. There haven't been any new settlements since the first year, and for good reasons."

"The camp is newer," I mused. "At least from what little I've heard about it."

"Yeah, but they started out with a huge advantage," she retorted. "They had a thousand people in their first summer, and four times that the next. We can't get those numbers to cooperate and stay in one place without bashing each others' heads in, so no can do for a rival operation, if that's what you are getting at. None of that matters now. As long as you don't stir up any shit there, you'll have a good chance it never need concern you. After all, all you want is your husband back, right?" The way she said that, it sounded like she didn't buy it, but I was too tired to protest now. Let her think whatever she wanted. None of that really was my business or concern.

We stopped once more about thirty miles away from our destination for a last meal and to make sure that no incriminating shit could be found in any of the vehicles. The heat was making me drowsy but the storm clouds rolling in from the east lifted my spirits further—also because I knew I wouldn't have to rough it in the rain but instead sleep inside a building tonight. That this kind of proved what Eden had explained right didn't sit well with me, but it wasn't like it had any impact on my life. I was an hour's drive away from being inside the same walls as Nate once more, and, who knew? Maybe we'd manage to find and spring him before midnight. I'd seen myself that patrols outside the camp were tight, but from what the scavengers had told us, not so much inside. That made sense in a way—and was something I planned on exploiting. Problem was, I was already getting the jitters, and I didn't want to waste that first evening coming down with the full impact of the withdrawal symptoms. I could always do that tomorrow to be sober the next day, should today turn out as a bust.

I really didn't care for Harris's sly grin as he offered me another hit.

I also didn't know what to make of Richards appearing at my elbow to take the bong from me to get some himself. The look he gave me held a certain amount of challenge. Who was I to deny him his downfall?

I hated how that fucked-up shit almost immediately screwed with my perception, but when we got back in the car and started on the last leg of our journey, I realized not all of that was negative. It certainly helped keep the latent anxiety—that was really different kinds of fear, but none of that I could admit—at bay. It could be a trap. Or it could not work. Or they could find us out ten minutes into the camp. I couldn't really plan for any of that, and even less plot a contingency plan, so why bother?

The storm clouds that had been gathering reached the camp about the time we topped a last rise and a familiar stretch of road led up to the checkpoint. My tree was farther back, to the north-west, the abandoned house where I'd slept to the south. It all felt kind of familiar but at the same time warped enough to leave me slightly disoriented. I idly wondered how many of the guards were under the influence of similar drugs. Maybe this wasn't a suicide mission. Maybe it would even turn out to be a walk in the park?

Yeah, right.

But the first hour or so of it turned out to be boringly uneventful.

It took us some time to make it to the checkpoint—which was a different one than where they offloaded their less-willing guests, I soon realized. There was another group ahead of us so we had to wait. Then came a variation of the usual check, although nobody seemed to care about potential bites and infections. Things sped up significantly after the guards took away two large sacks from the first vehicle, presumably the weapons and electronics that Harris had brought along as a bribe. I didn't get more than a passingly curious look, same as the other three people in the car—and then we were through the checkpoint with directions where to park the cars and to get instructions from the quartermaster what building we could crash in, should we not find accommodations elsewhere.

Nobody tried to drag me behind the next corner; nobody even gave me a weird look. Because of the gathering storm, few people were idling around but those that crossed the open yard did so without seeming hurried or intimidated, or ten kinds of skeevy. If my bias hadn't been heavily skewed by what I'd experienced here before, I'd have actually found the camp quite okay. Sure, everything was a bit dirty and run-down, maybe more so than in most settlements, but there were obviously lots of people around which came with the usual issues of civilization. What I also noticed was that there weren't children or animals freely roaming the streets, but considering the buildings around us looked either industrial or catering to visitors, it stood to reason that family dwellings were situated elsewhere.

In short, I fucking hated it, and even more so because it didn't look like the slaver camp I knew it really was.

In planning, I'd been concerned how we would manage to sneak away, but I needn't have worried. As soon as Harris had handed off the bribe and two of his people went to haggle with the guy designated the quartermaster over some other wares they had on board, the rest of the crowd slowly dispersed. Some wandered off toward the first tavern, right next to the parking area; others waltzed down the main street deeper into the camp; some went over to the other group to greet familiar faces or make new acquaintances, and the rest just milled around—no sneaking of any kind required. Already, I saw Santos and Clark head into the tavern, and Marleen was strolling toward one of the food vendors set off to the side. One of the Silo marines was gawking at everything but two of the scavengers quickly pulled him along to "give him the sightseeing tour," quickly finding an excuse for his behavior. Scott and his men were already gone. About time I did the same.

"Where do you wanna head first?" Richards asked from where he'd been standing next to me for the past couple minutes, surveilling our surroundings. "Chow and booze sound good?"

I wasn't hungry—ha, great surprise—and getting intoxicated on top of already feeling like everything was a little bit more hilarious than it had a right to be didn't sound like a great idea, but I dutifully followed him when he set down the road most people were gravitating toward. Within the first hundred yards we—both, on our own or together—had received several offers for more private kinds of entertainment, but also to go see rat and dog fights or join the odd poker game. I'd never been to the seedier parts of any gambling town before the apocalypse, but this was pretty much how I pictured how that must have played out—at least in a Spielberg movie. Being high came with the advantage that I didn't stare at every whore—male or female—in the face to try to discern whether they did this out of their own free will, and how drugged up they were themselves. To my slightly unreliable perception, it all looked pretty tame and consensual, maybe a little seedier than Dispatch but not remarkably worse. It didn't bother me that much that, after the third catcall from someone looking for some freebies—Red reached across my lower back and pulled me closer, giving off unmistakable "my piece of ass" vibes. It was actually quite hilarious, even more so considering that Nate never would have done something like that. Glared at everyone in sight who might get any ideas, sure, but no public displays of affection. My heart gave a pang at that thought, and my longing for him about tripled, suddenly going from a low, latent, easily-ignored sentiment to glaringly bright drive that made me want to take off down the street and run around like a headless chicken in search of him.

Up ahead, the road branched, and we ended up heading into the larger tavern that sat right there at the split. It was the size of a warehouse, the entire floor taken up by the serving part of the establishment, with private areas upstairs. Richards steered me toward one of the three bars that served the different parts of the floor, this one catering more to people who only seemed to drop by for a drink, it seemed. The scents of freshly cooked stew and grilled chicken made my mouth water, momentarily distracting me.

I blindly accepted the jug of beer someone pushed at me and drank a good half of it in one long go, my throat parched from the heat of the day even though I didn't exactly feel thirsty. A few unfamiliar male voices chuckled but looked away when I focused on them. I found Richards leaning against the bar next to me, too close to be mistaken for anything but my companion, which likely explained their behavior. Too bad; a good old bar brawl sounded very enticing right now.

"Don't even think about it," the bartender behind us spoke up, making me turn around. He mutely nodded at a sign behind the bar, spelling out "you fight, you get kicked out," in comically crooked letters. I gave him my sweetest smile and buried my face in the beer once more.

Richards eyed me with amusement and ordered another two beers, his own already finished. "Know anywhere rules may be less strict?" he asked, deliberately slurring his words slightly. At least I hoped it was deliberate. The beer didn't smell strong enough to affect someone half his size without increased metabolism, so he should have been fine.

The bartender looked from him to me, and back, frowning slightly, but then his expression brightened. "Your first time here?"

Red nodded while I gave the bartender another bright grin. "Heard a lot about this place," I offered with what I hoped sounded like real enthusiasm. "And it beats getting eaten out on the road."

"Sure does," Richards agreed, his arm back around my hips. I wondered if I should have discussed beforehand just how handsy I felt comfortable with him getting. Outside, I'd minded less as it helped get us from point A to point B quicker without any interruptions, but maybe him not sitting on top of me might let me snatch up some information.

"What are you looking for?" the barkeep wanted to know. "If you want to participate, sooner or later a fight will break out on the streets, although the storm might put an end to that soon. We have the betting dens where you can either bet on a contender, or jump into the ring yourself. If you prefer some more moderate entertainment, they should show a movie or two once it gets dark over by the warehouse. And then there's the arena, of course."

I wasn't sure why but that last bit made me perk up. "Arena? Sounds nifty. Don't tell me you're doing horse races, or some shit like that."

The barkeeper's lopsided grin grew, making me guess that it was a more sinister place than that. "Horses? Not exactly. Horses are useful and expensive. Nobody would be stupid enough to waste them like that."

My, didn't that sound promising? And a lot more like what I'd expected.

Red's fingers digging into my side made me look up sharply at him, only to be confronted with a bright grin. "Betting sounds like fun, right?"

"Sure does," I lied, happy to get my hands on another beer. It didn't, but since I couldn't outright ask where they might be keeping prisoners or records about slave sales, it was a starting point. It was only then that it occurred to me that Nate might not even be here any longer. Shit.

The barkeeper continued grinning with that not-quite benign sense of hospitality. "Don't forget to drop by later to celebrate," he reminded us before he turned to the next bunch of customers. I gave them a cursory once-over, but nothing remarkable about them. Most people here looked like somewhat run-down road warriors—all hard-hitting, hard-working folk. No farmers, from what I could tell. Nobody paid us any attention, the guys who'd previously tried to hit on me having found more interesting prospects elsewhere.

Turning to Richards, I leaned in close enough to make sure my words were swallowed by the din of the tavern. "You can stop pawing me now. I think you've established your claim well enough."

I got a smile from him back as if I'd said something sweet—or rather enticing. "I have to say, I quite like this," he said, making me wonder what exactly he was referring to. His hand remained on my hip, but since he didn't further try to feel me up, I dropped the point. Just two people getting drinks after being out there for a while, nothing to see here. Nobody could know that I normally used such occasions to take a break from Nate, not crawl into his lap. Until it was time for that, later. But this wouldn't have been one of the places where I'd be stupid enough to set out on my own, even if I'd gotten stir-crazy as hell on the road. Suddenly, Red's hand felt a lot more comforting than annoying. It was easy to rant about things not being fair that a woman alone would be seen as a free-for-all invitation, but long gone were the days when I let that color my actions.

"So, what's the plan?" I asked a few sips later.

Richards needed a few seconds to respond, still busy casing the joint. "The betting stints sound like a good place to start. People don't watch what they spill when they're concentrating on something else."

"Fine," I offered. "Know what's up with that arena?" Harris and his people hadn't mentioned that, making me wonder whether it was new, something they hadn't wanted to spill the beans on, or they usually got too drunk early on to make it to the attractions that required more attention than the first mug of ale and willing woman offering company. If I had to hazard a guess, the latter would be it.

We finished up and left, following a string of revelers in the direction the barkeep had indicated. There were more people milling about than I'd expected, but most of this still didn't seem like the picture I'd painted in my head when I'd sliced and diced my way to freedom. For a moment, I entertained myself with the idea that Nate had somehow wormed his way into the hierarchy that must be running this place, already only a step away from becoming pirate king. I was sure that Pirate Queen was a job I could pull off. Maybe not in a dress with ruffles, but I could rock a leather corset—would go great with my gloves. I knew all that was silly imagination only, but so much more comforting than what I was afraid was the truth.

Ahead, I saw Marleen in the thong of people, her arm around another woman's shoulders, the other wrapped around some guy's arm who looked like he'd just fallen out of a scavenger vehicle, paint and grime still in evidence. I hadn't gotten the sense that bathing was a priority for any of them. The crowds swallowed them up a moment later, too soon to point her out to Richards. Not that it would have made much sense to do so, anyway.

"What exactly are we going to ask about?" I asked Richards when I realized he was steering me toward an open yard to our left. "I know, I should have thought about this sooner, but I didn't really expect I could just chat with people casually."

"What others do for fun here," he responded, only briefly looking at me in favor of continuing to watch the crowds. "And disturbances. You know, remarkable shit people love to chat about? Nobody wants to recount their drab everyday job."

"You mean like a disgruntled prisoner causing a stir when he kills ten guards in one fell swoop?"

Red snorted. "Yeah, something like that. Although I wouldn't start with that line."

Getting through the mass of people—well over a hundred—wasn't hard, until we reached the very center of the crowd. I wasn't surprised to find a roped-off area—calling it an octagon would have been a bit much—with people all around screaming and laughing, in high spirits whether they seemed to be winning or losing. Just as we made the final push to the front, one of the fighters felled the other with a mean uppercut, sending him to the bare ground right in front of me, blood gushing from his mouth and nose. Cheers went up and the winner did a little victory dance, his opponent obviously knocked out. A few of the blood spatters had landed on my arm, making my dusty and grimy jacket even more appealing.

"Charming," I noted, turning to Red after watching all kinds of stuff trade hands as the bets were called. "Doesn't look like they have a common currency here." Like the wood-chip tokens Harris had given us earlier that Red had used to pay for our beers. "So what are we going to bet?"

Richards snorted, although he averted his gaze as he replied. "Since I want to keep my balls I'm not going to suggest what you might be betting."

"Har, har, very funny," I griped.

"I mean a kiss," he clarified.

"Actually, that's worse." In the press of the crowd, the last heat of the day was unbearable, and after a moment or two of hesitation I decided to ditch my jacket. Tying it around my waist so it wouldn't impede my reach for my knife or gun was a bit of a bother, but I managed, much to the amusement of not just Richards but also a group of guys standing next to us. "What?" I asked them as I straightened, loving the feel of the slight breeze on my sweaty arms. "Don't think I know how to use 'em?"

One of the guys, a little younger than me from what I could tell, gave me a bright smile. "No, ma'am. Wouldn't dare to presume that."

I rolled my eyes, turning back to Richards, but noticed the other two elbow their friend, making fun of him. It took me a moment to figure out why—without the jacket covering my torso up to my hairline, the X-shaped marks across the back of my neck were visible with only a tank top and sports bra covering the rest. The same went for the scars on my arms—a few from surgery, but also the bullet graze that had been the very first battle injury of my life, but also some from sparring, fighting, falling, and the well-healed gash along my forearm where last year a wolf had almost gotten the better of me. With the gloves covering my hands, the picture fit together perfectly.

"Yeah, that's not fake, either," I said as I vaguely pointed at my neck. "Why, want me to prove it?"

The guy was quick to raise his hands and decline, much to the amusement of his friends. Not so another, much burlier guy on our other side. "I'll fight you. Haven't had an easy win in some time."

A few onlookers noticed. One started to cheer, which the others quickly picked up. I sized up the guy—he had a good hundred pounds on me, most of it muscle but also a healthy layer of fat. That one wouldn't go down easily.

"What are the rules?" I asked, although I didn't really care.

The one who'd started cheering before was quick to respond. "Normal rules is hand-to-hand, so no weapons, until knock-out or clear win. No tapping out early, unless you want an exception?"

"Hardly," I chuffed, then smiled sweetly at my would-be opponent. "Better pretend I'm not a girl. That will make it so much easier for you to lose."

Just then, someone else staggered into me, forcing me to take a step to the side. I lost my balance for a second, needing a steadying hand on Red's shoulder to catch myself. I burst out laughing, not quite sure why. Red smiled back, the anticipation in his eyes obviously for what he knew must be coming. My stumble sure seemed to add to the agitation in the crowd around us. "I've got an idea," I told him. Much louder I called to the guy, "Let's do this!" already reaching to undo my jacket, followed by my knife and gun holsters. I dumped everything into Red's waiting hands before I ducked between the ropes and stepped into the ring. This time, I exaggerated the stagger, and for fun turned my hopping safe into a brief introductory jump, hands thrown up. The crowds cheered when they realized a new round was about to start, bets getting exchanged all around. I didn't try to catch on to it, but still heard the odds heavily swayed against me. Turning back to Richards, I grinned at him. "Bet for me, will ya? Momma needs some funds for later!"

The three guys from before had already closed ranks with Red, chatting animatedly. I pushed them out of my mind, instead focusing on my opponent.

He'd followed me into the ring and right now made a show of cracking his knuckles, making his pecs jump, and made sure everyone saw his heavily tattooed torso. I didn't miss the single X on his neck, which was the only passably good ink on his body. Sure, compared to Nate's it was easy for any tattoos to look cheap, but even mine held up well to that guy's. The referee called everyone to attention, then checked in with us that we understood the rules. Kicks and bites were allowed but no permanent damage, except accidental. I loved the phrasing, but didn't comment on it. I hopped around a bit to limber up but my body was already singing with anticipation of violence, no further pumping-up required. The referee told us to step apart further so he could give the signal between us and quickly duck away—and then, it was on.

As soon as I got the "go," I exploded toward my opponent, going for the obvious—a kick to the torso, trying to aim as high as possible to maybe get lucky and hit him in the face, thus ending the fight in under five seconds. He went with it—a sign that he knew a thing or two about fighting—and blocked well, not quite swatting me away. That was okay—my move had been mostly to test him; I hadn't expected the kick to go through. It hopefully made me seem like a trigger-happy asshole rather than someone who played the long game. Deception, half the fun of any sparring match.

I figured it was stupid posing rather than chivalry that made him give me time to come down, recover, and go for him again. Nate sometimes did that but it always ended up being a trap. This guy clearly underestimated me because no feint on his part followed. I pretended to go for another kick, but at the last second moved to the side to instead go for a punch with my left, aiming for his jaw. I'd never not be right-handed, but Nate had spent a lot of time and effort teaching me how to get the most out of what was left of my hands—and, surprisingly, I had much less reservations using my left than right in situations like these.

The hit landed, surprising my opponent, and this time I didn't give him a chance to recover or compensate. A well-placed knee to the groin, followed by a mean kick to the knee, and I got the first scream from him. It felt oddly invigorating.

The uppercut he aimed at my jaw—that I missed because of my triumphant grin—was a lot less so.

Both bloodied, we separated, all playfulness and boasting gone. I could tell that now he took me seriously—but probably not serious enough.

He made the mistake of trying to bullrush me, which gave me some good opportunities to use my elbows and joined fists. I still went down, but was up before he managed to pin me on my back. A quick twist and I ended up above him, a knee to the nose ending with some impressive blood gushing. I paid for that when he reared up and slammed me, back first, into the ground, his sheer size and weight something I couldn't compensate for. His elbow in my gut hurt, enough to make parts of my last meal come up. Ever the lady, I puked right in his face, much to the crowd's cheers. That distracted him enough to give me an opening to disengage, which I promptly did.

This was a lot more fun than I'd expected to have any time soon!

All bets were off now—and it wasn't like I could win playing coy—so I went right for him again, kicking and punching, earning myself almost as good a beating as I gave. My body definitely went with it, my state of alertness increasing and my stamina not something I needed to watch yet, but something was wrong—that laser-sharp focus I'd become so accustomed to was lacking, and while I sure packed a punch, I couldn't hit as hard as I wanted to. Hysterical laughter as in answer to getting jabbed in the nose wasn't helping, either. Whatever that fucking drug did to my system, it kept me from performing as well as I should have. The crowd loved it, though, so that was a bonus.

Time to end this farce.

I feigned the next kick—which he read correctly, getting ready to block or evade something else—but I followed through with it nevertheless, planting the heel of my boot squarely in his sternum. He expelled all the air in his lungs with an emphatic "uff" as he staggered back, but at the same time managed to grab my ankle and twist, wrenching my knee as he pulled me down with him. I did my best to cushion my fall, ending up sprawled on top of him. In a lucky break for him, he managed to grab my hair and slam my face into the dirt, my left cheekbone taking most of the brunt. Pain exploded through my head and my view got somewhat distorted as I rolled over and to the side, my world swimming as I came up. He was still on his back, gasping, so I did the only thing that made sense— pounding on him and pummeling his face with my fists. Blood and sweat went spraying, my opponent too sluggish to block my punches well—until his arm shot up and his fist slammed into my jaw from underneath.

I saw stars and vertigo hit me hard, enough to disorient me properly—and then something inside of me snapped. It was as if my mind took the passenger seat and some other entity took over. It seemed to have an easy time ignoring the pain, and punched twice as hard as before, while grunting like a rutting hog. It was quite bewildering to watch myself beat a man to death—because that's exactly what was happening.

This wasn't good. So not good.

I didn't so much try to wrestle for control as I suddenly snapped back into myself, pain providing a momentary clarity that had been missing since the day before. It happened just as two guys grabbed me from behind, pulling me up and off my unresponsive victim. I felt my body gear up to fight them but a conscious thought was enough to make my muscles go slack. "I'm good, I'm done!" I called out, surprised for a second why I was breathing so heavily. Right.

As quick as it had happened, that sense of clarity dissipated once more, but left me somewhat more in control of myself and my actions than before. The helpers let go of me, carefully stepping out of my reach. I looked down at my former opponent, feeling slightly relieved to see his chest still rising, the blood on his nose and mouth bubbling slightly as he continued to breathe. The crowd was cheering—particularly those assholes who'd bet on me, or a bloody ending—but I caught a few less-savory terms among the calls. "Glimmer whore" was amusing, though—and made me swear to never ever take a hit of that fucking shit again.

The crowd parted for me as I ducked back out of the ring where Red and his new friends were applauding enthusiastically. The referee was already calling for the next fight, people all over getting busy collecting their winnings and starting the next round of betting. I accepted a—passably clean—wet rag from someone and went to work wiping at my face, hoping I was clearing up the blood more than just smearing it around. "Here, let me," Richards offered, trading my weapons and jacket for the rag. His motions were gentle as he did, without a doubt, a much better job than I had, but I couldn't have cared less. With adrenaline leaking out of my bloodstream, I would have expected remorse and guilt to wash over me, but there was only a wicked sense of exhilaration. Sure, I intellectually knew that I'd pulled a dick move that had been completely unnecessary, but I didn't feel it. That disturbed me on so many levels—but nothing I could do about that, even more so as I still felt the drug's hold tight on me.

"That was fun," I heard myself say with way more enthusiasm than I should have felt. The three compadres agreed, grinning brightly. "Told him I'm the real deal. He didn't listen."

"Yeah, some guys just have it coming," one of them agreed. "But if I were you, I wouldn't accept a second bout with anyone. Most fight fair, but some are just out for blood." He snickered, looking at the guy to his left, who did a good job playing innocent. "That's really what the arena is for. Not sure why some people are that fucked-up to want to be a part of that."

Richards gave no reaction to that so it was for me to jump on it. "What's up with that, anyway? Arena, sounds pretty tame."

The other guy let out a snort. "It's really not. Unless you think a fight to the death is tame. You sure pack a mean punch, but those monsters would eat you alive."

"Maybe literally," the third chimed in. "I hear they don't feed them all that often, to keep them desperate for a win."

That didn't exactly sound like fun, but thankfully, my fucked-up brain still produced a grin. "How do they get people to sign up for that?"

"It's spectators only," the first guy offered. "Nobody really knows who the contenders are, but if you look around, you can probably pick out a few possible prospects."

"Yeah, I heard it's their way of law enforcement," guy number two enthused. "If you're just being a drunk asshole, they kick you out, no problem. But you can't run a tight ship in a place like this without consequences."

An idea started to form in the back of my mind, and it wasn't one I cared for—not at all. As I'd just demonstrated myself, there was a certain kind of people in this country who were really good at beating odds and surviving shit normal people wouldn't, or couldn't. So why not send out your hit-slash-collection squad to get your hands on new contenders?

Guy number one cut through my musing, slowed-down as it was. "If you're interested, tonight's the next round. Starts in about an hour. Time enough to grab another couple of beers and head over to secure a good spot. Maybe don't eat anything, it can get pretty gnarly sometimes." He then turned to his friends. "Do you know if they got fresh blood? It's always more fun with the rookies."

"Not sure," Guy number three responded. "I think I heard they got three new ones?"

"How long do contenders usually make it?" I asked, trying to sound less revolted than I felt. "This doesn't sound like a long-term gig."

"Oh, most die in their first or second round," Guy number one said. "Sometimes they also have wild animals in there, making it even more like the Roman gladiator fights. And you never know if some won't band together. They have some contenders who've been doing this a damn long time. People have even started petitioning a pardon for that one guy... how long has he been in it?"

"Over a year," his friends both provided.

"Exactly. That guy's absolutely insane! But I don't think he'll be fighting tonight. They do sometimes get to pass up a round because of more severe injuries," Guy One explained. He seemed to be waiting for something from us, but before I could offer anything, his face suddenly lit up. "You should come with us! It's always more fun as a group. Makes you feel more in the moment."

That sounded like the last thing on my mind but Richards already agreed. "Great idea! I still have some bets running but after the next two fights we're game."

Just then, the next fight started and everyone's attention turned to that. I used Red's momentary distraction to divest him of the bloody rag—and his duty to keep poking at my face—and set to arming myself once more. He leaned in once I was ready—and made a grab for my hip again. Since that kept me out of the press of the crowd, I didn't protest. Knowing whose fingers to break should they slip was better than anonymous groping.

"Sounds like a good place to check out next," he whispered into my ear. "Good deal with the fight, by the way. Nothing beats acting as expected when trying to throw suspicion for a loop."

I wasn't quite sure if that was meant honestly or as a jibe, but then realized that for this round, both opponents were female—and this so wasn't a spitting, hair-grabbing girl fight. I definitely fit in with that crowd. No harm done, except to my opponent's ego—and my peace of mind, but I had a certain feeling low in my gut that my own actions would be the least thing I found myself appalled at as the night progressed.

Chapter 20

Our three new friends—whose names I still hadn't had the brainpower to recall, if they even gave them to me—clearly weren't the only ones very excited about the upcoming arena event. About half an hour before it was set to start, the fighting ring crowd dispersed, and like a swarm of locusts moved on to the arena—which turned out to be an actual arena, amphitheater-style, only built into the ground rather than up from it, the likely reason why I hadn't seen it on my attempts of casing the camp from the outside back when we'd been captured. At first guess, the bleachers-like ranks held a good three thousand people and were over sixty percent filled, with more coming in every minute. The air was full of laughter and fun, reminding me of a fair or open-air concert more than anything else. Torches lit the entire event space well enough for me to see more than I wanted to, really.

Maybe I was mistaken. Maybe the assholes had exaggerated, and we'd just been dumb enough to believe them. Maybe this had nothing whatsoever to do with where Nate had ended up.

Maybe I could just go up to whoever was in charge, claim to be the Queen of the Apocalypse, and ask for my husband back.

The overall positive energy of the crowd changed when at the very bottom of the arena a gate opened and a pickup truck rolled out into the dusty ground. It stopped at the very center and two men in the back started unloading stuff from the truck's bed—weapons and gear, from what I could make out. It wasn't much, maybe what two people would need out there beyond the walls of the camp. It was a peculiar thing to do, and they left as soon as the last baseball bat hit the ground, to return behind the gate once more.

A series of shots fired scared the living crap out of me until it was followed by loud, booming music, making me realize it was a recording only. Hidden speakers and amplifiers—fancy, and not something I expected anymore even in a place like this that likely still had some limited electricity. The crowd went wild with cheers, the pitch rising further when a single figure walked out into the arena below, clad in a long, black leather coat and top hat—quite the ensemble, really. Tanned and lean, the man was hard to place age-wise but I would have put him around Nate's age, maybe a little older. He managed to both appear somber as he strode into the arena but also had a kind of flamboyancy about him that screamed showmanship from a mile away. He raised his arms and the crowd roared, then got as quiet as so many people would as he lowered them once more.

"Ladies and gents, welcome to tonight's festivities!" his voice boomed over the speakers, making me guess he was using a wireless microphone. Considering how rough bordering on archaic the entire camp was, the luxury seemed even more emphasized. The crowd roared, briefly drowning out the first crack of thunder overhead. They couldn't have timed it better had they staged it. If not for the unnerving feeling in my stomach I might have easily gotten caught up in the sentiment as well.

The speaker grinned into the cheering masses, clearly having the time of his life as he basked in all that attention. He playfully tried to shush them, which just got them roaring louder. Taking a brief look around, I decided I was easily the most sober person— Red excluded, maybe—here, which said something. More thunder cracked overhead, making me wonder just how safe it was out here in the open. The ringmaster seemed to be thinking along the same lines as he addressed the crowd.

"Because of the storm approaching, we will have to cut the entertainment part short..." Some boos rose, but mostly the crowd continued to cheer. "But that means double the trouble all at once!" His pause wasn't just for effect but because now they got really loud.

Leaning close to Richards so he could understand, I whisper-shouted, "I'm not sure I'm liking where this is going."

I got a surprisingly bright grin back from him that made me go back on my assessment of his sobriety. Apparently, getting punched in the face had helped my body clear out some of the shit that kept me loopy. Since he'd passed up that part, he seemed a step away from truly hammered. Damn, but we shouldn't have gotten that last hit just before getting to the camp. Well, now it was too late for regrets.

The ringmaster's boasting pulled my attention back to him. "I have a very special treat for you tonight. I know you were all waiting for the rematch from last week, but we got in fresh blood!" More cheering, now with a decidedly hostile undertone. "You all know what that means?"

With surprising accuracy, the crowd started chanting, "Blood! Blood!" in near-perfect unison. Some screamed, a lot whooped, and a few people down from us, a girl started clapping while jumping up and down.

"Exactly—blood!" the ringmaster called out, his expression a maniacal smirk. "Because we didn't want to deprive you of last week's winner, Brock is back, our main contender for this week! Six weeks and counting, he remains undefeated so far. He's getting the advantage, being allowed to wield a knife as he enters the arena!" Lots more cheering, if somewhat less so than before, and a few whistles followed. The ringmaster's smirk deepened. "And he will need it, because after they clear out the rookies, he will be facing one of your all-time favorites! Yes, you guessed it—I'm bringing the Nameless Terror back!"

If I'd thought the crowd had gone wild before, I got schooled as now the roar was deafening, enough to make me actually clap my hands over my ears. Our new friends were among those who seemed to lose it, screaming and clapping each other on the shoulders as if they'd just been told they'd won the lottery. When he realized Red and I weren't cheering, the closest of them leaned over, needing a few seconds to stop laughing. "You're in for a treat! He's a real monster! They usually only let him out when they have overwhelming odds that need to be cleared up! This is awesome!"

He didn't wait for my reaction as just then, the ringmaster disappeared through the gate the truck has entered before, leaving the arena empty for a few moments. The music still blaring from the speakers swelled to a crescendo, and the whole crowd chanted along with the countdown that followed—counting down from five, which was about the maximum mental capacity for most.

At the reverberating cries of "go!" several smaller gates spaced around the arena floor opened, spilling out people from three parts—two men on their own, and a group of three all together. It was obvious who the newcomers were, the huddle of three casting around frantically, ducked, clearly scared out of their wits. The guy with the knife had to be Brock—a well-muscled man in his late twenties, a little on the beefier side but the kind who'd sucker-punch you with unexpected speed and agility.

And the last was Nate.

My surprise was pretty limited, although I hated being right with a vengeance. He was still alive—which was great, of course—and looked to be moderately well, but leaned out to the point where his body was all cut muscles without much subcutaneous fat remaining. Might have looked appealing on an underwear model, less so if extra padding might have meant another month of survival with little or no food. All of that was on display because none of the men in the arena wore more than shorts, not even boots. Now it made at least some sense why they'd dumped full gear, including pants, jackets, protectors, and boots in the middle of the arena. Part of me could even admire the tactic for what it was—upping the stakes, and giving the viewers a much better look at most wounds that would be inflicted. But there was absolutely nothing about this display that I liked on any level. I was too far away to make out any details, but his skin was dirty with grime and dark smears that looked like dried blood, and there were bruises and half-healed wounds everywhere, either too fresh to have fully healed or his body no longer having the energy to do so in a timely fashion. At least he still had all of his limbs, and was moving with the fluid grace of a fully functioning predator.

I glanced at Richards, trying to gauge his reaction, but his attention was on what was going on below.

Brock, knife in a good grip in his right hand, had all of his attention on Nate as he stepped away from the gate, but took his time. Nate himself looked deceptively relaxed as he both glanced at Brock and the newbies, rolling his shoulders to limber up. The rookies were screaming and sobbing at each other, and then one of them made a mad dash for the gear in the middle of the arena, abandoning the others, who remained huddling right up to the now closed-again gate.

When he realized Nate wasn't going to make a move yet, Brock started forward, taking strong, ground-eating bounds toward the other guy trying to get to the middle. Their distance was identical, and the delay ended, making it even easier for Brock, who simply had to plunge his knife into the lower back of his bent-over victim, who'd been too scared and frantic to scramble for a weapon to care about his defenses. The knife went in straight to the hilt, roughly at the left kidney. The bent-over guy screamed—but not for long, as Brock pulled the knife back out, grabbed his screaming victim by the hair, and slashed his throat. Blood fountained everywhere, painting a dark semi-circle over the ground and some of the gear. The crowd went wild for several seconds flat. None of the contestants seemed to notice it, though, although the remaining two rookies looked even more scared, if that was possible. Brock briefly glanced up into the ranks, his face a mask set in stone. There was no satisfaction there for just having killed a man.

The crowd shushed when they realized more was going on below. It was hard to pick out, but when I strained my ears, I managed to hear Nate shout—at the newbies. His voice was hoarse and gruff, but so typically his that my heart did some weird things in my chest. That was likely due to the drugs as well.

"Help me take him out and I'll let you live," he told them, his attention still switching between them and Brock. Brock spared them a single glance before he stared back at Nate. I would have expected him to go for something from the pile, but he seemed happy to remain standing right there, guarding it like Cerberus the gates of Hades.

It took them a few seconds, but then one of the two shouted back, "You're just trying to trick us! We're not going to make it easy for you!"

Nate seemed less than impressed by that retort. "I don't need deception to do that." The crowd cheered at his statement. I didn't miss the disgust that crossed his features, but it was gone after a second, like a bad memory, easily disbanded. I felt my stomach knot up at realizing why they were all cheering—because they were waiting for that kill, and they knew it was coming. Of course it was—Nate was a rather accomplished killer, and from what I could glean of the setup here, he must have been thriving in such an environment—at the utter loss of his humanity. I had no idea how they'd gotten him to where he obviously was now because I didn't think anyone could simply beat it out of him, but I was sure they had their ways. This clearly wasn't anything new that they'd just started. This had the feel of a recurring event with lots of fans—an entire audience out for blood.

A shotgun boomed across the arena, making me jump and reach for my gun. Then I realized it had been the ringmaster, freshly appeared up in the ranks, overlooking what was going on in the area. The chatty guy next to me was helpful again as he explained. "When they're stalling too much, they get a one-minute warning. It usually helps."

So much for motivation—but I still had to ask, damn my morbid curiosity. "What happens if they keep stalling?"

"They get shot, of course," the guy offered, looking confused at me needing confirmation. "Not shot dead, just enough to wound them. Sooner or later, one of them grows tired of it and does something. Some use it like Russian roulette to hope it hits their opponents first and they can use it to their advantage, but you won't have to worry about it tonight. They're both seasoned players. They won't risk injury as the outcome is inevitable, anyway."

Very comforting to hear that, but I didn't say so out loud. Instead, I focused on the arena again. While we'd been talking, Nate had taken a few more steps forward, but not toward the gear in the middle but along the wall, in the direction of the newbies. He was just bending over—crouching, really, with his unprotected back to the arena walls—to pick up one of the many stones strewn across the arena. He kept eyeing Brock but mostly focused on the newbies, with the odd glance up into the ranks where the ringmaster was watching the proceedings. My guess was that he was biding his time but only until they forced his hand—literally.

A line of armed guards stepped forward below the ringmaster, which seemed to have been the signal Nate had been waiting for. Halting, he pitched the rock at the closer of the two rookies, hitting him square in the temple. He staggered, almost folding in half but caught himself against the arena wall. The other bolted forward, not quite at Nate but certainly steering away from Brock. Nate reached for another rock, seeming to consider pelting the running guy, but instead let him through as he further advanced on his now disoriented victim. Another perfect hit in the exact same place, and the guy crumpled to the floor, not even trying to protect his head with his arms. Bloody foam appeared at his mouth as he puked up blood. Almost at the wall, Nate glanced at Brock and the one who'd gotten away to make sure both were at a safe distance before he picked up a larger rock, hefted it over his head, and then brought it down to smash the downed guy's head in. That was quite fascinating to watch, with blood, brain matter, and gore spraying everywhere.

Horrifying, I quickly corrected myself, still unable to tear my gaze away from the gruesome display.

While I was sure the guy was dead as soon as the heavy rock smashed in his skull, Nate made a veritable spectacle out of it, to the beat of the crowd cheering him on. When he finally straightened, his head, arms, and upper torso were wet and shining, his eyes bright in the darkened, bloody mask of his face. He wiped one arm across his lower back, then used the somewhat less wet back of the hand to clear his face, but only so nothing would get into his eyes. The crowd watched with the same kind of sick fascination as did the runner, who'd stopped between the wall and the heap of gear, his attention torn between Brock and what Nate was up to.

Done with cleanup—if one could call it that, which really was a stretch—Nate made a show of cracking his knuckles before he took a step toward the runner. "Last chance to change your mind," he shouted. "Help me kill that asshole, and you might live to see another day."

The guy, frantic and scared, looked from Nate to Brock, who only had a shrug for him as he flipped his knife so that the blade was aligned with his arm rather than fingers. "They will only let one of us walk out of here, so your choice—do you really want to help your killer? And that you die is a given."

Nate didn't deny it, shrugging when wide eyes flipped back to him. "Suit yourself if you want to go down like a weepy little kid," he ground out, then turned to Brock, making an "after you," gesture with his right hand. Brock gave a brief jerk of the head as he declined. Nate's smirk was clearly one of derision, but it turned into something full of anticipation and darkness as he switched his attention back to the rookie. The crowd roared as he took a step forward, getting ready. Only that he wasn't done yet, instead turning around, both hands going up as he indicated the people all around him. "How do you want him to die? Give me your best shot!"

The cheering grew somewhat muted as suggestions started flying this way and that. The scared guy looked ready to piss his pants but darted toward the gear heap when he realized that Nate's attention was still on the crowd. He picked up the first thing he could reach, all the while nervously watching if Brock would change his mind and make a move on him. He didn't, only watching with amusement as the guy grabbed a hefty, long stick. I was tempted to turn to Red and ask him whether that counted as a tactical quarterstaff but decided against it; Richards was watching the proceedings with rapt attention, that in and of itself creeping me out. Then again, I sure hoped that the horror I felt wasn't painted all over my face and body language. Drugs would also explain why the rookies had all acted so damn stupid, unable to make a good choice, or one that would keep them alive a little longer.

"Beat him to death with his stick" and "break his back" seemed to be the two options most often screamed by the crowd from what

I could tell. Nate eventually dropped his hands, the smirk still there but more turned inward now. At least that was as far as I could read his face across the distance. The way he strolled toward the guy with his stick, slowly yet deliberately, reminded me of a large cat, a leopard maybe. Although I was intellectually horrified by the entire spectacle, I couldn't quite deny that my body found it… interesting. I would have loved to blame that on the drugs, or anything else, but it had been a while. Being so close yet still worlds apart created all kinds of frustration, and my way of dealing with that usually wasn't to reason it out.

As Nate advanced on him, the guy with the stick backed away, but there wasn't very far he could go, unless he wanted to get knifed in the back like his friend. The fact that he now had a weapon while his opponent remained empty-handed seemed to give him some backbone—but he was still slow, almost comically so, to defend himself when Nate made his move, coming directly at him. The stick should have given him reach—or at the least something to defend himself with—but instead, it got turned against him when Nate grabbed it with his right and punched the guy in the face with his left, gaining leverage through the weapon. Too stunned to react, the guy wasn't able to defend himself—but also didn't let go—and two straight, easy jabs later he fell to the ground, only partly held up by the stick that he was still holding on to for dear life. Nate grabbed the stick with both hands and kicked him in the side of the head, wrenching the weapons out of his slack hands. He dropped it, then bent down, picked the guy up, and threw him, back-first, into the sturdy wall of the arena a few feet away, uttering a primal scream that the crowd ate up. I didn't hear a crunch as the guy's body hit, but it didn't look good for him as he slid to the ground, lifeless. Kicking one end of the stick to make the other flip up, Nate easily caught it and advanced on the lifeless heap. Another kick to the shoulder had the guy flop onto his back. I realized I'd been wrong—he was still aware, letting out a scream, but he was unable to move. Nate pointedly looked at the stick in his hands, then down at the guy—and with a diabolical, twisted smirk rammed the end of it right through the guy's left eye socket. The scream cut off, some twitching ensued, and then it was over—seconds after it had begun.

Stepping away, Nate turned to the crowd, shaking the bloody stick—and then broke it over his knee, the sturdy wood splintering dramatically. "Who do you think I am?" he called out and threw the two parts away. "I don't need a flimsy weapon to win my fights!" Roars and cheers went up all around, chanting in places but it didn't take, the people too engaged to coordinate and concentrate.

Brock had watched the spectacle where he'd remained standing next to the bled-out body of the first victim, now no longer as relaxed as before. He watched Nate advance slowly, shifting his position a few times but not from nerves. The two men stared at each other, neither afraid but only Brock with a certain kind of apprehension in his gaze. Nate had turned full-on killer, no remorse visible. On the contrary, he kept his arms a few inches raised, moving his fingers up in turn with the ebb and swell of the crowd. All over, people started chanting again—"Blood! Blood!"—and now it took, like a terrible thrum of violence. I had no idea why he was egging them on, but it sure was working. They were eating it up. They were loving every second of it—and they knew that the real fun was only about to start.

There was no great lead-up. There was no testing, or taunting, or goofing around. As soon as Nate stepped close enough, Brock sprang forward, moving lightning-fast, his knife-hand even faster. Nate wasn't stupid enough to fall for it, evading rather than letting himself get sliced up by blocking to try to gain the opportunity for a punch, only to bleed out within the next minute. Brock was beefier—and in better physical condition—but Nate had a few inches on him both in height and in reach, and I knew he would bring them to bear soon. He gave Brock about a minute to tire himself out some, the knife getting nowhere near his skin. Both men were careful, neither underestimating the other, but it was only a matter of time until one of them would make a mistake.

I knew exactly when Nate was about to make his move—he didn't pause, or act any different, but there was something about how he balanced himself that triggered me. We'd spent a lot of time sparring, particularly over the last two years, and I knew his tells, few that they were, like nobody else's. Although, watching him fight now was something else. He never held back with me except for when he was teaching me something and had to wait for me to figure out how to best put knowledge to practice and commit moves to muscle memory—which was the reason why I'd had a relatively easy time beating that guy at the betting ring. I was used to always sparring with someone who was taller and heavier than me, with better reflexes and balance, a body not held back by missing bits and pieces. It was demoralizing as fuck sometimes, but beat losing in a real fight. But this now? This was something else. That should have been obvious—one would presume Nate usually wasn't keen on killing me when we got into a physical fight—but it still stunned me to watch it.

It was beautiful. Terrifying, sure—but also beautiful. The way he moved; the way he reacted; mind laser-focused, body in peak performance mode. Brock had never stood a chance, and he knew it.

Maybe Nate's tell had been more obvious than I'd thought because rather than continue to engage, Brock used that moment to step back and kick up sand and pebbles with his foot. Nate barely more than blinked as he went after him, having to move just a little farther because of the suddenly opening distance between them—

Brock fell for it, stabbing for Nate's ribs, the angle right and his speed too quick for Nate to parry. Only that Nate didn't even try but let the stab through, sacrificing a glancing slice to the torso—in favor of grabbing Brock's knife hand, a single twist enough to break his wrist. Brock screamed and tried to back away, the knife clattering to the ground. But Nate held on, using his opponent's weight for leverage to land a kick to the head. Brock wasted another few seconds trying to tear himself free which earned him a knee to the groin as well. Only then did Nate let go of his wrist, but only so he could twine his fingers and bring both hands together down on Brock's head. Brock staggered, and a kick to the sternum sent him toward the ground as he lost his balance. Nate screamed as he lunged after him, going straight for the face—and then his throat. Brock, bleeding profusely and in obvious pain, tried to pry his hands off but with only the fingers of his left working there wasn't much he could do. Rather than strangle him completely, Nate let up as Brock's face had turned a deep red in favor of a few more punches, his whole weight behind them. Blood and teeth sprayed—the crowd continued to cheer with every hit that landed. And then, when it was pretty much over, Nate grabbed the knife, plunged it into Brock's lower torso below the ribcage, rammed his left hand into his body almost up to his elbow—and ripped his heart out. The crowd screamed with triumph—as did he, I thought, but it was drowned out—and louder yet when he bit into the still-beating heart, never mind the blood spurting from the many arteries and veins attached to it, spraying blood everywhere.

And yes, he ate the entire thing, using his free hand to further fan the flames of the masses.

"You might want to consider doing some marriage counseling," Richards whispered in my ear, the words almost unintelligible. I turned my head, staring straight into his eyes, and let a snort be my only response. His brow furrowed, a look of bewilderment crossing his face. "Are you seriously turned on right now?"

The nice thing would have been a straight-out denial, but he'd held on to my ass one time too many tonight for that to happen. "Better not ask questions you don't want an answer to," I advised, almost breaking out into a fit of giggles when I realized how low and throaty my voice was. Queen of mixed signals, thy name is Bree.

Richards seemed relieved when I was the first to look away, quickly checking on what I'd missed in the meantime. Not much, from what I could tell—Nate was still standing there, letting the crowds cheer him on. No more cannibalism following, which I was glad to see. There was no disgust on his face but the passive expression told me all I needed to know—he wasn't proud of his actions, and he sure as hell hated the imbeciles who thought this was entertaining. But he was a part of this, clearly not by choice, and there was only so much he could do about it.

Just how much that was true became obvious once the crowds slowly started to calm down, and the gate opened to spill out yet more armed guards, the ones up by the ringmaster still ready for everything. Nate took a bow—deep and theatrical—which got him another wave of shouts and cheers, and let himself be escorted into the bowels of the arena underground. He did it walking tall, looking like a king with his personal escort, pretty much covered in blood from head to toe—but there was no mistaking who was in charge.

The ringmaster was back, but I tuned out the noise of his little thank-you speech, my attention still on the gate that had closed by now.

So close—and yet, so far apart.

The morbid part of me supplied that, at the very least, the serum would keep him from contracting all kinds of shit.

He was alive—and right now that was the best news possible. The only news I cared about.

"And, what do you think? Did we promise you too much?" Guy number one was back to pester us. I forced myself to stop gazing longingly at the gate and to focus on him instead. He looked delirious with excitement, which was a good thing because I wasn't sure how good my faking game was right now.

"That was definitely something," I offered, my mind too full of upcoming ideas what to do next. It must be easy to find some of the guards and maybe bribe some information out of them. Depending on how close they got to the Roman games, I could maybe even walk up to someone and say I wanted to fuck their monster and they'd let me in. That wasn't an idea I liked to contemplate, although I could take a good guess how that would have gone down—if only once.

They could hardly make a spectacle out of hapless whores being killed where nobody saw it. At least I hoped that was the likely outcome.

I really needed to get out of here and do something, or else I would drive myself crazy within seconds.

"Something you must have seen to believe," Red enthused, helping out when I got unresponsive, lost in thought.

Half turning to him, I nodded. "I'm weirdly hungry now. Let's grab a bite?"

Richards went ever so slightly pale, but did a good job fake-agreeing. "Sure. That one tavern had pork. I'd kill for a pig right about now." His hands remained pointedly at his sides. I had to bite down hard on the inside of my cheek when I noticed. This was too precious.

Our companions didn't seem to find it weird that anyone would want to eat something after seeing what had just gone down in the arena. "All kinds of meat available—the upside of coming here! Beats eating four-year-old canned food every day. Tell you what, why don't you come with us? We know all the best haunts around!"

I tried smiling sweetly as I geared up for my rejection but that didn't seem to work well, so I threw one arm around Red's neck and pulled him close. "Maybe we'll catch you later? I have something else on my mind right now." And oh, it was glorious to see—and feel—Richards squirm next to me, all the while trying to pretend like he was on board. Maybe I was going to hell for this, but at least I was having fun all the way there.

A trio of lewd grins told me they'd received the message, and nobody held us back when we split. It took us a while to leave the arena although we'd been in the upper third of the ranks. Throughout the fight, I'd pretty much forgotten about the thunder and impending storm, but as soon as we were out in the open, the wind whipped at my clothes, the first drops of rain pelting us.

"Let's find somewhere we can talk, and maybe not get drenched," I told Richards, staying close as not to get separated.

He inclined his head, adjusting his pace to mine to avoid me falling back. "Why didn't you just say how annoyed you were by my attempt to keep you off most men's radar? You didn't need to actively skeeve me out."

"Didn't need to, no. But maybe really, really wanted to," I teased before getting serious. "I get what you were doing, and maybe it was even working. Doesn't mean I had to like it. Isn't there anything in your psych profile of me about me acting out when I get uncomfortable?"

"I've been making you uncomfortable?" he said, as if that was impossible—and quite the opposite of what things had looked like to him. "You're the one who thinks getting punched in the face is fun."

I couldn't help but laugh, and it went on a little longer than it should have. Damn drugs. "Hey, you know who I'm married to. And I'm pretty adaptable where my standards are of what is healthy and normal." I paused, but simply couldn't help myself. "Why don't we continue this discussion after we've sprung him, so he can offer his opinion on the topic? Including your hand on my ass."

Richards was smart enough not to reply, instead focusing on something up ahead. "I think I just saw someone duck into that alley," he offered. "Looked like Marleen. Maybe she already found something out. We should catch up with her."

"Good idea. I'd love to hear her opinion on this, too," I quipped, laughing about my own joke. If Red ran out of luck, she'd agree with me. As part of this crowd, she'd probably been at the arena as well. I was sure she was the right woman to have a conversation about rare steak with right now. Oh, poor Richards—

I didn't notice the mountain of a man stepping into my path, nor his equally muscled companion behind me. My instincts gave zero warning. One moment I was thinking about how to best rag on Richards, the next there was a sack over my head and someone was holding me in a vise grip, and then it was too late to fight because they really knew how to tie knots. Brief—very brief, indeed—sounds of a fight coming from my left side made me guess Richards wasn't doing any better.

As they dragged us off to who knew where, I told myself that there was a silver lining to this—at least we wouldn't have to hunt down who was in charge here, but even got the VIP service of getting carried there.

Always think positive, I reminded myself—because right here, right now, the negative outcomes weren't anything I wanted to concentrate on.

Chapter 21

A short time and some quality vertigo later, I found myself dumped back on my ass, a quick kick to where my second kidney used to be convincing me that remaining down was a good option. They hadn't even bothered with gagging me, but trying to scream a few times had proven rather futile—not really a surprise. I hadn't been carried far, and most of that out of the wind and rain, the last minute or so through relative quiet. In the distance, I could still hear the din all the people in the camp made, which was strangely comforting. I'd kind of hoped they'd undo the rope my hands were tied with but instead, someone pulled my arms up and hooked the rope onto something, which made kneeling the most comfortable position—for now. I was still debating whether trying to get up was a good idea—and where they'd kick me next if I tried—when the hood over my head was removed, the light of a few torches blinding for a few seconds. The first thing I checked was whether Richards was still there; after all, this camp, me, and companions didn't have the best track record. But yes, he was there, right next to me, close enough that I maybe could have nudged him with my boot if I'd tried hard. One of the burly guys who'd lugged us here—wherever here was—removed his hood right now, leaving me to further explore the room.

There wasn't much to it. My hands were tied to some kind of iron frame probably used for just that cause—or hanging up laundry. The room was maybe ten by fifteen feet large, the only piece of furniture a small shelf at the wall to my left, mostly empty except for some odds and ends. It didn't look like the room got much use but there were three doors that I could see, one behind us and two in front. Through the right one the not-quite familiar figure of the ringmaster stepped, followed by a vaguely more familiar man. It took me a few moments to recognize the guy who I'd fought at the betting ring. He was silently sneering at me as soon as his gaze fell on me, or as much as he could see of me with one eye swollen shut. Those two increased the number of people in the room to twelve—making that eight guards, quite the overkill if anyone had asked me—leaving it quite crowded.

My thoughts were racing, the adrenaline coursing through my veins doing weird things in connection with fear and my body trying to gear up for a fight, while I tried so very hard to keep a clear head. Make that, clear my head so I could think. Fuck, but this didn't look good.

"What's this all about?" I heard myself ask—no, demand—out loud just as I'd wondered the same thing. Since I now had their attention, I decided to surge ahead, talking just a little too fast to appear relaxed—but then why would I be relaxed in my current position? "Don't tell me that sore loser ratted me out for a rule violation. Because, trust me, it was his own fault that he got his ass kicked. You can ask any of the hundred people who were there at the ring. I really thought you were better than those settlement pansies."

The ringmaster listened to my ramble with a slightly amused expression. Once I fell silent, he turned to the loser. "This is her?"

The guy nodded. "Yeah, it's her. I'd recognize that bitch anywhere. Fucking Glimmer cunt."

No reprimand followed, but the ringmaster looked vaguely bored by the expletives. Looking at someone behind me, he ordered, "Check her."

That didn't sound good. I tensed, but there wasn't much I could do, really. Not that much of a surprise when someone grabbed my head and pushed it down to reveal my neck; my jacket was still tied around my waist so my upper body wasn't covered by that much, making it really easy to get to the marks. "Three," the guy who was still holding on to me confirmed.

"Check her lower back next," the ringmaster ordered. Uh-oh. I really didn't like where this was going, and when the goon let go of my head in favor of pulling off my jacket so he could get to where my tank top was stuffed into my pants, I tried to rear up—to do what, I didn't exactly know—but when I felt the cool steel of the barrel of a gun against my temple, I froze. The ringmaster took a step forward so he was once again in my field of vision, a slight but not too nasty smile on his face now. "There's no need for violence unless you force our hand," he explained, sounding way too reasonable for anyone's good—and there was still the matter of the gun pressed to my head. "We just need to check something. Quick." He pointedly didn't ask my permission and neither did I give it, but I didn't resist when the goon pulled up my tank top in the back.

"Yeah, she got that one as well," he reported, without a doubt referring to my not-quite tramp stamp.

I tried to come up with a plan, but really, that gun was distracting as hell. As was the fact that, while afraid, I didn't feel anger or panic rising inside of me, my preferred triggers for all things smash and bash. It was weird as fuck to be both at one-eighty and feel kind of mellow at the same time. Seriously, no more drugs for me, ever. With luck, someone would sock me a good one soon and push my body into fight mode, but I wasn't so sure about my mind.

"I'm hardly the only one with that ink," I offered although nobody had asked me. "Was quite the rage some time ago, I hear."

The ringmaster ignored me, talking to another goon. "Check him, too."

Richards, of course, came up ink-free, which they verified by cutting off his jacket and the T-shirt he wore underneath. They didn't even give him the option of struggling first but went straight to the gun-to-the-head treatment. He didn't resist and also kept his trap shut, for now turning into the poster boy for good interrogation behavior.

Not that much of a surprise, the ringmaster turned to me, since I was so ready to spill my guts in the first place. "Explain."

That wasn't much to go on, but I figured he was hoping I would inadvertently divulge details useful to him, or even incriminating for me—not that I was too sure what this was about. I could guess—and really didn't like the first conclusion that came up where matching tattoos were concerned—but maybe I was wrong.

"Why he's all prissy, perfect skin and I'm not? Easy. He's an army reject and deserter. I'm the real deal. My people and I, we stumbled upon him a while ago and took pity on him. He's a quick learner but awfully lazy. I could tell you stories…" On cue, the ringmaster opened his mouth, and I quickly went on. "But you're probably already bored of us. Why not tell me what you want to know so I can leave out all the rest you're way too busy to concern yourself with."

The amusement from before was back. "You know who I am?" he asked.

"Great speech before the arena fight," I enthused, lying through my teeth. "And after, too, although I didn't really listen much to it. Sorry, but you must get that a lot, right? Adrenaline and all that. So, yeah, I know who you are. Great town you have here. Great entertainment. Not so great on the customer service, I have to say, but hey, misunderstandings happen. So if you just let us go now, we won't give you a bad Yelp rating. Hell, I'll even toast to you when we get some booze later. I'm really thirsty. Do you have any booze here?"

It was fun to see his eyes glaze over as he stopped listening, but the bright spark was right back once it was his turn again. "The name's Cortez. You said you're the real deal? Meaning what, exactly? That you were along for the ride in Colorado?"

I wondered if he'd just called me an imposter. "I sure as fuck was along in Colorado. Much good that did us, assaulting that base only to have it all grind to a halt an hour in with that fucking truce." From what little I'd talked to the scavengers, they weren't too fond of my actions back then, but I could understand why considering what had happened later. I briefly cursed myself for not having spent more time chatting with Harris—or Eden and Amos on the drive here, but then they seemed to be a pretty mixed bunch in general. Trying to emulate Eden, for what it was worth, I offered up a derisive snort. "Didn't particularly care for starving that winter, so I went to find some like-minded folks, and I've been roughing it with them ever since."

"Where?"

"Vegas, for the most part." Since that was the only scavenger base I knew, I had to go for it—and if anyone had already asked around, they'd suspect as much. "That's where we were last before coming here, too. You can ask at the gate, I'm sure someone must remember me. Well, maybe not me, but our cars are taking up a good third of the space you got there, so that's something. We can go there right now, if you don't believe me. I can show you my pack and gear. Or track down someone who can vouch for me."

Again, Cortez didn't really listen to most of what I said. "That won't be necessary." He turned to the loser of the betting fight. "You can go now."

He looked sorely disappointed but didn't protest. "A small reward, maybe?" Cortez just stared at him, and after a few moments the guy turned around and left through the door they'd entered through before. Cortez waited until it fell shut behind him before he turned back to me, for the most part disregarding Richards.

"You see, you're putting me in quite the dilemma here," he mused.

"I really don't see why," I answered, pretty much interrupting him. He didn't look pleased but let me talk. "Look, we haven't done anything wrong, right? I beat that sore loser in a fight, fair and square. My marks were out in the open, he was just too stupid to check and take me seriously. And maybe I got a little bit carried away in the end but hell, he could have tapped out sooner. Or not been that keen on planting his fist in my mouth. How's any of that my fault? We're not here to cause trouble. We just want to relax and have fun. It's never been an issue before. So, what's with the interrogation shit?"

Cortez pursed his lips as if to consider my words. I was pretty sure he'd already made up his mind. "You still think this is about that fight? It's not."

"Then what?" I asked, not having to feign the hint of exasperation that leaked into my voice. "We've barely been here for more than three hours. We paid our tab at the bar, we didn't molest or kill anyone, I won the fight, and we had fun watching the spectacle in the arena. I can't think how we could have possibly broken any other rules." I would have loved to strike a musing pose but moving at all seemed unwise, gun and all that considered. "Unless we should have molested or killed someone by now. My bad if it's that. Tell that fella to put away his gun and I'll make up for it in no time. Pinkie swear." To underscore that, I wriggled my right hand—the one pointedly lacking a pinkie, but since I was still wearing my gloves, nobody was the wiser of that. I at least found myself very funny. Fucking drugs!

Cortez considered briefly, then turned to another goon. "Get him up here."

Very cryptic, no explanation—and still, I wasn't surprised when, maybe twenty seconds later, the goon returned with two more who hauled in Nate, forcing him into a similar position to ours next to Cortez, facing us. They'd also bound his hands, and someone had passingly washed some of the blood—but not all—off him. The gash across his torso was scabbed over but still leaking fluids, and in the flickering light of the flames I could see fresh bruises forming where the fight had left more marks. From up close, he looked even more emaciated, and I could see a lot of scars I wasn't familiar with. He also wasn't wearing a stitch of clothing, which was disconcerting for so many reasons.

Because none of us was an imbecile, we didn't trade glances. Nate only looked at me until he recognized me, not even halfway through the door yet, and ignored Richards as steadfastly. With no more hooks available, one of the goons was forced to hold up his bound arms, and Nate did a good job slouching in on himself with the slack that left his body, becoming a lot of passive weight.

I knew I should have kept my trap shut—and I didn't feel much like talking since the track record for confirming my worst guesses was stellar so far—but Eden wouldn't have, and changing my demeanor now was the best confirmation Cortez could get for anything short of me telling him I was indeed Nate's wife and here to spring him.

Thank fuck, the drugs were making gushing uselessly very easy.

"Big fan of yours," I practically cooed in Nate's direction. He didn't react, which worked just as well—he hardly would have at a random, drugged-up bitch chatting him up. "Loved the move with the heart. That was awesome! Hey, can I get an autograph, maybe? You I'd even offer my boobs for that." One of the goons cleared his throat in what I figured was a suppressed laugh. Nobody else reacted. A shame, really. Cortez was watching both me and Nate like a hawk, not missing anything—only that there wasn't anything to catch besides my manic ramble.

Since I got no response, it made sense to turn to Cortez again. "Look, I really appreciate the meet and greet but this is getting weird. Just ask what you wanna know. Promise, I'll tell you."

Cortez considered, and his attention was on Nate when he uttered his next order. "Give them both another hit. Maybe that will get better results."

That didn't sound good—and felt even less so when, seconds later, the harsh chemical burn of an injection hit the side of my neck where it wasn't protected by my elevated arms. "Not this again," I heard myself grumble—but rather than feel myself go slack with some kind of paralytic or other, I felt liquid euphoria hit my body. It took me a few seconds to realize that the weird sound I was hearing was my own laughter, quite exhileratingly so.

Ah, fuck. Just what I needed.

"How much did you give her?" That came from Cortez, I thought. I couldn't be quite sure. Damn, but focusing on anything was hard!

"One normal dose," one of the goons responded. "Not even a large one since she clearly already had one."

Ha, that was something I could give my two cents to. "Two!" I called out before more laughter forced me to stop. "Three if you count last night. We knew we would be crashing here and Amos got driving duty so I figured, fuck it, I'm gonna have some fun!"

Someone behind me cursed, and I didn't catch what else he muttered. Looking around, I found Richards grinning stupidly at the ground between his knees but he seemed to have an easier time keeping his trap shut. Nate was still stoically ignoring everything going around him but I noticed that the tension was back in his body. He couldn't actually expect to be able to fight anyone, right? I sure as fuck was in no condition to.

"Doesn't matter," I heard Cortez declare, then louder, "Check if she has any other ink elsewhere."

Like before, they didn't offer me the choice of taking my clothes off myself but cut them away instead, until all I was wearing were the gloves as they were too lazy to undo the ropes. My toes and thigh got some less appreciative comments, but it was only when Cortez stepped behind me to check on my ass himself that I managed to get a grip on my weird mind once more.

"Interesting," I heard him muse as he straightened once more, his attention on Nate now. "So you do have a name after all."

"That's not his name," I heard myself blather, followed by more chuckling. At least it wasn't full-on laughter—yet.

Cortez, no longer that relaxed and easygoing, grabbed my hair and forced my head back until I was staring straight up into his face. It didn't get much prettier upside down, but I noticed a scar along the underside of his chin, as if someone had tried to ram a knife into his skull from there.

"Explain," he repeated, increasing the strain on my hair until I winced.

"Told you before, they're just stupid tats!" I cried out, adding a little more desperation to my tone than I felt—and was quite surprised that it actually worked. "What, you can't be that fucking stupid and believe this shit, right? Man, come on! Seriously?" Laughing in this position wasn't easy, and I only did it to prove a very small point. He really didn't look happy with me, but there was no going back now, since I'd already insulted him. "The names? Yeah, sure, I'm Bree Lewis and he's Nate Miller, and I'm here to spring him from prison! My army of five thousand people is waiting just outside your walls! Just how fucking stupid do you need to be to think that?"

I fully expected some painful repercussions for that, but he only let go of me as he stepped away, making me laugh in actual relief. Not sure this had been enough, I forced myself to keep going.

"It was a fun idea at the time. At least ten people I know got the tats. I have no fucking clue who that guy is. He wasn't there that night. Probably picked up the idea from one of the others. Or what do I know, maybe people are that weird independent of each other? Could be all the rage from what I know? I don't go around checking people's asses for tats. I mean, who does that?" Exhaling forcefully, I did my best to draw myself up into as dignified a position as I could manage, kneeling there, buck-ass naked, and too fucked up in the head to care, much. "You can't punish people for being stupid like that, or else you won't have any customers left here for your sick little games." Damnit! "And sick they are," I tried to backtrack. "I mean, sick, as in awesome! Never thought I'd see a guy eat another's heart, but here we are! Just let us go, okay? And thanks for the hit because this shit's amazing! But you're kind of killing my buzz with all that glowering and shit."

Cortez listened to me with the same relaxed patience as before but didn't answer. Instead, he walked over to Nate, looking down at him. "As usual, I won't be getting anything out of you, huh? We'll see." I really didn't like the nasty grin crossing his features as he turned to his men next. "Throw all three of them in his cell. I need those two more sober to be of any use. If I'm right, that should give them enough time to share stories and be in the right mindset to be more open to a certain kind of persuasion. If I'm wrong, maybe our nameless champion here gets to have some fun—or food. That little bit of muscle can't have been that filling, right?"

I tried to speak up—with what, I had no clue, but it didn't matter since someone hit me hard in the back of the head, and by the time I could think straight again, I was already being carried off, slung over a goon's shoulder.

Well, that could have gone better—but also so much worse.

Judging from Cortez's remark, worse would happen once the drugs wore off once more. Oh, what a lovely prospect to look forward to.

Chapter 22

I didn't struggle, which came with the small mercy of being treated like a sack of flour, meaning once we reached our destination I was unceremoniously dumped on the cold, hard ground, but without any extra kicks or shit like that. Light disappeared as a heavy door fell shut, the sound of several bolts being engaged following. I counted to ten in my head, then started working my wrists and hands, hell-bent on getting the gloves off. Tying my hands behind my back must have seemed so smart to them.

Fucking incompetent assholes!

At the count of seven, my right hand slid free, and then it was easy since that created enough slack in the ropes to get the other out as well. "Ha!" I called out in triumph, wriggling my fingers, then rubbing my wrists to help circulation normalize again. I was still seeing spots but my eyes were already getting accustomed to the darkness, not quite complete as it was thanks to some light coming in from somewhere above.

"Congrats on what must be the most disastrous rescue mission in the history of mankind," I heard Nate gripe from somewhere close by—the lump to my right, I realized. That must be Red closer to the door then.

"Oh, I don't know," I murmured, then scooted over to Nate and reached for the ropes on his wrists. A little more finger wriggling and waiting for my vision to clear up was required, but I soon set to work. "It took us all of three hours to get in here, find you, and be in a position to escape together. That's three to four days ahead of the most positive estimations." The ropes fell away, Nate already turning around.

I grabbed his face and kissed him as deeply as soon as I could, which was easily facilitated by cutting off the, without a doubt, snide response he was ready to deliver. I was met with zero resistance and some hefty, immediate response that made me want to crawl right on top of him and—

"Uh, guys? I can't get out of the ties myself, and if you absolutely must be getting it on now, at least free me first so I can hold my hands over my ears."

I was very reluctant to stop but Nate was already pushing me away, although I could feel his visceral regret in the way his hands continued to linger on my upper arms. I gave him a small smile—which was likely a huge grin, judging from how weird it made my face feel—before I pulled away to help Richards.

"Spoilsport," I muttered as I pulled on the knots, these ones just as easily undone as the others. Did no one know how to tie people up properly?

"You've already had your revenge on me today," he retorted, rubbing his wrists after the last rope fell away. It was obvious that he couldn't see as well as Nate and me in the almost darkness, which gave me a few ideas—that I promptly dismissed when I caught the serious look on Nate's face.

"Maybe you think that travesty of a plan of yours is working, but that ends here." I really didn't like his tone—it was way too dejected and desperate for it to be good news. Before I could object, his scrutiny of my face cut me off again. "Exactly how drugged up are you?"

"Very," I explained with way too much enthusiasm. "I might benefit from a punch or two in the gut. Any volunteers?"

Before Richards could even think about responding, Nate already growled, "If you even think about hitting my wife, I'll fucking end you!"

Red's hands shot up, the man wise beyond his years. "Not sure I could hit her right now. Hit, as in not miss. But I wouldn't. Besides, I don't think it works that way. Didn't work when she was in a fight earlier."

"Spoilsport," I told him again, then turned back to Nate. "I may blather like I'm drunk to the gills but my motor control is at ninety percent. Maybe eighty-five," I amended when I needed some extra balance to remain leaning against the cold, cut stone of the wall—not polished, but cut as in hewn. "Doesn't matter. You're alive. That matters. And we're now getting out of here."

I thought I caught the hint of a smile on Nate's face but it was gone when I blinked to further focus my eyes. He was way too serious for this to be any fun. I didn't care for how he was looking at Richards as if asking for help—with me—from him. Nothing came as I was starting to suspect that Red's reaction to drugs was to turn into a vegetable, while I got weird and hyperactive.

"There may be a way, but it's a slim chance," Nate muttered, more to himself than us. "But since it's our only chance, no sense in not trying. See that opening up there? I've managed to weaken the foundations the two middle bars are set in. Richards, you can maybe pry them the rest of the way out."

Craning my neck, I stared up at the window, for lack of a better word. I was seeing well enough to be able to make out the extent of our confines. The room wasn't very long—just so that we could stand next to each other without touching—and narrow enough that I could see how someone with longer legs and extra inches in height could have climbed up there pushing against the opposite walls. But what it lacked in both length and breadth, it made up in height, the opening sitting at a good fifteen feet above my head.

"Sure, I'll try," Richards offered after staring at the opening a little too long. "How do I get up there?"

"Hands on either side of the walls," Nate offered, validating my guess. "But since it's three of us now, it's probably faster if we try to build some kind of human pyramid. That way you won't fall right down if one of the bars gives."

"Why don't you do it?" I asked, feeling a little stupid. "You know your cell quite well, from what it sounds like." That guess was also supported by the smell.

Nate gave me a sardonic look. "I would, but both my shoulders are shot to hell. Dislocated one too many times without getting properly set and enough time to fully heal."

That irritated me for so many reasons, none of them empathy-driven—again, damn drugs! "Just an hour ago, I saw you pick up a guy and throw him several feet through the air."

"And now my shoulders are killing me to the point where I could hardly boost you up if I had to," he bit out, the venom in his tone clearly borne of hatred of his shortcomings, not because I'd asked.

"Well, that explains it!" I answered in the same heated tone, but lost it as I drew up short. "Anything we can do about it now?"

He shook his head. "It's set as much as it will go. Give me two weeks of rest, and I'll be good as new. Since we have maybe two hours, get the fuck up there and do something!"

Yeah, so much for tearful, emotional reunions. I hadn't expected one of those, but ending up pressed against the wall, standing on Nate's shoulders, somehow trying not to allow my knees to buckle under what felt like a ton of stone but was likely only part of Red's weight on my shoulders in turn was not what I'd envisioned. Richards did his best to cling to the more secure bars of the window, but there was only so much that he could do while he pulled with all of his strength. It sure made for interesting views—which I was hard-pressed not to comment on, and would take to my grave.

I was relieved when Nate broke the relative silence. Red's grunts weren't helping, really. "Let me guess—you don't have five thousand people ready to attack?"

"More like fifty," I offered.

"Sixty-three," Red corrected me from up above. "But not sure about all our spies, or how quickly we can activate them."

I felt Nate nod against my ankle. It got very distracting when he briefly—maybe even accidentally—brushed his cheek against my skin.

"How soon can you get them here?"

"Soon," I replied, deliberately not giving away more should anyone listen to us. With the drone of the storm and rain outside—which made talking between the three of us hard enough—I doubted it was something I needed to worry about, but you never knew.

"Good." The following pause was a pregnant one, making me glance down to Nate. He was staring straight up at my face, his gaze turning imploring as it caught and held mine. "Bree, you have to promise me. As soon as Richards gets the bars off, you're out of here, do you understand?"

"Sure, after I've found a rope and gotten you two out as well."

Only then I noticed how bleak his expression really was. "The gap's too small for either of us," he explained. "But it's large enough for you. Just get out, sneak out of the town, and get help. That's the best you can do."

I was already shaking my head, making Nate squeeze my legs—hard enough to hurt, if only for a second.

Just then, Richards gave a hard jerk, whooping in triumph as he pulled the first bar free. "Got it!"

"Keep going," Nate called up, only then making me realize that his revelation had been spoken too softly to carry up all the way to the top. But then Richards was smart, and I didn't doubt he'd soon come to the same conclusion, if he hadn't already.

I really didn't like this.

"By the way, Romanoff and Zilinsky say hi. I'm sure they'd whoop my ass if I didn't tell you," I offered conversationally. No response came, but then I hadn't expected any.

Richards saved the day when he pulled the second bar free minutes later, making me guess Nate had known they were ready to come off but had bided his time until he could get a third loose—only that he hadn't had the opportunity to. I was very happy to get Richards off me, and with a little scuffing we ended up on the ground once more to regroup.

I was already gearing up for the protest of the ages but Nate cut me off by gently cradling the back of my head and neck in his hand, leaning in so he could touch his forehead to mine. His eyes, so close to mine, stared at me imploringly. "Bree, I need you to be free," he whispered, barely loud enough to be heard over the rain and storm outside. "Trust me, after how long? Going on nine weeks—"

"I wish I'd managed to get here sooner," I offered, chagrined.

"Doesn't matter," he was quick to assure me. "You're here, and you brought backup, and after what little I've managed to hear from others, in this world with what's going on out there that's close to a fucking miracle in itself! I'd give anything to be out of here right this fucking second, but I'll hold out a while longer. Problem is, I don't have anything to give up, and the only thing that's kept me holding on so far is knowing that you're safe. That you're not here."

"How did you know—"

The shushing sound he offered made me fall silent. "Not important. I'll explain once we are out of here. My point is, if you're still here when they come back, things will get bad. Fucking bad, fucking quickly. And I'm talking your level of imagination bad, just so we're clear here. You'll help me the most by not being here. And don't bring up Richards, I know he'll agree with me once he gets what's at stake."

"No protest from me," Red, ever the traitor, provided.

Nate ignored him. "Promise me."

I really didn't want to—and not being able to feel real, deep-seated fear didn't help—but I swallowed thickly and nodded. "Promise."

"Good. Then up you go. In this weather, it shouldn't be hard for you to slip away unseen." Any and all protest I could have offered up he cut short with a deep, lingering kiss, and then they were already boosting me up to get to the window.

Damn fucking martyrs!

But considering Nate's stance on heroes and shit, he must have had a very good reason for his actions, and I had nothing to put up against that.

The window was barely more than a large slit in the wall, making it fucking impossible for me to find a way to pull myself through, but I somehow managed, scraping my stomach and back up good while maneuvering. It would be hell for anyone substantially more solid than I was, and not just because of the remaining two bars set into the frame. Part of the problem was that the bottom of the window was level with the ground, giving me next to no purchase. It would have been easier with a rope—or pretty much anything else—to cling to. Outside there was a large, open area, some kind of yard if I wasn't mistaken. Rain and wind assaulted me immediately but I didn't care, pushing and kicking until I was finally free. At least all that mud made me feel less naked.

I had barely straightened, hesitating in my decision whether to bolt or call down into the cell one last time when a piercing whistle made me jump. A single figure materialized out of the shadows at the other end of the yard…

Fucking Marleen!

"What are you doing here?" I whisper-shouted as she came over, her hair drenched but the rest of her looking warm and cozy.

"Why are you naked?" she asked instead of an answer, peering down at the gap in the wall that I'd just crawled out of.

"It's complicated," I offered, then thought better of it. "Or not. Whatever, not important." I looked at the shadows she'd come from. "Is that farm equipment?"

She glanced at what I was looking at. "I think they are using those trucks for bringing in produce, yeah. Why?"

"Any way you can get one working? One with a winch, and four-wheel drive would be best."

"What do you need it for?"

I pointed at the remaining bars. "Something that's strong enough to tear the bars out. Likely, a chain wrapped around them will do. Quick! We're running out of time!" From the outside, it was easy to see where the bars had been installed, set into concrete. A hard enough pull and something would give, either the bars themselves or their foundation.

Marleen didn't ask any further questions but instead ran over to the trucks to check up on them. I went to investigate the crates that were stacked up along the wall. No convenient stacks of clothes, sadly, but I found some rope and chains, and some roughly hewn wooden poles that could work well as makeshift weapons if one didn't mind splinters too much. The sound of a truck starting up made me cast around frantically, but no guards came running. Marleen was quick to drive it over in reverse and back it all the way up to the window so we could get the chain wrapped around the bars and locked on to the trailer hitch—and then it was time for some action. Also for me to lose my balance and land smack on my ass in the mud, but little did I care about my dignity right then.

Marleen started up the car, spraying water, mud, and gravel everywhere as she tried to go forward. Metal groaned, then screamed, making me look around, paranoid that now someone must be coming for us—but the yard remained empty. Something snapped, the chain suddenly no longer taut, and the car jumped forward. I was afraid the chain itself had snapped but when I checked on them, both bars were gone. Marleen was already backing up again so I could replace the chain with the longest rope I'd found and throw the other end down into the cell. It remained slack for maybe five seconds, and within a minute, Richards was proving my guess right that getting him through would be a tight fit. The mud seemed to help some, and another five minutes later, he was out. As soon as he'd caught his breath, we started pulling up the rope, not quite trusting the car for the job. Nate's obvious starvation diet had the advantage that he was out in no time, staggering to his feet with something between bewilderment and disbelief on his face.

"Told you time and time again—I'm amazing," I preened, but held back on the impulse to jump him then and there.

"You are," he simply offered, then frowned as the truck door opened. "Marleen?"

The assassin came sauntering to the back of the vehicle, giving Nate—and Richards, I didn't miss that—an appraising once-over.

"I already asked your wife why she's crawling, buck-ass naked, out of holes in the ground so I won't repeat the question, although I'm sure there's an interesting story behind that. Instead I'll say, damn, guy! You absolutely managed to find the one woman crazy enough to marry you, and she's continually proving the point! We really need to catch up."

I hated to rain on their parade—and found the pun hilarious enough to start snickering—but someone had to do it. "Can we maybe do this where we won't get caught and dragged off to God knows where in a sec? This fucking camp here really makes me realize that I don't have a nudist gene in my body."

Marleen squinted at me—and not my tits, that was for sure—and then Richards. "Shit. You're both high as a kite right now."

"Yup," I confirmed her guess.

"Perfect," she drawled, but actually looked excited rather than taken aback. For a moment only, I felt a hint of paranoia come up inside of me, but it was gone a second later.

"What's the quickest way out of here?" I asked. "Clothes would be nice but I've already spent a day running through the wilderness around here with my ass hanging out, I don't mind another if it means I can go where I want to." Nate gave me a weird look for that but didn't ask. "Can we get to the cars we came in with? We have clothes, gear, and weapons there. And the cars."

Marleen considered but then shook her head. "I'm still sketchy on the layout of the camp but we're pretty much on the opposite end. I don't think it's worth risking it."

"Where are we?" Maybe a stupid question from me, but I had spent a little time snooping around the outside of the camp. And if those were the trucks for the produce, maybe—

Marleen nodded at a large building at the other end of the yard. "That's one of the warehouses, and beyond that are the worker barracks. We could try the trucks here but I'm afraid they will make too much noise. Plus, there's a gate over there that's locked tight, and I don't think we can pull it apart like those neat little prison bars. But we can climb over it, no problem."

"Sounds like a plan," Nate agreed with her, talking right over anything I could have offered. I didn't mind. For once, I had zero objections.

"You might want to grab some clothes along the way," Marleen advised. "Love the view, but your lily-white asses shine in the darkness like nobody's business."

"Good idea," I replied. "If you happen so see a clothes line somewhere—"

Her dark laugh made me cut off. "Not in this weather. But I just told you, that building over there is full of people. Most of them like to wear clothes. The rest are likely not asked about their preferences."

"I wouldn't be too sure with these assholes," I muttered, ignoring the sidelong glance Nate gave me. "The barracks it is!"

Climbing out of the cell had been one thing; running and sneaking turned out to be quite another. Running without boots was weird for me on a normal day but tonight was everything but. Shivering from the torrential rain and gusts of wind strong enough to force me to add some extra steps to get where I wanted didn't exactly help. Without Marleen scouting ahead to warn us when to wait and when to run, things would have gotten complicated. As it was, it took us an ungodly amount of time to get to the barracks, which didn't bode well for the rest of our escape.

There were a lot of bolted-shut doors and windows with iron bars, but after rounding the building to get to the backside we found a door unlocked. It turned out to be a stroke of luck—a washroom, very basic, but we didn't need much. Threadbare towels to dry off a little were pure luxury. There were several hampers stored inside brimming with dirty, torn clothes—and no freshly washed ones, I checked every container available—but that was still better than nothing. Nate didn't hesitate for a second, and Red's delay seemed more because a thunderbolt outside made him blink stupidly into the rain than actual revulsion. Not for the first time in my life I was glad I couldn't catch normal diseases anymore and swallowed my reluctance. Even with the storm, it was warm enough that we wouldn't die of exposure, but it wasn't just predators lurking in the night that made me glad to have some clothes on once more. We didn't find any boots but nothing we could do about that.

Marleen appeared once more, having left us to our dressing efforts while scouting ahead. "You ready for a quick climb?" she asked, still way too chipper.

"You seem awfully familiar with the terrain," Nate remarked, still busy tying some extra rope around his hips as a makeshift belt. When Marleen—and I guessed, me as well—only stared at him, he looked up, raising his brows. "Correct me if I'm wrong, but judging from the so-far bungling approach to all this, you didn't have a lot of intel going in. So what's up with your great topographical knowledge?"

Marleen's expression turned smug. "I may or may not have tracked down Rita's spy and forced him to give me the deets," she explained. "Someone had to do the work, while others got themselves punched in the face and thrown into cells. I'm not throwing shade there—you did a great job cutting down recon time on that part of the mission, but it's a little sketchy on contingency options."

"Well, that's what we have you for, apparently," I quipped. "Can we move on now?"

We were just about to leave the building when a figure stepped through the door—Scott, I realized, followed by two more guys who looked vaguely familiar—likely his men. He ignored Marleen so I figured they'd already met outside. He briefly nodded in what must have been Richards's direction while I got a glance only, his attention flitting to Nate. I knew they could have handled introductions themselves but ever the cheerful socialite, I offered, "That's Scott, he's—fuck." And there went my memory. Nate, his attention on the newcomers, gave me a sidelong look. I shrugged. "If I say he's a marsupial, someone's going to gun me down in a sec, so I'll just leave it at that."

A hint of a smirk crossed Nate's expression. "Shit, I've missed you," he muttered in my direction, then louder, "MARSOC, I presume?" He turned to Scott, offering his hand. "Miller, as you probably already guessed. Glad to see some of the Raiders still around." Scott accepted the handshake, somewhat mollified by Nate's words but still finding the time to glare at me. "I'm not going to apologize for anything she says or does," Nate went on, now earning himself a glare from me.

"Understandably," Scott offered gruffly. "Would be a full-time job from what I've seen."

"Can we go now?" I heard myself whine, hating how that came out. "If you're done disparaging me, that is. We still need to find a way out and not get caught."

Scott had the audacity to look surprised at my straightforward approach but didn't protest—and, much to my surprise, handed Nate his backup gun plus holster and had his men do the same to me and Richards. I wasn't sure I should be using that thing right now but it felt great being armed with something besides a piece of wood again. Scott continued his explanation while we put the guns away. "We ran into Marleen just as she was returning. Something's going on out there, which may be related to your prison break, or maybe not, but we should use the distraction. Over the gate and up the hill is our best exit route. We've briefly connected with our contact here and that's the best way out they've settled on."

"Your contact's a woman?" I asked, flummoxed—and hating my own hypocrite ass for it.

Scott snorted but didn't deny it. "The more machismo the place, the less visible a female operator is. Unless, of course, she has to prove to the world that she has the biggest balls and is screaming for everyone to cut them off."

I took his criticism with as much stoic ignorance as I could. "No idea why you all keep ragging on me. So far my escape plan is working amazingly well! None of you could shine if I didn't set the bar this low."

Scott, ready to debate my claim, snapped his mouth shut and instead nodded at the doorway. "Let's go." It was only after we were all out and heading for the gate, using what cover was available, that he held Richards and me back. "Why the fuck are you both stoned as hell? None of us inhaled. Why did you?"

"First off, they also gave us a shot when they caught us," Richards objected.

"Because I'm not a pansy marsupial who has to fake it to make it," I hissed, although I was more amused than offended. "You do things your way, we do it ours. You would have stuck out like a sore thumb as we got in, we have slight memory and fine motor function issues now. That's how teams work. Can we please have this discussion once we're out of the camp? And preferably once I've had time to sober up, because I'm really not at the height of my intellectual capacity."

I was almost surprised—and a little disappointed—when no protest followed. Seconds into the thunderstorm, I was drenched to the skin again, and I slid somewhat awfully without boots in the mud and puddles, but we made good headway toward the gate as no one was out and about in this torrential downpour. With plenty of strong, tall men about, neither Marleen nor I needed to ask for a boost up, and Red was smart enough to simply keep his hands ready to help Nate without him requiring to, either. The grass on the other side was greener than in the yard—my own pun making me snicker, which got me a weird look from one of Scott's men—making dropping down easy, and then it was away from the camp, up the trail to the fields that I'd hidden by on my escape. Still no guards in sight, making me a little loopy with excitement—until I saw something ahead of us.

"Lights," I hissed to one of Scott's men who was walking directly in front of us. "To your eleven."

He squinted into the darkness. Without flashlights, it was pretty much walking blindly through the muck until someone broke a leg—unless the flashes of the thunderstorm blinded us. "You sure? I don't see anything."

Nate, previously behind me, caught up to us, staring in the same direction. "Five vehicles. All ATVs. They're headed in our direction."

"A patrol, looks like. They're going too fast to be searching for someone," I confirmed. They were driving along the same road we'd been following. "They'll be here in three minutes, maybe four."

"How the fuck—" the guy kept protesting. A quick prod with my stick made him shut up.

"Because we're so fucking special," I stated.

Nate, ever the spoilsport, explained. "Because she and I have great low-light vision. Comes with getting a little too cozy with the undead at times."

I was surprised that Nate admitted that; Richards—and thus everyone in the army—must have known about me by now, but even I hadn't known about Nate before we'd split paths as we'd hid on the destroyer to be later brought to the shore a few states south of the others' drop-off point.

"What's your plan?" Scott asked—Nate, of course, because I hadn't been running this mission so far. But I had to admit, his answer had been the one more instilling trust in someone than mine.

Nate considered. "How far is your forward base away?"

I shrugged, trying to remember. "A few miles outside of their patrol perimeter. Twenty miles?"

Nate made a face, staring back at the ATVs that slowly came closer. "We need those vehicles. At least three of them, four would be better. No shots fired unless we absolutely have to." A peel of thunder overhead must have let him see me grimace. "You have a stick. Use it."

So that's what we did.

Getting the ATVs under our control turned out to be easier than I'd expected. All it took was a few logs—conveniently stacked close by—as a barrier in the middle of the road. As soon as the vehicles stopped, it was bludgeoning time. Whether they'd gotten complacent, or only gone out with one driver and no backup because of the rain, but they were no match for us. I pointedly ignored how Nate didn't even try to incapacitate first but went straight for the kill. Of course I noticed—how could I not? But only two of the guards ended up breathing when we were done, and shallow enough that they might not live to see another morning. None of that was important. We now had vehicles, and thanks to my previous scouting somewhat of an idea of the terrain—and the direction we needed to be headed— so off we went. I ended up riding with Scott—or he with me, rather, since my better vision made me the designated driver—and Red with Marleen. I hoped that Nate's shoulders would be okay but trusted him to speak up before he was ready to fall off the vehicle.

We absolutely needed the lights; tonight was not the night for stealth. I sure as fuck hoped the ATVs' batteries would hold out long enough but even if they died on us two miles later, that was still two miles less we'd need to walk.

Lo and behold, fate continued to play nice, and all the ATVs made it out of the zone around the camp. And three hours of getting splashed and endless jostling later, I saw the shine of campfires up ahead, right next to the road we were following. A few tense moments of shouting later—mostly because nobody had expected us to show up for days yet—and we were safely through the perimeter of our forward operational base where Zilinsky, Romanoff, and Martinez were already waiting for us, never mind that it was way past two in the morning with rain still beating down mercilessly on the world. At least the thunder was gone now, and none of us had been struck by lightning.

I was ready to keel over, a weird fog making my brain less than useful, the drugs starting to wear off and exhaustion taking its toll. Or hunger—that I didn't feel—since I hadn't had much to eat since morning, I realized. While Zilinsky and Romanoff were busy hugging Nate, I happily accepted a cold bowl of stew from someone and started wolfing it down. Nate—and the others, too, of course— also got some chow, but while he dug into it with gusto, he forced himself to stop about a third of the way through. "Need to give my system some time to adapt," he explained as he put it away, looking like that was the last thing he wanted to do.

The base camp was pretty much a few tents around an old, dilapidated building, some kind of two-story shop or former apartment building, parts of it fallen in already as it couldn't have seen much commerce since the '60s. It lent some shade during the heat of the day and dry rooms out of the rain now—but that was pretty much it. I couldn't wait to crawl into a dry corner and get some shut-eye—but everyone else had other ideas.

I could tell that everyone and their mother wanted a sitrep update, but Nate cut that short three questions in, raising his voice to shut everyone up. "I know we have a lot to talk about, but unless it can't wait for another thirty minutes, I really need some alone-time with my wife right now."

Several people actually looked chagrined, and Andrej's chuckle was well-representing the rest. "Take forty-five. It's been a while for you both." I couldn't help but grin, although I had a feeling that wasn't Nate's intention for that ask. Nate's glare made Andrej chuckle harder, but murmurs from all around offered that they had other things to do, anyway—like sleep, in the middle of the night.

Turning to the Ice Queen, Nate instructed, "Have everyone who needs to be part of discussions ready in fifty minutes. The rest can stand down for now but we will be on the move soon after."

She acknowledged that with a nod and already turned to bark orders—if at muted volume—at people all around. Nate cast another longing look at the food but instead grabbed my arm and pulled me into the building, down the corridor that Pia had indicated where we'd find a few empty rooms. Far was it from me to protest.

Chapter 23

I barely made it through the door before Nate grabbed me and had me pressed against the sturdy wood, his hands everywhere and his mouth devouring mine. My mind was lagging behind several steps—only after a few seconds coming to the conclusions that no, we weren't going to talk first—but my body was very enthusiastically on board. I was very happy to shed the dirty, stinking, drenched clothes I'd later burn with gusto, and wrap myself around his strong, taut body, enticingly warm as it was, to reacquaint myself with everything that was familiar and discover every bump and scar that was new.

Someone had been thoughtful enough to leave some blankets and sleeping bags on the floor which quickly got repurposed. Frantic was the best way to describe it, and while I was very much on board with forgetting about all the time we'd spent apart, my mind finally did jump-start once more. I didn't mind being on my back underneath him but there was the matter of Nate's shoulders.

"Wanna switch?" I offered when I needed to come up for air.

Nate, clearly starving for more than food, was making me laugh—and moan—by kissing and licking his way down the column of my throat in the meantime, if anything annoyed at having to divert his attention to answer the question. He only stopped briefly to catch my gaze, his weight held up steady by his arms left and right of my face. "I'll let you know before I have to tap out," he growled, capturing my lips with his before I could come up with a response that wasn't required nor wanted. Fine by me. I was more than happy to abuse my position to let my hands roam down his back and reach for him—

Only that he shifted, leaving my lips and neck in favor of my breasts, then moving further down—and my mind was back at it again. "Uh, just saying. I haven't had a chance to shower or properly bathe in three weeks," I told the top of his head, currently getting busy between my spread legs.

His fingers dug deeper into my thighs—not that I'd tried to get away; I was too selfish for that, and quite too needy as well—holding me right where he wanted me. "Don't fucking care," he murmured against me and set to work—and, what could I say? It had been months, he was even more enthusiastic about this than usual, and the damn drugs did their thing to make it very easy to let go. And let go again because apparently absence not only made the heart grow fonder but also the damn bastard more ambitious than usual, leaving me panting and lightheaded, and thoroughly satisfied, when he kissed his way up my body once more.

"You smell so fucking delicious," he whispered into my ear—and at the same time thrust into me, deep and hard and hitting all the right spots to turn me into a whimpering mess all over again. No longer restricted by him holding me in place, I was happy to match his pace as I half wrapped myself around him, half moved against him to maximize friction in all the right places. It felt so fucking amazing but at the same time a part deep inside of me couldn't get enough, as if the time we'd lost needed to be made up for right this very second which was impossible on so many levels. He seemed to be thinking along the same lines—or maybe it was his shoulders protesting which kept him distracted too much—because just as I was about to lose it again, he flipped me over and onto my side so that he was spooning me with his entire body from behind, letting us both stretch out and relax but also kept our hands free. Well, mine weren't free for long as he pulled me flush against him, using his lower hand to grab my wrists and keep them there, while his legs entwined with mine. Just as he pushed into me from behind, his fingers were back between my thighs, strumming and stroking in perfect sync with—

Turning my face into his shoulder, I bit the inside of my cheek hard not to cry out loud enough to wake every sleeping asshole in camp, the dichotomy of pure lust and need on one side and feeling so wonderfully safe and warm and close to him on the other wiping my mind clear of thought and reason. And the same—in reverse—must have been true for him as well as it didn't take him much longer to finish, ending with us both lost in satisfaction…

Until I realized that it wasn't sweat—or rainwater, coming in somewhere—that was dripping into the hair at the back of my head. That he wasn't just holding me in place because he was a teasing asshole or for convenience, but pretty much clung to me like I was his rock and he was about to be swept away by the rough seas. With an iron fist slamming closed around my heart, I listened into the dark room, but besides our slowly evening-out breaths there were no further clues—no surprise since I was convinced Nate would rather die than sob once—but I didn't need further confirmation to draw the right conclusions.

My body might still be swimming in a cloud of endorphins and happiness, but my mind ground to a sudden hold, deepest apprehension warring with confusion and frustration.

Fuck.

The irony wasn't lost on me that we'd been at this exact moment before, only with our roles reversed. I now perfectly understood his frustration—with the circumstances, but also with me—after they'd picked me up from that blasted settlement in Nebraska after Taggard and his boys had kidnapped me, and words had been the most insufficient thing in the world.

I had no fucking clue what to say now.

I was a little surprised when, of all possible things, it was an echo of what he'd said to me then that made it over my lips. "You know that you can tell me everything, right? It won't make a difference for me."

I more felt than heard him laugh—and it was definitely not a mirth-filled outburst. "You wouldn't say that if you had the whole picture."

I considered but only for a moment. "There aren't many things that you could have actively done that would leave me horrified beyond what we could come back from. Together. And you know, I have a vivid imagination."

He remained silent for way too long to leave me feeling comfortable, but finally relaxed enough for me to turn around, not extricating myself from his arms but needing to be able to look him in the face. My heart seized up seeing his eyes slightly red, staring at me with a kind of desperation that I'd never seen before—fear of rejection.

Nate cleared his throat noisily, but didn't look away. "How about you tell me how you got away from there the first time, and I tell you how I knew you had gotten away?" he proposed, his voice cracking slightly. My turn to talk first. Fuck if my brain was ready to find the right words—but this I could do.

"Not really much of a story," I offered, trying to sound nonchalant but failing.

Nate's eyes narrowed. "The last thing I remember seeing was you lying there, tied up, completely helpless. And just so you know, even when you spend a shitload of time in solitary confinement, you get a chance to hear people talk. I know what their so-called kennels are."

"Then you probably know more than I do," I bit out, a little too sharply, but seeing the spark of annoyance in his eyes actually made me relax a little. "There's really not much to tell. They drugged me with some shit—might be the same they shot me up with tonight, I really can't say—"

"They are big on chemicals," he interjected. "Their chief chemist gets bored easily." Now that sounded like a story I both wanted to hear but really not at the same time. The light the discarded flashlight in the corner cast was creating weird shadows all over the room, but was by far enough that it would have been impossible to miss the track marks in the crooks of his elbows—and considering the rate of healing we both had going on, that must be from the past week only.

Distraction, right.

"Anyway, when they caught us, we must have done a good job killing a few of them because one of those that dragged us in had a score to settle with me. They were stupid enough not to properly tie my hands but used flimsy handcuffs. Then that idiot was even more stupid and started beating me up first, which sent my adrenaline into overdrive, and the rest is bloody history. I don't really remember much after I killed him, it's all pretty hazy. I woke up the next morning in a tree, covered in blood that mostly wasn't mine, still not wearing any pants. Apparently, drugged-out me had other priorities." No laughing at my bad joke from either of us, so I shrugged and resumed. "Took me some time to find water, food, and clothes. I tried to get close to the camp but the patrols were too tight. I stumbled onto their fields to the north but didn't find you there. I didn't want to leave but it was obvious that I needed help to get you out of there. So I hoofed it to the next settlement, hitched a ride, did a lot of bullshitting and grandstanding, and here we are."

Some of the disquiet had left his expression after hearing about my almost clean get-away, but I could tell that he was aware this was the heavily edited version.

"How did you get people from all over the armed forces to work together? I know two of the guards from the Silo, and I don't quite see Richards deserting."

I was tempted to point out that I'd already answered one question but since this was kind of important, I was happy to give him some leeway there—besides the fact that I didn't want to hear his answer.

"Pia managed to organize some kind of pow-wow between us, the Silo marines, Scott and his super fancy operators, and Richards brought some of his guys as well. Which reminds me—why the fuck did you never tell me that you were playing drop-off dump with him? They picked me up a day after I made it to the next settlement. Would have been great to know I could count on that."

As expected, my criticism bounced right off him. "Because I was hoping to hell that we'd never see him ever again," he supplied, grimacing. "I needed a loophole, some kind of backdoor entrance. I knew that between Martinez and Burns, Zilinsky would have known who to track down if she needed to reach us, and I trusted Richards the most to do the same if our people got into some serious shit." He pointedly didn't answer my question, but for once, I let it slide.

"It was a smart move," I admitted. "And no, I wasn't overly surprised that you set that up."

"Of course you weren't," he replied. "You're a smart cookie if you want to be."

That made me squint at him. "Exactly how drugged up are you if you use terms like 'cookie' to refer to this fine piece of ass?"

He gave that some thought—way too much, really. "Moderately so, I'd say," he assessed. "They always give us some crap or other before a fight. To keep things interesting, you know?"

I had no idea what to respond to that, and after a few seconds, Nate caught his lower lip between his teeth, stalling further—but then let out a loud exhale as he sagged deeper into the sleeping bag, stretching out in what wasn't really working as far as relaxation went. "I presume I won't get away with not telling you anything? I know how morbid your ideas can get. This time you'll probably get most of it right just guessing."

My, didn't that sound nice. I considered my words carefully, or as much as my addled mind would let me. "You don't have to. I get that you don't want to. I really do. And I'm not giving you some bullshit now like it will all be so much better if you share. But, you know—maybe you should tell someone. Doesn't have to be me. Can be Zilinsky or Romanoff, too. Or Martinez. But I'd really like to know why the new number one on my shit list deserves to be there."

Nate's brows rose slightly. "You're giving up your vendetta to defend my honor? Did you actually grow as a person and mature while I was gone?"

"Very funny." I wondered briefly how much he'd heard about the state of the world in general. "Hamilton's dead, so the top spot is vacant right now. I think my potential for emotional growth bottomed out around the time you told me to stop being offended about stereotyping cars. And things have gone pretty much to hell since we bugged out."

He took the news of his former friend's demise without a single blink. I couldn't imagine the news was jarring to him. "How bad is it out there?"

"Bad. What we tried to support all went to shit, except the large settlements in Utah and Wyoming. New Angeles is strong but cut off from the outside world—their choice. A lot of what used to be scavengers like us are the drugged-out asshole road pirates that are probably your biggest fans. Harris is one of them, but he helped us get in so I'm a little torn about placing judgment right now. Because Rita was at the meeting, too, and Dispatch is a bust. She didn't send a single box of ammo with us. So much for old flames of yours and support."

Nate snorted. "Well, Marleen is here, which I absolutely didn't expect. For her to survive, sure, but not show her face anywhere ever again." He paused for a second. "You know that she and I—"

"Yup," I quipped, cutting him off before he got any further. "She also banged Richards, just so you know. No hard feelings; she and I are getting along splendidly."

"No surprise there," Nate muttered, making me grin for a second.

"She's weird, but I can see why you'd want her on your side in a pinch," I offered. "If you're ever thinking about a threesome, I might be down with her. Maybe."

"No fucking way," Nate enthused, making my grin resurface. "At best, you'd both spend an entire night making fun of me. Worst, you'd get into an actual fight. Either way, no actual action for me. Not interested."

"Aw, not fair! Some guys like to watch, you know?" His pointed look made me chuckle. "Okay, no threesome with Marleen. Probably better this way. She did kill a president, by the way. We have apparently had some but the marsupials keep losing them."

Nate frowned briefly, needing a few seconds to decipher my remark. "That Scott guy really will shoot you if you keep doing that," he wisely pointed out.

"Marine special ops, whatever," I muttered. "I'd rather deal with the Silo marines, anyway. I may not be their personal best friend but they actually wanted to work with us. I'm not sure but I think Buehler has a crush on Zilinsky, in a completely non-sexual, awestruck because of campfire stories kind of way. I won't hold it against Wilkes if he doesn't let you or me personally into his fortress but they have skin in the game and aren't afraid to get their hands dirty. Richards, too, if you still think we can trust him."

"He sent someone to pick you up?"

I shook my head. "He did it personally, with Hill and Cole riding along. And some rookie whose name I keep forgetting. They were apparently searching for us since you missed a drop-off. I don't quite buy it but they were there, and they helped me, and I feel like their support, while rubbing some people the wrong way, helped get this party started."

Nate mulled that over for a second. "They must have been scouting out the city," he mused. "That we up and disappeared without a trace must have tipped them off." He paused, a light frown coming to his forehead, as if he was trying to remember something. "So how did you convince them to help get me out? I may be a conceited asshole sometimes but I'm very much aware that I'm just one guy among many. Personal affiliations aside, what do they want from us in return?"

I wondered how best to phrase it. "They think Decker is still alive. They think you might be our best bet of taking him out."

Nate nodded absently, showing neither surprise nor trepidation. "Any concrete info or just everyone running around like headless chickens, blaming the others for why everything has turned to shit?"

"The latter."

"Thought so." He absently rolled the shoulder I was partly lying on—making me wonder if maybe I should find a different perch—but as soon as he felt me try to move away, the hand that lay casually splayed across my lower back pushed me further into him. It felt like an instinctive gesture, and I relaxed against him once more.

"That will make things easier," he remarked, mostly to himself. I could practically see the wheels in his head turning.

"Guess when you told Pia to get everyone ready you didn't mean to break camp and run."

He gave a brief jerk of his head. "Nope." He let out his breath slowly, then caught my gaze once more. "You want to know how I knew you were gone?"

"Not particularly, but I feel like you need to tell me."

Nate thought about that some—or how to broach the topic—and decided to start from the top. "My first mistake was that I underestimated them. At the beginning, it was all pretty straightforward—throw a guy into a deep, dark hole, don't feed him, give him barely enough water not to die of thirst, and you don't even need torture to wear someone down. Although they beat me up pretty much from the get-go. I spent the first night after the damn drugs had worn off worried sick about what was happening to you, but then decided that I wasn't going to be any use to you if I did all the work for them, so I decided I needed to take care of myself first. I know how that sounds—"

"Smart," I interjected. "Put on your oxygen mask before you help others. Only makes sense. And I did a pretty good job taking care of myself, if I may say so."

A hint of a smile tucked the corner of his mouth up. "I've missed how humble and selfless you are."

"My best traits, for sure."

Exhaling slowly, he went on, idly stroking my back as he was staring up at the crumbling ceiling above us, as if clues were printed up there. "There was only so much I could do at first, but prideful asshole that I am, of course I thought I could easily take whatever they'd throw my way. I've been both on the giving and receiving end of shit like that before—of course I know how to play the game. How to outsmart them. I was such a fucking idiot."

He paused, but I didn't add a joke or objection—I could tell that he wasn't completely here with me anymore, and even drugged up I wasn't stupid enough to make an ass of myself if I could avoid it.

His voice took on a deceptively calm tone as he went on, still staring at the ceiling. "Cortez is one sick motherfucker. I thought I'd figured him and his operation out when they dragged me out of my cell that day. I'd started making a few connections by then—they keep us in solitary confinement but the cells are right next to each other, and you can talk to each other sometimes—and gotten my fair share of warnings. I thought I knew the perfect strategy to lie to him, to play him—but really, he was playing me. I didn't quite laugh him in the face when he told me in excruciating detail how he was going to rape me, but thought to myself, eh, amateur move, very expected. Confirmed all my guesses, down to the point where he explained that he was going to do it slowly and with plenty of lube so as to undermine my self-perception if, lo and behold, I did feel something besides utter revulsion. He'd even provide some extra help for that."

I had to lock down my muscles not to physically cringe as much as my mind was doing, but that confused me. "I don't get it. How should not destroying your ass wear you down any quicker? Just saying, I still vividly remember how Andrej explained to me in way too many words how to smuggle a knife in when you expect to be captured somewhere. Or two knives, if you're of the female persuasion. You just need a condom, some lube, and a little patience."

Nate grimaced, but mirth briefly lit up his face. Yeah, they'd all laughed their—probably not quite that tight—asses off at my reaction.

"Ah, that was my thinking also. Although there is something to be said about being gentle and nice to someone you torture sometimes. It can screw with their minds, get some good foundation for Stockholm syndrome going. I figured he was going for that and dismissed his skills. That was, until they brought in the girl."

Now that sounded ominous. I didn't miss how his hand had stilled on my back, and now dropped away to rest at his side instead. "At first, I thought it was you," he explained, voice empty now. "She was filthy, in bad health, clearly malnourished and abused. She could barely drag herself back to her feet, but then I noticed she still had all her fingers and toes and I felt a mountain of weight lift off my chest. For just a moment, I'd realized that—just maybe—I'd misjudged Cortez. That he'd been playing me all along, not knowing who I was and not really giving a shit; that he'd been biding his time, and that now his goons would rape you to death right in front of me— and that would have broken me. Nobody in that room would have survived—but that wouldn't have helped you. I felt like shit when I realized it wasn't you and I didn't give a shit about what happened to the girl. But they didn't rape her—at least not right then—but he instead told her to suck me off while he was doing his thing. You know, to make me feel even more conflicted. I was pretty sure he'd have her bite my dick off when she was done, but that was probably the drugs speaking. I wasn't quite lucid that day."

He paused, his jaw a hard line as he ground his teeth, and I didn't protest when he skipped ahead some.

"When I was back in my cell, I took a long, deep look at my plans and realized that I'd been mostly bullshitting myself. Everything he'd done so far was to test me, to get a read on me, and I'd been stupid enough to prove to him at every turn that I was smarter than him, playing my own game. But the problem is, how do you pivot when you're crouching in a deep, dark cell with some idiot's cum dripping out of your ass? I ran through every possible scenario, trying to model my behavior on all possibilities, but that in itself was the problem. He wasn't after some information. He wasn't trying to convince me of anything. He was simply delighting in the fact that he'd found someone who was trying to match him, trying to hang on to my self and humanity—and those are pretty fragile concepts when you think about it."

His voice turned dispassionate then. "I didn't know what to make of it when they dragged me into the arena for the first time. That was two or three days later. My shoulders were still in bad shape— that's where I dislocated them for the first time, because I did end up struggling because I couldn't hold still, and he had me locked in some kind of stockade that made it oh so simple for my arms to go in ways they weren't intended to. I didn't want to fight, and I sure as fuck didn't intend to be a part of anyone's twisted sense of entertainment. But, what can I say? After one of the assholes scored a bad scrape across my ribs, I had enough. The crowd was happy with the carnage but when they realized I hadn't killed anyone, they were displeased. So back into my hole I went, without food or water for two days, and next time he didn't use any lube or his kennel fluffer. Back to the arena it was, and they shot me up with some shit that fucked with me to the point where I couldn't see, walk, or think straight. Nobody intended me to survive that second round. Guess what? Surprise!"

I didn't know what to say so I remained silent, swallowing convulsively. Eating that stew had been a bad idea for sure.

"Like any beaten dog, I learned my lesson quickly after that. If I didn't fight, I'd spend the next days in agony—so I fought. If I didn't kill my opponents, I starved, so I killed them. Then there was a round that had me so fucking disgusted of the crowd and their champion who was catering to their needs, so I one-upped him and all but slaughtered him. That got me a lot of applause. It also got me fresh, warm food, and because Cortez was feeling generous—positive reinforcement 101 for you—they threw one of the kennel girls into my cell for the night. She was so drugged up that it took me a good hour to explain to her that I wasn't going to touch her, or let out my anger and frustration on her. She did help me with my shoulders, though, and worked some of the kinks out of my back where one of the fighters had stabbed me and I'd gone stiff. She eventually told me she'd studied to become a physical therapist before the shit hit the fan. She should have been a doctor or medic in Dispatch. Instead, she'd ended up there."

"Is she still alive?" I didn't know why I had to ask, but judging from his tone she'd been the one good thing that happened to him.

Nate shook his head, no explanation following. "I learned to work with the crowd. That sometimes got me a few days of reprieve, if I turned more aggressive, more brutal, more vicious when taking down my opponents. They sometimes even let us work together, particularly against the animals. The need for food turned into a rather strong motivator. The drugs—they helped. Sometimes they made me feel great, at least for a few minutes. Sometimes they were something I could fight. More often than not, they turned me dead inside." He paused, briefly licking his lips. I could tell that what was about to follow wouldn't be something I'd like to hear—and considering what he'd already told me, that was saying something. "I remember when it all changed. I was so damn hungry. They hadn't fed me for an entire week—my fault, of course. I'd tried being smart again. And the shit they'd shot me up with, it turned me very… susceptible to suggestions. I'd beaten that asshole into submission, and the crowd was going wild. As a last resort, he tried to take a bite out of me with his teeth. I got so damn angry—conversion-level fury, only that the drugs held me at bay—that I started cutting chunks out of his stomach and legs, and then forced him to watch as I bit down on one. It was warm, and I was so hungry, and I didn't give a shit about anything anymore except getting something to eat…" He trailed off for a moment. "And, truth be told, it didn't taste that bad, either. As I kept chewing, it actually tasted rather good—and as they say, the rest is history." He paused, offering up a mirthless snort. "Or should I say, it tasted pretty familiar by then, just like the strips of grilled meat and stew they fed me later when I was back in my cell. And that's when I realized what they'd been feeding me all along, since the very first meal they'd left by the door. Wouldn't do to waste any good livestock on us, right?" Another pause, then, "And do you know how it can get worse—and worse it got— from there? I really started to like the taste of it. What a convenient excuse that the crowds always love some extra gore?"

During the last part he'd turned his head to look into my face, his eyes never leaving mine. If he was waiting for me to bolt up in revulsion, he was going to spend a lot of time on his back. "Well, I think the average human body has something like eighty thousand calories. Not bad for a food source," I offered.

I almost cheered when Nate glared at me with real vexation. "I just told you I ate people and liked it, and all you have to say is a nutritional analysis?"

I shrugged, feeling less concerned with every moment that the topic was further digressing. "Well, you have been favoring meat somewhat more raw than well-done ever since we got back to the States. We didn't really talk about it but you and I both know that you didn't leave that damn underground lab the same as you went in." Then something occurred to me. "Wait, when we were getting it on and you told me I smelled good, did you just mean my natural musk and sweat that makes you feel at home and all cozy and warm, or dinner-is-ready kind of good?"

I really couldn't say whether he was fucking with me when he hesitated. "You do smell like home," he offered.

"You're a fucking asshole, you know that?" I grumbled, but refrained from punching him. He already had enough bruises and not enough padding left as it was. "You better not start chomping on my fingers, because I don't have any left to spare."

"Not even tempted, I swear," he offered, a slightly amused lilt in his voice.

"And no eating our friends. We have too few of those left to spare any, either," I pointed out. "Come to think of it, maybe don't tell that part to Martinez. I'm sure he has some great advice ready for hurt pride and annihilated self, but I think you'll lose him at cannibalism. Better not tell Andrej, either, because he will make stupid jokes about it until everyone realizes what is going on. Burns, too, although I think he'd be more guarded about it. Pia you should tell. Expect to find a bunch of meat of undisclosed origin waiting for breakfast. Plus if this turns into an out-of-hand urge thing, it would be good to have her in the know so we can find a way to pull you back from the edge. Pork might work. How does hunting a few wild boar sound?"

"What have I done to deserve you?" he griped—but did so with a smile.

"Did you really think that was going to be a dealbreaker for me?" I asked, a little insulted. "News flash—I saw you tear that guy's heart out and eat it, and I still kissed you half an hour later. And more just now. I may still not be quite coming down from that high, but I'm not that much of a lightweight. Give me some credit. If all else fails, there are always plenty of assholes around that we can prep for dinner. It's not like I can taste the difference, anyway."

"You're a horrible person," he observed.

"Hey, I'm not the one who'll throw morals and ethics overboard just to survive."

"I'm ninety percent sure that you just did," he pointed out.

I answered that with a loud sigh—and forced my stupid mind to quiet down again. Surprisingly, it did, after skipping over a couple of cannibalism jokes. Oh, it would kill me that I couldn't ever crack them where anyone but Nate would hear!

"So my guess is that you don't intend to walk out there and jump right onto whatever plan or leads they have been hatching out that they need your help for?"

Nate shook his head, clearly quite happy to change the topic again. "No. Which brings me to the next point."

"There are still points left? Cannibalism not enough yet?"

He snorted. I figured it was a good sign that at least a thread of gallows humor was left inside of him. "Let's put it this way—if you haven't demanded to divorce me yet, this may very well change your mind."

"Oh, please, do tell!" I crooned.

He ignored me. "Not yet. You'll hear soon enough when I tell the others. What I need from you is your absolute promise to fall in line with what I need you to do—no protest, no whining, no double-crossing me. I may look calm and collected right now but I'm a fucking mess, and I can't have you work against me and usurp me now. I wouldn't ask this of you if I wasn't convinced it was necessary—"

"Okay."

Nate blinked, confusing taken over from reluctance. "Okay? Just like that, you fold?"

I shrugged. "Of course. You need this. That's enough explanation for me. You have my unwavering, unquestioned support. I know I can be a pest, but that's usually my way of showing you how much I love you. Things may be a little more dire right now so I can leave it at adoring looks and kissy-faces when no one else is looking. Pinky swear." And, of course, I raised my right hand that conveniently ended with the stump of my ring finger.

Nate grunted, but it was a good-natured sound. Or so I hoped. It kind of did resemble a growl, even more so when he pushed himself off the sleeping bag and we ended with him perched above me, looking down at me, pinned underneath him, staring up at him.

"I know we've been talking a lot," I remarked wryly. "But we might have a little more time for round two. Unless that was only to prove to yourself that you still got it and—" I stopped, scowling at his expression. "Tell me that's not the truth, or I swear, I'll bury you in all kinds of meat until you die of gout!"

His lopsided smile was answer enough, but he still took the time to lean down and whisper into my ear, "Bree, it's been months. Do I really need a reason to want to fuck my wife? There's no force in the universe that could change that."

"Well, if that girl had bitten off your dick, that could have become inconvenient," I pointed out.

Another growl—and yes, this time it definitely was a growl—and he pushed himself up and off me, stretching to his full height. I ignored the hand he offered me, already scrambling to my feet on my own volition. I was ready to crack a joke—any joke, really—but the emotional weight on my mind was crushing me, keeping the humor at bay. Letting my breath out in one noisy exhale, I forced myself to utter what, out loud, sounded even more inadequate than it had in my head.

"Look, I know I should say something now—something supportive, or sympathetic, but I've never really been good with words and I feel like the events of the past years beat what little empathy I had out of me and—"

I could tell that, this once, Nate didn't delight in watching me squirm, and I was rather relieved when he lightly put a finger across my lips to shush me. "Don't. Just, don't," he murmured, sounding defeated for a second but quickly switching gears as he squared his shoulders, catching my gaze. "Wanna know what got me through it all? Every endless night, every day that made me dread what fucked-up shit would happen next? The knowledge that, for once, it wasn't happening to you. I've lived the past years with the constant dread that I'm to blame for every damned bad thing that happened to you, whether it was being hunted down or almost getting killed, barely surviving getting infected to rotting from the inside out, and having to deal with people who taught you the very definition of hate. I'm not stupid. I don't see this as some fucked-up kind of karma—but it was the one good thing in my life that I could cling to. And I know it's selfish of me, and kind of unfair to you, but I need you to be my rock, at least for a while. I need you to be your usual irreverent, hilariously not-funny self—"

"Hey, wait a minute! I'm damn funny!" I protested.

"You think you are, hence the hilarious part," he remarked, grinning wryly. "I need you to be you, as you are, as you've always been. That way I can tell myself that, whatever happened, maybe a part of me is still me, as well. If you suddenly turned into a caring, nurturing individual, I'd probably lose it. Just, don't. Please."

Biting my lips, I nodded, but then just couldn't hold back— and what the hell, he'd pretty much just told me not to. "You will probably bite my juicy ass for saying this, but your use of grammar has certainly been suffering. You disappoint me, kind sir."

Nate looked ready to bend me over his knee and spank me—and my, wasn't that a mental image that would never get us out of this room—but left it at a chuckle under his breath. "Why was I ever concerned?"

"Yeah, why were you?" I questioned, jutting my chin forward. "I'm like a dog with a bone. I keep gnawing on it, and gnawing—"

He playfully drew his brows together. "I'm not sure Romanoff is the one I should be worried about with the bad jokes."

"I can switch over to tasteful gay rape jokes if you prefer that."

He visibly shook himself—without a doubt regretting having ever pleaded to my more sensible side—and reached for the door. Outside, two stacks of clothes, plus boots, handguns, knives, and food waited for us. Grabbing the stack intended for me, I snorted. "See what I mean about breakfast?"

"And I've known Zilinsky for years and years longer than you—you can't have her," he snarked back, gathering his things.

"Please, let's keep this bickering up where she can hear us. I have to see the look on her face when we…"

I trailed off, but way too late. Pia gave me a pointed look as she handed me a bucket filled with steaming water, some clean washrags, and soap. I quickly accepted it all and backed into the room, and thus out of the beacon of her glare. Nate didn't bother with modest moves like that and remained where he was standing, dumping one of the rags into the water and then got some good lather going. "Bree already filled me in on the major points."

Pia gave a nod, the barest hint of a smile crossing her features. My, she really was happy to see Nate. "I know that you can be quite efficient about multitasking. That's not why I'm here. We have guests. They insist they are both Richards's spies. Since he's not quite in the right mind to debrief them, I figured you could make that part of the meeting."

"Sure thing," I answered just as Nate inclined his head. The Ice Queen looked from Nate to me and back, then turned on her heel and strode off.

"Get that sorted out before you join us," she advised. "The last thing anyone needs is to feel like Mom and Dad are fighting."

I stared after her, perplexed. "Did she just make a bad joke?"

Nate chuckled under his breath. "Looks like it. Burns must be rubbing off on her."

Which reminded me… "By the way, he got hitched. Not quite tied the knot but that's semantics only."

Nate considered but took the news with a small smile. "How big is the harem he's gathered?"

"Surprisingly, only one woman, but Sonia's feisty enough for ten," I gave my unbiased opinion. "I'd say I like her, but she doesn't really like me. I'm sincerely hoping it's just a random, unwarranted jealousy thing. We did tell her that even in a last-man-on-earth scenario, I'd rather have sex with Martinez than Burns."

"And what did Martinez have to say to that?"

I shrugged, grinning. "I think he's praying every night now that mankind doesn't die out."

"His word in God's ears," Nate murmured.

"Why, afraid your favorite snack is going to be too hard to find then?"

I totally deserved the washrag in the face I got for that, both his action and the look on Nate's face making me double over with laughter. And maybe the drugs, too.

A few minutes later, we strode back out into the corridor, ready to face the music—and I wished to hell that I wasn't wrong, and we would somehow make it through all this, together.

Chapter 24

We hadn't been gone that long—and it was still the middle of the night, with the storm howling across the land, rain falling in sheets—but the base camp had changed a lot in the meantime. Everyone seemed to be awake, and if not quite ready, getting there by chugging some coffee and getting a very early breakfast started. Zilinsky had gathered a good fifteen people in one of the larger rooms at the front part of the building where it was too exposed and drafty for sleeping but perfect for avoiding eavesdroppers. Marleen, Scott, and Richards were there, as were Blake and a few of the higher-ups of all factions, including Martinez, Burns, and Sonia.

I was just about to look around for the spies when I recognized them—and had to do a double take. It was two of the three guys we'd met at the betting ring who'd then—quite conveniently—invited us to come with them to the arena. I had to admit, it had been a brilliant move—not even I had realized that Richards had been doing more than chatting with random strangers. They recognized me as well as we joined the circle by the fire.

"Hey, it's you," one of them said, whatever number I'd previously assigned to him long forgotten.

"In the flesh," I offered, not quite sure what etiquette was in cases such as these.

His smile was bright and way too friendly—and froze a second later as his attention skipped to something behind me. The other one actually took a step back. "Whoa, why did you let that thing out?"

I was sorely tempted to check Nate's expression but the obvious fear on our spies' faces was too captivating. "Well, that"—I made sure to put special emphasis on the word—"is my husband."

The spies exchanged looks with each other. Then their attention snapped back to Nate, but they were clearly still only talking to me when the second guy said, "You fuck that? Aren't you afraid it'll rip your face off?"

I was doubly glad I had my gloves back on—it was one thing if I joked about him gnawing my fingers off, quite another if anyone else did that—and was still debating how explicit my response should be phrased when Nate spoke up—ignoring the imbeciles in favor of addressing Red. "Richards, I'm truly impressed by your selection of these fine individuals to base your intel on." The individuals in question gawked at him as if Nate had performed a neat trick. I couldn't help but grin—sometimes, his penchant for convoluted phrasing annoyed the fuck out of me, but now was a great exception to the rule.

Richards shrugged, looking more interested in the coffee he was nursing than playing referee. "They had to blend in, so I couldn't send in someone who was too smart or whose reflexes would have given them away."

The first guy took issue with that, apparently not too dumb to miss the implied insult. "Hey, now—"

A hard look from Nate was enough to make him shut up. Oh, how I'd missed this! And there was no doubt who was in charge, and not just because the others had clearly been waiting for him to join them. No, it was the way he held himself, tall and strong, whatever doubt he'd let me see just minutes ago gone. He was Nate the Leader again, the second reincarnation of him that I'd come to be familiar with, after he'd charmed his way into my pants—not that it had involved a lot of actual charming. It hadn't mattered back then that he'd almost died from being speared by a rebar; he'd always been in charge of us—across the country, to the bunker, through the winter, and as we'd set out into the free-for-all madness that our country had become. It was only now, looking back, that I realized how much his demeanor had changed after I'd almost died at the factory. Back then I'd appreciated him letting me hold the reins, at least sometimes, but this? This made me want to jump his bones right then and there, and screw whoever we made uncomfortable. And just like that, I'd realized how much I myself had changed as well.

Nate took a moment to look at everyone gathered in the circle around the fire before he crossed his arms over his chest and spoke up, his voice strong and clear. "Thank you for joining this operation. My wife has already filled me in on the broad strokes, and we will have plenty of time later to hash out the details. I'm correct to assume that your intention is that, together, we do something about the tsunami of shit that has rolled over our country? Good. It's about time that we, collectively, got our heads out of our asses." No cheers followed but also no objections, everyone watching with rapt attention. Why could I never get that kind of respectful response? Oh, right. Not my style.

"I know that you must have questions, but I'm afraid we are on a tight timeline with the deadline bearing down on us, and all that will have to wait. The most pressing matter now is that we get back into the camp before they can tighten security, or else razing it to the ground will become a matter of months with high casualty rates, rather than a lightning strike with minimal cost of life."

Scott, always the doubtful asshole in my face, gave a rather neutral nod. "You want to get revenge?"

"You can bet your ass on that," Nate replied with only the barest inflection in his tone, a hint of anger where I knew seething rage must be burning. "And before anyone thinks about calling me a selfish, vindictive prick, this is an opportunity that we cannot pass up on several levels. One, I think we can all agree that the camp, as it is, under current leadership, is a menace to whatever plan we will enact going forward. Two, under the right leadership it could become a base for our operations, but at the very least a stronghold that can provide shelter and provisions for any and all potential allies that might still be undecided. As you know, my wife and I have spent the last years living as nomads far outside of the ongoing conflict, but I've seen enough to realize that a steady supply of food can make a difference. And last but not least, three, we have the opportunity to recover certain assets from the camp that will both aide us in direct support, but may also be in the possession of key intel that we need going forward. Whichever way you look at it, going back in and upending the current hierarchy of power must be our next step."

Nods and minimal murmurs rose from all around, agreement turning into anticipation as Nate let that message sink in.

"We can strike in a day or two," Pia provided. "By then, our infiltrators will have had time to settle in and make contact with key personnel, and you will have had some time to rest up."

Nate allowed himself a pained smile. "As much as that sounds enticing, we need to move out within the hour." That statement was met with surprise—and not all of it positive, particularly from those who hadn't had a chance to crash tonight yet—but Nate talked right over any objection before it could even be brought forward. "Two reasons. The storm is still raging on. With no meteorological data, I cannot say for sure, but this looks like a tropical storm or maybe even hurricane to me, which means we have a chance that it will get worse rather than blow over before we get to the camp, making it much easier for us to move in and spread out. Nobody wants to be out in this weather, and guards will be more concerned with getting back inside than actually doing their duty. And second, as much as I would love to get more intel from our sources and infiltrators first, we have what we need, and we can't waste any more time. It may have come to your attention that several of us are under the influence of a variety of intoxicants—I'm one of them. I have no idea how long I still have until I will crash, but my estimate is around twenty-four to thirty hours, and it should be the same for the rest of us until onset of the worst of the withdrawal symptoms. Either we strike now, or we have to postpone the entire operation for a week, and by then the storm will be gone and the perimeter guards will have found our scouts or this base camp. As they say, the only way is forward, and we will get things started right now."

I could tell that his order made the Ice Queen want to rip his head off but except for a tick at the corner of one eye she didn't show it. "I will rouse everyone and get things started as soon as we're done with this briefing," she provided. "Everyone will be up and ready before sunrise."

Nate acknowledged that with the barest of nods, his attention still on the group at large. Turning to the spies first—who had been listening, mutely, in awe and a different kind of terror—he started on the instructions. "You, draw us a map. As detailed as you can make it. Buildings, guard posts, usual patrol rounds—whatever you can think of. Better to use too much detail than too little." They were quick to agree, and quite happy when Pia handed them some loose paper and pens so they could get to work right away and out from under Nate's attention.

"How many people do we have?" he asked Pia.

"Enough for five strike teams," she responded. "If we can reach all our infiltrators in time, close to sixty people."

Nate considered for a moment. "Even if we can't, that should be enough." The marines—and several of Red's soldiers as well—got twitchy, and Nate was quick to elaborate. "They have guards aplenty, and a lot of people who are part of the raiding parties, but the entire camp is set up to keep what's already inside in, and less to defend against an invasion. I doubt that many of the scavengers and other guests will come to their defense if we act quickly enough—that's why we need to strike now, before they can be rallied and convinced that it's in their best interest to die defending what isn't even theirs. Most of the normal inhabitants have no skin in the game if we don't set the entire town on fire. They won't care either way, or might even realize they are better off living in a town that's not under martial law. Our concern are the guards and their command staff. From what intel I've been able to gather, that's less than three hundred people, and half the guards at the gates and perimeter might be easily convinced that it's of vital interest to them not to make us kill them. The citadel guards are all loyal to Cortez, and I wouldn't hesitate for a second to blow their brains out once you encounter them. They will do you the exact same favor—and if not, you better pray that our mission succeeds, because the alternative isn't something I can recommend."

There was no need to explain what he meant, and no objections followed. Andrej cleared his throat, drawing Nate's attention. "How many prisoners do they have? And how many of them will be able to fight with us?"

Nate did a quick tally in his head. "Around fifty, give or take. Most of them will be quite eager to take revenge but unless we're losing badly, I'd keep them in their cells until we've cleaned out the citadel—that's what they call their stronghold in the mines below and around the arena. We'll have to do psychological assessments who's still fit to fight and that will take time. But I expect at least half of them will be happy to join us going forward."

Maybe it was just me, but I felt like he was forgetting about a cohort of potential fighters. "What about the labor slaves?"

Nate half turned to glance my way. "What about them? I presume that because of the storm they won't be herded out onto the fields in the morning."

His dismissive tone rubbed me the wrong way. "I've seen how many of them there are. Hundreds. If what you say about the guards is accurate, they alone could be enough to be an overwhelming force." As I said that, I realized that I must be missing something there—how could so few guards keep so many people under these conditions without an instant revolt? Particularly considering how tight their security seemed around the arena prisoners.

Nate looked at me as if I'd gone insane until something occurred to him, his frown turning pensive. "You don't know." He then looked at the others, meeting similar confusion. "They won't be able to help us," he finally explained. "Because none of them possess either the drive or mental ability required to." He shot another look my way, murmuring, "I know you're going to love this." Louder, he explained, "Remember when we had that standoff in Colorado, at the army base? Part of the conditions we demanded for the truce were that those soldiers who had been inoculated with a faulty version of the serum—that turned them into mindless husks most of the time, but sometimes progressed to full conversion—would be taken care of. Looks like someone found a way to keep them occupied."

I didn't know what to say at first, a sentiment shared by most of the others. Scott's glare over to Richards made me guess he was about as happy to hear about that as I was. While it was a sound explanation, it didn't completely make sense. "I spent some time hiding by the fields the first time I escaped," I pointed out. "And several of the laborers had scavenger marks on their necks."

Nate's answering smile was shy of nasty. "Harris isn't here to confirm my guess, but looks like whoever was working on the faulty serum didn't stop just because we kindly asked them to. What a surprise."

Which meant that, one—Alders, that mad scientist we'd found hiding in NORAD, hadn't been the only one, or driving force behind this after all, even though he had believed that himself. And two—I had an idea who might be behind it now.

"Ah, crap," I muttered. The suspicion that, inadvertently, my notes that I'd added to what we'd recovered from the lab in France might have directly factored into this really didn't make me feel great. It was easy to get lost in that, but something else he'd said made me pause. "Why would you need Harris to confirm anything?"

Nate briefly glanced at Richards, but since he kept his trap shut, Nate voiced his suspicion. "I've heard rumors from some of the other fighters. Nothing confirmed since all of us were either untreated or inoculated with earlier, working versions of the serum. But it sounds like whoever took over that project offered up newly developed versions to those looking for an advantage. You know yourself how convenient it is when you're constantly out there on the road and don't have to worry about a scratch or bite anymore. Side effects are reportedly issues with self-control and empathy, turning the newly inoculated test subjects hostile and prone to excessive violence while giving them a general 'why should I care' attitude about life. Sound familiar?"

It was mostly the impact of what he'd just said that made me cut down on uttering a resounding, "Fuck me," and instead go for a real answer. "What remains of the scavengers."

Nate gave something between a shrug and a nod. "Your guess is as good as mine, but that's my theory."

I couldn't help but glance at Richards for confirmation—with none of the scavengers a part of the briefing, we couldn't ask them—and we weren't the only ones, Scott and Blake both looking ready to pound the answer out of him. Richards looked less than impressed by the wave of hostility coming his way—probably due to the drugs still in his system—but he was quick to speak up.

"That's not on us. And before your wife jumps to conclusions, it's not what Emily Raynor has been working on in the meantime.

Just as she promised, she has been working on finding a cure for the zombie virus itself, and upgrading the serum to cut out the walking-bomb side effects."

I got what he meant, but Blake's frown told me he didn't. "That sounds an awful lot like what they just said about the braindead slaves."

Richards sent me a vexed look but I was more than happy to let him explain. "Don't ask me for the science shit—that's her domain. But our chief scientist has been on this since the very outbreak of the zombie plague. Lewis can give you a very accurate timeline for this since she's had all the information since that winter after the truce, when she and Miller helped us get that exact information. That was the reason why she agreed to help us, no unexplainable turn in loyalty as you may have been led to believe. Our science division has made progress but they are not even at monkey test level, let alone human tests. Someone else has been working on this." His gaze then turned to Nate. "My guess is that it must be the same people who have also managed to find and manufacture an astounding array of chemicals that make it through the normally impenetrable barrier the serum builds up."

Nate considered for a moment—and much to my surprise was quick to agree. "It makes sense. They also don't give a shit about what happens to their test subjects, and this way they can easily replenish their supply of laborers. And because everyone would blame you, seeing as you have already clashed with the scavengers quite publicly, it's the perfect cover. Who would suspect that a town that's full of drunken assholes and got popular by holding constant gladiator death matches is a secret bioweapon lab?"

I could tell that the others weren't quite convinced yet, but it made so much sense—and it also fit perfectly into our working theory. "You think that's where the other samples ended up that we brought with us from France?" That Hamilton had me pack at gunpoint—another reason that I was quite unhappy not to have been the end of him. "Our guess was that Decker must be using them for whatever nefarious purpose, and this entire fucking city sounds more and more like his stomping ground. Maybe not directly, but it fits too well to be ignored."

Nate was slow to offer his opinion, weighing his words but also the others' reactions first. "Cortez isn't running a tight ship so my first impulse is to say no. But it could be an extended, almost independent operation that's used for beta testing. I've fought and killed a handful of opponents who were a lot tougher than they had a right to be but had neither marks nor typical military training."

"Well, I've been wanting to have a word with their chief chemist, anyway. Sounds like that may be someone who might know more," I pointed out.

"He's on my list," Nate admitted. "And I'm very much looking forward to convincing him to sing like a bird."

But I could tell that something wasn't sitting right with him. "What has you hesitating to agree with me?"

Once again Nate was gauging Richards's reactions but obviously not getting what he was looking for. "Call me a conceited, self-important bastard, but if Decker is behind this, how they treated me doesn't make too much sense."

Blake, much to my surprise, had something to say to that. "What, disappointed that the golden boy wasn't welcomed with open arms?"

Nate sent him a less than warm look for that, but Blake wasn't wrong. "Seriously, they did a great job wearing you down and dehumanizing you. Isn't that like the first thing you told me you do to someone you want to break for good?" I got a weird look from Scott for that, which made me laugh in his face. "What, you still think I'm just a nice piece of ass? Give me some credit. We've spent two entire years twiddling our thumbs out there in the middle of nowhere, trying to be ready for whatever fucking shit we might get dragged into if our worst suspicions turned out true. Don't you think that shit like how to withstand interrogation and how to counter screw with your captor's mind came up in casual conversation?" Scott didn't dignify that with a reply, but I got the sense that he was taking me a little more seriously now.

"It's possible," Nate admitted, if grudgingly.

"And they didn't know who you were," I pointed out. "They may know now. Or not, thanks to my stellar acting skills."

"You were so high on drugs that you were spouting gibberish," he snarked.

"But not too high not to send them on a merry goose chase," I insisted. "Doesn't matter. We won't give them time to do anything with the information." More nods followed, making me guess that we were about to reach the end of our briefing.

Nate seemed to agree. "That leaves our list of targets. Once our map is updated, all we need is to pinpoint their likely locations for extractions, and strategize how to best wipe out the vermin. The list isn't that long. I don't have the name of their chief chemist but if possible, we should keep the entire drug production crew alive—underlings often know more than their bosses like to admit. There are a few low-ranking officers who I don't intend to let live but who are prime targets for interrogation." He quickly recounted seven names—all of which I forgot immediately, trusting that someone else would remember—but perked up on the eighth, and not just because it was a woman's.

"Say that again?"

Nate gave me a curious look but dutifully repeated, "Master Sergeant Cindy Cooper. Why?"

I wasn't sure what nagged me about it. Cole seemed rather amused as he offered, "She was part of one of the strike teams that defended the Colorado base. Tall, blonde, a little older than you, I'd say. We presumed she was killed in action back in Colorado."

"She's alive and well," Nate retorted, and I didn't miss the strained undertone in his voice. He hesitated at my imploring look but then spilled the beans. "I'm not sure of her actual position but she was the one who killed the girl who helped me with my shoulder."

It was then that my brain, usually so abysmal with names, brought one swimming up from the depth. "That fucking bitch shot me up with something before I managed to escape." And there I'd thought she'd been a well-meaning, equally enslaved worker bee for the slave-prostitutes' madam.

"Then you know who you're looking for," was his only response— no warning to keep her alive. Oh, alive I would keep her!

Just then our spies returned with their drawn maps, right on time to get that last part. They both drew up short, and I got a look not unlike what they'd given Nate when they'd recognized him before. "Was that about two months ago?" the more chatty one of them asked, sounding something between impressed and cautious.

"Around that," I answered. "Why?"

"I fucking knew it!" he enthused, slapping his friend on the shoulder. "I told you last night!"

"Yeah, you did," the other responded, a little annoyed. When he realized we were all staring at him, he shrugged. "A while back, a rumor started up but died pretty quickly, for obvious reasons. They quickly tried to suppress it so nobody got any stupid ideas. But from what we heard, someone killed eleven guards."

"Not just killed—they got butchered!" the first guy was happy to elaborate. "I talked to this one guy who was on cremation duty that day and he said that they had to literally bring in the bodies in pieces! There were betting pools going on for days who could have done it. The top bets were that one of the arena fighters had made a run for it, but the bookies insisted they were all accounted for. Turns out, that was pretty close, right?" He briefly glanced from me to Nate.

I couldn't help but grin brightly at him, showing a few too many teeth in turn. Inside, I didn't feel quite that triumphant, although I was sure I hadn't killed anyone who hadn't had it coming—but still. Eleven? That was impressive. "Still surprised that's my husband?"

"Nope," the one who'd been right offered. "I rest my case."

If anything, Nate seemed amused by the story—no surprise there. A few of our compatriots seemed confused or disbelieving. The Ice Queen, of all people, cast a concerned look my way but her features evened out into an impassive mask as soon as she caught me watching her. My, didn't those thoughts bring up the best of memories? Not much, but I suddenly felt really motivated to pay that camp another visit.

Nate left me to stew on my revenge plans in favor of completing his missive. "Back on topic—that leaves the prisoners. As I said, no guarantee about what physical or mental state they are in, and it may very well need a week or two for them to pull through withdrawal before we can say for sure who's of use and who isn't." As I'd expected, it was a longer list, fourteen names in all, a selection of the fifty or so he'd previously assumed could be useful.

And it was when he got to the very last name on the list—after sending me a sidelong glance and hesitating ever so slightly— that it became apparent why Nate had asked for my unwavering, unquestioned support.

"Cpt. John Hamilton."

Chapter 25

My very first impulse was to sock Nate a good one, on principle and because he deserved it, conniving bastard that he was.

But then I started thinking—and connecting a few dots that had seemed like random, inconsequential tidbits. I almost started laughing right then and there, and it was impossible to suppress a bright grin. "Fuck me! He's been there for over a year, do I get that right? He's their damn reigning arena champion, isn't he?"

I could tell that I was annoying Nate with my crowing, but he was smart enough to leave me that. "Yes."

"Oh, that's too precious!" My antics were definitely drawing some confusion, but I couldn't have cared less. Richards and his people looked surprised going on stunned, although that must have been because of the news, not me. As I kept pondering the ramifications, it was hard to ignore the glee bordering on euphoria that rose inside of me, enhanced thanks to the drugs. It only made sense to voice my thoughts. "I'd like to officially rescind my declared mission in life to take that bastard's life. May he live a long life and not bite it before the ripe old age of ninety, forever plagued by nightmares that must haunt him well into the next century—if he's still alive then. Which I hope. So very much."

"Are you done?" Nate asked once I fell silent, a moment away from gleefully rubbing my hands together in the ultimate villain gesture.

"Not for a long time," I preened, but forced myself to internalize my glee. "But you can wrap this up now. I'm good. This is great news. Why didn't you lead with that?"

Nate gave me a rueful smile, but it had an edge. "Because how could I deprive everyone else of witnessing your perfectly mature behavior?" I ignored his jibe, too exhilarated to care. Once Nate was sure that I wouldn't pipe up again, he went on. "I'm not going to play favorites but Hamilton might be our best bet where information is concerned. Unless something has changed that I'm not aware of?" That was definitely for Richards, who gave the slightest shake of the head. "It pains me to say this but if we can capture Cortez alive, we need to do that. He will know about any and all connections the town has. But if all we accomplish is to take out their entire leadership and end up without a single asshole to beat the information we want out of, I can live with that as well. Take-over is our primary objective. Any questions? Then get ready to move out. We will meet again before we leave with a more concrete plan of action. Until then, eat enough to get through the day and pack some extra ammo. This has the potential to be a quick op but might turn into a shit show of epic proportions. I hope for the former but we need to be ready for anything. If all else fails, maybe we get lucky and the storm takes care of it all for us. Share the important details with your people; we meet again in fifty."

The crowd, small as it was, quickly dispersed after that, with Pia the first to disappear to shoo everyone into a frenzy. I gravitated over to where Nate had taken possession of the maps, he and Romanoff already busy marking possible entry and exit routes. The spies proved to be very chatty, as were Marleen, Scott, and one of his undercover guys who had his own details to add. Come to think of it, I was surprised that Marleen had made herself scarce and spent the entire meeting munching bread and listening rather than speaking herself. There was time and opportunity for that now.

I mostly paid attention to have a good idea what would be going down, but felt my focus slip more often than not. Someone brought me coffee and more food, which helped but only so much. Nate appeared to be his usual calm, stoic self but I could see the mask fraying at the edges. No wonder—he had been injured earlier tonight, his body was severely lacking reserves it needed to heal, and I hadn't bothered asking him when he'd had the last good rest. His assessment of what kept him going—and how long—had been sketchy at best, and not something I liked to rely on. While the Ice Queen hadn't protested his insistence on striking as soon as possible, I kind of shared her true sentiment—this wasn't what was good for him. But at the same time, I understood why he had to do it. Why waiting now wouldn't just be a colossal waste of an opportunity, but also give his mind a chance to come down—and there was no telling how far he would plummet. Better get the shit sorted out first, we could all lick our wounds later.

Martinez seemed to be thinking along the same lines as he came sidling up to me, not quite pulling me away from planning but making it obvious that he wanted to talk. "How are you holding up?" he asked, trying not to sound concerned but failing by a mile.

I shrugged, doing my best to appear nonchalant. "Considering circumstances, pretty good."

"And how's he holding up?" No need to clarify who he was referring to.

I considered my words carefully, not just because I didn't want to blurt anything out that was better left unsaid, but also because I wasn't quite sure what to reply. That in itself seemed to be an answer already, making the frown on Martinez's face deepen, so I had to say something.

"For now? He's holding up, and I think that's the only way forward."

He grimaced, clearly not sharing my opinion. "You both need some time out," he muttered, staring into my eyes imploringly. "I mean it. I know you both think you can bullshit yourselves through everything until you make it, but—"

"No buts," I interrupted him, lowering my voice so nobody else could hear. "Is he toeing the line of insanity? Yeah, probably. When we were in the camp today, I watched him kill a guy with his bare hands and rip his heart out. And that seems to have been a pretty accurate representation of what life must have been like for him in the meantime. But honestly? I think he's right when he insists that he needs to act now. Fuck opportunities—he needs this. So I'm going to support him, if only so he knows that he has me a hundred percent in his corner. You know him as well as I do. You know that he will view opposition as lack of faith in him, and if he needs something above all else now, it's confidence in us to have his back." I forced myself to stop and exhale slowly to let my mind catch up with what I was ranting about, and channel my anger in the right direction. "You are right when you say that he needs a time-out. And I'll do my fucking best to make that happen, but after this is resolved. I know how he's feeling right now. I was the same after getting away from

Taggard. I could have done well with food and rest and some good old R&R, but I would have gone mad if I'd been forced into a state of inactivity. That was after a week. He's been through this for months. He needs this now more than ever. I appreciate your concern, but I feel like that's betting on the wrong horse right now."

Martinez certainly didn't like hearing my retort but didn't tell me to fuck off—which I appreciated. "You're probably right," he admitted. "From a medical and psychological point, I'd have to disagree vehemently, but I know that life seldom follows that course. Just—" He paused, looking a little conflicted. "Please come talk to me if you need help, okay? Neither of you needs to get through this alone. We're all here to help you. Whenever, whatever you need."

His concern wasn't surprising, but his vehemence took me a little aback. "I never doubted that. Why the insistence now?"

He hesitated again but then spilled the beans. "I know we never really talked about this in the past, but you changed after you almost died. On some level I've always felt like you blamed us because we couldn't protect you."

"That's bullshit—"

Martinez interrupted my interruption with a surprisingly stern look, unusual for him—enough so for it to work. "I didn't say it's the truth, I said it's how I felt. And I get that with everything that happened to you in Canada and France, and how I reacted, and how you thought you needed to hide to protect us—I get that by now that 'I need to be self-reliant' schtick has sunken into your bones. And maybe you're right and I'm wrong and you both just need to do your thing and eventually it will all work itself out. But, just maybe, consider that you're churning in the ever same ruts, and you need a good shove from behind to get out of that temporary hole. All I'm saying is that I'm always happy to shove you. Or him. And I'll stop now before you make a really bad pun out of this." His eyes narrowed then. "You're still pretty out of it. I know Harris insisted that it was vital that you appear stoned, but this is pushing it a little."

"Gee, thanks for pointing out something I already know and can do shit about," I complained but quickly offered up a smile to take the sting out of my words. "No fucking idea what that crap is, and even less so what else they shot me up with. If you know any way for me to come down from it quicker, please, by all means, tell me. But Nate was likely right there, too—withdrawal was a bitch the first time, and I need to function right now, even if it comes with some drawbacks. So unless you have any ideas…?"

"None until we know what compounds they are using," he professed. "But more coffee might help. Diuretics help flush out toxins through the liver. Just make sure you drink plenty of water."

"Yes, Mom," I quipped, grinning when he let out a heavy sigh as he left. Coffee was always a good idea, so I fetched some more for myself and my husband, and returned to his side. Nate accepted the thermos from me without comment and only the barest of nods, too engrossed in studying the maps before him. We now had five sets from various people, painting a pretty composite image. All I was interested in was that citadel and the kennels, and with luck the others would have cleared out the underground fortress by the time I was done clearing out the brothel.

In what must have amounted to record time, we broke camp— or as much as there was to break. A handful of people would remain as absolute last reserve and to guard the few things we wouldn't be taking, like the tents. Everyone else was split into groups, according to their specialties and group affiliation; Blake and Scott refused to work together, and when I dared select Hill and Cole as part of my group, only my old folks wanted to work with me—meaning Burns and Sonia, pretty much, since Martinez and Andrej would be staying with the vehicles as forward backup and triage station, and Nate and Pia were part of one of the citadel strike teams. The others were hopefully still safely getting drunk inside the camp, undiscovered and unbothered.

That's how I ended up being the boss of a bunch of army soldiers, which was hilarious on so many levels. I even considered changing my mind and going with Nate, but that damn bitch needed to be brought to justice. Also, as much as I wanted to constantly wrap myself around Nate now that I had him back, and brutally murder everyone who'd been responsible for what had happened to him, I didn't want to be anywhere near where he'd been kept. Somehow, seeing it all with my own eyes would make it real. I wasn't as big on denial as he loved to accuse me of, but if there was something important to be done that didn't involve me being slapped in the face with all that, I was very happy to tackle that instead. From his utter lack of protest about what job I picked, I presumed he was glad I'd be somewhere else when he started cleaning up that mess. In many ways, it had been fortuitous for us both that the first I'd seen him again had been strong, violent, and victorious, rather than a broken mess shivering in the corner. I would have dealt with both, of course, but if we could retroactively put a more positive spin on things, why not go for it?

Getting ready took longer than planned—when didn't it?—but it was still pitch black out there once all plans were plotted, routes fixed, gear loaded, and people readied. From what I could tell, the storm was getting worse, now strong enough to make driving sturdy cars fun; I didn't envy those who were pulling duty on the ATVs. Our plan of attack was laughably simple, but it might just work: a small group, including Marleen, Scott and his marines, and our two spies would enter the camp the same way we'd exited—across the fields and down into the agricultural part of the town. They would then either distract or take out the guards by the western gate—the one where the raiding parties usually came in. Once inside, I'd take my group over to the kennels while the others went deeper into the camp, two teams to check on the entertainment quarter to keep things as quiet as possible, and the remaining fire teams would head for the citadel. If the gate didn't open in the next two hours, we'd try to sneak in any way possible, which sounded ludicrous until we got close enough to see the camp in the distance—and the gale-force winds almost overturned one of the ATVs. We could likely have walked up to their palisades and simply crawled over them.

Since we'd already split up into the strike teams, I was sitting in the passenger seat of Martinez's snazzy electric car, with him driving and Burns and Sonia in the back row. The car had fully charged triple batteries from last week but the dark gray of the sky made me guess they wouldn't get any extra charge any time soon. Since we'd stopped, Martinez had given up on the wipers so we couldn't really see much of what was going on outside. Sooner or later, someone would have to get out and start checking with binoculars on the gate. I was sorely tempted to pull rank and send someone else out to get pelted with water and debris. The car was constantly shuddering under the onslaught of the elements, making it even easier to be morose and miserable. What I actually felt was the need for violence ebbing and flowing through my veins like surf in shallow water where it hit the beach. My higher brain functions told me to cut down on it, ignore it where possible and suppress it where not. The lizard part of my brain was screaming for blood. I was ready to heed the lizard, but still had to bide my time to let loose on the floodgates. None of that had anything to do with the drugs, although they made it so easy to want to give in to the siren song of blood and gore. I could tell that Martinez was a little concerned about the way I sat there, silent, brooding, but I wasn't in the mood for talking. Besides, we were both listening to Sonia and Burns bickering behind us, so it wasn't like we were lacking entertainment.

So much time wasted waiting—an hour now; days to get to the camp; weeks to rally backup; years hoping the day we'd need to do something would never come. And all for what? I was done waiting. I was done being passive. Today was the day for action, and act I would.

"You actually trust that Richards guy?"

Martinez's question made me tear my eyes away from the rain-splattered window and look at him instead. "Let's put it this way—he had so many chances to get rid of me by simply not doing anything to help. I'd say that, more than anything, shows that he's very invested in my continuing ability to be a nuisance. I know you have a lot of reasons not to trust any of them but—"

Martinez offered me a pained smile but made me trail off when he shook his head. "That's not why I'm asking. I guess on some level I'm glad that it looks like we're on the same side of the same conflict again." He licked his lips, briefly glancing at Burns in the rearview mirror before he went on. "If you look back, it was a fucking shame what happened those first two years. I think you said so yourself in at least one great speech—"

"I've given many of those. You need to be more specific," I teased.

I got a suffering look from him for that. "It should always have been humans against the undead. Never humans against humans, particularly if we've all come from the same walk of life. On some level I've never not seen myself as part of the army—I mean, shit. I've been a medic for long enough that Vitamin M is my standard answer for any problem, even things unrelated to pain. It's who I am. And I've always been proud to be part of the army. It never occurred to me that I wasn't when I threw in my lot with you at that intersection when Miller went one way and Hamilton the other. It was obvious, you know? Us versus zombies. And then that shit when they marked us up and declared us exiled to the road—I didn't take it seriously, you know? Just superficial crap, like you transfer from one unit to the other, or work with other branches on a joint op. And then suddenly we were shooting at and trying to kill the people who should have been our brothers and sisters. It's damn easy to react when you're afraid for your life. And there was a clear and present evil to focus on; that helped. But then you up and left, and suddenly you were working with them as if nothing had happened and I felt so fucking betrayed…"

He trailed off, giving me a moment to interject but went on when I remained silent.

"Didn't help that they all rolled out their best behavior when I got there. And I could tell that Jason and Charlie, when they joined me, had the same problems I did. Weren't they supposed to be raping, murdering, backstabbing assholes? Instead, they were the same bastards I've been dealing with for over a decade. The same lame jokes, the same lamenting over perfectly good food, the same lazy idiots who got screamed at by the same mother hen of a staff sergeant. Sure, we were acting like weary dogs sniffing each others' butts, not easy to trust at first, but that changed quickly. And even after that— when we got home to California—we've had some contact with them over the months that followed. Usually reserved, always cautious, maybe a little hostile, but that was it. And then you, of all people, get dropped off by a bunch of them who you're obviously friends with."

"I wouldn't call them friends," I offered, looking away so he wouldn't read the lie right off my face. Martinez knew me well enough that it didn't work, of course.

"They are, and that's okay. Might take us a little to function well together, but we'll work it out. You know, you can have more than two friends at a time, even if they might not get along great from the get-go?" He didn't miss me glancing toward the back row, making him flash me a brief grin but he was wise enough not to remark on any issues I might have had with Sonia. "Guess what I'm saying is that if you trust them, I trust them. We've fallen awfully short on people we can trust. It doesn't hurt to increase those numbers again."

That sounded smart—but also opened up the next Pandora's box. "And what about the scavengers? Harris and his people? They've been quick to help us, mostly because Harris knows us. But what about the rest of them?"

Martinez remained silent, considering, leaving Burns to step into the breach. "Well, if it's true that they're all acting like lunatic assholes because they got a faulty version of the serum, things might get a little complicated working with the people they will blame for that."

"From what we know, that wasn't the army," I pointed out.

Sonia gave a derisive huff. "I doubt they'll differentiate it. Then again, they seem to have a hard time deciding whether to hail you as a saint or burn you at the stake—you could use this gigantic pile of shit as an opportunity to kill two birds with one stone. Isn't that what you're notorious for? Unite lunatics under one banner to do your bidding?"

Turning fully so she could see my face, I gave her a mirthless, very toothy smile. "Guess I am, so nice of you to point that out!" I was already missing Marleen. She was so much easier to deal with. "But maybe you have a point."

"Maybe?" Sonia echoed, putting extra emphasis and condescension in her tone. "Of course I'm right, bitch!"

Burns snickered, making me want to sock him a good one, but Martinez rolling his eyes—for sure at me, as well—made me hold back.

"Not sure we have a choice, really," I went on, staring at the rain partly obscuring the tree getting whipped this way and that by the wind. "I think Nate was right when he said it was a good idea to leave the camp to the scavengers. I have absolutely no interest in managing brain-dead farm hands and planning planting schedules. All I managed to grow in two years was a patch of salad, and I never got to harvest and eat it. I think I'm way better at killing things than making them flourish. I'd better leave that to someone else."

Another chuckle from Burns. "And see, that's why you married the right guy. He hates salad."

I was tempted to tell them just how true that statement was, but decided not to. I didn't quite trust Sonia—not with something so personal and gruesome—and I didn't want to burden Martinez with Nate's change in eating habits, either. Maybe I'd pull Burns aside later. Or just leave it to Nate to tell Pia and let her deal with it. Ah, the joys of leadership—let others deal with the bullshit you tried so very hard not to think about. That this wasn't a good idea was obvious, but thankfully, I had something else to concentrate on instead.

My com beeped, making me reach down and switch it to sending and receiving. I'd turned it off to spare myself having Cole ream me later for having to listen in on our private conversations. I had the strong suspicion that, like the others from our bunch, they viewed it as highly entertaining distraction, but since Cole must have realized he could get under my skin with his nagging, he had no reason not to do it.

"Lewis here. What's your status?" I asked, trying to look through Martinez's window at the Humvee parked right next to us. All I could make out was a vague shape that wasn't trees or grass.

Richards answered me. "I'm sending Gallager out to check on the camp. You ready over there?"

I couldn't help but grin. "We're all cozy and warm and have no intention of leaving, so I guess, yeah?"

Even with the coms distorting his snort with static, I heard it well enough. "We're still fifteen minutes from the earliest estimate, but it never hurts to be prepared."

"So she said," I quipped. Someone else laughed on the open channel—might very well have been Cole. Richards wasn't going to come with us, but I could see why the soldiers were happy to stay bundled up in their Humvees until the very last minute. I considered switching the radio back off but refrained. There wasn't much I felt like chatting about, and the "go" could come any moment now.

Moments turned into minutes, but sooner than expected I heard Gallager's excited voice in my ear. "The gate's opening! I don't see the light signal but it's awfully murky out there." A pause, and even before he acknowledged, I saw a quick sequence of bright flashes coming from the gate. "That's the all-clear!"

Taking a last look at the others in the car, I took a deep breath, then ordered, "We are a go! Might still be a trap, so keep watching for anything that trips you up, but for now, let's get out of this damn storm!"

Martinez was already starting the car, and we rolled back onto the road right behind the lead Humvee with Cole, Hill, and the other two members of our team in it. It only made sense to let the armored half-tank take point. Across the field, by a different patch of trees, I saw shapes moving as the four vehicles that had been hiding there also made for the road. I was sure that the others followed behind us.

Nobody shot at us, nobody tried to force us to a halt, and we made it to the gate in good time, if with some sliding and slipping in the mudslide that the road had turned into. Marleen and Scott were waiting inside the gate, the heavy wood held open by two of the raider trucks wedged against them. I caught a few bodies slumped on the ground in a corner—and no prisoners visible—but didn't waste another second on it. As soon as Martinez brought the car to a halt, I flashed him a quick hand signal for "don't screw around" and got out, ignoring what he signed back.

The second the storm hit me, I felt my hair get drenched to the scalp, icy cold water sluicing away what sweat had accumulated since I'd dressed earlier. I did my best to ignore it as I stepped away and toward the side of the open square to gather my people around me and not get mowed down by the other vehicles following. Only a third would stay inside, the rest parked outside the gate should we lose control of it. Cole, Hill, and the other two soldiers were already waiting for us, so as soon as Burns brought up the rear, I gave the signal to move out and turned south toward where the hulking shape of the barn was barely visible through the sheets of rain. Since I knew where we were headed—and was the one with the shotgun since we were expecting close quarter combat—I took point, with Cole right by my side to clear up anything that was out of range for me. I saw a few shapes moving deeper in the camp but no alarm sounded, making me guess it was either our people or someone caught out in the rain, ready to get into the next dry building as soon as possible. It was early enough still that most people would be asleep, particularly with the storm making all outside ventures uncomfortable bordering on impossible.

Part of me hoped that meant we'd find the barn mostly empty, with only a few drugged-up, bleary-eyed whores sleeping there.

The rest of me was hungering for carnage.

Turned out, I needn't have worried that I had packed needless amounts of ammo. With nothing else to do, and the weather too hostile for raiding, the "kennels" were well-frequented. A few quick glances made sure that the prep room outside was deserted and quickly barred with a conveniently handy wooden bar that I figured was there to keep any girls already dragged into the main part of the barn from leaving; Hill was happy to kick the main door in for me, opening up the reception area for us. A good ten hairy, unwashed assholes stared back at us, all at least mildly, most heavily inebriated as they lounged by the well-stocked bar and on stools, waiting for their turn. Their presence was damning enough for me; I didn't hesitate one second after getting a good overview of the room. I was three slugs in when Cole and Hill opened fire, and by the time Sonia made it in last, there were only corpses left to step over. Burns and Sonia veered off to the left where the door to the prep room remained untouched to secure both exits of the room at once. I took the others with me to the corridor with the walled-off stalls. Storm or no storm, we'd caused enough of a ruckus that two half-naked men came stumbling into the corridor to meet a quick and grizzly end. I forced my mind to concentrate on the task at hand only, but my stomach seized up nevertheless as I kicked open the first stall door to my right and found another disgusting bastard on top of a limp girl who didn't even look up as I stepped next to her so that when I blew that asshole's head off, I didn't hit her with more than a spray of blood and liquified brain matter. What was left of him remained lying on her, pinning her to the cot, but I didn't have the time to drop my weapon and pull him off. We'd do that later, after we finished with the cleanup.

The boom of Hill's shotgun was nicely interspersed with single-shot discharges of the assault rifles as I stepped back into the corridor and got ready for the next stall, three partitions down. Cole was halfway down the corridor, keeping that clear as the rest of us went from door to door, working in tandem left and right, left and right. I figured it said a lot about the operation here that only four of the assholes came venturing out into the corridor to check or defend the others, and a single one made it halfway out a window before one of the other soldiers gunned him down.

We were almost to the last two stalls—one of them the one I knew best—when the door to the other opened but nobody stepped out. I advanced cautiously, letting Hill and Cole take care of the other doors. Inside the room I found several women huddled together, clutching each other, only one holding a handgun, and she dropped it as soon as she saw us outside. I didn't exactly recognize her from before—what little I still remembered was sketchy at best—but the simple fact that she and the older woman next to her were clean with decent going on nice clothes while the other girls were filthy and covered in bruises, their dresses barely more than rags, kind of made them stand out.

"Thank God you're here to rescue—" the older woman—the madam of this fine establishment—started to say. I blew her head to smithereens, hard-pressed not to smile at the splatter pattern it left on the wood behind her. Only two of the whores seemed lucid enough to realize what was going on and shied away, but with enough lag to make me guess they were too out of it to act. The blonde remained where she was, unmoving, but the way her eyes darted between us made it obvious that she was trying hard to assess the situation. A whistle from me and Cole came in from the corridor, nodding as soon as he saw her. That she didn't seem to recognize him in turn didn't surprise me, all buttoned up as he was with helmet and balaclava to save his pretty face from the storm and hail of blood.

"Yup, that's her," he confirmed for me.

Glancing back from him to the blonde, I gave a brief jerk with my shotgun, signaling her to get up. She did, slowly raising her hands, still playing the frightened innocent.

"You can take whatever you want," she said, her voice trembling, but I didn't buy it. "We'll cooperate. Just please, don't hurt the girls. They've already been through so much."

Cocking my head to the side, I allowed myself a slow smile. "And whose fault is that, exactly, huh?" She blinked slowly, still assessing. There was no recognition on her face. "Don't remember me? Well, too bad." My gaze fell on the satchel resting on the floor next to where she'd been crouching. "Let me repay the favor, huh?"

Another jerk with my shotgun had her step away further from the girls. I dropped my weapon on its sling and let Cole guard her so I could grab the satchel and root through it. Coming back up with a filled syringe, I fixed her with what was likely a malicious glare, judging from how she paled. Or maybe that was due to my smile? Hard to tell.

"Master Sergeant Cindy Cooper, it's time to pay for the crimes you committed," I declared, and aimed the syringe toward her neck.

She didn't try to fight me, but that would have been stupid with Cole's M16 in her face. All she uttered was a resounding, "Shit," as I plunged the needle into her neck and gave her a shot of her own medicine. She crumpled into a heap on the ground within seconds, her eyes wide open but her body unresponsive. The only reaction from the other girls was to move back enough so she didn't hit them on the way down. There was no hope or relief on their faces, but I hadn't expected either.

Cole got busy tying Cindy's wrists with zip ties behind her back as I turned to the two girls who seemed in marginally better shape than the others. "We're taking over the camp," I told them. "Every other customer in the building is dead. We need you to stay inside to stay safe. Can you help us get the other girls together?" Fear and more stoic passivity met me, making me realize I needed to explain better. "So you can help each other clean up, maybe get some fresh clothes and something to eat. We'll leave you alone after that. You're free. You just need to stay inside because there's a fucking hurricane coming for us, and we don't want you to get caught in any crossfire. Okay? Can you do that?"

They all looked lost—and the lucid ones suspicious—but then one of them nodded and slowly got onto shaky feet. "We can do that."

I nodded and backed out of the room and into the corridor. They all seemed calmer with no armed strangers in the room with them. Cole gave me a look I couldn't read before he joined the others in getting rid of the dead trash. While we were busy dragging the bodies into the front room, a few of the girls followed us to get the ones still in the stalls. They shuffled by and stepped over the corpses without a sign of revulsion or hesitation, as if they were nothing but piles of rags. Only one girl, her face so swollen that she could barely look out of one eye, kicked the corpse who'd been in her room as another guided her outside. It took some effort to keep my breakfast down but survival beat emotional turmoil any day. We were done in under half an hour, ready to depart and drop Cindy's unresponsive ass off with Romanoff by the gate. I met grim faces—or eyes, where nothing else was visible—all around, and Cole was the one who asked what they must have been thinking.

"This is where you ended up?"

I nodded. "And where I carved up the pig who wanted to take his anger for killing some of his friends out on me." I paused, glancing down the now empty corridor, only smears of blood left from the carnage. "I wish I could have done that back then, but didn't like the odds. I knew I'd have to come back."

"Good," Cole offered simply, pulling Cindy along with him as he turned toward the door. "Let's get this cunt's ass to the vehicles so we can join the fun elsewhere. Lots more assholes that need killing."

I'd never had less remorse about taking anyone's life before than here, and while my body told me that it had only just started, I kind of hoped that this would remain the worst we'd find today—but I had a certain feeling that wouldn't be the case.

Chapter 26

It hadn't gotten much lighter outside in the meantime, but the town had clearly been shaken awake by our arrival. We didn't meet with any resistance as we dropped our burden off, but the previously empty yard inside the gate was now filling with confused and hung-over scavengers, some of them already making their way into the wilderness outside, but a few ready to join the fight. I was surprised to find Eden and Amos waiting for us but probably shouldn't have. They were responsible for rallying their own people, and as soon as they saw me, they pawned off the task to someone else and told me in no uncertain terms that they were ready to rumble. So rather than set out with six sober, hardened fighters at my back, I had them and a good thirty drunk—on booze and the need for violence alike—scavengers in tow. Sonia didn't look happy about that at all but the soldiers took it for what it was—distraction and potential meat shields they could be using for cover. Eden in particular came in handy as she strode proudly next to where I tried to duck from cover to cover at first but soon gave up, joining her as she shouted at every scavenger who ducked his head out of a tavern door to see what was going on. The few corpses of gunned-down guards went mostly ignored, small signs of the progress of the other fire teams as they were.

Then we reached the end of the entertainment quarter where the betting rings were, a much larger group of people already gathered there. Dan Harris was shouting obscenities at another guy who looked as equally enraged and out of it as he did, both drawing up short as we arrived. Harris was quick to ignore his opponent and run up to me, grabbing my arm—barely giving me the time to drop my shotgun first—to pull it up and cry, "Here she is! Our savior, in the flesh!"

Hundreds whooped and screamed; equally as many scowled and remained standing there, glowering. Harris's grip was tight enough to make my fingers go numb but I didn't fight him. I sure didn't get any pointers from his mad grin. Apparently, he'd spent the night partaking in more shit that screwed with his system than I had, but judging from the mood of the crowd, he'd also been spreading his new gospel—whatever the shit that was.

Nobody was chanting, "Speech! Speech!" yet but there were a lot of expectant faces turned my way. As soon as Harris let go, I made sure to keep my arms to myself but stepped forward into the open space that Harris and that other guy had been using for their shouting match.

"I'm Bree Lewis," I called out, making sure that my voice carried. "And I'm here with an offer you can't refuse!"

Cheers went up all around, making me blink in irritation at first. They hadn't even let me get to the good parts first! Or any part, really, for that matter. I half turned to glance at where Cole and Burns were standing together but only got a blank stare from Cole and a grin from Burns. As per usual, no pointers from the peanut gallery. Guess it was a good thing that I was used to doing everything myself.

"Listen up, please!" I called, hoping they would quiet down a little. The opposite was the case, so I decided I needed to shut them up another way. "To cut to the chase, we're here to take over this camp! And by 'we' I mean a joint task force made up of yours truly and my old gang, the Lucky Thirteen!" More cheering. "Plus some of you fine folk, thanks to Dan Harris and his people!" More cheers. "We also got the finest examples of special forces from the army, marine corps, and some of the Silo's best!"

Some of the cheering died down at the mention of Red's men but was back by the time I got to mention Blake and Buehler's bunch. There were still frowns aplenty, but at least those were the ones who were listening to me. "As you can tell, we're quite the diverse group— and there's a reason for that. And the reason is that this camp here has a problem. You all know it as a place to relax and let down your guard, but it's the opposite for some people. That arena? That's a huge issue."

That got their attention—and me some less than favorable shouts. I ignored them. "Remember last night's fight?" I called. "The contender that you know as the Nameless Monster? I call him husband and bastard, depending on my mood, and you likely know him as Nate Miller, co-leader of the Lucky Thirteen and driving force behind our strike against the assholes that were stealing our women and gunning us down two years ago. And guess what? The same assholes who locked him up here and forced him to kill for your fucking enjoyment also drag people like you into this shit! And your women? They lock them up in a barn and rape them! That damn barn right there on the southern part of the camp, where none of you go because that's for the guards only. We just cleaned it out. Wanna know what we found? More than half the girls locked up in there had the same marks across their necks as you do! They are your girlfriends, sisters, mothers, and daughters!" Well, they sure didn't like that. Caught up in my own hype, I screamed, "And can someone fucking explain to me what it is with assholes and constantly thinking they need to lock us up and rape us?! There are plenty of us insane bitches out there who are happy to kill and raid with you, and fuck you when we're done!" A chorus of affirmative shouts, led by Eden, rose in response, making me grin. "I mean, I was more than happy to watch my husband tear out some guy's heart and eat it, and then jump his bones first chance I got! You like 'em strong, willing, and a little insane, well, here we are!" And just like that, I had the crowd back, and quite a few raunchy suggestions and offers that I ignored.

When I gestured at them to shut it, they quieted down, way too much attention on me to make me feel safe, but there was no going back now. "This hellhole of a town has its problems, sure, but that's why we're here. We want to clean it up, kick out the assholes who prey on all of us, but that doesn't mean we have to burn it all to the ground. Wanna know what Harris told me when I asked him about support to attack the camp? He would have followed me out of loyalty, but he didn't want to unless he had to. Because I know that a lot of you consider this your home away from home now. Well, I say, why not make it your home for good? Nobody has ever wanted the scavengers. It's about time we got a city all of our own!"

There was a poignant pause, long enough to make me afraid that I'd made a colossal mistake. But then the crowd roared as one, deafening even over the storm. I didn't try to quiet them down. That would have been impossible. Instead, I pulled Harris into a hug, both so I could talk to him but also grasp his hand in mine and pull it up. "Your new mayor!" I yelled, kicking off another wave of euphoria. To the man himself, I said, "Hope you don't mind, but you kind of had that coming, volunteering to help and all that."

His bright grin made me question whether he got the ramifications, but he sure seemed on board. "Whatever you need me to do, Ms. Bree," he shouted back at me.

"You have a lot of work ahead of you," I called back. "You'll have to get some kind of law enforcement set up that's not based on killing off every asshole who gets cute. You also really need to make sure that your people do better about consent than what the current leadership is going by. If we make this a safe haven for our people, we need it to be safe and a haven for everyone, not just the big brawlers who can force everyone else into compliance."

Harris kept on grinning. "Oh, don't worry about that! I'm sure Eden will scare the crap out of everyone who steps out of line easily enough. The last guy who got too forward with her she castrated in front of his whole clan!"

Eden, having caught some of that—probably just the castration part—gave me a bright yet evil grin. "I knew I liked her for a reason!" I shouted back to Harris. "We can help you hash out the details before we leave."

The crowd suddenly quieted, a wave of murmurs running through it, and already, the ones closest to us picked up a rather uncoordinated but no less loud chant of, "Stay! Stay!" Harris and Eden both were quick to pick it up as well, throwing their hands up and further working the crowd into a frenzy.

Burns and Sonia finally decided to lend me a hand and pushed through the people until they were behind me, Burns leaning in with a bright grin. "You've created a monster! I love it!"

I gave him the flattest stare I could manage before I turned back to the crowd. They even quieted down to let me speak. My chance to become a Pirate Queen for real, served on a silver platter.

"Okay, we'll stay!" Cheers, but they quickly went away when I raised my right arm, pointing my index finger skyward. "For now, but we have work ahead of us that will lead us elsewhere. If you want us here—and are willing to accept all of us—we'll be happy to consider this our new home base. I wouldn't mind getting out from under Gabriel Greene's shadow."

They gobbled that up with gusto. I wondered for a moment if maybe I should try to send someone for the citadel and let them know they should keep as many of the guards and command staff alive as possible, because I was sure I'd find a few volunteers to do away with them in the most mass-entertaining manner—or as food supply, should Nate prefer to not just let his anger out on them or watch someone else do the deed. But I abandoned that idea quickly enough. It was likely for the best to burn that arena down and be done with it for good.

Since they clearly didn't quite trust the crowd, I signaled the soldiers closer, pushing people away until I ended next to Cole and Hill. Hill was shaking his head at me, although fighting a smile. "I have no idea how you do it. Was it like that back before your last crusade, too?"

"Less drugs, less drinking, better food," I replied. "But besides that, pretty much. I have a gift."

"You have a problem," Cole enthused. "Ready to get back to work? Great that they won't try to lynch us, but we haven't actually liberated the city yet that you so grandly promised them."

"It will feel like more of an accomplishment for them if they help doing said liberating," I let him know, but he had a point. Seeking out Harris—and finding him looking even more loopy than before—I instead gestured Amos to come over. "Think you can keep them in check?" I asked, nodding at the people all around us. "We still need to help the rest of our people at the citadel. I know someone who has a massive score to settle, and even if I'm late to the party, I'd like to see the aftermath of it." I absolutely didn't but Cole was right.

"No problem," Amos shouted over the ongoing din. "Need some extra hands? Give me five minutes and I can have another fifty people to help you. All far less out of it than you yourself."

I gave him a bright grin in return—scowling would have been impolite—and nodded. "Sure! Meet us at the northern end of the square. And then get the people out of the storm. We don't need anyone to be struck by lightning."

It took us closer to a quarter of an hour to get things sorted out—and when the rain became even more punishing, people were more than happy to return to the various taverns and bunkhouses to keep celebrating inside—but we ended up with enough backup to fill the entire street as we moved back the way we had come and then on toward the citadel.

Halfway there, Marleen suddenly appeared out of thin air—more likely she stepped from a side street, but all that screaming and getting cheered on had gotten a few wires crossed in my brain—Richards and the rest of his fire team trailing behind, followed by a bunch of the Silo marines.

"How are things coming with the fortress?" I asked, shouting way too loud as I was still used to that from before. The much smaller crowd behind me still cheered; I wondered what I'd have to do to make them stop short of sending them away. Richards looked quite disturbed, but Marleen seemed to find my entourage incredibly funny.

"Well, good for you that you finally get the recognition that you deserve," she remarked. I had no idea what to make of that but chose to ignore it in favor of letting her reply to my previous question. "It's actually quite fortunate that you arrive with backup. We're kind of at a stand-off at the citadel so we went out to look for something to tilt the scales. Hello scale tilters!" The last she called out loud enough for the scavengers to hear, who were happy to cheer to her as well. "They are quite convenient, at least if you need to make some noise," Marleen admitted. "Come on, this way."

Rather than use the street they had all come from, she started down the main road toward the arena—and that was exactly where we ended up. The entrances to the ranks were all barred, but the scavengers immediately set to either climbing over them or using all kinds of utensils for crowbars, including a few actual crowbars that were blood-splattered and rusty enough to make me wish for a tetanus shot. Marleen watched them for a bit before turning to me. "We need to get down below to help clear up the tunnels. Think you can set them to making sure nobody gets out of the arena, or the two exits here and here?" She pointed to where less flimsy gates led into the rock that made up the very top of the mine I knew was below us.

"I can try." Amos was nowhere to be found but I recognized one of the younger scavengers who'd been part of Harris's group as well, and explained to him what we wanted them to do. I wasn't sure if he got it but he nodded very enthusiastically and immediately started shouting orders at those nearby, clearly considering himself deputized. At Marleen's satisfied nod, we split up again—my team going to the left entrance, and Richards and Marleen heading toward the right. I found the door barred, yet as soon as I rattled on it, I heard a squeak coming from my radio.

"Lewis here. We're coming with backup," I said, waiting for someone to acknowledge my message. Instead, they opened the gate, two cautious Silo marines peeking out. They lowered their weapons as soon as they saw us, making room for us to surge inside. There was a pile of dead guards to step over—and one corpse, carefully pulled to the side, belonged to Buehler's marines also—but beyond that, the corridor hewn from rough stone was free. The constant howling of the storm cut off as the door fell into its lock once more, but that only served to make the shots echoing up from further into the bedrock sound all the louder.

"Status?" I asked the closer of the marines.

"They're making progress but keep getting pinned down at every intersection," he explained. "We didn't bring enough explosives to smoke them out, and besides, we can't use them without endangering the prisoners. Sgt. Buehler said to tell you that they are working on chasing what is left into the arena. With luck we'll catch them before they can slink off."

"Yeah, no chance of that," I muttered, grinning. When he looked back at me with confusion, I nodded toward where the arena lay next and below us. "We found a couple of scavengers happy to help us. They are currently taking over the ranks of the arena. Nothing will get through them." At least I hoped not. Suddenly, having Amos out there was a relief. I doubted he'd be susceptible to any bribes from Cortez and his men after I'd just promised them their own kingdom to govern as they saw fit.

"Richards is coming in from the other side," I told the marines. "We'll see if we can help below. You're good with holding that door?"

"Perfectly fine, ma'am," the marine acknowledged.

I was tempted to threaten him with violence if he ever did that again but left it at a glare, much to some of the others' mirth. Sonia ignored it but Burns and Hill were grinning at me—and each other—while I got a vexed look from Cole.

"Loosen up some," I told the surly former delta operative. "If you keep hanging around, you better get used to my leadership style."

"That would require you actually doing any leading first," Cole griped—but fell in behind me as I got ready to move on.

Even with flashlights, the tunnel was dark enough that it made sense for me to go first. I paused before every intersection to look at the crossing corridors and have someone else sweep the intersection, but we moved a good three hundred feet before we found anything except more dead pulled to the walls not to be an obstacle. Buehler and two of her marines were there, one of them guarding the others while the other was fussing over the bleeding bullet wounds in her leg, the sergeant herself less than thrilled with being fussed over.

"Go on down below," she called out to us. "That's where the real shit show is going down. We've already cleared the upper level. Just needed to fall back when one of the assholes strafed me."

Following her advice, we switched from the tunnel to the ramp leading down into the bowels of the mine, closer to the staccato sounds of rifles eating up bullets. The acrid twang of urine, feces, and unwashed humans hit me as soon as the ground evened out below, making me realize that we must have reached the cell block.

The corridor looked the same as the one above, only with a few sturdy doors along the walls. We must have come from the other side when they'd hauled us into Nate's cell, but even though I didn't recognize the tunnel, I sure remembered the stench. Most of the doors were open, making me guess that our guys had been recruiting on the spot. A few of the dead we went past were naked, verifying my guess. I pulled up short when I recognized two bodies from the California settlement but couldn't remember their names. Every foot of the tunnels seemed to have been paid for in blood, and I realized another reason for why Nate had seemed quite happy to let me go shoot rapists—so I wouldn't be the one paying the ultimate price here.

Then we reached the first intersection, and to the right was the corridor the shots rang out from. I let Hill take point as we moved forward. He paused five steps in, then gave us the go-ahead. The reason why he'd halted so soon became apparent when I glanced around his powerful frame and found two of our people, anxiously looking around between us and the forward position behind them. I stepped around them and moved up to where I found Zilinsky playing backup with Rozen and Calveras.

"Status," she whisper-barked at me before I'd even come to a halt next to her.

"We cleaned out the brothel and delivered that Cooper bitch to Romanoff for safekeeping," I reported. "We also got some backup. Oh, and I promised Harris and hundreds of scavengers that they could have the city once we're done here. Hope that's okay?"

For a second, her eyes went wide but Pia caught herself quickly. It wasn't the first time I'd pulled a stunt beyond what we'd planned.

"As long as they don't hamstring us, I don't give a fuck," she enthused.

"Actually, they are right now taking over the arena and blocking the surface access gates. We ran into Marleen and Richards on the way over. They should be around here somewhere, too."

The Ice Queen gave a brief nod to signal that she'd understood, her eyes already trained forward. "Go ahead and see if you can make it to Miller's position. I think he could use a voice of reason."

I didn't like the sound of that. "I'm rarely known as the voice of reason."

"Maybe that's exactly what he needs now," she stressed. "Unless you want to stick it out with us here."

"Nah, getting shot in the face sounds like fun," I offered, already taking the next step forward so she couldn't shove me. Somewhere behind me I heard someone chuckle. It was anyone's guess whether that was Burns or Hill. Damn, but maybe I shouldn't have let those two pair up, particularly outside of where Richards might have kept at least his people in line. Being fabulous like me came at a price.

It took me a while to make my way to the very front of our outstretched line—not quite sure whether it was defense or attack. That I wasn't the only one with that problem became apparent when I managed to make that last dash and press myself against the wall behind where Nate was crouching, low enough that he could use the two doors that they were barring the tunnel with for cover. They had seen me coming and made me wait with my last dash until they gave the signal, yet just as I came to a rocking halt, Santos and Clark next to me shot up out of cover, assault rifles firing on full auto. It was only when a dead—and naked—body toppled onto our side of the door barrier that I realized what was going on.

"Fuck," I whispered. "Are they seriously using the prisoners as meat shields?"

"Something like that," Nate muttered. "They found out quickly enough that we are trying to keep them alive. Some they managed to convince to fight for them. Some are too far gone to be able to make sense of friend or foe. Some just want to die. So we have to wait and see whether they come to us and just want out—or even want to get revenge right here—or want to tear our heads off. We're bleeding ammo, and it may well take another hour until we can force a push."

I carefully craned my neck until I could see over the door. Almost immediately, weapons went off ahead, making me duck, but it had been long enough for me to get a gruesome picture of what lay ahead. The tunnel floor was full of twisted, filthy, naked bodies, only a handful of guards among them.

"So what's the plan?" I asked, then added, before he could speak, "I hope you don't mind that I promised Harris and the scavengers that they could have the city. Didn't seem like a memento worth keeping. Some of them are right now securing the arena outside to make sure nobody escapes. They seemed mighty fond of the idea to get their own city in exchange for us doing the cleanup first."

I expected at least a hint of scorn from Nate but all he did was nod after a moment's consideration. "Smart thinking. And no, nothing here has sentimental value for me."

A few more shots from ahead followed but the wood held them back well. I realized they must have used the doors from the prison cells, reinforced with sheets of steel as they were.

Looking around, I noticed the corridor leading away to our left a few feet behind our position. "Where does that go?"

"Straight to the arena," Nate was too quick to respond. It was clearly a part of the structure that he was familiar with. "That's the main gate they use for the trucks when they dump the gear. Or the animals."

That made me think of something. "Why didn't they try to go down that way? If that leads to the arena, what's up ahead?"

"Oh, they wanted to, but we discouraged them of that notion," Nate said, his smile more of a grimace. "Ahead is their armory but they already raided that before we pushed them back. There's the kitchen for the cells and a guard room. And the interrogation room where they dragged you and Richards in. No access to the actual mine because that's in the opposite direction, back where Zilinsky is guarding the ramp to the upper level."

"Right." I tried to bring up a mental map of the information he'd just offered, but my mind drew a blank. Maybe this was a stupid idea. Maybe I should keep my trap shut. Maybe the Ice Queen had ordered me not to, so here went my brilliant plan. "How about we let them into the arena so we can pin them down there?"

Nate gave me a somewhat suffering look. "And how exactly are we to facilitate that? They won't just be stupid enough to follow us if we withdraw."

"But maybe they will if I do this." And because smart and cautious had never worked for me, I started shouting loud enough for my voice to carry beyond the growing heap of bodies—and without first consulting Nate. Maybe I should have done that. Now it was too late. "We have to fall back! They're about to cut us off!"

Nate glared at me, looking a moment away from strangling me for real this time, but dutifully called back—needlessly close to my plugged-up ears—"Who's cutting us off?"

"The fucking scavenger assholes!" I shouted. "They already killed our backup squad! We need to move!"

Santos and Clark were both looking at me quite confused but Nate was already signaling to them that we were trying to bait a trap for Cortez and his men. And it looked as if they were buying it, if a new barrage of shots hitting the doors and going over it was any indication.

"Fall back!" Nate ordered, shooting back over the barrier as two marines grabbed the door in front of him to do just that. It was awkward, remaining in a deep crouch as I backtracked the way I had come. More and more bullets bit into the wood and the rock of the tunnel walls, spraying us with shrapnel and splinters. At Nate's gesture, I hightailed it into the intersection and around the corner, happy to be able to get up for a second. The shotgun was useless, the reach too short to do any damage, but I still sent a few slugs down the corridor in my valiant effort to guard our "retreat." There were a good thirty of us down there and Nate ordered the marines to bar the extension of the tunnel to force whoever came after us to use the route to the arena instead. We all had to back up further since our opponents weren't stupid enough to let themselves get shot like fish in a barrel. When they finally made their break for it, they laid down heavy cover fire, forcing us all to flatten ourselves to the cold, dirt-strewn ground.

"Move forward!" Nate hissed, the command reaching me over the coms rather than directly although he was only a few feet ahead of me. I followed suit, almost running after the guys with the movable barrier who were quick to secure the intersection once more and clear the tunnel. Nate and his strike team were already moving in on the arena exit, only stopping where the gate became too narrow to use the barriers effectively still—

We spilled out into the arena like a hedgehog made of angry humans with weapon spikes protruding outward, ready to meet our opposition—or what was left of it. With the firefight raging on, Cortez's people were down to fifteen men, who were now, for the most part, gawking at the arena ranks still filling with scavengers. Amos and several of his people were standing on the very edge of the front rank, weapons pointed into the arena ground. They were quick to change their aim away from us as we entered, making me breathe a little easier.

So far, so good. This could be over in five seconds flat. Pew, pew, pew—easy peasy.

One look at Nate was enough to realize that no, that wouldn't do.

A closer look at Cortez—and who he had kneeling, naked, with a tight noose around his neck, the other end of the rope casually wrapped around Cortez's hand and forearm—told me why.

Could things never be easy?

If I'd thought Nate was in bad shape, Bucky was way worse off. True, I'd never seen him completely naked but getting into the hot lab in France had required a quick change of clothes, and I'd been close enough to him to know that, two years ago, he'd been quite the fit specimen. Now he was all wiry tendons and mottled skin stretched over bones that showed too prominently to be healthy. His abundance of beard and hair didn't make up for that. I wasn't exactly feeling sorry for him—I'd need drugs way more potent than what I was rocking for that, if it was even still possible, which I kind of doubted—but that was one miserable shadow of a human being. A year spent mostly in darkness had turned his skin deathly pale, and if I hadn't known he was still alive, I would have guessed that he was a months-old shambler. But there was intelligence lurking in his dull eyes as they stared in our direction, and hope so clearly human that it was easy to make out the difference. The irony that Bucky was happy to see me, of all people, wasn't lost on me. Well, maybe not me personally, but for once in his life he didn't sneer at or taunt me—which I found oddly disappointing. Really, this whole reneging on my revenge thing wasn't shaping up as I'd been hoping.

"Ah, the prodigal son returns," Cortez called out, the phrasing making the hair at the nape of my neck stand on end. Was it just a weird thing people said? Greene had called out something similar to me. Was that just my natural paranoia talking? Or my bias? Or the drugs? Or had we all been one bunch of naive lunatics to trust the self-declared leader of New Angeles for so long?

Nate didn't react at first besides continuing to stalk forward to where we had enough space to spread out, both to make harder targets and to not shoot each other should this actually end with a quick round of "pew, pew, pew" which I still hadn't given up on. I'd killed Taggard in a split-second decision—why couldn't Nate do the same? Not that I didn't understand his need for vengeance—it was just inconvenient.

Not for the first time this week I wondered just how full-circle we had come that I had to sympathize with Nate's past annoyance at actions I'd set and considered fully acceptable.

At least today there would be no foul truces and hidden agendas.

Finally satisfied with our formation, Nate gave the signal to halt but took another step forward, as if all the attention wasn't on him yet. "Any last words?" he called out to Cortez, ignoring his men completely. They seemed to have realized that they were going nowhere, and were hoping that if their leader got sacrificed for the common good, maybe they could slink away somehow.

Cortez was smiling, but it was a tight smile. He didn't seem to have any illusions about what was about to come next, but I had to admit, it took some backbone to stare down Nate in full-on bloodlust and not cringe away.

Rather than respond, he asked a question of his own. "You truly are the creature I have forged you into. Marvelous. Deadly. Magnificent. If it's my time to leave this mortal coil today, I'm ready." He added a dramatic pause. A muscle ticked in Nate's jaw, making me guess that was his usual MO. "But know this—the moment you attack, your friend here dies. Oh, indeed. I know who he is, and now I know who you are, as well. You are aware that if he dies because of your actions, a part of you will die as well. Is your soul worth your vengeance?"

I was starting to wonder if maybe I should shoot Cortez—before he could strangle Bucky—and call this a day. The rain and wind were only partly kept at bay by the layout of the arena, once more drenching me through and through. I was also hard-pressed not to call out whether he always talked such bullshit, but didn't want to rain on Nate's parade.

Nate's mouth twisted into a smirk, his attention straying to Hamilton. "What do you say, Buck? You ready to die so I lose my soul?"

It took Hamilton a cough or two to clear his throat, and his voice sounded like gravel, but was still surprisingly strong as he replied. "Fuck, no. You don't have a soul. Else you couldn't stomach continuing to stick your dick into that mutilated hag of yours."

I couldn't help it. I had to utter a low yet emphatic, "Yes!" at Hamilton's taunt, earning me a sidelong glance from a few of our people, mostly the Ice Queen. Her expression clearly told me that she was disappointed in me not being able to exist above such pettiness.

I couldn't tell whether it was Hamilton's jibe or my reaction, but Nate allowed himself a small smile—that froze as he glanced back at Cortez. Rage took over his eyes, that same deep-seated, visceral, burn-me-up-in-flames-of-hatred rage that I also felt boiling in the depth of my stomach. It was only then that I realized I'd never seen Nate lose control before. Not really, not completely. Not deliberately. It scared me to the bone but also held my attention like few other things I'd ever witnessed. It made me want to let lose as well. Abandon all things human and just become the purest, distilled essence of vengeance. As I was standing there, watching him, I could even feel my mind slowly flipping the switch, my body ready to gear up—

Only that I didn't. Because that was his fight, his victory—and there was a chance that he'd need me to find his way back, and for that I had to be lucid, and calm, and ready to pull him away from the chasm, not launch myself into it right after him. That was a sobering thought, and not one I particularly cherished.

Proving that he still had more control over himself than I would ever master, Nate continued to talk rather than let his rage take over.

"Oh, come on, be nice. Or is your ego really that fragile that you can't even say thank you this once when you'd still be rotting in your cell if not for her?"

Hamilton still refused to look at me, his attention quickly flipping to the gathering crowd. "Lots of violent maniacs? Yeah, sounds like her doing." His attention turned back to Nate, and from one moment to the next he was serious—and surprisingly enough the most worthy of the rank he held that I'd ever seen him, malnutrition and his state of undress easily ignored. I realized Bucky Hamilton was ready to die—after doing the right thing for once.

"You can go ahead and kill that asshole. He doesn't have a fucking clue about anything. His chemist is the one you want. He's the one I delivered the samples to, as instructed. If you can't, I left a backup sample with Raynor. Cortez is nothing but a sadistic fuck, a puppet and a figurehead. He's—"

Nate sprang, moving almost too fast for me to see. One moment he was standing next to me. The next, he was halfway to Cortez—who was ready. He suddenly had two knives drawn, one in each hand, and as Nate came sprinting toward him, he yanked the rope hard, pulling the noose tight around Hamilton's throat. Bucky's hands were tied behind his back so there was no way he could fight the mounting pressure, his face already turning red. Nate was still carrying his assault rifle, and I fully expected him to use it to at the very least bash the knives out of Cortez's hands—but instead he threw it away.

Right. Create a monster, get killed by that monster. But really, I wished right there that I'd married someone with more common sense and less need for drama.

Nate was fast, and he was deadly, but Cortez still had those knives and knew how to use them. Because of the rain, I couldn't see where exactly he slashed at Nate, but even across the distance I saw the weapon in his left hand come away bloody from the engagement. Yet it cost him the one in his right that Nate kicked away, likely breaking a few fingers in the move as well. Cortez, knowing that his chances at survival were slim and advantages slimmer, followed right up with a stab at Nate's back, ignoring the pain that must have been paralyzing his other hand. He hit, the knife going in to the hilt, making Nate roar with agony. I felt myself go still, real fear licking up my spine. This couldn't be it—this couldn't be how Nate would die. Not hours after I'd gotten him back, a little chipped around the edges but overall okay.

Cortez pulled the knife back out, ready for a quick repeat—but never got to it. Not because Nate was stepping out of his reach, because he wasn't. No, because Hamilton threw himself forward, using his weight to pull Cortez off balance, buying Nate the second he needed to pivot and sidestep—at the cost of the last remaining slack in the rope. Nate noticed but Cortez was already coming for him again, forcing him to block instead, which brought him further away from Hamilton where he lay on the floor, gasping for breath that wouldn't make it into his lungs. Cortez was quick and merciless, stabbing and slashing, moving almost as fast as Nate could have had he been in better shape, but wasn't. A kick that landed in his abdomen and Cortez staggered backward, but was at it again a moment later. By the way Nate's movements became fluent once more, I could tell that he was doing a great job pushing the pain from his injuries away—yet he was several feet away from the dropped knife now, even farther from Bucky, and there was no way he could get to him in time.

"Who exactly declared that we were letting this be a fair fight?" I asked no one in particular, but got a few flat stares back from my compatriots. A muscle moved in Pia's cheek and I realized she was about to smile. Yeah, right—not me.

I knew there was a chance this wouldn't end well, neither for me nor Hamilton. One of Cortez's lieutenants could see this as provocation to act, but I wasn't going to let Hamilton die. The irony of that conviction wasn't lost on me—or him when his eyes, about to bulge out of his head, fell on me, coming for him. I didn't bother hunting for the dropped knife but instead pulled my own from its holster, dropping into a crouch over Hamilton.

For just a moment, I was tempted as I saw him there, helpless, partly twisted on his back, baring his throat to me. One quick stab underneath his chin, and Bucky would be no more. He knew it. I knew it.

This was even better than Christmas and Easter combined!

With no time for being dainty, I sawed at the rope with abandon, ignoring the blood that welled from the inevitable shallow cuts I was causing. I knew the rope was about to give when Hamilton let out a pressed grunt but I kept going until the pressure underneath the blade suddenly ceased. And because I wasn't a complete bitch, I only halted to make sure that nobody was about to clock me over the back of a head with a rifle butt before I stepped over Hamilton's prone body as he lay gasping before me, and cut through the rope that held his wrists behind his back. I considered trying to pull him away but there was that utter revulsion thing going on about touching him in the back of my mind, and besides, he would be fine right where he was now. He already had enough air in his lungs to be able to glare up at me, not a smidgen of gratitude in his gaze. I allowed myself a satisfied smile—this would henceforth be known as the day I condemned Bucky Hamilton to a lifetime of knowledge that it had been me, and me alone, who had saved him. Nothing beat that knowledge, least of all lies coming from the asshole's mouth.

Nate had noticed my actions, driving his attacks, and now also did Cortez—and that one moment of split attention was enough. A hard punch against his sternum, followed by another straight to his jaw, and Nate managed to grab the hand that still held the knife and twisted it. Cortez screamed as Nate kept twisting, and pulling, forcing the other man to his knees. Just as I thought he would pull his arm out of the socket, Nate let out a roar and let go, only to grab Cortez's head—and with a powerful twist and lunge that looked like something out of a cartoon he wrenched it off the neck, blood spurting and tendons, nerves, and a bit of spine hanging from the gruesome trophy. The rest of Cortez's body sagged into a kneeling position, then fell over, the rain quickly mixing with the blood still spurting from the neck.

It took me a few moments to realize that the sound in my ears wasn't coming from my racing pulse but from the stands, the crowd going wild one last time for their champion. Nate held up the severed head, then dropped it and kicked it up, out of the arena and into the crowd, much to their continued delight. And then he fell to his knees, hunched over, one hand pressed to his side, the other to his lower back where Cortez had skewered him something good. I was running over to him before I realized it, ignoring the Ice Queen giving the order to fire, and fourteen more bodies hitting the ground.

There was blood on Nate's hands, and more running down his back as I pulled up his jacket, but less than I'd been afraid to see. That still didn't mean anything—stab wounds were great for causing internal bleeding as well—but since all I could do was pull off his jacket and then his shirt to wad that up and hand it to him to staunch the bleeding in his stomach, and then do the same with my clothes to have something for his back, that's what I did. Pia dropped into a crouch next to me, already pulling Nate's hand away to check on the abdominal wound, not looking happy but less concerned by the minute. It took me a moment to realize that Nate wasn't shaking from the cold or pain, but he was laughing silently, his head thrown back, the rain pelting his face.

"He'll live," the Ice Queen declared after checking on the other wound as well. Without the jacket, a few more shallow cuts had become visible, blood slowly seeping from the wounds but quickly getting washed away by the rain. "That needs stitches, but it's already slowing. Unless he starts pissing and shitting blood, he'll be okay."

"And how am I supposed to know about that?" I asked her, a little perplexed.

She gave me another disapproving look. "You're his wife. You make him tell you." She paused for a moment, her hand squeezing his shoulder, but then turned and left without saying another word.

I suddenly didn't know what to do. My eyes fell on Hamilton, still lying on the floor, getting cozy with the puddles. When I looked back at Nate, I saw him glance at his friend as well. "Go to him," I whispered, not quite sure where the words were coming from because I, of all people, couldn't be uttering them. "He needs it. You both do. I'll wait inside. Come to me when you're ready."

I lingered a little longer before I turned to go. Nate's hand, warm and strong and sure, catching my arm pulled me back around to face him. I'd been afraid to find his gaze empty—or borderline insane—but while there was sadness, there was also hope, and gratitude, and above all else the drive to live. "Bree—thanks. I know that couldn't have been easy. Saving him. And I know you didn't do it for him."

The smile came easier than I'd expected. "Of course I did it for you," I huffed, playfully frowning at him. "But I can't very well watch him suffer for a long, long time if he's dead, right? I was already planning on hunting down his undead corpse to be able to kill him after all. This is a million times better! Don't thank me yet—you'll have to live with the both of us hating each other's guts, now probably more than ever."

Nate snorted, shaking his head slightly. "And there I thought you were ready for the high road."

"Oh, please. Me? Never. Now go do your bro bonding thing. I need to check in with the others and find out if someone knows anything about that chemist." Glancing at the bodies on the floor, I heaved a sigh. "Maybe we should have kept a few of them alive."

Just as I'd said I would, I left, pausing just outside the relative safety from the elements that the gate provided, looking back over my shoulder. Nate had made his way over to Hamilton, right now pulling him to his feet, neither of them looking too stable upright. They stared at each other, unblinking. Nate said something but the storm was howling too loud for me to catch it. Hamilton responded, looking just as exhausted as Nate. Then they hugged—and it wasn't just a passing slap on the back or playful goofing around, but a full torso-on-torso action, each clinging to the other for strength and support.

Whatever Nate might have told me—and I was sure that he'd already spoken his piece—there was nobody who could understand what he'd been through... except for someone who'd been in the same boat. Who'd suffered through the same agony, who'd had to watch himself degrade and turn into something he loathed from the bottom of his heart and soul. Spiteful me might be doing a happy dance that Hamilton must have had it so much worse, his ordeal going on for such a long time, but I was surprised to realize that I didn't wish any of it on him.

Sympathy for the devil—where would that lead?

Nowhere today, and since that was about as far as my mind was willing to plan ahead, I dropped the point and slunk inside, happy to be out of the rain.

There was much to do—weapons, ammo, and gear to secure, an entire town to be boarded up for the storm that was upon us—but I found myself dragging my heels, lurking outside of where Pia could get a hold on me and put me to good use. I wasn't the only one, clearly, as I stumbled onto Richards just inside the gate, smoking a joint of all things.

"Does this shit even do anything for you?"

He looked at it, then held it out to me. "Doubt it, but the scent triggers memories that help me relax."

I hesitated but shook my head. "No, thanks. If the last days have taught me anything, it's that I'll never become a fan of anything that screws with my mind. Or body."

"Suit yourself," he remarked, taking another drag.

Looking around, I found the corridor deserted. "Say, any update on how many of our marks we found? And what's up with that chemist everyone keeps mentioning?"

Surprisingly, Richards could give me an answer. "He got away." At my raised brows, he snorted. "Not because we were too slow—Scott and his people found the lab and raided it, but there was only one assistant there, level intern from what I hear. They have him secured for interrogation. I think they appointed you for the task, seeing as you're the only one who can make sense of pretty much anything he says. Turns out his master left three days ago on an impromptu mission. Nobody knows where or why he went, but the timing is suspicious."

It took me a moment to work out. "You think someone who was at our meeting tipped him off?"

Richards shrugged. "Makes sense, now, doesn't it? I doubt he was afraid of the storm. And my people tell me he never leaves."

I didn't like any of that, not one bit. "Even if we knew where he went, we can't leave with the hurricane about to tear everything that's not bolted down apart. By the time that blows over, he'll have a week's head start."

Red nodded. "He could be anywhere by then."

"And this doesn't concern you, at all?"

He shook his head, his slight smile silly enough to make me want to put that damn joint out on his face—so much for my mind finally snapping back to normal. "Concern? Yes, but there's nothing I can do about it right now. First, we have to regroup, weather out the storm, interrogate the prisoners, and try to make sense of the notes the chemist left."

That was a good plan, even if I didn't like it. It sounded like a lot of work, and not the kind I wanted to do right now—or ever. "Does that guy have a name?"

"None that we know," Red provided. "Wouldn't be surprised if he went by Keyser Söze."

Silence fell, neither of us knowing what to say next. I was tempted to ask him about what Bucky had said in what may very well have ended up being his last words—that he'd left some of the samples of the bioweapon, not just the cure, that we'd fetched from France with Raynor, but I doubted that Red knew anything about that. I wasn't even sure if the good doctor herself knew. I didn't put it past Hamilton to sneak into storage and dump it into a liquid nitrogen tank with only him the wiser.

"Guess I should make myself useful now," I said, meaning that as goodbye for now, but Richards held me back.

"I should probably not tell you this," he started, pausing until he had my full attention. "But you keep complaining about me being all uptight about the file I have on you, and if this helps establish trust between us, why not?" He halted again, making me want to wring his neck, but then I realized he wasn't being dramatic but actually uncomfortable. That made me instantly suspicious.

"Just spit it out. It can't get any worse than what I've been through, or your people have already done to me."

He took another drag on the joint, looking at it, then the smoke he blew out, before focusing on me again. "It was just a scrawled note I caught in Emily's surgery protocols. She's very thorough, you know?" I must have looked a second away from outright violence as he quickly offered up the rest. "You know they had to remove one of your ovaries? The other's likely still working since you don't seem to have any hormonal issues from what I can tell. That was her guess. The updated version of the serum is more balanced than the old ones, factoring in that women's metabolisms work slightly different than men's. If you ever feel the urge to test out the theory that you and Miller would have beautiful but extremely violent babies, go hunt down a doctor or nurse with a working ultrasound, or an obstetrician who really knows what he's doing. The outcome may very well surprise you."

That said, he dropped what was left of the joint and ground it out with the heel of his boot, and without another word walked away, leaving me standing there, quite stunned.

No. That couldn't be true. My first thought was denial. After that came the urge to yell after him what was up with his people and putting things up my privates that I hadn't consented to. Then came paranoia—why was he telling me this now? I knew that if I asked the Ice Queen—who was the first, and likely only, person I'd want to discuss this with, at least until I made up my mind. I already knew what she would tell me: it was a distraction, plain and simple. The most effective way of taking me out of the game—as in making me want to drop out and never come play again. And last, almost drowned out by the cacophony of thoughts and ideas racing through my mind, there was a flicker of hope, so small it could be blown out like a candle by a hurricane with just a single word. Did I dare believe him? Could I even let myself, under these circumstances, in this world?

I didn't know the answer, and I sure as fuck wasn't going to waste any energy on that now—and even less, tell Nate and add one more heap on his plate that was already too full. But as I turned to go look for someone to give me a more detailed update, I realized that

I didn't need to decide right now—because that flicker had already turned to embers, quietly glimmering away at the very bottom of my soul, impossible to extinguish.

Well, as they say, the only way is forward—and forward I would go.

Acknowledgements

Wow, this book was a tour-de-force start to finish!

First off, thanks where thanks is due—my editor and beta readers, who are the best, and still talk to me after getting through this tome of a book! You have my eternal gratitude!

I pretty much wrote the book in a little over 1.5 months, with 3 months from the end of chapter one to uploading the polished version to Amazon. It's the second longest novel I've written, and it sets up what I consider to be the final trilogy that will make up the Green Fields series (if you want, you can split the books up into a a sequence of trilogies, theme and plot-wise). I absolutely loved writing it—whatever that says about the state of my mind.

As you probably know already, I've started my own Patreon last summer, and I'm happy to report that I've had a blast writing a novella / short story each month and providing some extra behind-the-scenes content. If that sounds interesting to you, why not check it out here? But no worries—you won't be missing any vital information for the novels if you only read those. Patreon has become a happy, little side project for me that has kept me surprisingly motivated and productive since the release of the last book.

And now, there are only two more books in the Green Fields series remaining! As you are reading this, I'm likely already writing on book #11. I hope you're just as excited about it as I am!

Thank you so much for sticking with me, Bree, Nate, and the gang—let's get the last leg of the journey started!

Thank you

Hey, you! Yes, you, who just spent a helluva lot of time reading this book! You just made my day! Thanks!

Want to be notified of new releases and updates? Sign up for my newsletter:

www.adriennelecter.com

If you enjoyed reading the book and have a moment to spare, I would really appreciate a short, honest review on the site you purchased it from. Reviews make a huge difference in helping new readers find the series. Seriously, they do. Wanna make a difference? Now you know how you can!

Or if you'd like to drop me a note, or chat a bit, feel free to email me or hit me up on social media. I'll try to respond as quickly as possible!

Email: adrienne@adriennelecter.com
Website: adriennelecter.com
Twitter: @adriennelecter
Facebook: facebook.com/adriennelecter
Patreon: patreon.com/adriennelecter

About the Author

Adrienne Lecter has a background in Biochemistry and Molecular Biology, loves ranting at inaccuracies in movies, and spends increasingly more time on the shooting range. She lives with the man and two cats of her life in Vienna, Austria and is working on the next books in the Green Fields series.

You can sign up for Adrienne's newsletter to never miss a release and be the first to know what other shenanigans she gets up to:

http://www.adriennelecter.com/
Email: adrienne@adriennelecter.com
Twitter: @AdrienneLecter
Facebook: facebook.com/adriennelecter

Books published

Green Fields
#1: Incubation
#2: Outbreak
#3: Escalation
#4: Extinction
#5: Resurgence
#6: Unity
#7: Affliction
#8: Catharsis
#9: Exodus
#10: Uprising

28718772R00258

Printed in Great Britain
by Amazon